John Shelton of Virginia
d. 1726

William Shelton

John Shelton   John Henry
d. 1777

Sarah Shelton II - m. Patrick Henry   ELIZA
("Sally")   1736 - 1799   HE
d. 1776   1749

m. (1)   m. (2)
WILLIAM CAMPBELL   WILLIAM RUSSEL
1745 - 1781   1748 - 1793

Delilah's Mountain

Novels by Gloria Jahoda

Annie
Delilah's Mountain

DELILAH'S

MOUNTAIN

by Gloria Jahoda

The Riverside Press Cambridge

HOUGHTON MIFFLIN COMPANY BOSTON

1963

Ja

First Printing

Grateful acknowledgment is made to Mrs. Flora L.
McDowell of Smithville, Tennessee, for permission
to quote the song "Shoot the Buffalo" on pages 58-59.
The extract from Charles Bickley's war record which
appears on page 238 is taken from material in the
office of the clerk of the Russell County Court in
Lebanon, Virginia.

Library of Congress Catalog Card Number: 63-13683
Printed in the U.S.A.

To my mother, Adelaide Love,
and to the memory of my father,
Chase Whitney Love

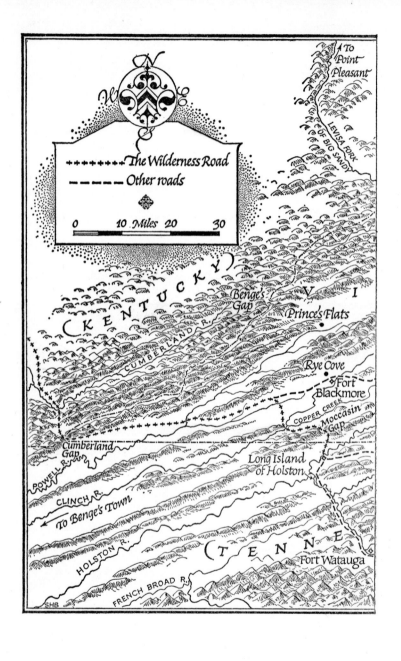

The Wilderness Road

++++++++ The Wilderness Road
-------- Other roads

0   10 Miles 20   30

To
Point
Pleasant

LEVISA FORK OF BIG SANDY

KENTUCKY

V I

Benge's
Gap

Prince's Flats

CUMBERLAND R.

Rye Cove

Fort
Blackmore

COPPER CREEK

Moccasin
Gap

Cumberland
Gap

POWELL R.

Long Island
of Holston

CLINCH R.

To Benge's Town

HOLSTON R.

T E N N E

Fort Watauga

FRENCH BROAD R.

SHB

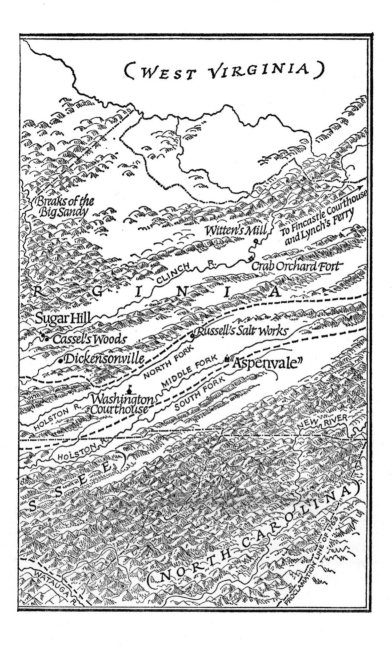

Foreword

In 1763 Great Britain concluded a treaty with the Indian nations west of the Allegheny and Appalachian mountains which guaranteed that no new settlements would encroach upon their territory. The treaty proclaimed a dividing line — the Proclamation Line — which separated Indian land from the settlements of the east. In Virginia, the Proclamation Line ran roughly from Fort Chiswell, near modern Pulaski, in the south to a point near present-day Morgantown, West Virginia, in the north. Beyond it no man could legally farm land or build a home.

But the land-hungry people pouring into the colonies from the Old World — the Scotch-Irish, Alsatians, Palatine Germans, Highlanders, English yeomen — as well as eastern Virginians growing poor on tobacco-exhausted soil, were in no mood to respect such a barrier. They recognized neither the line on paper nor the geographical barrier of the vast ranges of the Indian wilderness. If the Indians could not hold their land, argued the would-be settlers, let them lose it.

In southwest Virginia the Clinch River valley was such a wilderness: legally forbidden, actually fertile and beckoning. The white man came in defiance of the law, and for a time the Shawnee and Cherokee tribes, busy fighting each other, made only sporadic raids on his settlements. Cabins and clearings began to dot the Clinch valley. But in 1773 Daniel Boone attempted to lead a party from the Clinch still deeper into the wilderness — into Kentucky. The Indians, seeing the danger of further land losses and resenting the depletion of the game on which they lived, killed Boone's son. Rumors of an impending Indian war began to circulate. The settlers were adamant. They were prepared to defy men they considered savages, the King's Law, and their governor, Lord Dunmore, alike. What land they had seized they meant to keep. The Proclamation Line had only increased their impatience of English rule, and they were determined if necessary to die both for what they already had and what, in the future, they meant to get.

I

"All I want in this creation
 Is a pretty little girl and a big
  plantation
 Way out yonder in the Cherokee
  nation."

—*Frontier Song*

Sugar hill was not the highest mountain in Virginia's Appalachians. Delilah Winfield had believed it was the first time she had ever climbed to its crest. She was a child then, fresh from Williamsburg and the flatness of the eastern seacoast. Now in 1774 she knew better. She was twelve after all, nearly a woman grown. She had lived on Sugar Hill for four years; Williamsburg was becoming daily a more distant memory. But she still wanted to believe Sugar Hill was the highest mountain in the whole west, whenever she stood here as she was standing now, because the mountain was hers — hers and her father's. He himself had claimed and won it from the wilderness.

The August afternoon was hot and sticky. Impatiently she shook back the thick mane of her black hair. Then she swept her eyes once more across the landscape she had learned to love: the winding, silver-flecked Clinch River below and the cluster of cabins on its far shore, beyond them the rows of jagged, silent ranges covered gray-green with unbroken forest. She used to believe, too, that this wilderness was the end not only of Virginia but of the world. In truth there was no end to Virginia. It stretched away forever west, through the Kentuk country of the Long Hunters to unknown rivers with strange names like Chenoa, Kanawha, and Ohio. She had been afraid, once, of a world without limits; she was not afraid now. She could think of those rivers like the Clinch, speckled with light, shouting and tumbling over worn stones. Few men had ever seen Virginia even as far west as the Appalachians, but she had. Still fewer lived in them, but she did. The frontier! There was magic in the word whenever her father spoke it, letting the "r" linger proudly on his tongue. He would make a real plantation of Sugar Hill some day — for her sake, he said, but she knew it was for his too. He loved the mountain as much as she did. All the Tidewater and Piedmont, the Settlements, would be wanting the yearly run of tawny, sweet syrup from its maples. In the dream, she had lost her fear of a world without towns, without church spires, without watchbells at night or the reassuring roughness of red brick under her hands at a gatepost. She could still remember these things from the Settlements, but she did not often, any longer, deliberately try.

When she heard the clopping of horseshoes she was surprised. Her father's bay nag Chickamo was not shod. But she settled herself on a fallen maple log, spread her skirts, and began to husk corn, watching from the side of her eye. When she saw Charles Bickley swing down from his Arab stallion she smiled politely. She had envied the miller that stallion with its flaring nostrils and crook tail and high neck ever since she had seen it on the journey west. It was a beautiful horse, chestnut and sleek. Secretly she longed to ride it down Sugar Hill and through the Clinch and across all Charles Bickley's fields, the wind in her face and her hair blown back. There was wildness in its eyes, a spirit not easily tamed. She wondered whether he had broken it himself as a colt, or if he had bought it afterwards. She had never asked him. He could very well have broken it. He had a tall, lean hardness about him made for riding, and he wasn't as old as her father, who always said breaking colts was for young sports and fools. The odd patch of gray in the dark hair at Bickley's right temple belied his twenty-one years. Still, he had worked long hours at his grinding and surveying and planting since he had come to the Clinch in Captain Russell's party with her father and herself. Everybody worked long hours on the Clinch.

Bickley smiled back at her; he had a quick smile. He didn't speak, however, as he hobbled his Arab with a strip of whang leather and then went round to the front door of the cabin to knock. When he started to scrape the mud from his high Russia boots, his forelock falling across his brow as he bent, she frowned. She would have to scrub the stoop again. Gran was getting too stiff to do it often.

> *"As I was going down Shinbone Alley,*
> *Hoozen John, a-hooza,*
> *As I was going down Shinbone Alley*
> *Long time ago . . ."*

Her lips began to move silently in Gran's shucking catch while she stripped cobs after Bickley had gone in, but her mind strayed. What did he want here? He wasn't a visiting sort of man any more than her father was. Nobody made visits in summer, and Bickley seemed to keep himself too busy in winter to mix with his nearest neighbors, let alone the Winfields this side of the Clinch, who mixed with nobody. Visits, in Delilah's mind, belonged to Tidewater, that now misty world of other years, to candlelit drawing rooms and warm dusks, not to the windy forests and stump-pocked clearings of the west. Whenever her father plowed he still had to go round the remnants of the giant sugar trees he had girdled the first year and then hacked away, one by one. It was a wonder, what he had done — felled trees, hewed logs, built a cabin and stirred chinking, all with only Delilah and her Grandmother Mackinnon to help, and a wandering hunter hired for three months. (The hunter's breath, Delilah remembered, had smelled of corn whisky.) The settlers across the river had helped Ben Winfield with the barn raising alone. Delilah knew they felt slighted at his choice of land away from their midst. He liked his solitude these days; too well they understood. His hands, the hands of an ex-schoolmaster, would bear the marks of his first desperate and triumphant summer on the Clinch forever — froe and axe blisters, cuts and gashes from wild briers. But he was as proud of the marks as Delilah was, doubtless as proud as Charles Bickley was of his own scars, to judge by the way she had once seen him at a wedding infare over the river, not hiding his palms but spreading them on the table before him. It didn't matter about Ben Winfield's crooked corn rows. What mattered was living: growing enough food and flax and fodder to survive in the wilderness as the Old Testament prophets and John the Baptist and the first Romans and the ancient planters at Jamestown and even the Indians had all survived in theirs. "Many have gone before us, Delilah." Her father would straighten his heavy shoulders and put his arm around her waist as they stood together on the mountaintop. "Many have had need to leave their kind." No, she wasn't homesick. The dream of the plantation was a great one. The God of the Presbyterians, Gran's God, to which her father had been converted from the English Church, had led him to it after what Delilah always called, in her mind, the Trouble. She had perfect confidence in her father; there was no wariness in her trust of him as there was in her trust of God. Her father had never failed her.

She tried to concentrate on the cobs in her lap, piling the green shucks neatly at her feet to be dried and crumbled as litter for the Dominecker hens during the coming winter. But she longed to know what was happening between Bickley and her father. The date for the milling of her father's corn had already been set. What else was there to arrange? Why didn't he call her?

I'm not a child! she decided angrily, as she decided several times every day; I hate being left out! She jumped up, bunching the cobs in her tow apron. Beside the stoop she piled them carelessly on the harvest bench her father had sawed out last summer. Let the old black rooster get some scratch if he wanted it . . . She smoothed her hair and tightened the yellow ribbon around her head. Her face felt flushed as she came into the cabin's large room. Then her lips parted in surprise. Nobody was saying a word: not her father, not Gran, not even Bickley. And when she looked at Bickley he stared right through her. He wasn't even trying to smile now.

Her father, in a tannin-stained butternut hunting shirt, was holding a paper in his hand. He was holding it far away from him, his jaw jutting squarely above his thick neck. His pale eyes narrowed as he peered at it in a dust-dancing shaft of light from the greased-paper window. His forehead was seamed with lines. He lifted a hand to the clubbed knot of his gray hair. Then he raised his chin in a motion Delilah recognized as defiance.

"I want to see." She moved closer.

"She had better see." Gran's voice was hard, her thin

mouth almost immobile as she spoke. She was sitting by the stone hearth, her blue-veined hands clasped in her lap.

Delilah took the paper from her father without a word. The print slashed its whiteness large and straight.

MEN OF FINCASTLE COUNTY! The House of Burgesses will without all Doubt enable his Lordship to reward every Vollunteer in a handsome manner, over and above his Pay: as the plunder of the Country will be valuable, and it is said the Shawanese have a great Stock of Horses.

August 10, 1774

WILLIAM PRESTON
Colonel Commanding

She did not understand. Who was "his Lordship"? Lord Dunmore, the Governor in Williamsburg? What did he have to do with the Shawanese Indians and their horses?

"Mr. Bickley would have your father go to war, Delilah." Gran's voice was colder than ever, in her anger heedlessly burred with the Scotch-Irish accent which returned whenever she forgot to be careful. "To a trumped-up war for no reason. I have told him he has not the right to ask it."

"But — but Papa couldn't go!" Delilah knew the paper had floated from her hand, yet she did not stoop to the puncheons to pick it up. Suddenly, accusingly, she turned to Bickley. "Why?"

"A chief's family has just been killed by a fool of a hunter, Delilah," he answered quietly. "You remember the scalping of Jim Boone and Henry Russell last fall. You know what could happen now."

"Mr. Bickley believes the Indian nations are about to rise." Even as Winfield said it he kept his hazel eyes intently on Bickley. "He tells us Lord Dunmore means to wipe them out once for all."

Of course Delilah remembered the scalping of Jim Boone and Henry Russell. Who didn't? It had happened only thirty miles away, in Powell's Valley, just after Jim and Henry had set out for Kentuk and the lands Captain Russell so madly claimed from the savages there. He wanted the lands settled. So he had hired Jim's father to lead out the first party. Instead Dan Boone had led his own son, and the Captain's too, to their deaths. The rest had turned back fast enough after Powell's Valley. They'd learned. Delilah didn't want to remember the massacree: not now, not ever. It was over! She hated being afraid. Desperately she searched for the familiar words she had so often heard. "They were going to the Indian country, Jim and Henry. They had no call." After a moment's silence she cried the old consolation: "It's different here. It won't happen to us!"

Bickley's voice was slow and soft, in the manner of the Settlements, but to Delilah it sounded ruthless. "The Indians are gathering on the Ohio — Shawanese, Mingoes, Delawares." He stiffened, as if bracing himself against a thing he did not want to meet but knew he must. Sticky chunks of resin clotted the sleeves of his shirt. His sun-browned hands were streaked with meal from his mill. "The Cherokees could march from the Tenase to the Ohio in a week."

"But not my father!" Delilah knew she was gripping the edge of the table. "Not my father, to go there — to the Ohio."

Winfield's laughter was quick and sharp. "I speak for my-self." His smile skewed from amusement into irony.

She leaned toward Bickley. "Why did you come here?" Her cheeks were burning, her own chin came up. "Why did you have to tell us?"

"Was ever a thing stopped by not telling?"

Her hand hardened on the rough pinewood. Gran got up too, pulling at her patched apron so fiercely Delilah heard it rip.

"Would you trust Dunmore, Ben? When he has the tax troubles in the Tidewater and the Sons of Liberty at his throat? Does he care for our skins or his own? Answer me!"

"In time, Madam. This isn't the moment."

"No," Bickley agreed levelly. "It isn't. No governor would deliberately start a war with the savages, Mrs. Mackin-non. You must know that."

"Ah!" Gran's dark eyes were flashing as they narrowed. "Not even to be a hero and make people forget everything else? You're a harebrained Tory, young man. I'll give none of my family to your nonsense."

"Mr. Bickley is our guest, Madam."

"And loyal to my governor and King, sir." Bickley started toward the door, his voice apologetic but firm. "In honor. I see it's useless to ask you. May I have the paper?"

"I dropped it," Delilah said as icily as she could. Thank God her father wasn't going, thank God . . . Bickley stooped to pick the paper up. She thought, for a moment, that he was going to dare to grin at her with that ready charm of his. He could turn it off fast enough, certainly, like the spigot on a cider barrel; maybe he'd actually try to turn it on. But instead he looked across to Winfield. "I don't blame you, I guess. My sort drove you out here. And your child — it makes a difference."

"I'm not a child!"

He did grin, for a maddening instant: "No?"

It was not until he was outside that Delilah heard the unbelievable words from her father, the crisp words which froze Gran into a statue and which seemed not to be coming from Winfield at all but from a hidden corner of the room. "Bickley — I'll go. Wait." The cabin door hung open. Leaves were stirring in the hot wind. A catbird was jeering, and a jarfly buzzed. Bickley stopped and turned.

"You can't, Ben." Gran whispered it at last. And then, tightly, shrilly: "It's a fool's word, honor!"

He gave no sign he had heard her. With a long stride he went to the door and his visitor while Delilah watched the wind shake the branches of the sugar trees over Bickley's head and listened to the heavy breath of her grandmother who still stood at the hearth, motionless in impotent rage.

Delilah went outside that night when she couldn't stand the quarreling any more: Gran's voice hoarse and desperate, her father's thundering stubbornly. Honor . . . a will-o'-the-wisp, Gran rasped, a thing like the light glowing in a Tidewater swamp, a dream-thing that wasn't real, not as real as home or people who loved and depended on a man. Would he have left his wife too if she had lived to come to the Clinch? Maybe her swamp fever had been a mercy after all.

— This is a war, Madam.

Gran's pleading was useless, Delilah knew. There was never any changing her father when his mind was set. Even the Trouble hadn't changed him — the Tidewater jail where the justices had put him because he wouldn't go to the English Church every Sabbath as the law demanded and wouldn't pay the fines the court set. "I'll change no principle," he'd said then. "You, Madam," he'd told Gran, "should be ashamed of mouthing what you don't believe."

"I've a reason," she'd thrown back tartly. "I've a grandchild to rear. Your child, and my daughter's."

"She shall be reared in the west."

"So? Where the jailbirds go? Beyond the King's Proclamation Line?"

"You think little enough of the King, Madam."

That had been one of the other arguments; and it hadn't done Gran a particle of good. She'd come west too, naturally, to the land proclaimed closed to settlement but in truth being taken up not only by jailbirds but by younger sons, adventurers and speculators, roamers shy of the fetters of civilization, and people who called themselves True Believers — of various sorts. Delilah believed in her father. So had the pupils in the tiny Williamsburg academy he had kept on South England Street, though they had paled at his bellow and at the slap of his ruler across their knuckles. On his last day of classes, before the trial, they had brought him their tributes: a morocco-bound pocket Homer, a pair of pinchbeck shoe buckles, a glass paperweight with tiny red flowers that sparkled in the sun . . . the tributes of tradesmen's sons. The boys had realized he always shouted at the people he cared for, wanting them to understand what he called his conscience. But it was sometimes a fearful thing, that conscience. Now it was leading him to a war with the red savages who had scalped Jim Boone and Henry Russell.

Over the Clinch the stars were gleaming in a black sky as Delilah walked alone. She sought the constellations: the Seven Sisters and Heavenly Twins, the Chair around the polestar, the Great Swan and Orion the Hunter, all the patterns her father had taught her on summer nights when they had stood on Sugar Hill, arms linked under the whispering trees. She and he had been a part of the mountain then, of its sounds and pungent smells: woodcocks and whippoorwills, scraping katydids, ginseng and pokeroot and wild raspberry roses and foxgrapes. At such moments she could think of herself growing like the trees, straight and strong. Some day she would be a woman. The very knowledge of it ran like sap in her body and her heart, surging upward, tin-

gling in her veins. She was ready now for life; she wished
her father understood that, and she tried to tell him how she
longed for womanhood instead of this hated no man's land
between childhood and true life.

"Enjoy your childhood." He would only pat her hand.
"You've time yet for life."

But to live was to be listened to *now*, to be able to give all
her love without being laughed away or turned off and told
she was a queer baby. Sometimes her father talked to her as
if she were a woman, but he was only pretending she was her
mother. It was the one thing standing between her and Ben
Winfield: his blindness to her growing . . . She breathed
deeply, and ran her right forefinger along a heavy brow. The
wind murmured in the sugar trees . . . War, her father
had said. Gran knew war from General Braddock's time —
stockades and Indian raids in the Shenandoah Valley from
which she had been driven to Tidewater in order to escape
horrors hinted at but never detailed. Men died in war. Delilah clenched her fists until the nails dug into her palms.
Charles Bickley mustn't lead her father to death on the leaf-
strewn floor of some distant forest, like the forest where Jim
Boone and Henry Russell had been massacreed. Charles
Bickley was a Tory, he didn't care about other people's dying. He'd fought cruelly with that soft voice of his, using
the word that would touch her father and take him
away . . . Honor! Delilah hated the word. Now she hated
Bickley too. What were his King and Governor to the Winfields? He'd defied King and Governor once himself to cross
the Proclamation Line and claim forbidden land. Was that
his precious honor, even though the Governor shut his eyes
conveniently to the western settlers? Surely it was more
honorable to break the law if you hated the King who'd made

it. Oh, she'd face Bickley alone as soon as she could, she'd tell him his kind of honor meant nothing. His honor was what *he* wanted, and no more. She herself would go to his mills. She would prevent death from claiming her father even as Gran had tried and failed. It's my turn now, she thought; I'm grown enough for that. The stars flickered sharp and clear. She stared up at them, tautening, knowing the burden she had taken upon herself.

The next morning when she said she wanted to ride, her grandmother nodded. Margaret Mackinnon saw defiance in Delilah's bright blue eyes, in the set of her full mouth and firm chin. But Margaret Mackinnon also knew the defiance wasn't for her. Delilah wanted instead to defy life and events; and how vulnerable she looked, standing there, for all her height and her big hands and broad shoulders. Ah, child, her grandmother longed to tell her, there are times a body can't fight; I only hope you learn it. Feeling the catch at her heart, Margaret bit her lips. This tall, beloved, clumsy, eager child with the heavy black hair and the fair face that waited so expectantly for love and praise to happen to her: was there a way to save her very eagerness from hurting her?

"I'll not be blaming you, Delilah. I'll boil the copperas this afternoon and we can dye the linsey for your new gown tomorrow." We'll go on living, Margaret Mackinnon was trying to say; we'll do the things we've always done. A thing has happened to us that can't be defied; your father will go to war and you can't stop him. God expects endurance and suffers no rebellion.

Delilah saw only the blue rings around her grandmother's

eyes. The cords in Gran's neck were working, but she kept on stirring cornmeal mush in the black caldron on its crane over the hearth. "Your father's hoeing," she added, her voice brittle.

Delilah's father saw her as he grubbed at pussley and iron-weed in the clearing, but he only nodded. The mare Chick-amo picked her way undisturbed down rocky slopes under trees dripping with dew and laced along the path with shimmering spiderwebs. Fiercely Delilah smacked at a mosquito on her bare arm, but she was too late; soon her arm would swell. It was a nuisance, the way her skin never toughened. At the river ford Chickamo whinnied and then plunged while the water broke in a shining spray at her shanks and Delilah bunched her skirt at her knees to keep it dry. The water tingled coldly on her legs and seeped into her moccasins. She had forgotten to take them off; her cheeks heated with annoyance. At the far shore she let down her skirt again, smoothed it, and flexed her toes in her wet shoes, trying by the act to will them dry. She straightened herself in the cracked sidesaddle and tossed back her hair, loosening her hold on Chick's frayed reins. Charles Bickley, at least, must think her a woman, certainly not a fretful and heedless girl.

His settlement was called Cassel's Woods, after the Long Hunter who had roamed it in early days. As she rode in, Delilah heard the staccato sound of hammering coming from behind a cedar-covered hill near Mill Creek, but she couldn't see what the men were building. When she came to the mill the hammering was drowned by the rush of water over the millwheel, the steady thumping of the gears and shafts, and the vibrating of the millhouse floor. Where the water gushed into the millpond it quieted immediately, the ripples spreading out until they merged into the glassy surface at the edges. Bickley's coming to Sugar Hill yesterday had been like that: a surge not breaking her life's surface, though like the water her life was roiling beneath. Inside the millhouse the noise deafened her until she wanted to put her hands to her ears and shut her eyes. Pulleys and belts rattled at her from overhead. A black man was standing at the lever, watching the speed of the giddy burrs as they ground, the runner burr circling endlessly over the bedder. She raised her brows at the slave and he pointed to the sawmill room beyond. She picked her way over scraps of wood through a trail of corn grains and buckwheat groats and sawdust. When she found Bickley he was in his rolled-up shirtsleeves, helping two more blacks to dog walnut logs under the saw. The muscles of his upper arms were bulging. He did not see her. The saw began to whine, the sound of it cutting through her like a knife. When she called to him he did not hear her. As the saw stopped she called again. He turned. She was suddenly aware of the smells of green wood and bread from the mill and from him as he came over to her.

"I want to talk to you," she shouted. She heard her voice crack.

He thrust out his lower lip, arched his dark brows, and then motioned to her to come outside.

They stopped by the millpond in a patch of snapweed. Water squished in her shoes as she shifted her weight. "It was noisy," she stammered stupidly, her hands spread on her skirt.

"D'you think a tree saws itself in silence?" he laughed. "Have you brought me early corn?" He seemed taller than ever as he stood before her. She wasn't fooled by his laughing, wasn't beguiled; not this time.

"Go back to Papa. Tell him you don't want him to come."
She heard her voice rising: "Please!"

Sobering, he looked down at his mealy hands, then wiped
them on his hips. "Your father is one of us, my girl, whether
he likes it or not."

"He'll be killed!" She went toward him. "I know it." She
kept staring at him, and beyond him at a thin thread of water
spilling from the millrace onto a worn rock. "He's never
been in a war, don't you see?"

"I haven't either. You and your grandmother couldn't
manage alone — is that it?"

"I could." Her chin came up. "I'd plant and hoe myself!
It's not us, it's Papa. Tell him you didn't mean it, about
honor. Tell him! It's just a word you used!"

"You're a strange child." He moved closer, his blue eyes
fixed on her searchingly. She drew back.

"I love him," she whispered. Her lips were parted, her
breath was rushing faster through them and she could feel
it hot on the tip of her nose. A dull pain began to nag at the
pit of her stomach. She tightened her hands.

"Every man here is expected to go. If I excused him the
others wouldn't — Captain Russell, Dan Boone, the rest.
Don't you see it?"

"Papa doesn't care about people!"

"Oh, but he cares about you. Lord Dunmore has just com-
missioned Dan Boone to bring back the government surveyors in Kentuk if they're still alive. The hammering — we're
building a fort." His voice softened. "Your father wants to
defend you, Delilah. He wants his war on the Ohio, not
here on the Clinch. You must try to understand."

With a great thump, the millwheel ground to a stop. The
weight of the silence fell on Delilah. She could feel the

tears pressing behind her eyes, tears she dared not shed. "Please — " she tried again, forgetting her hatred to beg.

"Your father won't die." At once she felt Bickley's hand on her shoulder, heavy and warm. And she didn't move. She couldn't. "I'll try to see to that. I promise you."

"You're a Tory," she whispered. The tears did start, stinging her cheeks. When they turned to sobbing she felt Bickley's arms coming around her, but still she made no move. His arms were strong and firm.

"I was born a Tory. But I'm not the devil, you know. You mustn't do this. Hush." Dimly she heard his tenderness, but now she was lost in her tears. In the loneliness of her grief she was pressing herself against the only refuge there was, the only warmth. Soon the pain tore at her whole body, spasm after spasm of it. She didn't care where she was or what she was doing. She began to think of her father already dead, began to think she had lost him as Gran had once lost Grandfather Mackinnon. She twisted her fingers in the cloth of Bickley's shirt. When he put his hand on her forehead she had a brief, amazed instant of respite and tried to break away, but a fresh rush of agony swept over her and she stayed limp against him, crying out the tears she hadn't been able to cry the sleepless night before or this morning. "Hush," he said again. "I'm sorry, sweetheart."

It ended imperceptibly, the sobs dying at first in her throat and then in her breast. She stared up.

"Better?" His thumb was under her chin.

She gasped. Then she backed away. Her body felt cold as she did it. "Oh! You — Oh! You — "

"I'll look after your father," he broke in. "I promise you. And we won't tell him about this."

"You don't care! You couldn't!"

"That's not true, Delilah." Their eyes met. She didn't want to know he was almost as unhappy as she was, but she did; he was sorry for what he'd done. But now it was too late.

"I c-came to stop you." She dabbed at her eyes. "There's no reason for a war, Gran says."

"If there weren't it would be criminal. Tell Gran I know it. And tell her I'll bring your father back."

She shook her head, the tears brimming. "You can't. Maybe you'll die too."

Creaking slowly, the sluice gates parted. A stream of water rushed over the millwheel. The rolling began once more, the swish of spray and the mad banging of the gears. He took her hands in his, and she could just hear him: "I won't die. Don't be silly. Go back now." The sounds and his words merged in her head as she watched him turn and leave her. She hated him still! But she was suddenly lonely for the comfort of his warmth against her, and the comfort of his sureness that a war, like his mills, could be managed easily and well.

3

Sugar hill turned scarlet that autumn, brighter than it had ever been before. Delilah saw the leaves of the trees flaming on the trace as she rode restlessly over it, past tiny fern-ringed waterfalls and clumps of gentian. But as she listened to ravens croaking out the approach of winter she shivered. She was trying to forget the war — Lord Dunmore's War, people on the Clinch called it — but she could not. She tried to see only the long tunnel of rustling leaves and black trunks ahead of her, and the hot blue sky above, and the red clay of the winding path at her feet. Instead she saw visions of guns, of smoke and her father's bulk crumpling wounded on a path like this one. She could almost, at times, smell powder as she had smelled it on dead game he had brought in. Then she knew she was only smelling witch-hazel and ginseng, that the smell was nothing like powder at all, that the sharpness in the air was from the mountain's herbs. A heaviness half pain and half weariness stayed always in her throat. Her comfort was in remembering Bickley's promise to bring her father back. It was the only thing to put dependence in while he was away.

Late in October the weather turned sweltering. Hard marching weather, Gran said before her evening prayers. Always, now, Gran prayed for the troops, for that column of men which had trudged away into the steep forests, their

Deckhard rifles gleaming in the morning sun, their shotbags and powderhorns and pemmican envelopes jigging on lean hips and wide shoulders . . . her father had said his rifle was heavy. Delilah remembered that. He hadn't been used to a rifle — only his fowling piece and battered musket. How many rifles felt heavy? Did Bickley's?

Often Delilah rode down to the river to bathe away the perspiration on her body, letting the cool water cover her arms and legs while Chickamo pawed softly at the cane on the shore, her bay coat dappled with light. The last time for swimming: this was a wooded hollow, a secret place where nobody could see Delilah and she could hang her homespuns on a willow branch. The wash of the water over her hard, white limbs brought momentary peace; but she soon remembered the war again, her father's absence, her father's danger. Was it like this for Gran, waiting too? Were the women at Cassel's Woods across the river feeling the same things? Was any woman waiting for Charles Bickley? Did he have parents, brothers, or sisters back in the Settlements? Delilah realized she didn't know. Lucky Mrs. Boone! She at least had her husband with her because he had brought back the surveyors and now commanded the Cassel's Woods fort. Everybody else was bereft: wives, daughters, mothers. And they had each other, but Delilah had to stay on the mountain, sharing the waiting only with Gran, who never said what she felt. If Indian sign were seen Dan Boone was coming to Sugar Hill to get them both and bring them down to the fort. "I'll live in no stockade," Gran rapped. "I've seen 'em on Shenandoah — people lumped together and snapping at each other, and a stench no decent woman would tolerate unless she had to. If a savage comes skulking round I've a stout gun and I'll use it. I'll not be pent with the rest down there like a herd of cows."

Winter came in a stark morning of snow flurries as a gray bank of clouds rolled in from the west. Where was Ben Winfield now? Wind whistled through bare trees and the brittle cornshocks she and her grandmother gathered and tied in the clearing. The sheep baaed restlessly in their slatted pen and Delilah nailed its loose boards, pounding hard, over and over. The brindle cow began to give less milk, scarcely a pailful a day. The smell of the last wild mint was mixed with the smell of the crabapple butter Gran stirred in a caldron in the cabin yard, her woolen shawl wrapped tightly around her thin shoulders, the smoke spiraling in a white drift to the bleak sky. In the first real snowstorm Delilah went outside to bring buckets of snow to the hearth for melting into drinking water. She hated going to the spring in the cold. Always her father had done that. Huge, wet flakes slanted down for days. Then the snow melted, and streams roared from the mountain's creeks down to the Clinch only to freeze once more. Her fear and her hope were like that. For her, indeed, the winter had come before the frost. She waited, warming the cold of her fear in the labor of routine: milking the brindle cow, kneading bread, scrubbing the puncheons, polishing tables and chairs even when they shone already.

She tried to pray too. *Let Papa come back, God. I hate waiting for anything. You know that.* God was a large, white-bearded gentleman with a stern face and gimlet eyes who sat in the sky watching people. There was nothing you could hide from Him; and when you prayed, you had simply to hope He would decide to be kind.

The biting day her father did return she wasn't looking for him at all. Her grandmother had promised to show her how to quilt, and she was sitting at the long frame waiting with her needle, wondering, her grandmother knew, what patterns she would put across the bare expanse of white tow stretched out so tantalizingly in front of her. A long strand of her dark hair brushed her shoulder, and she was biting her lips in concentration as she bent forward: thinking hard, doubtless, wanting to make out of nothing a thing of her own that was truly pretty, hers especially. The seams of her gown were straining at her shoulders again. It was a wonder, the way her body grew. She was slim enough, though, all clean frame. Her face would have been a beautiful one but for that chin, just a bit too proud and aggressive. Her nose was big too but it was in scale. And her eyes were dreaming eyes, sometimes, as now, so intent on whatever she dreamed that their blue depths were an impenetrable sea. It was those eyes that would draw some man to her, if looks were to draw at all. He would want to break their mystery, to make them shine for him, to make them dream his own dreams . . .

And Delilah mused, unaware of her grandmother's scrutiny: Did you have to use a pattern somebody else had made, or could you invent your own? She would rather do that; she hoped Gran would let her. Suddenly she heard the door, and she heard heavy steps that weren't Gran's. Then all she knew was that she was in her father's arms, her feet deep in batting. Soon he was lifting her up, his hands hard under her armpits, and she was laughing and hugging him while Gran stood to one side, her eyes red-rimmed with tears of happiness, her feet full of flax tufts too. Delilah couldn't cry; but she couldn't stop laughing.

"Look at you, Ben!" Gran scolded joyfully. "Filthy!"

"Oh, Papa!" Delilah kept on laughing until he put his hand on her mouth and pressed her closer. She ran her fingers along his shirt fringes while she heard Gran begin to fly from cupboard to hearth, clattering pewter plates, unstopping the year's foxgrape wine, lifting strips of pickled venison from the crock. When Delilah heard Bickley's voice she turned in surprise, but she went on clinging to her father.

"Aren't you going to welcome me too, Delilah?"

She drew in her breath when she saw the bandage on his bare arm. His sleeve had been torn off, and the bandage was brown with bloodstains. Quickly she reached up to her father's arm, but it was all right, there was no bandage, *he* hadn't been hurt! Her world was safe. "I — " She went to Bickley at last. She had remembered. "You kept your promise."

"Am I forgiven?"

She nodded. "Your arm — "

"Grazed. Nothing much. More cold than sore." He shrugged, his smile fading.

She turned to her father again. "You won, didn't you?" As she looked up at him the sharpness of Bickley's laugh made her shiver.

"Oh, yes. We won." She wheeled around, and she saw his face distorted with bitterness: crooked mouth, empty eyes, rigid neck.

"What happened?" She pressed her hand in her father's calloused one.

"A battle. A great victory, with God's help. You'll hear of it later. Go to your grandmother." It was dismissal, and so she went. It didn't matter, really, Bickley's bitterness. Nothing mattered except that her father was safe.

During dinner Gran piled their plates with fluffy biscuits, with venison and smoked chicken and roast pumpkin and blackberry jelly (the last of that, but who cared!). Delilah kept her eyes on her father. How thin he was! There were hollows below his prominent cheekbones; the cleft in his chin was deeper. Yet his very thinness emphasized the solidity of his frame. His gestures had a new deliberateness in them too, a sureness gained as some of Charles Bickley's old sureness seemed to have been lost. There was no bitterness at all in his face. Instead, Delilah was aware of a look of satisfaction she could never have put into words but which she felt, and from the feeling could draw strength of her own. Yes, her father nodded between mouthfuls, he'd had the bloody flux on the march. Everyone had. His clothes were stiff with mud, his square fingernails were rimmed red-brown with it. At the hearth afterwards he sat close to the fire and Delilah sat at his feet, seeing his boots, ripped and sleazy, while he spoke of the march as if its remembered rigors gave him pleasure: first the long, steaming days upcountry, the sun glaring white-gold in men's eyes until they scarcely saw; then the nights when mists circled the mountains round and round like rings and penetrated into every bone in the men's bodies; at last the days of winter, relentlessly freezing blistered feet, numbing fingers, making the troops desperate for soup and hot meat when all they could stop to eat was pemmican because fires weren't safe in Indian country. All this he had survived. "With God's help, Delilah," he repeated. "We must pray for His continued favor."

"Yes, Papa. But you won. There won't be the Indians any more."

"We won," he echoed proudly, raising his gray head.

And again she heard Bickley laugh, this time dryly and quietly. "You'd better tell her how," he said.

She bit her lip. Her father hunched his shoulders as he bent down over her. "We marched to the Great Kanawha to meet Dunmore." His voice thickened with anger. At once she knew he was talking not only to her and Gran and Bickley, but the whole world. "We marched deep into Shawanese country to meet the troops we needed to fight the red men. For days we risked ourselves in a trap because Dunmore would be waiting: the Governor of Virginia in the field, himself."

"But — "

"He wasn't there. He never came. We had to win without him."

Her hand flew to her lips. "Then — "

"The place he'd sent word for us to come — Point Pleasant — it's exposed on three sides. The Kanawha meets the Ohio there. No enemy could have wanted a better target. Aagh!" He shook his head in disgust. "The morning after we reached it the Shawanese whooped down on us in a horde. Dunmore knew, I tell you! He was in their towns making a treaty. He *must* have seen 'em go. And he never sent a warning." He let out a sharp breath.

"So." Gran's bone knitting needles clicked in the silence which followed. "A deserter and a murderer both, then."

Bickley turned to her, but his eyes were still clouded. "Yes. All that, Ma'am."

Her needles went on clicking, but she made no answer. Delilah laid her head against her father's knees. She wanted to keep touching him, to be sure he was real and alive. "The old army men said it was worse than Braddock. We lost twice as many as we killed. Once Bickley jumped in front of me — that's how he got the arm."

"Hell, Ben, it was an accident. Let's spare the details. May I have another biscuit, Mrs. Mackinnon? I'm hungrier than Ben." Bickley laughed this time as if trying hard to do it.

"If you watch your tongue in front of ladies." Gran grudged a smile as she passed the platter. When the realization of what her father had said broke on Delilah she could only breathe to him: "Then you almost died. You almost did die." She heard the shudder in her voice. "I knew. I don't want to wait like that again, Papa. I couldn't."

"Waiting's most of living."

"Spoken like a schoolmaster, Ben." Bickley tried to keep a chunk of butter from slipping off the top of his biscuit. His knife gleamed briefly in the firelight. "I don't blame Delilah. I hate waiting too."

"Come with me, Ben," Gran broke in. "I'll burn every stitch you have on. Somebody should do the same for you, Mr. Bickley." She stood up, smoothing her skirts. She was still angry with Bickley, Delilah realized; she was scolding him mildly and indifferently, not as if she owned him, which was Gran's way when she loved someone. But what did the past matter? Only the present was real, only the leaning against Ben Winfield's scratched boots and hard legs. Bickley had taken him away, but he was back. Her life could go on. He would continue to fill it. Yet — had Bickley's act been just an accident? Or had he really saved her father's life? If he had, oughtn't they to thank him as well as God? This new thought struck her as Bickley shifted awkwardly in his chair and answered her grandmother.

"My blacks will clean me up, I expect. One night I dreamed of old Isaac bringing me a bowl of hot water and a clean towel."

When Winfield clumped after Gran into the cabin's second room Delilah took her father's chair, even then reveling at the heat on it from his body. Bickley set his plate of biscuits aside and put his elbows on his knees, his hands on his temples, while he stared at the floor. "It was a good

welcome," he said at last. "The way you came to him."
Then he looked up. "He fought well, you know. He's got
an instinct for a rifle."

"Tell me the truth," she heard herself saying slowly. "Did
you really save him?"

"I don't want any thanks from you, Delilah."

There were new lines at Bickley's eyes tonight, even sug-
gestions of lines running from the corners of his mouth down
to his jaw. How many years ago had he gotten the gray
patch? She couldn't remember. Her father was here, and
that was what mattered. Bickley said he'd fought brave
and she must keep her mind on his deliverance and —

The name broke into her consciousness like a shot. Dunmore.

"The Governor — your Governor — you really admit he
was wrong?"

Bickley rose and began to walk in the room, his shoulders
rounded, his hands clasped behind his back. "I have to admit
it. I saw. I'll never forgive what I saw — the tomahawks
and scalps, decent men from Cassel's Woods turned into
savages themselves. I try to think why he made it happen
and I get no answer but betrayal."

"So you're not a Tory any more."

"No, I gave that up. The last link. Your father helped
me through it." He sank into the rush chair again, its plaits
creaking from the weight of him. "But it wouldn't interest
you." Abruptly he grinned across to her: "I take it you'll let
me stay here tonight. In the morning you can say 'I told you
so' all you like. That's what a woman wants most, isn't it?"

At least, she thought afterwards, he hadn't this time called
her a child when he teased her. And whatever else had happened to him, he could, after all, still tease.

4

H E BEGAN coming often to the cabin; his mills were idle because the creek was frozen over. She would hear Mercury stamping in the yard while he tied him, then hear the familiar rap at the door. Sometimes she would find him staring up at the flying squirrels huddled in chattering bands in the sugar trees as if he had never seen them before.

"It's been so long since you've cleared you can't remember 'em, Charles?" With a mocking smile her father would tap out his long clay pipe in its dish. "Noisy varmints. You'll be thinking I'm slow at clearing, but I haven't got blacks."

Charles flushed. (They all called him Charles now, even Gran when she thought of it. He had asked them to.) Delilah could remember her wonder at his blacks on the journey west: the slouching phalanx of bare-chested, heavy-muscled field hands, the woolly-headed body servant called Isaac, and a skinny house slave whose hair was knotted in corkscrew curls, each tied with a faded pink ribbon. In Cassel's Woods Charles's blacks must have become a familiar sight by now. Delilah had once seen the Negro woman trudging from the springs there with bucketsful of water to his cabin; had seen her, too, sitting on the stoop as she tied a cornshuck broom, her eyes large and white as if they sought something beyond the mountains to the east . . . Delilah

began to wonder more than ever why Charles had come to
the Clinch. He wasn't poor; he couldn't be seeking to become what he already, apparently, was — rich. Perhaps he
was running away from something or somebody, as so many
people out here had done.

One afternoon when her father was cleaning the sheep
pen she walked with Charles to the spring. Tiny bunches
of mistletoe were swinging from the oaks overhead. She
watched him look up, then scoop a handful of white berries
from the tufted ground.

"Didn't you have mistletoe at home?" She drew her cloak
more tightly around her in the wind.

He shook his head, his eyes oddly wistful and boyish.
Then he scattered the berries away. "You'll have a good sugar bush here some day. Your father can buy blacks when
he trades his runs to the Settlements."

"Have you ever sugared?"

"No." He scuffed his boot at a rock, then kicked it away.
"I've read about it, though. I grew tobacco." She waited,
hoping he would go on; but he didn't.

"Did you have a plantation of your own?"

"My father did." He kept his eyes on his boot as he turned
up twigs and leafmold. "He had everything. Green Springs,
our place was called. It was in Louisa County. You could
just see the Blue Ridge from the house."

In the silence which followed she knew he wouldn't say
more, and she didn't want to ask, to intrude. She only said,
to break the silence: "It's funny — your seeing the Blue
Ridge and wondering, then knowing after all, going over it
and beyond."

"So you know I wondered." He smiled. " 'Come on, then,
boys, it's one to ten/ We'll all turn into gentlemen/ To

prance and strut as well as they/ Over the hills and far away.' It's got a thousand verses, that. I suppose you don't know it. Our militia twisted it out of *The Beggar's Opera.* I remember sitting in the playhouse in Williamsburg with my uncle once and hearing a verse — 'Were I sold on Indian soil . . .' And here I am. I never thought it then. Well — this isn't helping your father, is it? Life's a rum business and no man changes it. You'd better go in, you're cold. I'll earn my dinner by making myself useful in the pen." With that he strode away from her, beginning to push up his sleeves. That night Gran heated a caldron of water, and he and her father scrubbed dirt-caked hands and faces and brushed the straw from their buckskins.

"Charles can sing, Papa. Did you know it?"

"I can read, too." Charles grinned. He drew a paper from the pouch which hung at his waist. "I've read this."

Dinner was finished. Delilah went to stand over her father's shoulder while he studied the paper in silence. The words of the flowing script were jumbled: "We . . . men of Fincastle County . . . free exercise of our religion . . . liberties and properties as British subjects . . . loyal . . . but . . ." She squinted:

> . . . but if no pacifick measures shall be adopted by Great Britain and our enemies will attempt to dragoon us out of those inestimable privileges which we are entitled to as subjects and to reduce us to a state of slavery, we declare that we are deliberately and resolutely determined never to surrender them to any power on earth but at the expense of our lives.

She felt Gran's breath close by: minty and warm. Gran was reading too.

"Why — 'tis treason, Ben! Breaking with the King — all that on paper for the world to see." She straightened. "You'll not sign that. You've a daughter. There's never been a thing like it! We've liberties anough where we are."

"I've not been asked to sign, Madam. Russell has signed for all of us. But I believe what it says and I'll tell him so. So do you believe."

Delilah did not understand what new liberties her father wanted; perhaps this had something to do with the perpetual tax troubles back in the Settlements. But she was proud of his resolution, of his deep voice, the set of his head. The liberties to him, doubtless, were Principles. And Principles in turn were things a body could hold to, could cherish even in a wilderness of baffling trees and rank woods and crude frontiersmen — Cohees — who sneered and scoffed at books. She was glad her father had Charles to talk to now.

Charles clasped his hands. "I've already told Russell I'll back him, Ben."

"Have you lost your mind?" Gran snapped at him. "Lord Dunmore could grant your cornright and Ben's too to a court fop tomorrow to punish you both. He'll hear of this. He hears of everything, I'll warrant." Then she stalked away to her flax wheel and began to thump at it vigorously.

"Let him try to move us out," Winfield grunted.

Charles put one hand firmly on the arm of his chair. "Never." Delilah saw his knuckles whiten. "No man alive can take my holdings, Ben." And the coldness of his tone as he said that sent a shiver down Delilah's back.

"You'd better hope your people have influence in Williamsburg." Gran was biting her lip, her feet moving harder at the treadle. "You're young yet. They could pass you off as a silly boy."

"They have influence. But I'll do for myself, Mrs. Mackinnon." Charles reached for a book which lay open on the table and began to turn its pages quickly until he came to a place he wanted. Slowly, a sense of peace settled over the room as the shadows of its rough-hewn furniture danced on the chinked walls in the firelight. Gran didn't like risks, Delilah thought as she began to mend one of her aprons, drawing her needle in and out, over and over; but that's for my sake. She thinks Papa and Charles are fools for declaring but she likes them for it too . . . What book was Charles reading? Perhaps her father's copy of the *Letters of a Farmer From Pennsylvania*, which were against the Parliament across the sea. Captain Russell had brought this from the Settlements on his last trip. Now Charles's face was bent close in the dim light of the betty lamp beside him: high forehead, with its falling black forelock, long humped nose, square chin which rested in his knuckles. He was scowling in comic concentration, as if trying to memorize strange exercises in a new school. Well: he hadn't declared for Principles, after all, only for his anger at Lord Dunmore's meanness. She'd tried reading the *Farmer's Letters* herself once, but they were so hopelessly dull she'd never gotten beyond the first two pages. Her father had begun reading too, and was making sharp notes in the margin the way he always did, his goosequill scratching out its pokeberry juice. The copy of the Fincastle Resolutions lay still open on the table, its physical reality forgotten. But its meaning was everywhere. It was a symbol of the bond between Ben Winfield and Charles Bickley. Charles had told Delilah a little about his past this day. Once he had grown tobacco in Louisa County. He had a father and an uncle, and he'd been to the opera. But he'd really told her nothing. She realized that.

A plantation, relations — not what he felt for them. Had he loved his father as she loved hers? What did he want from his living? (What do I? she wondered suddenly.) Why had he looked, outside, as if he were trying to memorize every tree on Sugar Hill? (What *do* I want? I don't know!)

The lamp sputtered, sent up a cloud of greasy black smoke, and then died, throwing Charles's face in shadow. She thought he might have been smiling again, but she couldn't be sure.

"It's agreeable, you know," he said later. "Not to be always alone." And then he laughed, as if half at himself. "Heathens tolerate Presbyterians right well, don't they?"

Her father, reading, didn't hear this last. Neither, fortunately, did Gran, for she had gone to bed.

When Charles brought Dan Boone to supper Gran made a potful of raccoon stew. Dan loudly smacked his lips over it. He always wore the same black-dyed deerskin shirt around the fort, Charles said. He had bulging eyes and a thin face, a soft jaw and quiet voice. His table manners were terrible. "Goin' to have a fire hunt," he announced with his mouth full. "No Indian sign yet. I'm for Kentuk against spring comes, so we'll have us a fire hunt by way of celebratin'."

"I want to go!" Delilah pleaded quickly. "Papa, please. I've never seen fire hunting."

"She'll bring us luck." Dan munched on his meat. "She's a peart one for thirteen, ain't she?"

Delilah liked Dan Boone for all his roughness. He wasn't bad looking. He didn't have the black rotten teeth most of the hunters had. Sometimes he stared off dreamily, the lids half down over his eyes, and she wondered what he was thinking then. "It's Eden, Kentuk is." He leaned back in his chair. "Empty and waitin'. So much peter dirt a man could make his own powder. Oh, it's fine — the cane and the trees, and peavines so thick you'd not need to feed aught else to your stock. I saw."

"You're not afraid?"

"Because of Jim bein' skulped? Why, honey, Jim would want me to go. I'm buildin' a chapel here so you folks can remember Jim. Say a prayer for him an' one for me now an' then, will you? Any man in his right mind is afraid of Indians. It's best so."

Kentuk was Dan Boone's Eden, but Sugar Hill was hers. Perhaps there would be peace forever. Perhaps Chief Benge and his Cherokees, the closest Indians, would stay on the Tenase and let Ben Winfield and Charles Bickley and the others have the Clinch to themselves. The Shawanese had been whipped by Virginians at Point Pleasant, hadn't they? Surely the Cherokees knew it.

"Don't you count on peace," Dan grinned. "Benge's a redheaded halfbreed with itchy fingers. All this land used to be his, before old Jake Cassel got it for a butcher knife an' then gave it away for a musket."

If there has to be more war let it be in Kentuk, Delilah thought quickly before she could stop herself. Then she flushed in shame. She didn't want to wish Dan Boone dead either.

The river was plashing at the shore the night she stepped into the long canoe in front of her father. She clutched her skirts as the canoe rocked in the waves. Then she scrambled down beside Charles Bickley's legs, pushing back her hair and breathing deeply. What an adventure this was! When her father needed game he went alone, afraid she would frighten it. She was happy tonight because he trusted her.

"You're quiet." Charles bent over her. "Hadn't you better say us a charm? You ought to know some good Scotch ones."

She felt herself blush. "It isn't fair to tease all the time." Then she turned away.

When Dan Boone handed her father the burning torch she forgot to be quiet. "Oh, let me hold it!" she cried so loud the men laughed. She could hear even stern Captain Russell laughing boisterously, his reddish hair and beard shot with gold in the firelight. He hadn't laughed much, people said, since his son Henry had been killed . . . Again she blushed, because she knew he was laughing at her as Charles had been. But she took the torch and raised her arm high. Yellow flames soared into the deep blue above. Dan Boone and one of Russell's sons began paddling into the river. She felt droplets jab at her face but she was concentrating all her energy on keeping the torch steady, though her arm was beginning to ache from its weight. A curious deer would come to the shore, her father explained. They'd shoot it then. Overhead the stars were hazed by April mist. Wind played in the naked gray branches of the sycamores, flapping the peeling bark strips on their trunks. The torch crackled.

"There!" someone whispered. She saw her father's neck and jaw muscles tense with excitement.

"Hold the torch where it is." He took his fowling piece, its fittings gleaming coldly. When she turned her head to the shore she saw two small points of light, the eyes of the deer. Just as he raised his gun she cried out hoarsely: "No!"

But he didn't hear her. The gun cracked out in a flash of white, the smell of powder hung around her, and the men began turning the canoe to the shore, their elbows bent furiously as they struck their paddles downward. "Heave her!"

"Got him!" Dan Boone whooped.

Delilah felt her father snatching the torch from her, heard it hiss as he doused it in the river, but she couldn't think of that. She had never seen a deer shot. There had been something so wild and appealing in those two points of light. Now they would never shine again. The deer was dead. And she hadn't wanted it to be dead at all. It hadn't deserved to die. What was she doing here?

The men scrambled out of the canoe when they beached it on the mud. She let them pass stumbling over the corners of her skirt and cloak. In the dim light of their smoking lanterns she could make out the tawny stretched form of a doe. The doe had come to the river to drink and had been shot. Why had she wanted to see this? Her father was kneeling down, beginning to skin with the other men. He'd killed; and he didn't even care! She could hear knives cutting at the flesh, could smell the hot blood; she swallowed down her nausea and tried not to see her father's head bent over the flanks, his arms moving in long, firm, slashing strokes as if he relished his task.

The venison plopped as the men threw bundles of it into the canoe. The fresh smell rose headier. When they brought the skin, rolled and tied, a corner of it rubbed past her face. It was hairy and warm. She bent her head to her knees, squinching down. She was sitting that way when she felt the canoe gliding out, back up the river toward home.

"What's the matter?" Her father leaned over her. "Delilah, what's come over you?"

She huddled away. "I wish I hadn't come. To kill her when she only came to drink — you didn't care!"

"Delilah." All the affection left his voice. "You're being

squeamish. I won't tolerate that. We needed meat. You know how we get our meat, I trust."

It was just meat when I saw it before! she wanted to shout. But she did not. Her father's voice was brusque and clipped: "I shot while you held the torch. Remember that."

The canoe floated on; the men talked and grunted with pleasure among themselves; Captain Russell told a story of two buck deer locking antlers outside his cabin last summer. When she felt a hand on her head she knew it wasn't her father's. The shapes of its scars were familiar from another time . . . She didn't move. Charles kept his hand in her hair, his fingers hot and moist as he tightened them.

At the Sugar Hill shore, she fled before the canoe had been tied. She ran through the icy water to find her hollow, but she heard a quick step after hers, and she turned. Charles's face was blue-white from the light of the half-moon, his eyes wide and dark. "Delilah — " He stopped before her, getting breath. "Are you all right? Are you sick?"

"No!" She swallowed hard. "I mean — " her hand flew nervously to her cloak pin — "they couldn't tell I almost — "

"No. I could, though." Slowly, he added: "Your father shouldn't have said what he did about the torch. It was cruel."

"He didn't know." She swallowed again, trying not to show her hurt or even what was left of her queasiness. "He only meant it was my fault too. And it was, don't you see?"

"I'm afraid not." His mouth was as grim as his eyes were gentle.

She raised her face to his. "But, Charles — "

"Yes?" He bent so close she could feel his breath on her forehead. "You're sure you're all right?"

She nodded. "Thank you for coming."

"For God's sake don't thank me." His voice was rough as he straightened. "I wish I could help: this and — other things. That's all." Abruptly, he turned and left her, the dry twigs of last autumn cracking under his jackboots as he made his way back to the boat.

It was only when she lay under her quilt in the dark loft of the cabin on Sugar Hill that she remembered his return from the battle so many months ago. Outside, a titmouse was whistling at the moon. In the slender shaft of light from the loophole above her, she could see Charles's face not as she had just seen it, concerned and kindly, but as it had looked that night, the night she had flung herself at her father and had all but ignored him. She could see the loneliness of drawn lips and puzzled eyes as she had never seen or understood it before. Of course he had saved her father! He must have; and she'd barely stopped to be grateful, she'd made him say that he wanted no thanks from her at all. He'd said it then, and said it again tonight. Always her father's love and his care, his principles and his God had been the center of her life. Yet tonight they had all failed her. Tonight it was Charles who had come to care for her and comfort her. *It wasn't Papa who came but Charles* . . . Over and over that thought began to run in her mind. At last she fell into a restless sleep, punctuated by the steady rumble of her father's voice as he prayed aloud below in gratitude for a successful hunt. He had prayed that way too, she remembered, after the battle.

5

THE DOGWOODS bloomed early on Sugar Hill, and the air grew heavy with the scent of its fire cherries. Soon the azaleas were flaming orange in the hollows. It was going to be a summer of intense heat, stifling like the waiting for Indian attacks that might, or might not, come. To the south there were Chief Benge and the Cherokees: enemies of the Shawanese, but Indians too. Once Benge had owned the Clinch, before he had traded it to the hunter Cassel for a butcher knife. Benge might yet decide to take revenge on the white men, to join the Shawanese if the Shawanese broke the treaty they had made with Lord Dunmore.

"Dunmore." Charles gritted the name in contempt every time. Dunmore, in his camp after the fight, had shown himself to be a swaggering sandy-haired lout in a tam. He had treated the militia privates as if they had been dogs to be spat upon; "rattlesnake privates," he'd called them. He'd treated the Indians like dogs too; surely they had known it, seen it. Dunmore had goaded them into war. Would they forget their war now, Delilah wondered? Or would they, as Charles said he feared, sweep down from the misty ridges to the south, the west, the north, their blood fired and their hands twitching on tomahawks and on the rifles traders sold them along with fresh-stilled whisky? He'd seen those Pennsylvania wagons with "Baynton, Wharton and Morgan" painted across their blue bottoms. Traders cared for money, not lives, excepting their own. She wanted to talk to Charles; but he began to stay at his mill to dress his burrs for the new season, to saw out hominy blocks for the fort, and to peg the last bedsteads for its cabins. A year ago she would have wanted to talk to her father. But that had been before the fire hunt. She could not forget the hunt, would never forget. Her father had blamed her for sharing in the kill and Charles hadn't. How could her father fail to understand she hadn't known what killing was, what it meant?

"You will eat that venison, Delilah," he'd said when Gran had aged it. She hadn't dared not to eat it, but it had stuck in her throat. Otherwise he hadn't spoken of the hunt since. What hurt was not so much the death of the doe as his blindness to what was in her heart.

She saw Charles briefly the day Dan Boone left for Kentuk. First she stopped with her father at the chapel for which Dan had given the timber and Charles the labor of his slaves. Then she stood with her father and Charles to watch Dan stride off into the woods, whistling as he went. His pale, dark-haired wife and his cluster of children followed, riding Captain Russell's workhorses, a last gift to them. Dan's wife and children were silent and hard-faced, not whistling at all. Perhaps they were remembering their first start. Mrs. Boone held her head very high, but her forehead was creased with lines, her brows were raised petulantly, and her eyes were like those of a mournful squirrel, small and sharp and sad.

"She knows, I reckon," Delilah heard Charles tell her father. "She won't stay in Kentuk either. Dan's not the staying sort." The little train wound away while the wind stirred the cedars. Delilah felt Charles's hand ruffling her hair. "Would you like to see Kentuk?"

"No. I mean to stay home."

"Ah! So do I."

On Sundays, the men — all except Charles — took turns leading prayers at Boone's Chapel, which smelled strongly of resin and oil. The benches were hard, the walls bare. Charles came, but he belonged to the English Church, and didn't seem to know the prayers and hymns Ben Winfield often led himself, standing at the front of the center aisle, his hand raised:

> *"Who knows how near my life's expended?*
> *Time flies, and death is hasting on;*
> *Who knows how soon, the battle ended,*
> *May heave my last expiring groan?"*

A Pennyslvania preacher had written that hymn before a massacree. He'd been scalped in it, but the hymn had spread down the Alleghenies and Appalachians even so . . . Charles always sang with the rest, and after the service he would stay to greet the Winfields. But then he would leave, doubtless to eat dinner alone in his cabin. He worked in his mills even on Sabbath afternoons, having no principle against it. That was wrong, of course, though Delilah's father said Charles's religion was his own business as long as he didn't preach it. She could never help smiling at the table grace Charles said a man ought to use when his wife got sudden company; it was more cheerful than the massacree hymn.

> *The Lord be praised! I am amazed*
> *To see how things have mended.*

Biscuits and tea now I see
Where mush and milk were intended.

She had laughed so hard at that, and he with her; they'd been outside together; but later when she heard her father's grace, slow and solemn and reverent, she felt guilty.

It was Captain Russell, not Charles, who rode up Sugar Hill to bring the latest news. "This is it," he said shortly as he swung down from his horse. "Massachusetts men have fired on British soldiers at a village near Boston. I've had a letter. Washington of Mount Vernon will head a Continental army." Russell's mouth widened in his long sunburned face. "Oh, yes, and Dunmore's pulled one trick too many. He seized the powder in the magazine at Williamsburg. Town was in such an uproar he had to flee with it to a British warship off the coast. We've a new governor now — Patrick Henry. The Parliament's been told so, at least."

But that, Delilah thought, wasn't news of the Indians. What did the Settlements' doings matter out here, or the Parliament's either? She wished it had been Charles who had come.

Russell pulled thoughtfully at his beard. "Bickley — is his rebellion genuine, Winfield?"

"He backed the Resolutions. We can't ask more."

"Pity if he hadn't. Do you trust him?"

Delilah, at her quilting frame inside, felt her cheeks reddening. "I do! He isn't either a Tory — he told us he wasn't." And when she heard Russell and her father both laughing at her she wanted to stamp her foot under the frame. The men turned away and began to talk: England off their necks, no quitrents, no tea tax, no Proclamation Line, no Dunmore . . . but it didn't seem real. What were the Cherokees close by going to do?

"I wish we *knew,* Gran," she sighed that night when Russell had ridden off.

"*I* know," Gran said. Then she began knitting faster, her needles flying in tightened fingers.

The clearing yielded a good harvest. Delilah could smell the nutlike tang of Charles's wheat, too, every Sunday in chapel. After the service she saw the green-timbered stockade beyond, with a row of cedar water buckets lined up at its gate. Sometimes she stayed with her father and Gran to watch Captain Russell gathering the militia for drill. The young boys and old men tramped on the ground while Russell shouted: "Cock firelock — make ready — take aim — fire!" They didn't waste powder; they made believe. The men who had fought at Point Pleasant naturally knew already how to shoot. Delilah shivered when she heard her grandmother murmuring to Russell: "I'm a ready hand at running bullets, Captain. I've not forgotten Shenandoah."

When word came from a trader that the Cherokees were planning to raid Rye Cove fort, twenty-five miles down the valley, Delilah's father wasn't called to go but Charles was. For days she wondered what was happening to him there. He didn't like fighting; she knew it. He even hated hunting — or had he made her think that out of kindness? She could see him in her mind as he marched: his lean body, the way his forelock kept falling, his long step and his large eyes and his smile, and his scratched hands that felt soft at the same time they felt hard . . . The leaves crackled under her feet when she went to feed the chickens each morning, her water bucket hanging on her arm, her thick hair blowing back in the wind, her cheeks reddened and her eyes bright with the cold, her body braced straight against it. In the poultry house she set down her bucket to scoop kernels from the sack. Then she bent easily to fill the water pan. She always smiled to watch the hens picking busily at her feet. Chickens were comical, foolish in their self-importance, bobbing in little jerks and clucking as if each feeding were an event of which they must tell each other they approved. Chickens weren't lonesome, no; they had plenty of company to peck at and talk to. Her eyes grew vague as she wondered again about Rye Cove. On the way back to the cabin she swung the empty water bucket and took long strides through the dry leaves, listening to the swish of them at her feet, her head bent to see her ankles covered by them as if by sea waves.

"Learn to walk quietly, missy," Gran said dryly. "It's useful knowledge these days."

It had begun to snow by the time Charles came back. Her eyes were so blinded by whiteness as she scattered crusts for titmice that she could hardly make out his figure on Mercury until he was almost before her and she heard the stallion snorting and stamping.

"Oh!" She ran to him. "You're safe! What happened? Tell me!"

And then he was laughing, not at her but as if to share a joke, and he was taking her hands in his the minute he had jumped from his saddle. "Not a Cherokee in miles. The march was a false alarm." Charles's shirt smelled like her father's: tobacco and lye soap, leather and sharp tannin from its lacings. "Are you glad I'm back this time?"

"You *know* I am!"

He stopped laughing to stare at her. She *was* glad, he realized. This time, she really was. Her eyes were shining, her full mouth smiled at him with eagerly parted lips, her hands were warm and moist in his own. The way her dark hair was caught back in its ribbon emphasized the clarity of her features and the paleness of her skin, and especially those

deep laughing eyes. She was a strong, lovely child, her welcome now like a blazing fire at which he was suddenly asked
to warm himself. This warmth, this — was it a kind of love,
her gladness? — were for himself, for Charles Bickley. She
loved him today as she loved her own family, and the knowledge of it gave him a wave of pleasure that was indeed like a
fire's warmth. Slowly, he smiled back at her.

It was to Delilah a baffled smile. Couldn't he believe she
was really happy? She'd never seen quite this sort of puz-
zlement in him before, as if he wondered how anybody could
care for him at all.

It grew too cold to quilt on the far side of the fire, and the
snow was often too deep for Charles to come up the mountain or for the Winfields to go down to the chapel. So Gran
spun flax and Delilah watched her, night after night. Some
day I'll be old like Gran, she thought: I'll be sixty myself. I
want to look like her then — straight and small and thin. I
wish I were shorter. I'm fourteen and I still don't stop growing, and I wonder if Papa thinks I'm clumsy . . . Delilah
looked down at her moccasins and wrinkled her nose. Her
one pair of slippers was far too small now. They pinched her
fearfully though Captain Russell had brought them from
the Settlements only three years ago. Moccasins made her
feet look even bigger than they were. Did Charles think she
was clumsy? She wondered how to make her hair behave
when she washed it. On Tidewater Gran had used lavender
water and dried it with an immense Turkish towel; but the
heavy towels had all worn out and lavender didn't grow on
Sugar Hill and Gran hadn't brought any seeds of it, not having room in the saddlebags. Delilah had to wash her hair

with the lye soap instead. Her whole head smelled like medicine, and her hair felt ever so coarse and was hard to tie back . . . Had the women been pretty, where Charles came from? Had they used scent, back in Louisa County below the Blue Ridge?

When Russell came again to Sugar Hill it was to tell them there had been a raid at Fort Blackmore. "Our neighbors, Winfield. A man killed. Start packing. I won't have a child murdered here by those yellow dogs of savages."

"So the worst begins, does it?" Gran's sigh was bitter. She was to stay in the fort with Delilah while Winfield, with armed men to help him, began his first plantings by day and returned to the fort at night. Then he'd help other men plant, and once every fortnight he could hoe for himself. "If necessary you'll give that up," Russell added. "We'll raise enough to carry you."

The fort seemed almost a sort of game to Delilah. The women, chatting and clustering, drew lots for their turns at tasks: going to Big Spring Branch for water, pounding corn and sweeping the yard and spelling the watch while the men were sleeping. Families who lived nearby kept running back and forth to and from their cabins. On sunny afternoons the men stood lounging in their linseys and buckskins against the stockade. When Joe Sawyer's youngest boy began pulling at the bellrope everybody laughed. But the laughter died when Russell stalked up to him, smacked him across the cheeks and bellowed: "Fool child!" Then he flung the boy aside and stumped away.

"He's turned mean, Cap'n has," Mrs. Sawyer hissed. "Don't pay e'er mind to him, Billy. Hateful Tuckahoe dandy so proud of hisself it pleasures him making folks dance to his tune. Just on account he brought us out here he ain't

Goddamighty." Billy Sawyer whimpered at his mother's faded skirts; but he never pulled the bellrope again.

Charles was living at the fort too, but every day he was at his mills. The sound of the wheel and saw came steady now from the first flush of morning into the blue dusk. At night he was making maps for Captain Russell; sometimes Delilah could hear his quill scratching when she passed his cabin on her way back from feeding the chickens . . . It was hard for her to believe in the war when nobody she cared for was threatened. It even seemed strange that one family, the Cowans, had chosen such a quiet time to leave the fort and go back to the Settlements.

She was seeing new people and making new friends: the helter-skelter batch of Sawyer children, and a boy of fifteen named Simon Oscher who began to carry her water bucket every afternoon when she went to Big Spring Branch for Gran's washing. Captain Russell had decided to let people drink only from the tiny spring inside the fort; but everybody knew how *he* was. Simon Oscher laughed with her about Captain Russell's fears and proud ways and asked her questions about Sugar Hill. "Ever since I come out with Mam and Pap I wanted to see it. I heard the miller — Bickley — talking about it the other day. He said it's a prime sugar bush. Said he'd admire to own such hisself." Simon had a high shock of yellow hair as dry and stiff as cornsilk. He had sinewy arms under his shirtsleeves, and a friendly crooked grin which lighted his freckled face. He always stood very straight. His eyes were brown and big over a long nose and chin. There was a tiny red vein in the right eye which had burst, he told her, when he'd hoed too many hours under the sun last year on the farm his pap had rented back east in Louisa County. "It hurt some," he said modestly.

"We had to work most as hard for the landlord as we do here for our own selves. But a man's got to stand such." He arched up on the balls of his feet and swayed back and forth.

Twilight was falling. Fireflies were beginning to sparkle. She stood with Simon at the fort gate, swinging her hand idly. She felt peaceful, contented. A line of women were washing clothes at the cedar tubs in the corner with a steady ploshing and dripping. The sound of pounding came rhythmic and dull from the hominy blocks. She was surprised when she felt a familiar hand on her shoulder and looked up to see Charles standing over. In his other hand he held a small, reddish ball of fur hardly bigger than a baby rabbit. It was too red for a rabbit; but it was alive.

"Let me see!"

He held it toward her in his palms — a tiny fox, not more than a few weeks old, its body pulsing with the quick breath of fear, its bushy tail bristling. Its brown eyes had an intense dignity even when it jerked its head. "Take it. I found it in the woods — curled up in a hole in an elm tree. Somebody probably shot the mother. It isn't hurt but it needs food."

She could feel its heartbeat, fast and panicked. When it tried to jump down she tightened her grip. "Oh!" How sharp its claws were! If she could keep it, if she could! Her father could make a leash, and a feeding bowl, and — but Captain Russell wouldn't want it near the chickens in the fort. Her heart sank. She stroked the fox and held it close to her breast, feeling it hers already, not wanting to lose it, fearing she must. Its ears were small and pointed. The tip of its black nose was wet. Its fur was so soft!

"The chickens — "

"I'll make a cage if you want one. I thought of that."

She could give it milk from the brindle cow, smuggle it pieces of her own meat when it was older, pick poke greens for it. She began rocking it. It was shuddering. "It's so scared, Charles — look! Oh, Gran's got to let me keep it. I'll need a big cage, and — " She swallowed, remembering her manners. "Thank you very much."

"What a proper little Calvinist you are." When he walked away she watched him for a moment, stung by his flippancy. Then she turned back to the fox. Reynard: Gran had told her tales, she'd call it Reynard. When it was old enough she'd let it go — oh, she surely would, she wouldn't pen it up forever. But to have a pet, her own! And a cage! She had forgotten Simon completely until she heard him kick a stone, suddenly and furiously. The fox started and yipped. She grasped it hard.

"Well, if that doesn't beat all!" Simon burst out. "Miller, so high and graceful, bringin' you a thing I could've brought any day. You should've told me you fancied such."

"Hush, you'll scare it!"

"You got no call to take a thing from the miller. My pap says he never does e'er thing for a man unless he wants something. You know who the miller is? My pap does! Used t'see the miller's uncle back in Louisa ridin' in a carriage with a plume stuck in his hat — a British 'Sir,' he was. You know that?"

"It's not true!" Her hands tightened on the fox.

"Ain't it? Well, my pap asked the miller the minute he heard his name, the first day we come. Pap said, 'You kin to Sir Will'am Bickley?' And the miller said yes, he was, but he didn't want nothing said. Gave out he wanted to make his own way. But Pap says if the King fights us all he'll tell. The miller might be a spy. You know what folks said about

Sir Will'am Bickley in Louisa?" Simon bent close to her. "Said he used one hand to carry the English prayer book and the other to carry a whip. I'd never put dependence in the miller. Maybe he's bein' nice to you just so he can get your pap's land. He'd do that."

"Don't be stupid." She drew herself up. How nasty Simon was! Jealous and selfish, hatefully selfish, not to care what she'd been given. It couldn't be true about Charles. Could it? Was it? He'd said he was a Tory. But now he'd changed, he'd said that too. Oh, it was mean of Simon not to trust him.

"Ask how miller got Dave Cowan's cornright," Simon growled. "Dave had a washout and couldn't pay for log-sawin' with his crop as he'd promised. Miller took his farm instead. Made Dave sign a paper. You just ask, Delilah Winfield. He drove the Cowans away."

"It's not true," she repeated, clutching Reynard all the while. When she heard Gran calling her to supper she held Reynard tight while she ran toward her cabin, and when she had slammed its door the words poured out: "I've got a pet, Gran, and Charles is going to make a cage — and Simon was nasty and told stories about Charles getting the Cowans' farm, and — "

Gran turned around. Her mouth opened. Then she started laughing. She came to Delilah, peered at the fox, and touched the ruff of fur at its neck. "Well, let him down, child. He's scared half to death of you."

"Can I keep him if Charles makes a cage? He promised! And, Gran, it's *not* true about the Cowans, is it? They wanted to go, didn't they? They were afraid." She stooped to free Reynard. He stood motionless, as if he doubted his legs could carry him anywhere. But just as she reached to pet him he scampered behind her father's trunk, his claws scratching the puncheons as he wobbled and slid away. Gran laughed again.

"One question at a time. 'Twill take some doing to tame it. Keep it, eh? And if I say no, do you think I could abide by it? Child, I've ever had a weakness for varmints, Lord forgive me." She went back to the mutton stew she was making; she'd traded flax to Mrs. Sawyer for a sheep's neck. "Mind you make your father fix a leash tonight. Walk the beast in the yard. Foxes stink."

"Will Papa let me — "

"He will," Gran said firmly. "As for the Cowans, what does it matter for your fox, eh? It may well be true; but I'd not spread the talk. What Charles Bickley does is his own matter unless he takes your father into a war where he's no business going. Enjoy your fox." Gran's ladle circled in the caldron, round and round. "Foxes, coons — they make good pets. I had a coon once. The smart way that coon used to get under the bedcovers — " Her laughter died. "My mother hated it, though. It was a little thing. But she hated it. Said it was a sin to love a varmint. I don't know — " Her voice trailed away.

Delilah filled a mug of water at the piggen. "It was mean of Simon, Gran. And he told me — " But, no; she wouldn't speak of the part about the uncle . . .

Gran kept on stirring. "You're always wanting to grow up, missy. Maybe you're doing that. There's pleasure in being a woman; but mind you don't enjoy it too much, the way menfolk behave like buck deer."

That night Ben Winfield turned a pair of frayed bootlaces into a makeshift leash and collar. Reynard strained and yelped and then curled up exhausted to sleep at the hearth.

Delilah felt her father's arm come around her waist as she watched. And as she pressed herself against him, she felt the old closeness between them. "Happy? I'm glad you've a thing to care for." Was he, too, thinking of the dead doe? When Delilah crept to the hearth to stroke Reynard, the fox trembled, but slept on. Her father stroked him too, over and over, as if wanting her to see him do it.

She didn't ask her father about the Cowans' farm. She didn't tell him about Simon's gossip. Pleasure in being a woman, Gran had said . . . her very feet felt smaller, her hands smoother, and she reckoned even her waist looked narrower below her swelling bodice.

Simon Oscher, of course, wasn't a man at all, like Charles. He was only a boy.

Captain Russell marched away with a detachment of militia the day after Charles finished the cage, its pegged walnut bottom and sides shining in the sun from the polish he'd given them. He'd even polished the ashwood slats on the sliding door. He went with Russell; a scout had ridden in from the Watauga settlements below the Virginia line with word that Benge was massing his Cherokees far down the Holston River. The men had let out whoops of joy. Cassel's Woods was safe! While Russell took his small contingent into the valley, those left behind propped the fort gates open with boulders. The women began packing bundles to take back to their houses: cookpots, trenchers, ladles, quilts, sassafras brooms. The battle would be somewhere else — and weren't half the captains of Virginia, men from every frontier county, going down to stop Benge? Maybe Benge would sign a treaty himself: who knew? The Winfields went back to Sugar Hill, loading Chickamo with bags of meal, Gran driving the sheep and hogs toward the ford, Delilah leading Reynard on his leash like a tiny dog and shouting to the brindle cow to move, because they were going home. Simon Oscher came to say goodbye as if nothing had ever happened, as if he had never been rude at all. Well, what did she care? Silly freckleface! As for Charles's British uncle and the Cowans' leaving, she wouldn't spread talk. A man's past was his own business, her father always said.

6

When the militia returned her father went down to the fort. There had been no battle, he learned, but a treaty at Long Island of the Holston. The Cherokee chiefs had been ranged in a row to make their marks. How many there had been, besides Benge. It surprised and disquieted a body, that crowd of savages. Benge, the halfbreed with flaming red hair; Hargis, the white renegade who always fought with him and could actually write his name; Attacullaculla, called "the little carpenter" because he built peace and friendship between the red man and the white . . . Old Attacullaculla had been laden with silver gorgets and British-made medals.

Later, at her hearth on Sugar Hill, Delilah could hear all the privates' tales in her father's repetition of them while she sat before him. Her father could make things and people come alive when he talked of them; it was why you remembered a thing when he taught it to you.

"Russell says" — Winfield moistened his lips — "that the Congress in Philadelphia has gone the Fincastle Resolutions one better. They've declared independence from Britain."

Delilah heard Gran gasp. The spell was broken. "No!" Gran breathed at last. "Ben, no."

He nodded, his hands stiff in his lap. "It's come. I'd have been on my knees if Russell hadn't said what I was thinking about the Cherokees."

"An army," Gran said dully, turning away. "A British army in the backwoods. The treaty gives 'em time; then they'll fight for the side that pays most and takes no land. The side that gave 'em the Proclamation Line we'd not heed." At once she wheeled to face her son-in-law. "We'll go back now! Back to Tidewater. We must!"

"I'll not leave my land, Margaret Mackinnon. Never. I can fight."

"You'll not live to plant it — nor Delilah to see it done."

"I'll fight, I say!" he shouted. And Delilah knew another quarrel was in the making. Quietly, she went outside with Reynard on his leash, because she already knew how the quarrel would end. Staying would be, naturally, a Principle.

When Simon rode up to ask her to the dance celebrating the treaty and Independence, she consented to go with him. Gran said they all might as well dance; what else was there to do? Simon said it had such a fine sound, Independence, and that he'd kill every Indian in sight when the time came. It didn't pay to be gloomy like Captain Russell, whose wife had died of milk fever in his absence. Of course the British lobsterbacks would arm the Indians — they had a post at Detroit on the Northern Lakes from which to do it. But what American couldn't whip a lobsterback or an Indian? Mrs. Sawyer, as she carefully picked her teeth with a dogwood twig, said that it was hard to believe even a Britisher would pay straight out for — well, for scalps, as she'd heard tell. Up to a few weeks ago, they'd all at Cassel's Woods been Britishers themselves, hadn't they? No man, wherever in the world he was born, would be a hairbuyer. Hadn't the miller, too, said the British wouldn't do that?

When Simon, in the fort yard, started to answer Mrs. Sawyer, Delilah jerked his arm. "Don't!" she begged under her breath. "Please, Simon."

He stopped. But she knew she had better not look about for Charles, at least when Simon could see her doing it. She'd tied Reynard outside before leaving Sugar Hill, had fed and petted him, thinking specially of Charles. Now she could smell the resiny split logs of Charles's mills. The strings of a fiddle began to squeak and twang. She smoothed the skirt of her yellow calico gown, the new one Gran had worked nights to make her and then press out, fold after fold, with a burning-hot sadiron. Gran said the gown became her, with her black hair and her paleness, and was full enough for dancing even with wild boys who stamped and swung every set.

Simon thought her the prettiest girl in the room. He wanted to touch her hair, to see what made it shine so. Her eyes were mischievous and flirting: for him? Her even teeth were very white when she laughed, not brown and jagged like his mother's. Little curly black wisps framed Delilah's face at her forehead and cheeks. She smelled of soap and starch and herbs, her skirts rustling as she walked.

Delilah loved to dance. Some people said it was mortally wrong, but Gran said it kept folks busy, and a jig or a reel harmed nobody. So Delilah sailed with Simon down the row in the opening reel; and though she was tall for her age she knew she was prettier than Ann Neece, for instance, whose hands were cut from pig butchering and plowing and whose nose was peeling from sunburn because she never wore a bonnet. Ann shouldn't wear pink when her face was so red.

"Rise you up, my dearest dear, present to me your hand,
And we'll take a social walk to a far and distant land

Where the hawk shot the buzzard and the buzzard shot
    the crow.
We'll rally in the canebrake and shoot the buffalo!"

How hot the night was! Delilah wiped her forehead as
Simon wiped his. Ah, there was Charles — dancing with
Ann Neece now, his feet heavy as if he wasn't used to reels.
He seemed to be enjoying himself, though; she could hear
his laughter. Perhaps he'd be her own partner later, and she
could teach him to be lighter on his feet.

    "Shoot the buffalo, my dear, shoot the buffalo —
    We'll rally in the canebrake and shoot the buffalo!"

The dancers all grew redder; the fiddle squeaked faster.
From outside the stockade came the tittering of a girl strolling
with her lover. Gran wasn't dancing herself, but was chattering to the Sawyers and watching with Winfield . . .
Now Charles was doing a do-si-do with old Grandma Sawyer, who was puffing and gasping in a red flannel petticoat
and purple shortgown. The flaps of disused fort cabin windows rattled in the breeze. Men gulped from their flasks of
Monongahela and corn whisky. The tittering came again,
and between sets Ann Neece whispered to Delilah: "Listen
to that Jezebel outside!"

When the shrieking began no one at first believed it.
Heads fuddled with drink cocked at the walls. The fiddler
scratched out a few more tentative notes. Pairs stayed arm
in arm. Then came the screams of the couple outside: "Fire!
Indians!"

Delilah stood paralyzed beside Ann Neece. When she
raised her feet from the earth in an effort of will, still she

could not believe what was happening. From the gate she could see flames rising suddenly high into the night sky. A cabin was burning! Where? Whose cabin? A new wave of Indian shrieks rushed down from the hill beyond.

Men began snatching their rifles, lined against the posts. She saw Charles tripping over her father to get his. She heard Joe Sawyer swearing at a rusted flintlock . . . The mills! Oh, no Indian would dare to burn them! Why didn't Charles rush to Mill Creek, to his flour and grain and rails? Almost in that moment Delilah could hear the word he had once used to her father: honor . . . And how strange she wasn't afraid for herself at all, or for people, but only for things: houses, mills, barns . . . Sugar Hill! Would it be burned: her father's fine cabin, the sheep pen, the pigsty? Where was Reynard?

"Git back!" Simon screamed at her. "Git in a cabin! You, Delilah!"

Whiz! A flaming arrow sailed over the wall in an arc of blurred light just as the gate banged shut. How close the savages must be! Minutes ago she'd been dancing a reel, and they'd been close then too . . . From the corner blockhouse a boy screamed and fell suddenly to the ground as a rifle clacked. She could only stand watching, hearing and seeing and not believing yet. She'd seen a doe shot, but this was a boy, a person as much as she was, and surely it couldn't be so easy for human flesh and blood as alive as hers to cease to be . . . Two men started dragging the boy away. Women began to scream too, clinging to their men until they were pushed back. Skirts ripped as they dragged each other into cabins. Simon was trying to drag her now, but she shook him off and ducked. Another arrow flew by and set fire to a hominy block. Charles plopped a bucket of water over it and the flames hissed and died. A gust of wind came up. At a loophole Simon was ramming his rifle pan shut and stuffing bullets down the barrel. Then he shot; but Delilah heard laughter outside.

Women were crying, children howling. Over the madness in which she stood rigid came a taunt from beyond the gate: "Long Knives! Benge is come!"

She wanted Gran. How much, how suddenly, she wanted Gran! But Gran was at a loophole herself, biting bullets, her arm steady and her chin raised. Gran was shooting, Gran knew how. *She thinks I'm inside* . . . her father was shooting too, and he was smiling a fixed smile. Delilah heard flames crackling behind her, and more water hissing them out, as she stared at him. She wanted to run more than ever but still she couldn't move, and Gran couldn't help her. A new, ominous silence settled down. The shrieks beyond the stockade stopped entirely. Whimpering children and crying women within grew silent too, waiting. Grandma Sawyer, from a cabin door, cackled nervously. The wind rose again. The smell of trampled crabapples floated up the hill. An owl hooted. Delilah blinked. The wind stopped.

She walked woodenly, unseen, to a loophole and stood beside a man she didn't know. By the starlight she tried to make out the forms of the Indians. She couldn't. The man moved aside to let her look. She saw nothing at all until she saw what the rest must see, what Charles must see . . . the flames licking at the millhouse on Mill Creek. She blinked again. They were doing it. They really were burning his mills. The flames were tiny at first, barely reaching to the lowest windows. Then, in a burst of gold, they soared to the sky, lighting the antlike forms of the looting red men, their torches dimmed to false stars in their hands.

She heard the frantic stamping and snorting of cattle. Barns were burning too. Their wood crackled while horses whinnied, sheep baaed high and brokenly, and pigs squealed. Dogs began to howl to a sky turned orange and shimmering; the cows mooed and stamped. The sounds of the chaos rose higher and higher into the night. She saw and heard her father start to shoot again, then everyone: the high cracks of rifles, the hollow boom of muskets. Her father was firing wildly, and Simon, and Gran, and Charles, ramming down one bullet after another at her father's urging, snapping fire-pans over and over.

Somebody was praying. "O God of battles, Lord of hosts, be with us — " Was that her father too?

The screaming, crackling, smoking madness went on as the night went on. The millwheel lit up in a dazzling circle of yellow before it crumbled into the creek in scraps. The trellises, the flumes and the millrace fell tearing and wrenching in a shower of sparks. She could feel the ground under her feet trembling as it had once trembled under the galloping hoofs of a buffalo herd. Were the Indians driving off horses? Were they on Sugar Hill yet, or had they been there already?

When the slow dawn painted the horizon beyond the outermost hills with streaks of pink, and the silence fell once more, the ground grew still. The smoke of what had been Cassel's Woods hung down like the very mist which had given it place. Delilah stood at the loophole alone. When she saw the open gate she walked through it in her hideous dream toward the river, toward Sugar Hill.

Millstones lay cracked and useless along the creek. Corn and oats everywhere were parched to a charred powder. Iron tools — hoes, hammers, mauls — were twisted into grayed wrecks. She stumbled over them as she walked on. What had been oaken plows were hot iron points among the cinders. She burned her feet but hardly knew it. The bodies of

black men were strewn, scalpless, at random among pieces
of surveying chains which had been wrenched apart. Log
walls had turned into dying embers. Bits of curved board
were floating down the creek toward the river: the last of
the wheel. The sluice gates rode the water like black rafts.
Festoons of bedfeathers hung everywhere in the cedars.
Feathers drifted over ashes and blackened half-logs and the
dismembered corpses of stock: cows, sheep, hogs. Not an
animal in Cassel's Woods settlement had been spared. She
tried to keep her eyes on the ground, not to see any more.
Near a well she found a canvas bag. She could read
the rough paper tied at its neck: "Lok inside," a scrawl of
charcoal. Mechanically, under a compulsion she felt but
could not stop to wonder at, she pulled the rope apart and
started to open the bag; then she saw a tuft of kinky hair and
a scrap of pink ribbon and she dropped the bag with a
thud. Charles's black woman . . . Quietly, bracing herself against a tree, Delilah vomited; then she went on, her
bodice stained, her eyes dry, her soiled skirts whipping at
her ankles in a fresh breeze. When she heard a soft whinny
she turned. From the edge of the woods trotted Charles's
stallion Mercury, his chestnut tail singed black at the tip, his
eyes bright, his nostrils still flared with fear. She let him go
by, up the hill toward the fort.

At the edge of the Clinch, where the water gushed endlessly over the stones as it had always gushed, she stopped.
Slowly, she raised her head. Then she saw the smooth,
sharp-cornered logs of her father's cabin and barns shining in
the light through the maples high above, intact. She drew a
deep breath. But as she stood there on the riverbank, the
dazed rigidity of her face revealed what she herself did not
yet know. In the coming of the war to Cassel's Woods, she
had truly at last left childhood forever behind her.

7

FROM THE DAY Charles moved into their cabin she knew he hated it. Once he had come there because he wanted to. Now he spent his time outdoors, away from her father and from her. All winter he rode Mercury up and down the zigzag traces far into the back country, those folds of land toward Kentuk so dark with monstrous trees that the men who had ventured there said the sun scarcely touched the earth at all, and you could hardly tell when it was high noon. At the sheep pen and chicken house, her cloak blowing as she struggled against the wind with her feed buckets, she would see Charles tall and erect in his buckskins and a fur cap, disappearing over the far hump of the rise toward the west where the wind came from. What drew him there? Was he trying to forget the raid as hard as she was trying? Had he seen those bodies, and her father's strange smile? At night Charles gave hours in the barn to the brushing and currying of his horse. Once he said lightly, "Mercury's my fortune, Delilah. I'd better take care of him, don't you think?" She wasn't fooled. He didn't mean to be light. He took over the milking of the cow: surely no man's work, but he insisted so firmly Gran gave up her protests. He ate his meals morning and evening with them all unless he were riding too far. Sometimes he told a joke or two at table about Dan Boone's singing offkey, or the recruits in

Dunmore's War who hadn't been able to tell the sound of a smoothbore musket from that of a grooved rifle. Courteously, he let Gran know whenever he would be away past supper. He made routine conversation about frosts and thaws and woodcutting; he listened at prayers and bowed his head; but several times when Delilah was watching him she saw him staring into a shadowy corner and she knew he wasn't hearing her father read the scriptures at all. None of Charles's jokes were real. The lines at his eyes had deepened, the creases in his forehead had set, as if to tell her so.

"I'll rebuild," he said quietly. Beneath his brows his eyes were pale and hard.

"Of course you will. But, Charles —" She bit her lip and then asked the quesion: "How?" She was sitting on the milking stool in the barn — tagging after him, Gran had snapped — while he rubbed down his horse. He went on rubbing in long, regular strokes.

"I've written to my father. He lives near Lynch's Ferry now. He'll send me more blacks." It had been easy to have letters delivered to the Settlements after Benge's raid. So many families had been going back there.

"I'm glad you don't have to worry." She scuffed the toe of her moccasin in the wisps of straw at her feet.

"It'll take some worrying to pay the debt." Still he rubbed; Mercury's hide had begun to shine in the yellow light of the lantern. The stallion stood motionless and patient in his stall.

"He'd give you what you needed, wouldn't he — your own father?"

"Yes. But I don't like charity."

That was surely a slap in the face. Charity! *Her* father didn't count it charity to have Charles here. He'd have ex-

pected Charles to do the same for him. And surely she
wouldn't call it charity to ask her father to help her if she
were a man and needed his help. But it galled Charles, apparently, to accept any gift from anybody, though he could
make gifts when he chose. She had never realized how
much pride he had. Pride was like a chain on him, dragging,
chafing, cutting at him until the anger he tried to hide made
her as miserable as he must be, because she saw in his grim
eyes and stiff throat and wary defensiveness that anger at
fate, at what God and Benge had done to him. She could see
it sometimes in his very hands when he clenched them at
table as her father spoke excitedly of revenge. She didn't
want to share the anger, but she had to because Charles was
here, he was with her. He never grew excited himself when
he talked of revenge. His voice had instead a deadly calm,
resigned but determined, that made her want to shudder.

She'd thought at first that he would enjoy the antics of
Reynard. Reynard was such a clever little creature, just like
a dog, ever so tame with his sly begging ways and his sneak-
ing up to the loft to be with her at night, a warm ball curled
next to her chest. It had taken Gran weeks to find out he was
doing that, and then she'd shrugged and tried not to laugh.
But Charles only glanced vaguely at the fox as if he had had
nothing whatever to do with him. *Right now he wishes I'd
go: he wants to be alone.* If only she could tell him how
sorry she was; but somehow she didn't dare.

"The things of this earth are taken from those who covet
them too much," her father warned her. "I know. Charles
must pray for grace to bear his losses. I bore mine." *My
mother,* she thought . . . Every night, by the light of smoking bettylamps, his voice boomed out: "Lord, we thank Thee
for preserving our lives as Thou didst preserve Israel,

who took his journey with all that he had and came to Beer-sheba, and did offer sacrifices to the God of his father Isaac. Help us to suffer our chastisements . . ." He didn't look directly at Charles, but his meaning was very plain. Half the world, he told Delilah with bright eyes, was damned.

"But not the people Ben really loves." Gran would smile wryly afterwards. "Only the others."

In March Charles announced at breakfast over his mush and ham: "If you all want to start sugaring this year I'll help. It's a crime to have this place and not begin using it." When he had started to hammer out ashwood slats for sugar boxes he seemed happier. He laughed once at the way Reynard reared up on his hind feet when Gran started stirring soup for dinner. Reynard had a provoking way of scattering chips, but Charles didn't seem to mind. When he hit his thumb with his hammer he roared out "Damme!" but he quickly flushed, and grinned lamely to Gran: "I'm sorry, Ma'am." He taught Delilah how to chip the boxes herself, guiding her hand to turn the openings so that the sap would flow straight into them. Six hundred buckets could be tended by one person. He figured the yield by the fire, how long it would take to drill the southeast bush, and how many days of freezing temperature might safely be lost until the end of the first run. From time to time he blew back the hair falling across his forehead as he scratched at his paper. He hardly seemed to realize when it was bedtime. Maybe it's making him forget, Delilah thought; I wish I could forget too; and I wish Papa wanted to.

The day the sugaring began she was up at dawn. Outside, the wind was keening in the bare trees. She shivered; Chickamo whinnied. They all went deep into the bush, Gran pulling tight at Mercury's reins to manage him. By midmorning

Delilah was hot in her wool cloak as she covered box after box, slamming the lids tight to keep the syrup from souring. At noon when she tasted her first sap she wrinkled her nose. "It's like burnt bacon."

"Of course, sweetheart." She started; Charles hadn't called her that for a long time. "We'll boil it and strain it."

Her father kept on emptying boxes into cedar buckets. She and Gran helped him while Charles piled rocks for a fireplace wall to keep the wind out. When he had finished that he built a half-faced shelter of hickory poles and brush, and rolled a log into it. They could all sit there during the boilings.

"You'll be building soon now at Cassel's Woods." Her father stood up to ease his shoulders.

"When we've finished here." Charles blew on his hands and rubbed them. "D'you notice the lay of the hill? It's made for sugaring, this mountain. So steep there's not enough sun to make the sap buddy. I envy you." He stamped his boots on the ground to warm his feet.

"More like it I'll envy you when you've got mills twice as big as you had. You'll do that, I suppose?" Her father was only half serious, but Charles shot back: "Dead right I will — if I have to sweat the rest of my life for it." Then he gave the log before him a savage blow with his axe, using every pound of heft he had to split it though it was half rotten and would have needed only a few taps.

The night before the boiling it snowed. By morning there were several inches of snow on the ground, sparkling in the white sun. Gran said it was too cold for her to go, lent a ladle, and called after them: "Mind you bring it back!" All day they carried the heavy buckets of sap, poured them into Gran's biggest crabapple butter caldron, and then sat by in the shelter while the liquid steamed and simmered slowly, thin and brown and foamy. In the cold the sap stuck to the mesh of the wire strainers and Delilah caught herself whining with vexation until she realized she could boil them clean again. Her shoulders and arm ached. Yet by the time the sun was tipping Sandy Ridge in the west the run wasn't nearly finished. She saw and heard her father's teeth chattering even as he stamped his jackboots in the shelter. Charles threw fresh logs on the fire, and fresh tinder of sticks and leaves.

"Go in, Papa. We'll stay. Please. If you get sick Gran will be angry."

"No, Delilah. I'll sit it through."

Charles turned. "Don't, Ben. There's no need. You won't worry if we're late — you'll see the firelight from the house." He didn't say anything outright about the Indians. But they wouldn't come, of course, when snow was on the ground to show their tracks.

As darkness began to fall Delilah stirred the caldron silently, over and over, her arm hot and tired and sweating, her back stabbed by the wind, while Charles strained the early batch. She was glad her father had left for the cabin's warmth. Patches of gold shifted through scudding clouds. The trees loomed black and gaunt against the eerie light.

Suddenly she thought of Williamsburg at dusk: Bruton Church spire under a sky like that, clipped catalpa trees, yellow lights going on in the glass windows, townspeople in red and green cloaks hurrying safely along Duke of Gloucester Street beside the picket fences . . . Stupid. She kept stirring, thankful for the heat on her face, saying not a word until Charles had poured in the strained bucketsful and she could go to the shelter to wait an hour for the boiling to begin again. The air turned grayer; the snow darkened from white to blue, broken only by footprints and the tracks the horses had made. Chick snorted, and moved in her hobbles closer to the fire.

Delilah turned to Charles in the shelter. "You're happier working — doing something."

He smiled a little. "Was I bad before?"

"Terrible. It made me afraid, the way you put us off. It wasn't like you. And if you hadn't offered to sugar, Papa mightn't have asked you to."

"I'm sorry." He began drawing patterns in the snow with a stick, great circles overlapping each other. "I've been a nuisance, I reckon. But it's not pleasant to hear God visits me personally with punishment He spares your father."

"Papa always — judges. But you make people hurt for you."

"I didn't realize that," he said softly, after a pause. "That I made you hurt for me, Delilah." He went on scratching with his stick: circles, triangles too now, fantastically intricate designs within designs.

The moon came up over the river, silvering its surface in short bright streaks. Together they raised their eyes to it in silence. He threw aside his stick. She saw his eyes studying her. Then he got up to check the syrup, shrugged, and sat down again to stare moodily at the ground. Watching his sadness — for it wasn't anger now — she grew unaware of what she was doing. When she put her hand on his he opened his mouth as if to speak, but he didn't. And when she realized her gesture, still she didn't move to take her hand away.

"Please talk to me." Her words, unplanned, sounded oddly natural to her. "I'm not afraid of you now."

"No?" He smiled faintly again.

She shook her head. They leaned back against the warmed boughs. As the darkness gathered deeper the firelight became redder, and it outlined his features: the crooked nose, the wide-set blue eyes flecked with green, the straight mouth, the patch of gray at his temple. His face had, just now, the ascetic look of a dreamer. Were his dreams of the past, or of the future?

"You've been bitter and sorrowing. You came to me once when I needed it — you knew about the doe, that time. But you won't let me know anything about you."

He closed his eyes, his lashes dark on his cheeks. He patted her hand. Still he said nothing.

"Simon Oscher told me who your uncle is. Your uncle's got an English title. It doesn't matter."

His eyes opened, and he turned to her. "They doubt me, then — the others? They would, of course."

"I wouldn't. Ever."

"God notwithstanding?" His lips were fuller when he smiled. "Perhaps you wouldn't."

"I don't mock your religion." She stiffened. "It's wrong to mock ours." A branch creaked overhead.

"What should I talk about?" he asked her finally.

"Oh — what you're thinking. Where you came from. Why you left." As an owl called she finished: "What you mean to do at Cassel's Woods when you've got your mills back."

"Why, plant it." Was he teasing her again? "Work it until I'm under the ground, Delilah." He sobered. "I've eighteen hundred acres already. Did you know that? Yet in Louisa I would have had twelve thousand." A note of bewilderment crept into his voice. "Sometimes still I catch myself thinking of quarter-sections at Green Springs. It was the name of our place, did I tell you? I learned surveying there. I laid out every tract for my father, some of them three times over. I still start to do sums in thousands on my plats, until I remember a man fights like hell out here for every hundred."

"And dies, maybe." She shivered.

"Yes. I've learned that."

Silence. Shutting away her own vision of the raid she asked gently: "Was it beautiful — Green Springs?"

At first he didn't answer. But then a fresh smile lit up his face as if the very firelight had grown brighter, and he said simply: "Yes, my dear. It was the most beautiful place on earth. I used to ride over it every morning, watching the blacks topping and suckering the tobacco. I knew it would all be mine, you see — the trees and the dirt, the creeks, the house, everything. We grew Sweet-scented. Everybody in Louisa did. It's only near the ocean you have to grow Orenoko." He leaned forward. "The house was a frame copy of our English place, Attleborough Hall, the one my great-uncle gamed away. It had big windows in the drawing room and you could see clear across the lawn to the fields even on rainy days."

"Then why did you go — if you cared for it so much?"

"Why?" The thinness of his echo belied its casualness. "Because my father sold it, Delilah." His voice hardened. "My own mother died when I was a baby, and after a long time he married again. My stepmother had a better plantation near Lynch's Ferry. Richer ground, he said. So he went there to live — on her bounty."

"Wasn't that — wise?"

"Wise!" he shouted at her suddenly. "Christ, when all he had to do was stop mooning over fripperies he couldn't have

— cravats and coaches! He should have set to caring for Green Springs. It wasn't a gold mine to be plundered for buying trash, it was a plantation. He'd let the prizing screw rust, he'd never bothered learning to grade even the bright leaf decently, he never manured the old fields but just kept shifting without rhyme or reason. Second-growth pine was spreading like a blight. I used to beg him: let *me* try. I'll make money for us, real money; you've only got to be patient a few years, pinch a while, rotate your crops instead of letting all those acres go, make more of your tools and grind your own grain. But" — his voice sank as if the energy of his bitterness was flowing out of him — "he wouldn't listen. He always laughed. He said I thought like a clod instead of a gentleman." His own laugh had no humor in it, and no force. "So he sold Green Springs first and told me afterwards when he gave me my share of the cash. My brother and sister had known all along."

"Oh, Charles!"

"I remember the day my father handed me that bag of gold. We were in the drawing room, just the two of us — "

The wind rose in the trees. When he spoke again she could hardly hear him. "We'd always been poor, you see. It was that scraping sort of poverty that keeps up appearances and lives high when the neighbors are watching. Every time my father had a suit of clothes made for any of us he'd say 'Do you know how much this cost me?' I used to wonder how long I had to say thank you to match the price even. It's why I hate gratitude. You feel it, it's enough. I can't stand hearing it from people, taking pay. I even had to keep thanking him for selling Green Springs because I got money for it. I was the eldest. I got the most." His mouth screwed down.

At once, achingly, she wanted to make him forget his

shame and his loss, to make everything up to him. She wanted to be close to him, because he had to have somebody, and she was there. She held his hand more tightly; she was afraid he might yet snatch it away. But he didn't. "You'll have it all again. You must believe you'll have it — here."

Had he heard her? "Mills weren't plans for gentlemen, my family said." Fresh bitterness edged his tone. "Tobacco's a thief, Delilah. It ruins your land and it brings only the prices those rascals of factors set in London. My Shelton cousins have already lost their fleet at their place on Tidewater, Rural Plains; they've got to pay shipping now — living on a river like the Pamunkey. My father has to pay too. I could show you miles along the Pamunkey and the James and the South Anna gone to scrub. Out here we've got more sense. We raise vulgar things like corn and wheat and cattle and sugar. We make what we need to raise 'em. If I'm a clod for that, it's how a man's got to make a plantation today. I'd have done the same at Green Springs. Maybe that's why my father did what he did. And now I have to crawl to him for help. Tainted by trade, he'd say. Jesus!"

The wind rose colder through the boughs of the shelter. The fire sputtered and sparked and sizzled as flakes of snow were blown into it. The sweetening smell of the syrup floated in the air. Charles hunched back as if exhausted by his last outburst. He grinned abruptly after a while: "You're patient. I've spilled out the whole mess like a brat robbed of sweets. I've never done it before."

"I'm glad you chose me," she whispered, raising her face to his. "Are you?"

His grin faded. He didn't answer, but his eyes never left hers. At last he said, slowly: "Yes."

It was in that moment, that word, that she knew a flowering in all her body. Her eyes could meet his without hesitation or embarrassment, without anything at all but the longing simply to see him. When he got up and walked to the fire again her eyes followed him. His feet crumbled the leaves and twigs where the heat had melted the snow. He stirred the caldron and came back to her. "It's late." He sat down again, farther from her than before.

She remembered the day at the mill when she had been in his arms. Now she wanted to be in his arms again. He would realize then he wasn't alone. On impulse she reached up to draw him down, his head in her lap. Amazingly, he let her do it. He even let her press her fingers to his temples as she bent over him, her breath growing tremulous and unsure. She could feel his temples throbbing, see their raised veins pulsing in the firelight. The familiar smell of tobacco came from his shirt. A drop of syrup bubbled over the caldron and hissed in the flames; she heard it. A loose sugar box scraped against a treetrunk; she heard that too. Then she heard herself whispering "Charles," once, twice . . .

When his hands came up to circle her neck they were strong and warm, as she had known they would be. His mouth found hers, demanding and tender. After their kiss he sat up, pressing her head against his chest and stroking her hair, while she heard the drumming of his heart. When he kissed her again she felt a wave of emotion so strong and so unfamiliar it startled her. This time his mouth was not gentle. He gripped her tighter. She felt his hand cupping her breast. Soon he drew apart her cloak and kissed her throat. She heard his breathing start coming as quick as her own, and felt it on her throat, her shoulders. She began groping, trying to draw herself closer still.

When he threw her back it was brutally and without warning. His eyes narrowed into crescents. Roughly he wrenched his hands away. She tried to cry out but she could not. His grating breath was all the sound there was until he rasped: "Go back inside."

Her cry did come brokenly then, but his fingers caught at her arm and pulled her toward Chick.

"Get up!" he ordered. "Look to your gown, for God's sake." She could feel her body moving, doing what he was telling her to do, but she could not believe she was doing it. Her hands were numb as they fumbled at the hooks of her bodice. "I'll leave tomorrow." His teeth were clenched.

"No!" She stumbled toward him.

"D'you think I'm mad?" He gave her a look of rage, his mouth twisted in the orange light of the flames. Her eyes blinded with her tears. Dumbly, she reined in Chick while he freed the mare's legs in clumsy jerks. Along the trace she could hear the syrup beginning to boil over. At first she could hear the crunch of his footsteps through Chick's plodding, and the hard striking of his ladle on the caldron. Then the sounds died, the firelight faded. There was only the light of the moon, frigid and bleak. The wind came up, stinging her throat where it was still bare. Chick's breath streamed white into the blackness.

He hadn't wanted her. She loved him and he hadn't wanted her.

The cabin was cold in the corners but smoky and warm near the fireplace where Reynard was curled at her father's feet in a tight ball. She managed, she thought, to sound calm when she forced her excuse: "He's still working. I'm going to sleep, I'm so weary." She kissed her father goodnight and kissed Gran, and when Gran squinted she turned

away and scrambled up quickly to the loft where the heat
and the smoke swirled over her pallet in the chimney corner.
She waited for Reynard to come but he didn't. She lay stiff
while her father began to read aloud to Gran below, his
words fuzzed and merging without meaning or sense:
". . . amongst men no distinct judgment between the
prophet and the fool . . ." When he had finished she
heard Gran going off to her bed. Later she heard Charles
stamping snow from his boots and mumbling briefly to her
father, and her father's answering: "No, didn't seem chilled,
she went up —" And soon: "Tomorrow? When we haven't
finished? . . . Of course, the mills to start . . ."

Charles wasn't telling. She'd been afraid, stupidly.

When the cabin was dark she sat up and started to throw
her cover off. She'd go down to his pallet and beg him to
explain to her why he couldn't want her. What did I do?
she'd ask him . . . No; she was afraid of him again, and
her father might wake up; she couldn't go. Shutting her
eyes, she dreamed briefly of trying Gran, laying her head on
Gran's arm and telling her everything and listening to what
Gran would say: soothing words to bring the peace back . . .
But Gran wouldn't soothe at all; this thing was the second
in her life beyond Gran's comfort as the raid had been the
first. No help anywhere. She lay back and covered herself . . .

When the tiredness of Delilah's body drew her at last into
the sleep her mind had tried to deny her, she dreamed of the
firelight and the snow and the smells of woodsmoke and tree
sugar. Never in all her years — she knew when she blinked
in the first weak sun of morning — would she forget those
things. Later she heard the crunching of Mercury's hoofs
in the snow, and she knew that Charles had gone away.

8

A STRANGE procession wound one day not long afterwards into Cassel's Woods from the Warriors' Path along the river. At the head of the procession rode a short man dressed in a blue broadcloth cloak, with stiff ruffles at his sleeves and neck. Instead of boots he wore black pumps with buckles that might have been pinchbeck but — Delilah decided as she stared at him — must be gold, so brightly did they shine in the sun. He wore a silk cravat and on his head sat a white wig with every sausage curl in place. He had bushy chestnut eyebrows, a practiced smile, and a broad nose that wrinkled when he saw the ashes of the cabins and barns and mills everywhere around him.

"Bad, by Jove," he said. "But no mind."

It had been silly to ride all the way down Sugar Hill to see him, for she had seen settlers come in before. Not this year, though . . . He must be brave, this plump and ruffled dandy who said he was Henry Dickenson, a lawyer come to stay. You could tell he'd never held an axe in his life. Half the people of the fort were staring at him, and Ann Neece giggled when he bowed at her as if he were the English King greeting the Queen.

His packhorses were swaybacked with their loads: piles of threshing flails, nails and plow points and hammers, bags of seed, feed for his cattle, pigs, crated chickens, and the sheep that were stirring up dust on the path. Muskets and rifles gleamed in whole bundles. Pots, kettles and pails were crammed with knives and ladles and red flags, roped by surveying chains. A broad-backed brown ox labored and puffed with the burden of a high spinning wheel. Neck bells jingled as the other oxen and the horses stamped restlessly. A fat Negro woman in a gunnybag shortgown shifted on the squat back of a donkey, the rolls at her middle shaking like pudding. A brown-skinned girl in faded calico gaped, fingering the fuzzy curls behind her right ear. Slave men sullenly flicked flies from the pigs; a tall one scowled as he stared at the ruins.

"Seems like we git every man-jack o' the Tuckahoes in Cassel's Woods," Granny Sawyer wheezed to Delilah. "Hope he sets some o' them Neegurs to buildin' for us."

"You got a blacksmith with you, Mister?" Henry Neece, Ann's father, asked, wiping his horny hands on greasy linseys. "We need tools bad. Can't make do without we got new tools." The men were clustering around Dickenson, who pointed to a burly, bare-chested mulatto with arm muscles that swelled as if they'd pounded at many a forge. The crowd shouted at Dickenson about the raid, each man fighting to tell first what he'd lost. Captain Russell and the miller, now, they were with a salt-making party over Clinch Mountain on the north fork of Holston, but they'd be mighty glad to see those goods . . .

"Mr. Bickley's the miller, isn't he? Some of these things are his. His father sent them, and the blacksmith."

Delilah froze, remembering. Had he sent a bill of lading too? . . . She wouldn't have come here, of course, if she hadn't known about the salt-makers' being gone. Her eyes darted around her; even now she must be sure Charles wasn't here . . . But, oh, if he were, just to see him once . . .

Ann Neece thought the newcomer looked right silly in his wig and cloak. Nobody but a fool would pretty up for Cassel's Woods. Simon Oscher said he doubted the lawyer would know a squirrel from a fox; he'd probably get himself killed before the summer was out, not knowing Indian sign when he saw it, not knowing how to walk in the woods so the redsticks couldn't hear twigs breaking, not knowing how to follow game or to heat water so it would warm the blood and keep away the fever. Captain Russell might be a Tucka-hoe, but he'd been in the militia a time and a time, and even the miller had learned from Jake Cassel and Dan Boone in the early days, just as Simon's pap had learned from the folks here; but that lawyer didn't look like the learning kind, with his curls and fine lawn. Granny Sawyer, her eyes beady from the depths of her sunbonnet, said she reckoned the lawyer would last about a year even if he did live. For her part she'd admire to see him hoeing alongside his blacks the way Captain Russell and the miller did . . . And every-body asked questions about the Settlements: what about the war? Was Patrick Henry still the governor? Did Mister Dickenson have any coffee with him, by chance, or mus-covado sugar? Had he come by way of Bottytot Courthouse, and did he know who else had been burned out? The folks at Abb's Valley and Witten's Mill and Crab Orchard up the Path, were they safe, or had Benge been to them too?

The lawyer talked briefly of the war on the King, of vague victories and losses in distant places; he talked of Governor Henry, whom he'd seen in Williamsburg in the palace old Dunmore had fled; he told what clearings were still worked, and what ones were abandoned; but everybody seemed most interested when he unwrapped a small parcel of real Spanish coffee to give to the women, and unwrapped another to hand out single hard lemon drops to all the barefoot children while his gray gelding swished flies from its tail.

So Charles would build again, truly: gritting his teeth, no doubt, at his father's largesse . . . Soon Delilah heard he'd gone up to Brushy Mountain with a brace of slaves to quarry quartz for burrs. Lawyer Dickenson began building his own cabin. He laid out a great floor plan with walnut trunks, hollowed out two windows even though her father warned him it was madness with Benge so close, and instead of a loft he built a regular second story with a staircase and two real rooms. He didn't need a house raising, what with his slaves; no more did Charles. The first time Dickenson met her father Delilah heard him say, "An honor, sir! I had no idea you'd turned frontiersman. I remember the Winfield Cause. I'd have liked to plead it for you."

"I could only afford to plead for myself," her father said crisply. "Do many leave the English Church these days?"

Dickenson said he thought so, though maybe men were just starting to own to beliefs they'd long held in private. There were nervous Church parsons up and down the Settlements who feared they'd be turned out of their vicarages now. But, as all Virginia knew, England for years had sent her clerical dregs to the colonies, and Patrick Henry had been right when he'd said many a Church parson would steal an old woman's blanket when he went to her sickbed. Delilah smiled; but her father turned on her and growled: "It was no laughing matter. It wasn't to be borne, to be told how to worship by a pack of fools or worse. Some of them pocketed the tithe as fast as they got it. I know. I saw. Gentlemen, they called themselves."

When the Winfields were getting in their second seeding of corn Simon Oscher came up Sugar Hill full of gossip and ready to gulp the last of Gran's cider. "That lawyer — " he shook his head. "He says he means to lawyer us here too. But he goes around talking to folks about patents and grants and *pre*-emptions when anybody knows a cornright's good enough, specially with the war and all. Can you raise four hundred acres of corn, you buy a thousand more with pelts or whate'er you got. He sold Joe Sawyer his land all over again — said it was in another name with the land office at Washington Courthouse, some Englishman's. He keeps goin' over the mountain to Washington Courthouse to pry into folks' business. Joe was a fool for paying. Forty shillings he give. My pap says maybe the land office never sees the money, only the lawyer. He says the lawyer's prob'ly laughing at us. But Joe says he wanted to be sure, what with the old Fincastle County being split up. It's a marvel the lawyer hasn't been skulped on Clinch Mountain when he travels it."

Listlessly, perfunctorily, Delilah served Simon a bowl of cream and a dish of wild strawberries. She wished he'd talk about Charles but she wouldn't ask, she had pride too . . . Charles would learn that. He'd have to.

"All I want in the world," Simon spooned up his berries, "is a cornright to call my own. Four hundred is enough for anybody. It's not the place for blacks out here. Your pap's thoughty to save his sugar money for tools. I'll build a fine house some day, I'll grow my crops and raise my younguns and kill e'er Indian that shows hisself in my woods. Captain Russell and Lawyer Dickenson and the miller, they'll never be able to seed all they got already, and they're always want-

ing to get more. Some day they'll be fighting amongst their-
selves the way they talk about fighting Benge now."

Delilah wished Gran would come back. Gran didn't *have*
to dry pease today. What did she know or suspect about
Charles? And why couldn't she see that Simon was making
a nuisance of himself?

"It goes hard," Simon said, wrinkling his freckled nose.
"Seeing some get help from the Settlements."

"Charles Bickley built once right with his blacks. I saw
him. Wouldn't you let blacks help you if you could?" Delilah brushed a stray wisp of hair from her brow.

"The west ain't the place for blacks," Simon insisted stubbornly. "My pap says the Settlements are sot on blacks because they help a man live like folks in England, in a big
squire's house in the country. But this ain't England." He
pushed his chair away from the table and went over to stare
down at Reynard, who was sleeping near the window on a
pine stool. "You ever walk him?"

Delilah nodded.

"Some day," Simon hesitated, "maybe we'll both of us
walk him."

She nodded again, not knowing what else to do.

"The miller's signed to survey the Wilderness Road, clear
into Kentuk. Make hisself money to pay for what his folks
sent, so he says. Seems funny, don't it? He could send back
buckskins besides — every one fetches a Spanish dollar now.
Lawyer says so. Upcountry they're tradin' in bucks."

Delilah's hand had tightened on the pitcher of milk she
was carrying. "How long — "

"Miller? Oh, year, maybe more. His men'll work for him
here. But I thought you were such great friends he'd have
told you." He smoothed his yellow cowlick.

"No." Carefully, she set the pitcher down. For a minute

the world went dark. A year . . . then the sun blinded her from the window, the gold flecks on the leaves outside danced and shifted, the wind hit her quivering jaw, and she sat down, feeling her lips form themselves into a smile at Simon Oscher, whom she wanted to slap so hard across the mouth he would scream with the pain.

For Delilah it was a year of waiting to be sixteen, because her father and Gran counted growing in time. It was knowing too that Simon came to court her, that Simon wanted to wed her. She could tell. Could she ever have seen herself as Simon's wife, sitting at a cabin hearth to welcome him from a day's planting, sharing his dream that had fixed limits and listening to his Cohee talk? Even before Charles, could she have seen herself that way, when she'd been reared with her father's books that held the dreams of all the world (though she preferred dreaming her own dreams)? Ben Winfield wanted more than a tiny cornright. He wanted enough to make it possible for him to build a house with real cedar weatherboarding some day, and a library room to read in, and a pretty bedroom for herself, and — perhaps — a schoolroom to teach in, when he had time to letter all the children of Cassel's Woods.

"Tell Simon if you truly can't bear the sight of him," Gran warned. "Find the words. Otherwise think. And don't tell your father anything. He'd be angry at any man alive daring to court you so soon."

She would never (she was sure) love any man save Charles. But he was a coward himself because he refused to face her. If she could have cried about that it would have helped. But she only went on churning butter, winding flax, carding wool, gathering beans and squash and pumpkins and corn. She wished she had a mirror, to see the growing of her body, to see if she were by some miracle turning beautiful so that when Charles saw her next he would have to love her as she loved him. Sometimes she went down to the river to her hollow, but whenever she tried to see herself the water rippled and all she got for her pains was a mocking distortion of her thick brows and wide-set eyes.

"Don't moon, missy," Gran scolded. "Get to hoeing your sallet patch."

Delilah and her father and Gran carried buckets of water from the springs to the clearing in an endless round, wetting down the crops that would otherwise die of drought. Not a trace of Indian sign was seen anywhere. Across the river, cabins were rising once more. By harvest the mill was rising too as a swarm of Negroes hammered and planed and drilled and rived and hoisted great walnut logs in grapevine slings. Sometimes, when Delilah couldn't sleep, she got up before Gran or her father had stirred and went outside to see the sun come up over the new buildings while the heavy folds of mist parted at its heat.

All winter she dreamed at night that Charles was colder even than she became in her loft. He was alone on the road in the wilderness where he had no friend save Dan Boone at the end of it . . . She wouldn't avoid Charles when he came back. No, she'd go to him, tell him, forget all her pride and beg him to love her. He'd been hurt himself, so he'd understand. When her father started going out to strap sugar boxes to the trees she began tracing out her first quilt pattern: a great yellow circle for the moon, yellow dots for the stars, and red slashes for the leaves of the sugar trees. She would call it Sugar Fancy. She found her pattern didn't bring to mind a scene at all but was instead something in itself, with its own wholeness. Gran sniffed that there were enough quilts to choose from, right pretty ones like Whig Rose, and why a pesky girl had to think up a new one she'd never know. The moon wasn't yellow anyhow. It was better to follow a scheme that had been tried. But Delilah kept working, drawing the long needle in and out, over and under.

"I'm tired of seeing you mope, missy." Gran put down her knitting. "I think I'd like to know now what happened. You know what I mean."

Delilah stopped her piecing. "Nothing."

"I should hope not."

"Charles — he kissed me. And then — it was the night in the bush, Gran — he made me go." She heard herself telling of the kiss, knowing Gran hardly needed to hear Charles's name to understand, hoping Gran understood no more. She longed not to be telling even the fragment but she couldn't stop. "I love him so much," she whispered. "He told me why he came here, how his father took his place away from him and he built a new one and then Benge burned it. And the night of the fire hunt when Papa didn't care I hated the killing, he did. He came to me."

For a long time Gran didn't answer. Then, slowly, she said: "I'm sorry for this." In a moment Delilah felt her hand on her shoulder, bony and hot. "I'll speak no nonsense of first love never lasting. A woman feels at sixteen what she feels at twenty-six. But he's a man that would bring happiness to no woman. He lives for that place of his on the river; for that only. People don't count. Simon, now — he'd care for you to the end of his days. Simon has room for people as well as land grants in his heart."

"I don't want to be in Simon's heart. Not in anybody's but Charles's. Am I so ugly, Gran?"

Gran smiled, seaming her brown-spotted cheeks. "Never. You're a mite powerful, but it's right for this place. You're not a field to lay out exactly to Charles Bickley's taste. You might interfere with his plans. He'd love you if Sugar Hill were your dower instead of all your father has in the world. I've seen him looking at our trees."

"No!" she shouted. "That's not true! He — "

" — sent you away," Gran finished quietly. "And could do that. And thinks he lost nothing by it." She took her hand from Delilah's shoulder and went back to her knitting.

Gran hated him, then . . . Ah, what did Gran really know about loving? What could she? How could she sound knowing when she was old, old! Delilah, seeing the blue veins at Gran's temples below her cap and the brown spots on her cheeks, asked the question mutely, feeling her mouth turn down in contempt. What did Gran know when loving was so far behind her? "You don't understand." Delilah muttered the timeless, trite words at last, true as she spoke them because she believed no person could have lived through a trouble like hers to any age at all.

"We all have our own ways," Gran said, her needles clicking. "He — my husband — and I were raised together, but I don't think I ever told him how I cared for him and he never told me. I knew, though, the day he left with Braddock; I knew how much. I didn't want to soil his coat because my hands were floury and he said, 'I'll think of your hands.'" Her needles stopped, and she shut her eyes. "Your father — he took my God and my church when your mother died. He needed something to hold to. Your mother was no beauty, child. She was plain. But he never saw that. There were less prayers and more laughing in her day." She opened her eyes, and her old mouth curved into a smile again. "When you love" — her smile faded — "you never turn a body away. Don't you know that? You take him to you greedy and selfish for everything of him you can get. It's so with women and so with men. Love's more than being lonesome and sorry for yourself on a winter night when you're sitting with a chit of a girl who'll listen to anything you tell her." Gran smiled patronizingly this time. So it was no use saying any more.

Raids began at Rye Cove, but both the Cherokees and the Shawanese left Cassel's Woods alone. Delilah never knew Charles had returned until a May afternoon when she was riding Chick near Mill Creek. Crabapple and dogwood blossoms billowed in vast white clouds near the new millhouse, its overshot wheel grinding through the water in a steady rush. The mockbirds had begun to sing. She was sitting loose in her saddle, letting her reins lie in the hollow of Chick's withers. When she heard footsteps and she turned and saw him she couldn't manage a word.

"I'm looking for a freshet and not finding any. No flood this year." He smiled at her so casually the thing between them might never have happened. Quick pain pressed behind her eyes. Then she forgot herself. She scrambled off Chick and went to throw herself into his arms. And the miracle happened: he held her. His hands went round her and when she looked up he was smiling at her still. She wanted him to kiss her, but it was enough to be with him, held, cared about.

When he put her away it was to look at her, as if to take in her changes. "Thank you, sweetheart."

He had said it! She laughed in the joy of his thanks, needless and silly as they were. Then her words poured out: "I missed you enough to die! You went without telling me. Why?" She threw herself against him again; but he didn't put his arms around her this time. He only touched her shoulder lightly.

"You shouldn't ask me that," he said gently. "I felt bad that winter. It was a setback. I did things that weren't — sensible. But I ask you to understand. Can you?" His eyes had fixed on hers.

"Yes." She buried her face in his shirt, breathing in its smells of flour and resin and meal and tobacco. "I'll understand anything. Yes."

"This is enough." He pushed her from him slowly but firmly. "Tell your father I'm coming to see him."

"You're staying. You have to stay." She was hungry for every detail of him: the line of his jaw, the way the gray patch was spreading in the brown of his hair, his scratched hands, the worn places on his sleeves where his surveying chains had been looped, the baggy knees of his faded leggings.

He shook his head. "I'm going back, sweetheart. Colonel Clark is leading an expedition to the Indian towns."

"You can't! You hate fighting!" She tried to go to him but he kept her back.

"I have nobody. I must go, don't you see? My men and buildings are valuable not only to me but to these people. I must take my part in defending 'em and I'm better able than most. What I hate doesn't matter."

"You have me." Her body was shaking; her hands were

stiff at her sides by an act of will; her chin trembled as she held it up. "I showed you!"

"Listen, Delilah." He put his thumb and forefinger under her chin. "You're good and dear. There's not a selfish bone in your body. You care for everybody, even a sour fellow like me. You get carried away. But you must be careful."

"You can't go. I don't care for everybody! You can't leave me alone again!"

He bent over her. "You aren't alone. You know it."

"You aren't either!"

"Thank you," he said again: slowly, deliberately. "I hope I always will have you. But I do ask you to understand — what I mentioned. I'm sorry. I can't say more."

You aren't alone . . . I always will have you . . . She heard nothing else — not his goodbye, not the time for her father to see him, not the wind racing through the meadow or his steps on the path. For he had just promised himself to her, hadn't he? In his own queer way? He thought she was too young yet, but when he came back he wanted her always! He loved her too. He was sorry he had turned her away. What was it Gran had told her? Gran and her husband had never spoken about love at all, that was it . . . Charles hadn't kissed her today; ah, but somebody might have seen . . . He had asked her to understand. Oh, she did! He was sorry. But he needn't be any more. She wanted to sing as she rode splashing through the river and back up the mountain. Then the cold passed over her. He was going away to Kentuk not to survey but to march on the savages. He couldn't always live. He might be killed. He might smile no more, might never have his dreams or touch anybody again but lie cold and oblivious . . .

Death. She'd seen death in the raid; she'd seen the black

bodies and the corpse of the white boy . . . Death, on the Clinch, was murder. It would be murder in Kentuk too. Jim Boone and Henry Russell had been the first. Death wasn't candles burning in a parlor at a closed bier, as it had been when her mother had died on Tidewater. It wasn't even a doe at the river's edge. No, it was scalpless heads and rivers of blood and the screaming everywhere, it was fire and retching and gunsmoke . . . Would God spare Charles? He wouldn't spare himself. He hated murder as much as she hated it. He was a planter, not a soldier. But he wouldn't flinch. And she couldn't beg him to stay behind.

Soon she began a new quilt with twined blue rings in the center for their promise, and sheaves of yellow wheat at the corners for his plantings, and white dogwood stars in a circle around the rings for the place they'd made the promise. It would be her marriage quilt.

9

It was not until a week later that she found a chance to tell her father or grandmother anything. Always they seemed to be working apart — Winfield at his wheat clearing and Gran at airing the shuck ticks and quilts — or else they were in the field pulling wild onions from the rows of young corn while Delilah mixed batter inside the house. The hot evening in the cabin when she did stammer out her news that Charles Bickley had proposed marriage to her, she was not prepared for the reaction she got. Her father didn't question her; he didn't rage or bellow at her at all; he didn't congratulate her or even seem surprised. He just sat in his slatback chair and started to laugh. His laughter wasn't mocking, she realized. It was simply the laughter of fond amusement. His eyes crinkled at their corners over his stubbly red cheeks; his forehead lost every line of worry it had ever had.

"Delilah! How lonely you must have been all these years."

If she wanted fancies, he went on, smiling indulgently, she must read them in his books. Why, she was mooning over the first presentable man to say a pretty word of flattery to her. It was Charles's way to flatter, to say courtly things. Naturally he wasn't to be believed. What a child she was after all, in spite of that sturdy look and those roughened

housewife's hands. Naturally too, Charles hadn't said anything to him, her father. Charles himself would smile if he
could hear all this. It wasn't possible he'd consider wedding
a child like Delilah. In time he'd marry one of his own sort
— a cousin, most likely. That was what Settlement planters
generally did to keep land and money in the family. In time
she'd marry one of *her* kind, a Scotch-Irishman who shared
her faith. That was that. So she must keep her imaginings
to herself if she didn't want to be humiliated by the guffaws
of every Cohee on the Clinch who liked to watch a giddy girl
sigh over a militiaman.

"I'm not imagining! He said it! He said 'always.' "

Gran held her peace until Winfield had risen to go outside
and fetch water in the cedar bucket. Then she began to card
wool by the cabin window, her hands firm on the combs, her
lap heaped with greasy matted fleece. "It's a word easy to
say, 'always.' Doubtless Charles used it easily, missy. Try
living it." The lamp beside her flickered in a breeze.

"You don't believe me either!"

The teeth of Gran's combs ripped firmly at a yellowed puff
full of cockleburs. "No, I don't. I can't see what use you'd
be to Bickley now. If it is true I wish you the best of him,
but I'm thinking it isn't because I still have my reason. So
start shelling your pease. I'll not tell your kissing secrets —
you may rest about that."

"Papa got married." Delilah felt herself flush as she lifted
a heavy wooden tub piled with Gran's first crop of cherished
blue rouncevals.

"Ah!" Gran's ruthless laughter floated out in the room.
"He did that — a penniless schoolmaster hanging round my
cottage stoop every day until I thought he'd eat the last scrap
of side meat I had. And I knew before your mother did, my

girl. I bore her blushes and primpings and your father's promises to teach himself into riches until I sent for the Dominie from despair." Her carding slowed. Tenderly, she added: "I pray it will come for you as it came for your mother. You could read it in every line of her face and his too when they were together."

"But — "

"I've heard enough myself." Briskly Gran threw aside one bundle of fleece and took up another. "Your father won't laugh next time you prattle. Mind that, if you've any sense left."

So Delilah minded it. They'd both learn. The dignity and the pride of her silence would have to tell them what her words could not. Yet when Lawyer Dickenson sent for her father she went too, hoping for news of Charles, though she told her father it was because she wanted to ride with him. In the moist stuffy cabin of the lawyer she could scarcely draw breath. She gave her head a shake from time to time, trying to keep the heavy strands of her hair off the back of her neck, but it wasn't any use. Lawyer Dickenson had taken the paper out of both his windows, yet still not a breath of wind eased the oppression. She felt as damp and sticky as the lawyer's stack of papers looked. The lawyer had no news, she found out within the first ten minutes of her coming. There was only the one disturbing rumor that George Rogers Clark's men weren't in Kentuk County at all. Where, then, could they be? North of the Ohio, in that tangle of forest unbroken by a single white man's settlement, peopled only with painted red men who would leap out from behind the trees to massacree any invader who dared to tread their paths? She didn't want to think about it too much. She drummed her feet quietly and restlessly, and knew the heat was only a part of the heaviness in herself.

She didn't understand what the lawyer was saying. She ought, of course, to care enough to try. She ought to be thinking of her father's business some of the time, not just Charles's. Dickenson's dry, even voice was tediously hypnotic. As he droned on of cornrights and counterclaims he almost put a body to sleep. She couldn't see what all this had to do with herself or her father anyway.

" — I thought I ought to tell you," the lawyer finished.

"Tell me what? I'm thick on Virginia law. Are you trying to say I don't own Sugar Hill? If so, you're being ridiculous. I've got a clear cornright to four hundred acres and I can pay soon for an extra thousand. In time I'll buy up the rest of the mountain. Bickley's already surveyed it for me."

"Virginia law." Dickenson smiled his dry smile and pushed up his wig as he leaned back in a slatted chair. He rested his elbows on the writing table, which was raw from the hewing of a black man's axe, and fitted his long fingers together at the tips. The black cambric of his coat sleeve shone dully in the ray of light from the window. "What is Virginia law? In 'seventy-four the English courts held that titles purchased from Indians were full and sufficient — the Camden-Yorke decision. Later Dunmore started giving grants of his own; Governor Henry gives them now. There are old crown grants; there are cornrights. All these overlap. We're fighting England with the other colonies, but are we a colony, part of a new country, or a country ourselves?" Softly, he laughed, as if pleased with his own joke. "Ah, no, sir, there isn't such a thing as Virginia law."

"Then there's justice. I don't care what record you saw at the court. No Englishman named Smith owns Sugar Hill. He's never seen it, never had it surveyed, never planted it. If there ever was a royal grant it's not valid now. I'll not line your pockets with a fee, and empty my money chest to buy land I own already."

"Bickley emptied his," Dickenson answered quietly. "Did you know that? He bought up the crown grants of a Shelton cousin. He's got those, and his cornright, and the trade with the hunter Cassel; he's clear three ways. You're not. You'll be sorry for it."

"Nonsense. Cassel's Woods isn't the place for the subtleties of courtrooms. I came here to get beyond the reach of 'em. I'll stay beyond. My mountain's my freedom. You can be sure I'll keep it."

"In your way," Dickenson mocked.

"In my way, yes." How strong her father looked as he stood there in his hunting shirt! His sturdy body was outlined in the sunlight: broad waist, stocky legs, and a head so large in proportion to his height that it always seemed too heavy for his shoulders to bear. Yet Dickenson, at his table, also looked strong. His was a strange, almost a devious strength. His mild gray eyes had a careful cast to them, as if they were waiting to see something about to happen. His hands were delicate and fine, yet Delilah wondered if their grip wouldn't close slowly over a thing and never let it go.

"No man is beyond the law." Dickenson smiled again.

"I make my own laws." Delilah, standing, felt her father's hand tighten on her shoulder. "My God is my law, and my daughter. As you say, we've no country. So I won't rob her to satisfy laws which don't exist." He bowed; and then, with Delilah, he left. All the way to the river's edge he walked in long, firm steps, saying nothing. Delilah could match his stride, for she was as tall as he was and her legs were longer.

At the Clinch she longed to plunge into the water, but there wasn't time to stop. Her father untied Chick at the blacksmith's shanty where the mare had been left to be shod, and they both climbed on, Delilah riding pillion behind as they jogged along the mountain path.

"I thought Bickley would have more sense than to heed Dickenson's bid for a fee."

"Charles wants his plantation more than anything else in the world."

"Precisely. But I want mine too, and I've got it." Chick clambered on, beneath the glossy sunlit leaves of the sugar trees. The buzzing of the jarflies heightened, and above it soon came the flat sound of Gran beating out counterpanes in the cabin yard. Delilah wondered what Gran would say to the lawyer's advice. At dinner, over cornmeal mush and bacon, Gran's eyes narrowed until they were small dark coals in her weathered face, and she pursed her lips.

"I'd not heed the lawyer so much as Bickley, Ben. If he bought, you must."

"Nonsense." Winfield reached for the wooden platter on which the bacon slabs were lined in a neat row. "If we win the war, Virginia will confiscate English lands. If we lose, fighting in courts won't keep us here. We'll have to fight on our stoop."

"So? Put money by. The Lord helps those who help themselves. I've always minded the meek inherit the earth when the rest are through with it. If you don't save, I will."

"You have that privilege." He smiled. "Both my ladies seem to need a deal of humoring of late. They grow blasphemous or moonstruck." He was breathing heavily, but he went on eating his slice of bacon, cutting it neatly with the pewter fork that had been his wife's. The fork was one of the few things rescued from the Shenandoah when Gran had had to take her daughter to the Tidewater.

Simon Oscher, too, laughed at the lawyer. Delilah knew she ought to tell Simon she was promised. He wouldn't think her a child; he'd believe her. But she didn't want him growling and frowning over it, and besides it was for Charles to tell at Cassel's Woods. So she said nothing, hugging her knowledge, smiling with Simon over the lawyer's attempts to get money from everybody, and walking Reynard after all with Simon on the trace. She began to feel so guilty about Reynard's leash that she took it off; and to her delight Reynard stayed at her heels and wouldn't stray an inch from the path.

"He's free and he stays, Simon. Look!"

"You fuss over him so much he wouldn't know what to do, free." Simon's mouth screwed into the familiar grin, white and ingenuous. "He thinks he's a dog." He threw a stick, and Reynard chased it for a few feet but then stopped, his tail upright as a ninepin. "He don't even retrieve. He's a house dog fit for a Settlement lady. You surely love that fox a power. It's ruint him."

"It hasn't either." She couldn't help grinning back.

"I like to see the way you care for 'im. If a body cares for creaturs he cares for folks, I always think. Some day I'd like a pet. I might catch a coon. My mam doesn't want the work of a creatur, but when I have my own cabin I'll have one." He sobered. "Dammit, I hope Clark whips the redsticks once for all. Seems like you can't feel a place is really yours. You catch yourself wondering when it's going to be burnt. When I help my pap saw tables I try to plane 'em smooth, and then I wonder what for."

Simon longed to fight. He would have gone with Clark's men if his mam hadn't taken on so and his pap stropped him in the shed until he promised to wait another year. That would be fine, fighting with Clark. That would be a man's work. He was tired of house chores. He was a man grown, wanted to stand and fight with men, and clean up the Indian mess so he could farm his own cornright when he took one, and not forever be taking orders from his pap. He'd shown him a thing or two a couple of days ago. The boys were playing snick-a-snack, the game where everybody let fly their hunting knives at once; he'd been the last one slashed, the winner. Proudly, he showed Delilah the still-raw gash on his arm. Oh, his pap had been proud too. And even though his pap had stropped him for wanting to go with Clark, he thought his pap admired him for it. Against spring came he'd ask for his own cornfield. It was high time he did for himself.

Sometimes Delilah walked the trace alone or with her father. Whenever the morning sun rose scarlet through the white mist over Copper Ridge across the river, just above Cassel's Woods, he would tell her it meant a clear day. Charles, when he'd been living on Sugar Hill, had generally announced his plans for the day after scanning the ridge. But all she cared for at such times was seeing the red glow in the sky, and the pink shadows running through the mist, all lighting it like the shiny seashell she had brought from Tidewater. Sugar Hill changed every day, its trees pied like a patch quilt in the sunlight or muted in the shade. The river changed too. Sometimes it blinded her with dots of gold; on gray days it ran dull and quiet, foaming white only at the rocks thrusting up their worn gray tops at intervals. Some day she'd show everything to Charles. She'd make it his too in that way. She enjoyed trying likenesses of the things she loved in Sugar Hill in her quilt patterns. It wasn't just having the power of making them come back to her, but re-

membering the feeling of them, calling back the times she'd
been happy on the mountain by creating them all over and
letting them sift through her heart. When she put what she
loved and felt in a pattern, and the overflow of herself, it was
an easing. But maybe nobody could make just happiness.
There were wolves and painters on her mountain, barking
and screaming on long winter nights. There were, often,
wind and a driving rain that slanted cruel and cold. There
were deadly plants like nightshade and poison ivy. There
were pits full of the bones of unwary fawns. You couldn't
reason why, she guessed; you couldn't control or reason out
all the world; you had simply to be a part of it. When it
changed you changed too, as you watched and smelled and
felt and heard. Living, Delilah decided, was like being on
the mountain; you were a part of life because you knew it
through your senses. Thinking about it wasted time you
could be feeling it. And not to feel anything would cheat
you of the good times if it saved you the bad. Maybe it was
better to see raids and wait for Charles and stand both, and
remember the years of peace and Charles's promise. A thousand Principles and verses of scripture couldn't alter the bit-
ter-sweetness of living itself.

Whenever Simon came, Gran fed him her best cuts of bear
meat she'd traded from the Sawyers, her pickled venison, all
her preserves and her persimmon beer. She baked rolls for
him until Delilah frowned, "You make him feel too welcome,
Gran. I'm promised!"

"Don't you like Simon?"

"You can't *not* like him, I suppose," she shrugged. "But
you're making it harder for me when I have to explain to him
about Charles."

"Your knight," Gran's smile mocked.

"Why *won't* you believe me?" Delilah snapped angrily at

the table where she was paring apples. She swung around to her grandmother, who was laying apple slices on huge wooden trays to be dried in the winter sun.

Gran's smile died. "I'm afraid to believe it." And then she added: "Simon's hungry, Delilah. I like to feed him because I can see his pleasure."

Delilah's father told her once that Simon made him miss his teaching days. There was good stuff in the lad. He worked hard and went to chapel and had a solid friendly way about him; it was a pity he couldn't write his name. Surely he could be taught that. The frontier took some things away from people. It took the chance of learning, and made drudges of the young. But it gave more: it gave the right to follow your beliefs, to toady to no snuff-pinching planters and justices in satin coats or to hard-riding Church parsons who knew fetlocks and foxes better than the Word of God. All his life he, Ben Winfield, had sought the right to be himself: first in London's cobbled alleys, where he'd not wanted to pass his days as a tailor's apprentice and where he'd spent every farthing of his meager portion on books; then in Williamsburg, in the new land where he'd thought he would teach for the rest of his life . . . finally here on the Clinch, which had been a forest unbroken by the hand of civilized man but which now echoed with the whisperings of a hypocritical law clerk.

It was Simon who brought the real news of Clark's whereabouts. Clark had tricked his men into going clear to the Illinois Country. Henry Neece had had it from a hunter. With only a handful of troops Clark had taken Kaskaskia and Cahokia, the old French settlements on the Mississippi River that were British forts. He'd won all the west for Virginia, land so far away that it puzzled a body even to think about it. Folk gave out there were hardly trees there.

It was clear beyond the trees. Instead it had great seas of grass that grew higher than a man on horseback. "Not a man lost!" Simon exulted. "Oh, that Clark! I wish I'd been there." The rumor going the rounds now was that Clark planned to take Fort Vincennes on the Wabash River, then Detroit. Detroit was where the hairbuyer general was, the man who paid British sterling for every American scalp his Indians brought him. If Clark took Detroit the British and redsticks would skyte off, the wars would truly stop forever, and a man could tend to his clearing —

"You'd have liked to fight at Detroit, Simon?" Gran looked up from the night-rail she was mending.

"The rest are there, Mrs. Mackinnon. I'd like to show those British I can lick 'em."

No one knew for sure what was happening in the east; for the east seemed as remote as the grassy plains to the west. Russell was a delegate this year for Washington County in Williamsburg and a settler named Jimmy Bush had charge of the fort. By spring the Cherokees had begun to raid on the north fork of Holston. A Holston boy riding to the Clinch to warn Cassel's Woods was shot on the way and only his companion got through. But Benge (it was Benge again) didn't come after him. Instead Benge killed a captive white woman on the spot and threw her baby down a cliff and went back to the Tenase, to his "sacred town" of Chota. Some of the Cassel's Woods men went to bury the dead boy and woman and baby, Simon with them. They dug the bury-holes in a spot of lashorn trees, dark and quiet, where you could hear the streams and the wind and it was hard to believe Benge'd ever been there at all. The wolves had been crying a lot nights of late, and Simon went wolf-hunting to get bounty for the pelts. "I aim to prosper," he told Delilah.

They walked along the trace with Reynard. Beside a spring they stopped. For a moment Simon stared at her. Then, before she knew what was happening, he pressed her into his wiry boy's arms. She screamed. She tried to fight, kicking, pushing, but she was powerless against him. His mouth closed moist on hers; she clamped her mouth shut. Then she heard him laughing softly. She could feel the scratching of his shirt against her throat, the pressure of his thighs against hers. "Let me go!" she screamed again. His fingers felt like clumsy claws over her back as they started to work in the tow of her gown. But they stopped when she cried at him: "Beast! Let me *go!*" He stopped laughing. His arms dropped at his side. He stared at her again, at first puzzled, then sadly. Tentatively, he reached out his hand; but when she shrank back against a boulder he made no move to come to her.

"You mind — that much?" She could hardly hear him.

"Leave me alone!"

"I didn't aim to scare you." He took off his coonskin cap, scratched his head, and then turned away. "You meant 'beast,' didn't you? You weren't just sayin' it. You looked so pretty. I didn't aim to scare you."

"Hush yourself!" she hissed at him, twisting back her gown, smoothing her ribbon.

"Now you'll tell your pap." Listlessly.

"No! I'd be ashamed."

"Of what I've done? Or of me, Delilah?" His voice was steadier but still dull. "Maybe you ought to tell me which, I thought you liked me some."

"I don't! I do, but — " She couldn't say it; not now, not here.

"We'll go back." Simon picked up a fern and stripped its

stem. "You needn't worry yourself." And there was a new dignity in the way he walked with her to the cabin. He said not a word more. She had hurt him! He had hurt her, too. He had dared to fumble at her, and she'd never forgive him for it, never! He left in the yard without eating any of the hoecakes Gran had fried out for him. Inside, Delilah splashed cold water from the ewer on her face. Her father was down at the mill today, thank God, and Gran was tending new lambs in the barn. She felt a murderous rage in her heart at Simon and at herself. She longed to tell her father so he would punish Simon.

Yet afterwards, while she listened to the peepers croaking and the river running, she knew Simon had done what any boy down at Cassel's Woods might do. He had tried to steal a kiss from a girl he liked. Sometimes she herself had fancies and thoughts of Charles that made her blush on her pallet, but she couldn't stop them even if God did know she dreamed of lying in bed beside a man and loving him . . .

Fort Vincennes was taken after a terrible march through miles of flooded prairies. Half Clark's men, said the trader who stopped by on Sugar Hill with the report, were down with fever. (Delilah would nurse Charles, she determined, when he came back; she wouldn't leave his side; but he couldn't have fever, not Charles. And how could that heartless trader wolf down so much pork when he knew men with Clark were hungry?) A few French, the trader added between mouthfuls, had joined Clark when they heard the French King was coming into the eastern war for America. The Governor was dawdling over giving Clark more troops for Detroit, but kept writing Clark to get him blooded horses from the Frenchies for his Tidewater plantation. Governor Henry had changed, folks were saying, had gotten prideful and extravagant. At Vincennes Clark had found and captured the hairbuyer general himself.

"Gov'nor better give him a good reward for that," the trader said. Then he sighed. "Other hairbuyers back in Detroit, more than likely, just as wizzen-hearted. And capturing one hairbuyer don't help dyin' men. Clark's waitin' to take Detroit while they moan on their cots, and Henry don't send him the troops to march."

Charles can't be moaning on a cot, Delilah thought quickly. She had to keep believing that, to remember the time in the crabtrees and the dogwood when he'd asked for her, to remember every line of his face, the way folds of skin lapped at the outer corners of his eyes when you looked close, the way he smoothed his hair, the little nicks in his cheeks from his close shaving, and the slow smile that was so different from his company smile. The slow smile was the one that hesitated as if he wondered you could really care for him, but was so pleasured that you did . . . And he always smelled of tobacco but he never smoked in front of women, he was so polite . . . Oh, of course he'd come back! If he were dead she would feel it; and she didn't. A man like Charles couldn't be born wanting to plant and build, couldn't live through being cheated of his first home and then being burned out by Benge, couldn't live through the fighting he hated but had to do, just to die far away on a strange prairie in a strange fort.

She began to pray harder, commanding God to save him. She made herself eat to stay strong and whole for him, she kept at her marriage quilt (it was almost finished), piecing in the dogwoods and the rings and the sheaves, and she believed with every fiber of her body that she would be in her lover's arms again before the summer was out.

He was the center of her life now and all life meant to her. Nothing and no one else were real any more.

When the scattering of Clark's men came back from Vincennes, Lawyer Dickenson himself rode up the mountain to summon the Winfields. Without thinking of her father or Gran, Delilah raced out to saddle Chick and rode with the wind down the trace, through the swollen river, past the mill and Copper Ridge to the fort. He was there! She saw him! He was standing in his journey buckskins, tall and new-bronzed, laughing with Joe Sawyer. How clean his buckskins were, as if they had been washed! And she had forgotten the way he kept his hair tied so firmly in a club with that faded piece of black grosgrain that was more gray than black. She didn't bother to hobble Chick at all. She didn't care how she herself looked or who was standing around. She heard his deep laughter and she pushed aside Granny Sawyer and everybody else and threw herself straight into his arms. He let out a startled breath, but then he laughed again, and she laughed with him, and he lifted her up. The sun was hot; she could feel it on the top of her head. Everybody else was laughing now. When he put her down he gave a pretend-gasp as if she were too heavy for him. And then he said: "Dear girl! How I missed you! But where's your father?"

She put her hand to her mouth. "I — forgot. Oh, Charles, I forgot!"

From the corner of her eye she could see a strange woman and a short swarthy man with waxy mustachios and a double row of fringes on his shirt. The woman was young and pretty; her reddish-brown hair glinted in the sun. Granny Sawyer stood next to her. Granny's petticoat was stained at the hem with mud. She was grinning toothlessly and trying to smooth out the snarls in her dirty white ringlets. Well, let them all grin; they'd learn the truth any minute; everybody would. Simon would, standing there not grinning but with a mouth looking as if he'd tasted a sour apple.

Charles put his hand on Delilah's arm as if to lead her. And so she followed him to the pretty woman, who had a pale face and was very short beside Charles. The top of her head didn't quite come to the fringes at his shoulders. She wore a gown of real polished cotton — pale green cotton, here in Cassel's Woods. *Why am I seeing that?* Delilah looked to Charles, wondering why. She herself at least came to his forehead. Her eyes were level with his mouth. She could see the thin seam beneath his lower lip . . . And he stood before her, unharmed, hers at last.

He said: "Delilah, this is Mam'selle Hatler. She and her father have come with us from the west. She asks me about my family, you know, and I tell her you're that — you and your father and Gran." He took his hand from Delilah's arm and put it on the woman's shoulder with the ready movement of habit. "You must call her by her name, Marie. We're to be married here."

II

"Never pay a lad ninepence to climb a tree and look into the middle of next week. 'Tis money thrown away."

—*Love's Herald*

10

"No." Delilah heard her voice come stupidly at last.

"Sometimes I've work to believe it myself, sweetheart." Charles's hand moved protectively toward Marie's white neck. "A rattlesnake private hardly deserves my luck. I'm trusting you to be her friend, you know. She'll feel very strange away from her countrymen." He talked on; he said something about Marie's father going down to try his fortune in Watauga. He spoke of finding a Scotch parson on the Holston or in Watauga as soon as he could — any would do — and of starting his blacks at planting his wheat and corn. Delilah hardly heard him. She stared instead at Marie, at the small dainty woman in the cotton gown. Marie smiled a polite smile. Soon, however, an understanding seemed to be dawning in her eyes, for her smile grew more fixed.

"You are surprised, Mam'selle Winfield?" Her voice, touched with its French accent, was ever so soft when it came. But it was also triumphant. Very slightly, her smile curled upward.

"He can't," Delilah said dully.

"But he will." When Marie looked up at Charles her smile gentled. "He has, as you see."

Evidently Charles did not hear her, for he was speaking to her father.

It was then that Delilah felt Simon's arm close roughly on hers. She felt him pulling her back, and she let him. She did not know what else to do. "Come on, Delilah. Your pap's here now, and the lawyer." And while she stood between Simon and Granny Sawyer at the side, she saw Charles actually turn his back on her to be congratulated again by the Sawyers, the Neeces, the Bush family, Dickenson, the others. Soon her own father was clapping Charles on his shoulder. It was not until Gran led her away from Simon that she realized how hard her breath was coming.

"Don't let Bickley know," Gran murmured. "Come back with me. Keep your head up."

Delilah didn't cry as she rode through the river behind her grandmother. She still saw the sharp outlines of every new leaf on the trees, and her father's cabin and barns high above, and the clay of the trace. She smelled the blooms on the hobblebushes, and the rank leafmold of the forest. She heard the songs of the birds. But she began to feel as if she were not a part of any of it, that she had a separate existence, that an invisible wall had sprung up to bar her from the life of the world around her. Inside the cabin, where Reynard slept in a square of sun on the floor, her grandmother sat her down firmly in a chair and put a tumbler of foxgrape wine to her lips.

"Drink," Gran ordered.

Soon Gran was saying other things: things about a girl's foolishness, and the way men were, and a woman's pride and self-possession, which were what turned a silly girl into a true woman. Delilah listened, but the words seemed a thousand miles away, not as if she were hearing them now but had heard them long ago and they only hung suspended in her memory. Her eyes moved to the quilt folded on her trunk in the corner: her marriage quilt, with its blue rings and white stars and sheaves of gold. She must put it away. She wouldn't need it now.

"I wish I had lavender. For the quilt, I mean."

She felt Gran's arms tighten on her shoulders. They were very strong; Gran was kneeling beside her. "Hush," Gran whispered. "You'll forget. Go to sleep."

She must have slept some, because when she looked out the window again she was on her father's pallet and it was dark outside. Her head ached. He was standing over her, his brows knitted in a line of worry. He bit his lip. "I tried to warn you."

She sat up. "I'm fine," she heard herself assuring him in a brittle voice. "Don't fret, Papa."

"God in His wisdom brings us these trials when we're young. But they teach us. You'll get over it. You'll be the friend Charles meant you to be when he said 'always.' He did say that?"

There was no God. There couldn't be.

She got to her feet, straightening herself, passing her hand across her forehead. "I must put my quilt away. She won't have it. She won't have that."

"Delilah, that's hardly generous — "

"Will you *hush*, Ben!" Gran rasped out.

"I hate her," Delilah announced levelly as she walked to the corner, gathered up the quilt, and put it on a table next to the trunk. She lifted the trunk's heavy lid and then laid the quilt inside on top of a bolt of faded calico. For a moment she looked down; she could see a white dogwood spray, and a blue ring. Then, firmly, she slammed the lid of the trunk shut and heard its echo in the room. Once more she straightened. "I know how she got him. She'll see I understand. It will hurt her. I'm glad."

"Hate is wicked, Delilah. It — "

"Hush, Ben, I say!" Gran's voice was sharp.

Delilah walked to her grandmother. "I'll go to his wedding, Gran. She'll see me there."

"Naturally," Winfield grunted. "Very proper."

"No. Not very." Gran began stitching a moccasin for him beside the bettylamp. Outside, a whippoorwill started calling, and the smell of ginseng floated in, sharp on the cool night wind. "She'll have to do it, though."

Charles Bickley and Marie Hatler were married early in June, on a morning when the sun blazed down on slicks of pink laurel in full bloom along Copper Ridge and on the young shoots of corn in his fields below. The very shadows of objects were nearly transparent. Everyone in Cassel's Woods had turned out early, the men and boys in their brightest hunting shirts. Gran wore a new-made muslin cap trimmed up in blue satin ribbons, and Ben Winfield the shiny blue broadcloth coat and yellowed white Kersey breeches he had taken from his own trunk in the cabin loft. He had carefully arranged a black silk cravat so ancient it rustled like tissue whenever he turned his head. He had polished the cracked leather of his schoolmaster's pumps with their princhbeck buckles that flashed in the sun as he trudged along the path to Boone's Chapel, now rebuilt larger than before. Delilah smoothed the skirt of her newest gown, dyed brown last week with walnut juice. She had had to bleach her hands with pokejuice afterwards; they felt rougher than ever. She had tied back her hair with a brown band. At her throat she wore a silver circle brooch which had been her mother's.

She heard Marie laughing ahead. The boys had set her high on Mercury, and she was trying to cover her ankles in the stirrups of her sidesaddle. "Please!" she cried gaily. "Oh, Charles, your horse is not used to me!"

But Charles would see that Mercury didn't bolt. He had the rein firm in his hand as he walked beside her. Her flowered dimity skirts were billowing. Her hair glinted redder than ever. Her father, Sebastien Hatler, walked on the other side of her—a comic little Alsatian dandy who had been talking incessantly of starting a vineyard in Watauga.

"Suh-basteen." Simon grinned. "Isn't that a name? He won't be trading for fancy Detroit goods like her wedding gown when he goes to Watauga." His grin softened. "You'll sit by me, Delilah. I'm glad you came. You don't mind all that much now, do you?"

"No." She felt her mouth working itself into a smile. She concentrated on the smile, thinking out each detail of it: the little sound of laughter, the narrowed eyes. All along the cedar-lined path the boys of Cassel's Woods had strung grapevines from the treetrunks on either side. She saw Charles and Hatler hurrying to untie them, one rope after the other. Fluffy clouds were massed across the sky. Crows were cawing, and Mill Creek tumbled brightly down in the distance toward the river. The world had not changed after all. Granny Sawyer, just ahead, was wheezing that English Church the miller might be, but he'd taken a good Scotch-Irish dominie fast enough to say the marriage-words over his lass. Church parsons never went where there might be Indians. A dominie might not be lawful in the Settlements, but the miller didn't seem to be worrying about Settlement laws today. Right anxious he was; oh, she'd seen him walking with his Frenchie girl in the woods, the pair of 'em so close a body couldn't see the light between.

The dominie—it was Parson Doak from Watauga—read

out the service in his black robe. "Dearr-ly beloved!"
he shouted into the chapel and at the crowd gathered outside on the steps and in the yard. When he had finished
the ceremony he preached a sermon about wifely obedience
and man's sacred duty to hate eternally the English King and
his hirelings the red heathen. Afterwards Charles bent over
his bride and kissed her on the cheek. The parson gave her
mouth a resounding smack, and he never blinked when he
saw the big barrel Henry Neece and Joe Sawyer had rolled
into the yard not thirty paces from the chapel door. With a
gourd ladle, they began dispensing whisky. "Cheers!" yelled
the men to Charles and Marie. "God be wi' ye!" "Thumping luck, miller!" Some of the younger boys began to dump
girls from their saddles on the way to Charles's cabin and
laughed uproariously when Ann Neece raised her fist from
the ground. Delilah walked erect between her father and
Simon, behind Gran whose cap ribbons bobbed with each
step. Her father had just bought her a gelding of her own
from Lawyer Dickenson, which he called Farmer George.
He was a slow horse but a determined one, like the English
King after whom Ben had named him in derision. But she
had tied the horse at the river's edge. She was glad of that.
She wished she had taken some whisky herself. Ahead,
Henry Neece was standing on Charles's lintel and was hold-
ing up a leather flask tied with a white streamer.

"Black Betty!" he yelled. "Race for Black Betty, boys!"

Over stumps and stones they dashed, pell-mell across
the ground until it shook with the hoofbeats of their horses.
Charles and Marie were caught in the chase. A boy who
beat everyone to the flask raced back with it to the bride,
and Marie grimaced and laughed at the same time she drank.
"Oh!" she wiped her lips. "It is so strong."

"Strong corn, Marie!"

Black Betty went the rounds. "Snick-a-snack," someone cried, and the boys' knives began flashing in the sun. "Blaze away!" they shouted. "Your turn, Tim Fraley. Blaze away!"

"Don't look," Simon muttered to Delilah as a knife streaked by. But she kept looking because she was hardly feeling anything today and that was best, and if she looked at this she wouldn't have to see Charles with his hand on his wife's shoulder again.

"Oh, I'm fine." She formed her smile. Charles's head bent closer to his wife's. He was whispering something to her, perhaps also telling her not to look. Soon the two of them would be alone. Even now he couldn't keep his hands from her. Soon he would take her because she was his, because a parson from Watauga had shouted a few Bible words over her.

In Charles's large new grain barn his guests started forming a reel. Fiddles scraped under the walnut beams, his black men twanged their bangers, feet stamped, the laughter rose higher. Opposite Simon, Delilah began moving her body in the figures.

" 'Devil's Dream!' " came the shouts. " 'Hang Out Till Morning!' Let's have the wedding song!"

Once Charles waved to her. She didn't wave back.

> *"Fire on the mountain,*
> *Run, boy, run!*
> *Fire on the mountain,*
> *Run, gal, run!"*

Charles and Marie were dancing together in a "Swing Your Partner" call. He kept his hand at her waist, and as she clung to him her eyes looked up at him adoringly. Her dimity gown floated out behind her as she whirled in a cloud of flowered blue. Her red hair shone brighter than ever in the long rays of light from the loft loopholes. Her tiny slippered feet were keeping perfect rhythm.

"He is very rich, my son-in-law." Sebastien Hatler beamed at Gran. "He has many slaves. He told us, and it is true."

This is really happening, Delilah thought. I am watching and hearing it happen with Simon Oscher. I'm not screaming. Maybe that's because Charles turned me away in the sugar bush, and I really knew then . . . Did Marie want him only for what he had? Or for what he was too? He was happy today. Delilah had never heard him so gay, never seen him so easy with the people of Cassel's Woods.

"Oh Simon," she gasped brokenly, trying to go on dancing.

"You're tired. You got to stop." He led her to the wall. "No, please. I can't — "

Charles waved to her again. She waved back this time.

Soon she and Simon were watching a whooping brace of boys rush on Charles and begin pushing him up the pine ladder to the loft. Children were squealing happily, the women laughed louder, Marie gave a breathless little scream as she was pushed after him, and the boys began to roar out ribaldries that made Simon color under his freckles and scuff his boots on the barn floor. "Your turn, miller!" "Big children!" The dancing began again, and the daylight faded. In the darkness of the barn, lanterns began sputtering. Gran and her father were talking now to Lawyer Dickenson and Sebastien Hatler in a corner. Delilah waited for Simon to bring her a trencher of jerked beef and hot cabbage and bacon. The smell of the cabbage crowded out the smells of grain and sweat. She tried not to think of what was happening in the loft above. It was just a joke, this part. It was supposed to be very funny. The two of them would only be waiting there. Her time with him hadn't come yet, it wouldn't come for a while. The noisy madness and the music continued through the night into morning. Delilah ate, and she drank the persimmon beer Simon brought her, and she heard herself laughing while she danced on. At dawn Marie and Charles were allowed to flee to his cabin, but a crowd of boys followed them with cowbells for the chivaree. When Marie came back in a russet paisley-printed infare gown that matched her hair she was still smiling her brilliant smile. Charles was trying to smile too, but the line between his eyes showed he was growing angry at the crowd, wanting them to leave him. Still the fiddles scraped. The dancing began again, and the singing:

"Rise you up, my dearest dear, present to me your hand,
And we'll take a social walk to a far and distant land . . ."

Couples bobbed at the cubes of tree sugar hanging on grapevine strands overhead. They kissed each other and giggled. It was very handsome, the miller's infare. Delilah didn't move. Her father came to stand with her. He was frowning too as he brushed a fleck of sawdust from the front of his best osnabrig shirt. "Last time they danced this one they were burned out," he growled.

"The more they deserve to dance now, Ben." Gran pulled her cap straight. "I think it's time we go back. We've done our duty."

At the riverbank Delilah raised her head high and said: "Thank you, Simon. It was nice."

"He could've danced you one dance." Simon's mouth set. "I was real proud of you."

"Were you?" She turned on him what she hoped was the brightest smile of all, brighter than Marie's. "What for?" Then she climbed on her gelding and followed her father and grandmother on their horses — Gran's was borrowed from the lawyer — to Sugar Hill, while the river rushed down and away toward the wilderness in the west.

Several times Charles rode up the mountain, but whenever Delilah saw him coming she quickly contrived to be in the woods gathering poke greens and ginseng by the time he could reach the cabin. He wanted her to come down to see his bride, she knew. He had said that. But she told Gran to answer she couldn't be spared. Gran promised to say no more . . . Perhaps there had been a night at Fort Vincennes; perhaps he'd talked to the French girl Marie about Green Springs there, had needed her as he had needed Delilah Winfield once, and the French girl had known better how to show him she was no child . . . When winter came Delilah was glad. It meant he would not come again. He had come through snow once because he was lonely; but he wouldn't be lonely any more. He had a wife.

She blessed Simon for not coming at all, for understanding. She forgave him everything.

The winter soon turned to the most bitter one the Clinch valley had ever known. When the snow started, it never stopped. Blizzard after blizzard howled across the brooding ranges and dumped window-high piles of snow at the cabin's chinked walls. The air was so cold it stabbed in bitter pricks. Delilah found she could not stay outside for long without first rubbing her face with Gran's beargrease salve. Her father learned this too when his close-shaved cheeks just missed being frostbitten. The sugar trees boomed like huge guns as they cracked apart intermittently, their sap frozen solid. Delilah helped her father and grandmother jam the stock into the barn: the sheep, the brindle cow which was with calf by Lawyer Dickenson's bull, the pigs and the black Dominecker fowl. Each day she did her share of fighting through the drifts with water-buckets which froze in an hour, even as the snow froze stiff on her cloak. The rats were cold, too, and voracious, for when they took refuge in the barn they began chewing through the gunny fodder bags, and her father had to chase them with a stick and begin heaping his cornmeal into Gran's iron caldrons while he cursed under his breath. Down at Cassel's Woods, Delilah knew, there were people who had not finished their cattle barns. What were they doing? Simon's father had not finished his. She thought of the Oscher cows and sheep growing scrawny as they staggered through the drifts, perhaps starving to death. On a frigid, palely sunny day her father tried to get down the mountain to the river where he could gather shoots of cane to fatten his pigs. That way, he would save corn. But he couldn't manage to drive Chick or the gelding into the snow at all because the drifts at the stable door were higher than the horses' bellies.

"Doubtless others have thought of the cane." Gran stirred a bowlful of chopped venison stretched with meal. "There may be none left to take by now."

And at last Delilah began to feel emotion again: pity for her father whenever she saw his face muffled in scarves against the wind, his topheavy body bent from fighting it as Gran's body was bent. He hadn't been meant for this. Gran kept the fire blazing high in the grate and Reynard slept ever beside it, twitching his bushy tail from time to time. As the winter wore mercilessly on they all started sleeping beside the fire. Her father chipped out ice chunks for water, and Gran fanned the flames to melt them faster. The food store was dwindling. Delilah knew it even as she slipped scraps to Reynard, and she knew her father and grandmother knew it. Gradually Gran cut down the sizes of portions at meals, but they did not talk of this. One night they found one of their young rams frozen stiff in the barn; it had stayed too close to the loopholes. They dragged it by its legs through the snow and inside the cabin; there they thrawed it out, dressed it, and began eating its rank meat. Reynard grew thinner, his short legs sticklike and awkward. Once her father went out on his snowshoes to try to find a dead deer, but he could not, and it was long since buffalo had roamed Sugar Hill. Some mornings Delilah saw wild buzzards rigid in the high branches where they had frozen at roost the night before. By February Gran was cooking them after Winfield had shaken them out from the trees with his stick. Somehow the family would hold out until spring without killing the stock they needed to breed more; after that they would hold out until harvest. But how? On buzzards?

"Oh," Gran gestured, "I'll learn to boil a savory plantain, I reckon. I've a piece of fine lawn in my trunk, Delilah. Would you like to edge it for a cap?"

Delilah shook her head. "I don't need to be kept busy, Gran. I'm all right now."

"Perhaps you are." Gran kept stirring what she politely called the turkey soup; and the smell of even this was pungent and tormenting to Delilah's contracted stomach. After dinner her father prayed: "My misdeeds shall prevail against me: O be Thou merciful unto our sins . . . O God of our salvation, who in His strength setteth fast the mountains, and is girded about with power . . . Thou providest for the earth, Thou waterest her furrows, Thou sendest rain into the little valleys thereof . . . The folds shall be full of sheep, the valleys also shall stand so thick with corn, that they shall laugh and sing . . ."

Does he really believe that, Delilah wondered? Does he, when we're hungry, and the winter never breaks? How can he believe it? We'll freeze and starve; but I don't care.

Oh yes, you do, the voice in her mind began to mock her. You still want Charles Bickley; you'd take him tomorrow if you could. Long ago you decided nothing would ever stand in your way.

When spring did come the sounds of it were eerie. The Clinch thundered like cannon as its ice cracked. Sodden days succeeded frosty nights. There were mornings when Delilah, her stomach gnawed by the hunger that never left it now, looked from the cabin door with Reynard in her arms to a world where every tree glittered with a coating of ice. Once a large flock of passenger pigeons darkened the dawn sky and when they roosted, too briefly for slaughter, on the brittle branches there was a sound of popping that echoed like rifle fire. Thousands of tiny twigs fell to the hard earth. The pigeons cooed in a great rush when they left, as if the whole world were breathing. Then the snow melted. It poured down Sugar Hill to the Clinch to swell it until Delilah could see the river flooding many of the fields at Cassel's Woods.

"You'll help me clear," her father said. "They may need growing space if they lose much topsoil down there."

And so she learned how to chop and split trees. She

hacked at logs, and lifted them, and at night she ate boiled greens and the thin meal-and-water paste Gran called light bread, and she watched the scars on her hands covering themselves with yellow calluses so hard that when she pricked them, sewing, she felt nothing. She had her father. He would not be able to buy the mountain's extra acres now; too many sugar trees had frozen. Well . . . She had him, and she had Gran who knew some of what was in her heart but not all. She had a fox which shared her lean times as it had shared her good ones, and Reynard too was something to love. Delilah was eighteen, and she had learned how to fell a tree and split it into firewood by herself. She would soon learn how to guide a plow in the new clearing when her father had to follow with the dragtooth harrow. Her hands were harder, her body leaner and tougher.

She was tending the emaciated brindle cow, due shortly to calf, in the barn alone the day she looked up and saw Charles at the door. He was thinner too, and looked as tired as she felt. The cords of his neck were gauntly prominent, his knuckles and wristbones large knobs in his hands. He walked slowly toward her. Then his old smile lit his angular face. "My dear," he said softly.

She didn't move.

"I've brought your father meal. I've worried very much." He was standing directly over her; still she knelt in the straw beside the cow, its ribs rising like ridges at intervals in its taut flesh. "We — had extra. I wanted to see you."

"Thank you, Charles," she managed.

"I wish you'd come down to us some day." His voice was touched just then with the boyish wistfulness she had heard in it long ago. "The winter was hard for her — for my wife."

"Your wife." Delilah heard herself repeat it mechanically.

"She misses her father. A woman of her own sort, well — " He broke off. Then he added: "I'd like to see you too, of course. You know that, sweetheart."

"Would you?" She was very careful to keep her hands palms downward on the cow's swollen belly, and she was glad her cloak hid her old yellow calico gown, which was patched and bleached from years of use. Her cloak was newer. "I might come," she smiled slowly at last.

To herself she thought that night: I'm not really proud at all, the way Gran thinks, or brave. Today I loved him more than ever. I'll take anything he gives me. If I can only keep on loving him, maybe that's all I can ask of my life.

11

Sʜᴇ ᴄᴏᴜʟᴅ feel Gran's eyes burning into her when she told her she was going down to Cassel's Woods to visit Marie Bickley. But when Gran asked, bluntly, why, Delilah explained carefully that Charles had begged it. He might not even be there himself; probably he would be at the mill. *But I'll stop by the mill first. I have to.*

"And you can see her, missy, and behave decently to her?"

"Yes, Gran. It's over. I told you."

"You're lying to me." Gran clamped a square of new-woven tow into her tambour.

"No." With an effort, Delilah kept her hands limp at her sides. "I'm only tired."

They all would have been more tired, Delilah and her father and her grandmother, more hungry too, if they had not had the extra meal. Had it been extra for Charles? Or had he stinted himself? She had to find that out.

"Let me go, Gran," she pleaded listlessly. "Truly it's over."

"Remember that, then." Gran bit off a madder-dyed thread on the towel she had started embroidering and knotted a length of indigo. "I trust you not to make a fool of yourself again."

The trace to the Clinch was soggy. Several times the new

gelding, Farmer George, mired, and when Delilah reached
the Clinch she saw its water sweeping widely down what
had been its banks and its cane stands. The willows of her
hollow had been submerged a quarter of the way to their
tops. Willow logs were floating down the river; one was actually blooming as it was carried by. The leaves of the sycamores and the creeper vines that twisted through them hung
utterly still in a windless calm. But even so the river swept
on, carrying its cargo of logs and weeds and trash from last
year's crops the Lord knew how many miles up — perhaps
all the way from Witten's Mill where it had its source. The
soggy cornstalks would be borne downriver into Chief
Benge's Tenase, perhaps, and a world away into the great
Ohio, then into the Mississippi beside which Charles had
spent half a winter in one French fort before he had marched
back eastward to another, Vincennes . . . Delilah took off
her moccasins but the water was deep at the ford, and her
skirt itself was soon soaked. It didn't matter; the brown dress
was drab anyway; she hadn't any truly pretty gown. Still,
she wouldn't let Charles see her hands this time either. She
could feel her face still smooth, and she had brushed back
her hair. Farmer George plodded laboriously through the
mud of what had been cornfields at Cassel's Woods until
they came to the mill. The wheel was churning up great
sprays of foam in Mill Creek, which itself had widened into
a river. Inside, Delilah found Charles bent over a large
leatherbound ledger, making notations with a frayed quill.
The mill smelled moldy. Its storage room was empty. But
its gears were banging and clattering, its pulleys buzzing as
usual.

"Delilah!" He looked up. "You've caught me reckoning,"
he shouted over the noise. "We'll need your father's extra

field." Then he rose and walked over to her. She could just hear his next words. "I've got a few more acres but they're mud at the moment. We're grinding the last of our corn."

"I'd like to see them." She moved closer, her throat strained.

"You'd be bored to death," he laughed quickly. "We've lost some families to the Settlements, fortunately. We couldn't have managed otherwise without slaughtering stock." He smoothed back his forelock. It, too, had started to gray. She hadn't noticed that in the barn. If only the noise would stop.

"Your meal — it wasn't extra." She had to shout too.

"It was, sweetheart. We'll leave it at that. But don't let me keep you. Go on to Marie. She'll be very happy." The gears thumped away over the whirring of the burrs in the room beyond.

Are *you* happy? she wanted to ask. But she made herself smile too, and when she reached his cabin she realized it would be her first time in the house where he lived. The infare had been held at the barn. Suddenly she wanted to break into hysterical laughter. She'd dreamed of living here herself, but she'd never been inside.

The fat old Negro woman came to the door and motioned to the cabin's largest first-story room, its parlor. With a shock Delilah recognized the moment she saw her on a settle that Marie was pregnant. Marie's face was pinched and white; her small body was distorted under her loose white gown; but her green eyes still sparkled, her hands were still soft, and her hair still fell in a cascade of tawny red-brown waves about her shoulders.

"My baby will come in three months," she said without blushing. "Please sit down."

They talked at first of the past winter, of the threat of raids, of food shortages and the stock and the weather. "My father's got extra land cleared," Delilah bragged. "Did you know it? It ought to help." They drank sassafras tea together when the Negro Marie called Maum Silvey passed it shuffling softly and noiselessly. All the while Delilah knew Charles's wife was watching her as she was being watched. Marie's eyes, from time to time, narrowed into a slight squint. It's not just your baby, Delilah wanted to remind her; it's his too; you needn't look so satisfied.

"Charles does not know you were attached to him," Marie smiled at last. "I have not told him. He can be very stupid, my Charles." There was tenderness in her voice; Delilah grudged her that. But she felt her hands tightening in her lap. Then she heard herself repeating the sentences she had so often cried out against: "I was younger. He was the only man I knew beside my father. And" — she couldn't help adding with a tiny thrill of malice — "he was lonesome. You'll understand because I know you've seen him that way too."

"Naturally." Marie kept on smiling; if this meant anything to her, she did not show it. "I was lonesome myself, at Vincennes. We came there from Canada the year before, Papa and I, after coming from Alsace." Sebastien Hatler had tried trading at several Canadian forts and disliked the Abenaqui Indians, who stank of beargrease gone rancid and cheated him every chance they got. At Vincennes he had "naturally" preferred the American milita of Colonel Clark to his British masters, and had heroically smuggled powder from the fort to the American lines. He was very clever, Marie's papa. He had known who was going to win. I am clever too, she implied, cleverer than you . . . Cassel's Woods had been disappointing to her. But then, there had been a raid, had there not? Was it very bad to see a raid? Some day her Charles planned to change the settlement's name, to make it Bickley Mills. He would build a very great plantation here, buy many new slaves, add rooms to his cabin and board it over and raise pillars and send for fine silver from the east. She would join his English Church — she was not so firm a Huguenot, truly — and they would require a parson to come and stay, as in the Tidewater. Soon Charles was going to start trading ginseng to the east, Indians or no. It would be so convenient for the people who could not afford to tithe their corn and wheat; they could pay by the work of digging in the woods, especially the children of large families. It was certain that the ginseng — "sang," as people called it — would become very dear in the Settlements because of the Indian trouble and the war. Everyone knew what a tonic sang was, how it warmed the blood and strengthened the heart and healed men's wounds. Marie's papa had known it did not grow east of the Blue Ridge, and Charles knew too.

"But he wouldn't send children into the woods to dig it for the Settlements, not in summer! Not just to pay for corn milling." Delilah tried to keep her voice down; the house, unlike the mill, was so very quiet.

Marie's small red mouth widened in her white face. "It is better for the little ones to be busy, is it not?"

"Or killed!" Delilah snapped.

"Please." Marie stirred her tea. Promptly she began to ask Delilah the names of trees she had seen on the ridges, and the use of each. Charles only came in an hour later, when the sun was shining at a long angle through the open window of the room. He pulled off his muddy boots and put on clean moccasins. Then he went to stand beside his wife. Delilah saw her press his rough hand to her breast and smile softly up at him. Was he tired? Did he wish something? Delilah felt herself blushing furiously. He loved Marie. He had begotten his child in love . . . Delilah forced her eyes to sweep the room. There were few signs of him in it. His rifle, hung on the wall; his powder horns; a musket and fowling piece in their brackets; two riding whips; a closed morocco case on a trestle table, perhaps with his surveying instruments and map dyes inside. He had been burned out. That was why he had nothing from his old home, Green Springs, nothing more intimately his.

At the door, alone with him, she asked aloud before she knew she had done it: "You're happy?" And he took her hands, looking down at her, not noticing her calluses at all. "Very happy." He shook back his forelock in his characteristic gesture. "Tell your father to come down too."

"The children — not to dig in the woods. She told me, Charles, but — "

"You don't think it's a good plan? We'll guard 'em. It's lucky I can provide work this year. You'd never think a pretty head could be so full of planting notions," he laughed genially. "I had no idea any children had asked about digging until Marie mentioned it to me. It ought to save land for a few of their fathers."

"Otherwise you'd take it?"

"Yes, my dear," he answered quietly, letting her hands go. "I would."

Go back to her, then! Delilah wanted to shout. Let her be beautiful for you and let her drive you into meanness and play on your wanting more land so she can be rich. She doesn't love you; she only loves what you can give her.

That's what you wish, the inner voice answered; but she does love him. That's why you hate her more than ever, because loving him she can still be cool enough to take what she wants. You can't; you only wait here like a stupid clout of a girl, like any Cohee.

"Bickley Mills." Delilah's lips were dry as she repeated the name.

"It sounds very grand, doesn't it?" he laughed. But he soon sobered, and when she had gone outside she heard him shut the door quickly and willingly.

She didn't think she'd come back to that cabin.

It was a hunter who brought word that Benge had begun raiding downriver. Delilah's father started to carry his rifle whenever he went to harrow his cornfield; he would lean the rifle against a butt close by, glancing at it from time to time as he guided Chick down the rows. He forbade Delilah to pick greens alone. Gran took a fowling piece with her whenever she went to rake out her seedbed of flax. But Benge still hadn't come to the mountain by midsummer. Perhaps he did not think the crops on this part of the Clinch worth burning over, Winfield joked grimly; the fields at Cassel's Woods were cracked and the corn shoots stunted; his own would yield poorly too. Benge wasn't supposed to be bringing many Indians with him these days. He had harried Martin's Fort near the Cumberland Gap with only a handful. There was no need, Jimmy Bush had told Winfield airily at the mill, musket in hand, for everybody to come to the fort he now superintended. Jimmy had heard Benge was raiding mostly with the renegade Hargis.

"For a fact," Winfield mocked Jimmy's Cohee accent. "He says if a man bolts his door carefully and keeps his water buckets ready by his barns and hayricks and never lets his gun out of his sight, he can manage to stay in his clearing and raise victuals for himself and anybody else who may need them. Which means Bush wants our crop, meager as it looks." Russell was in Williamsburg for the Public Times, the meeting of the assembly; he couldn't quarrel with what Jimmy Bush decided on the Clinch . . . Even as she listened to her father's mimicking irony Delilah could not help a smile. How was it he could never understand her, when he understood other people so well — so vividly, whether kindly or cruelly.

Yet stories soon began to come from the couriers who rode in at intervals from Fort Blackmore and Rye Cove: children massacreed and their severed limbs hung on trees; outlying families killed and burned, their young girls taken captive to Chota, Benge's town. To be taken was the worst fate of all . . . Any day now Marie's baby would be born. Oh, Marie might yet see a raid! It was strange; Delilah hated her, but still she could fear more for her than for herself. Charles would not want to lose his child. And so many were the horrors any woman heard about out here that she got hardened. What the first raid had begun for Delilah the stories now finished, until she felt that her very heart had an overlay to prevent any stabs of terror she might feel from wounding it. Still, there was the night she and her father and grandmother heard twigs cracking outside. She went rigid then in spite of herself. She could see her father's lips move in a prayer and his hands harden on his rifle stalk while he smiled his humorless smile. The noise died. Perhaps it was only a deer or a vixen smelling Reynard's spoor. Later she remembered the thrushes had sung unusually long.

What was an outlying family? Was it a family like her own?

Benge came the second night, but again he came to Cassel's Woods, not Sugar Hill. From her cabin window Delilah stared across the river at the tiny pinpoints of his torches and knew them for what they were. But no flames soared up while the faraway rifles and muskets popped. Occasionally a long whoop floated up the mountain to die in the wind and the darkness, but the sky across the river never turned red as it had once before.

"We'll shoot if they come here," Gran said doggedly. "If they think this mountain's worth climbing for one family, they'll find out not. We can hold 'em." Her fowling piece lay on the table beside her, but she went on pounding cornmeal in her pestle, never missing a stroke even without a lamp to guide her hands. And Benge didn't climb the mountain the night of his raid — not that they knew. By morning there was silence. After sleepless hours of watching Delilah started when the silence was broken at last by hoofbeats. She darted back to the window to see Simon leaping down from his cob. "Delilah!" he breathed at the door. "Thank Goddamighty! I had my mind to you all the time long."

"What happened?" She moistened her lips; her tongue felt furry. She tightened her fingers on the water piggen she held.

Simon swallowed; she could see his Adam's apple bobbing up and down. "Maybe it's true Benge thinks this is a holy mountain. He knows it has a clearing here, surely. You're truly all right?" Inside, he stumbled over the words of his tale, his face flushed. "The miller's blacks at our place — they came out with muskets. The lawyer's did too. He and the miller were ready, seemed like. E'er time the redsticks set a fire the Neegurs doused it and we doused it with 'em. But the miller's wife started screaming uncommon bad. You could have heard her for miles, I reckon. It fair curdled my blood. The miller ran in his house to her — couldn't fight after that. She was — she'd been taken, you see." Simon turned away. "I spoke with Granny Sawyer after. The black woman Silvey, she was shooting redsticks from the loft — she was screaming too and wouldn't come down to help. He was alone with her. He had to — "

"What *happened?*" Delilah's fingers went white on the piggen's rim.

"She was bad, Granny says. He told her. It was twins — right in the shooting and the firing and the black woman crying. He did what he could. He didn't know — "

Delilah felt the muscles in her stomach grow stiff. She started from her chair; then she forced herself to sit back. A slow shallow breath came from her throat. "She — died?"

Simon's head came up. He peered at her. "Did I say it?"

She knew Gran was watching her now, her father too. "No," she whispered.

"She'll come through." Simon's voice was suddenly listless. "She nearly did give up, but he brought her around. She's addled some, Granny told. The boys — they lived too. A pair of little Tories to do the rest of us out of our own in twenty years' time. It's what Henry Neece says." He tried to grin. "It is sort of funny when you think about it — twins, and he not knowing a thing, and — "

"It's not funny at all, Simon." Gran began stirring mush in her cauldron, her spoon sloshing in the silence which had fallen.

"Not very, Ma'am," he admitted lamely. "No."

"You're hateful," Delilah snapped at last.

Gravely, he kept his eyes on her. "Am I? I'm right patient too. Remember it." His look was so deep she wanted to flinch. Yet she only watched him get up, go outside, and mount his cob once more, fingering briefly the blaze on its forehead before he rode away, the sound of the cob's hoof-beats echoing hard in her ears as he spurred it down the trace. When he came back a few days later it was simply to tell her that Sebastien Hatler himself had been massacreed on the Watauga River. He had gone to tend his grapevines with-out a gun, a trader had given out. The miller had had to tell his wife before she had gotten up from her pallet. He felt a mite sorry for Mrs. Bickley, did Simon. His eyes squinted at Delilah as he said that.

When the stranger came to Cassel's Woods Simon came up to fetch her to see him and she rode down gladly enough because it was a thing to do to break the routine of her chores. With Simon, too, she wouldn't have to stop to see Marie or her babies yet; she could put that off. Her father went with them, jogging along on Chick while his rifle jogged in its saddle holster beside him. When they reached the mill a giant of a man with red hair was already raising his fist in the air, bellowing at the knot of men and women gathered around him. He had come, he said, from the Holston to bring them news. The British Colonel Ferguson had sent a message to the west to submit to the King or be hanged to a man.

"What d'ye think of it?" the giant shouted. "Ferguson marches now. He'll march to the Holston and Clinch and past every overmountain man who lets him. What will ye do about it? Will ye let him too?" His burr thickened in pi-ous outrage as his voice rolled on.

"William Campbell," Delilah heard Lawyer Dickenson muttering to her father. "Calls his place Aspenvale. You'd better listen." He smiled his laconic smile. "His wife is Gov-ernor Henry's sister. He's colonel of our militia now."

Campbell's Scotch face was growing redder as he cursed out the Scotch infidel Ferguson. Submit or be hanged indeed! Ferguson didn't know the overmountain men. They would be the hammer of the Almighty. They would fight while their women cheered them on. They would march to Ferguson himself and teach him that Washington County, Virginia, submitted to no one except the Lord Jehovah, and its people were His Elected Saints . . . All around her Delilah saw the men and women of Cassel's Woods beginning to stir at the recruiter's ringing challenges, astonished that the eastern war was reaching west. Hadn't their part of the war been England's Indians, Simon asked her in a puzzled voice? But if that King was sending his very own officers to make threats, it was too much; that was what it was. Surely Simon would go with Colonel Campbell and fight; oh, he would polish his rifle Sairey and he would set his mam to running bullets, and he only hoped he would be the man to strike down Colonel Ferguson while Colonel Campbell looked on. His pap had just given him Sairey; he had traded some prime pelts for it. That was to make up for Clark, it might be. Delilah's father would go too, wouldn't he?

"You can't, Papa." She touched her father's frayed sleeve. "There's Gran."

"We've had that out, Delilah." She saw his jaw set.

Campbell went on crying at them from his stump. Campbell and liberty. Death to Ferguson. Death to the English King. Remember Dunmore! Remember the men of Oliver Cromwell a century before, who had marched against another tyrant King, another antichrist . . .

When Charles came forward to sign the muster he was alone. He, too, had forgotten he had a family . . . Slowly, carefully, he put his name to the foolscap laid out on a walnut butt, its corners flapping around the stones which weighted them down from the wind. Soon Simon and her father left her to sign. She thought of Dunmore's War, and her waiting with Gran, and the dreams she had had of smoky battlefields. She had waited so much; now she had to do it again. When several of the women began chattering around her of following their husbands and sons as far as Aspenvale she knew right away she herself would go there if she could. She wouldn't lose sight of Charles until she had to. Dimly she recognized Granny Sawyer's wheeze as she talked of following Joe to the Holston in her buckboard; there wouldn't be so many women dared to do it, and surely the miller or the lawyer would loan a handful of blacks to guard them on the way back.

"I could see Joe e'er day until the colonel turned us back. He's careless against the damp, Joe is. I'm always at him to wear a scarf at night. I'll give 'im some cheer, right enough. You goin', Delilah? Your gran, you reckon?"

I'll go. I can hear my lies already as I tell them to Papa. I lie so much these days. When, afterwards, she saw tenderness filling her father's eyes she flushed in shame. She knew she had won her own battle before starting it. Even so, she was able to smile also at Simon and was able to see his own eyes soften; he was thinking she might care for him too. Simon did love her, then . . . Even when Gran peered at her that night she could bear her shame. Charles was going. That was what counted. Gran could go to the Oschers' and help them fatten what cattle they had left. A brace of women were riding to Aspenvale; Granny Sawyer was, and Ann Neece for her father, and Mrs. Bush . . .

"Dear girl." Winfield patted Delilah's hand. "Your

mother, God rest her soul, would have wanted to come with me too. I'm proud of you."

The worst of it was, she longed all the while to be honest.

They started on a hot afternoon bright with goldenrod. The Clinch sparkled between its shores. Soon the troops began tramping east toward Moccasin Gap. Delilah rode sidesaddle on Farmer George, her skirts whipping at her ankles. Her father and Simon were on foot, as was even Charles, marching in his down-at-heel Russia boots beside pudgy Lawyer Dickenson. The sun burned in the meadows. Delilah was glad she had worn her bonnet. It was only in the pale, green-washed hollows she could take it off and shake out her hair while she watched redbirds flitting through the brush on each side of the trace, the tramp of feet startling them from their nests. The lawyer kept passing his hand across his brows and shifting his rifle from one shoulder to the other. Without his wig, his hair was dark auburn. Charles never shifted his gun. How straight he kept himself! At the head of the column, when it wound over a meadow, she could see Colonel Campbell himself in shirtsleeves on his gray charger. The amethysts on his silver sword hilt glinted in the sun. Trusty Andreferrara, he had called his sword; the women snickered. Behind him an aide in buckskins carried his claymore. Campbell meant to charge Ferguson with a claymore to show himself a Highland man, to show Ferguson the Scotch of overmountain Virginia had not forgotten how to fight the Scotch hirelings of a Hanoverian King. "Death to Ferguson!" Campbell sang out to his men and to the women behind them on nags and in hay wagons and buckboards, their babies whimpering at their breasts in the heat. And all the while, stopping beside creeks to refill their water flasks and chew at strips of jerky, the men muttered admiringly: who by now hadn't heard of William Campbell of Aspenvale? He had courted and won Elizabeth Henry of Williamsburg. He had brought her over the Blue Ridge to the west. Why, once he was coming with her from Parson Doak's meeting on a Sabbath morning, holding his babe in his saddle while she rode beside him. He saw a green-coated Tory rider, so he handed the babe to Madam Campbell, chased the Tory, caught him and strung him up on a tree. Then he took the babe back, said a prayer, and went riding peacefully home to Aspenvale . . . Campbell and liberty. Liberty or death. This was a leader, Ben Winfield said. This was a man to be trusted and put dependence in, a man to believe.

Near Seven Mile Ford the Holston ran lazily along its wide valley, a gentler valley than the steep one of the Clinch which Dan Boone, grinning, had used to call the Face of Hell. Delilah gave her horse his head a little until she was riding nearly beside Charles. He smiled up at her with astonished eyes but went on talking to Dickenson who had grown panting and red-faced. Yet how young Dickenson really looked after all without his wig, for all his broad nose and stout trunk. Perhaps he wasn't much older than Charles's twenty-seven years . . . Charles had filled out the past summer to his old figure, muscular and firm, not ganted at all: probably on her own diet of plantain and pork, mutton and sang tea. Always he marched as if he had done nothing else all his life, as if he didn't hate it one bit. Tonight she would talk to him — somehow. She would make him notice her.

She was still close to him when the great log house called Aspenvale came into view. In its dogtrot stood a big woman who must be Madam Campbell. Delilah saw Charles jerk his head as if startled. Then he left his column and started toward another. What had happened? She tried to follow him but she couldn't because a host of militia barred her. Troops were beginning to mill in from every direction. Soon they were shouting and laughing and drinking Mononga-hela in their butternuts and gamy-smelling buckskins, clutching battered muskets and long Deckhards, gathering in noisy circles to dice. She couldn't find Charles at all for the rest of the afternoon. So she stayed with her father, re-membering to press his hand while the men clustered at last in the great meadow to hear Parson Doak pray over them. Tall Madam Campbell was reading to herself the names on the muster: memorizing them, Simon said, for her own prayers.

"God bless your weapons, Campbell!" shouted the parson while his old greeny-black robe billowed in the wind. "Carry the sword of the Lord and of Gideon!" Everywhere rose the echo: "The sword of the Lord and of Gideon!" Leaves trem-bled in the rush of new wind and the loud voices. And the men laughed when Campbell barked at his wife: "I promise ye a scalp, Betsey! If they send the redsticks on us, I'll bring ye a handsome scalp."

At nightfall the campfires dotting Aspenvale meadow sent up spirals of fragrant hickory smoke into the gathering dark-ness. Delilah ate her venison beside her father and Simon. Her father's eyes were bright, his chin firm. Simon was happy too, his grin crooked and touching. *They might be killed too; I must realize that . . .* Simon shifted on his haunches. In the firelight, his freckled boy's face took on a sober look of waiting, as if he expected her to say something. He blew back his cowlick. But she did not speak. She wished she could pray for her father and Simon as well as Charles; but she couldn't pray any more at all because there was nothing to pray to.

"I'll be back soon."

"I know, Papa."

When the stars came out to flicker in the deep sky she crept from her blanket and began to walk aimlessly in the summer night, wondering where Charles was and how she could find him. The tall grass brushed wet across her skirts. A lantern was shining in the dogtrot where two men and a woman were sitting. She kept on walking. When she reached the front path she saw one man's face in the long light. It was Charles's. She drew in her breath. What was he doing here of all places? Beside him sat Campbell and his wife. Delilah bit her lip. In a second she decided, and squaring her shoulders she went straight up the steps.

"I came to say goodbye," she announced. How clear her voice was!

Charles swung around. "Delilah! Wh —"

"You went away this afternoon," she challenged, not caring who heard her now.

"Say he ran away." Madam Campbell's laugh boomed out like a man's. "My Tory cousin — I had to find him. How pleased Patrick will be."

"Your cousin?" Delilah gave her hand to Charles when she came up to him.

"This is a family talk, Delilah. I expect — discretion."

"But what is there to be discreet about?" Madam Campbell smiled, her smile as broad as her husband's. She turned to Delilah. "Surely he boasts of Patrick. I do. Patrick's wife, you know — poor Sally, she was a Shelton, his cousin too. I've been telling Charles of her last days — she took the coughing sickness. We're all cousins of one sort or another on Tidewater. How we quarreled over Patrick in those years." Her smile faded. "Too like many another family, I fear."

"Sally was sixteen," Charles said stiffly. "She was a child — too young to wed anybody."

"Certainly to wed a treason-monger, eh? I'm proud you're a treason-monger yourself now, Charles. Nonetheless I hope you'll make it up with your father some day. He meant well, selling out. You may not like to be forgiven, but he does." She adjusted her starched cap.

Why hadn't Charles told Cassel's Woods about his kinship to Patrick Henry and Madam Campbell? Because he "wanted no thanks"? The old words leapt from nowhere into Delilah's mind. "You have to tell," she stammered heedlessly, her hand on his arm. "People won't hate you any more." Then her hand flew to her mouth. Why had she said that?

"I'll stand alone, Delilah. I must do for myself. They ought to know I'm loyal."

"I mark your people all breed proud, Betsey," Campbell chuckled, puffing at his long clay pipe. "A good thing." He turned back to Charles. "This is your wife." It was a crisp statement, matter-of-fact.

Charles drew a sharp breath. The silence which followed echoed that breath from every corner of the dogtrot. His wife! *Oh, Colonel, I should be, I nearly was . . .* But she sat straight and composed. It was Charles who coughed nervously.

"But she's not one of our connection." Madam Campbell's voice was puzzled. "I don't think I remember hearing of a cousin who — "

"No." Charles forced the word. "Not at all — not my wife, I mean. Or cousin." His own voice was flat. "Delilah's my — my good angel." His laugh fell thinly on her ears. He seemed to be searching for an explanation. When it came, the flatness was still in it. "Her father's a friend of mine." After a pause he added: "She'll keep my secrets, if I promise her I'll return. I try to keep promises like that."

No one answered him. Colonel Campbell only puffed thoughtfully at his pipe.

The strangeness passed when a Campbell slave brought out tall tumblers of spring water. Madam Campbell chatted for a while of her family and her husband and her child, a girl. She teased Charles again for her having to find him. His face was flushed when he answered: "I knew you'd be here, Betsey, but all the same it was a shock to see you." Her husband asked a few sharp questions about the terrain at Cassel's Woods. Then he got up and stretched, and Charles seemed glad for the signal of dismissal.

"I'm not an angel," Delilah couldn't help snapping on the way back to the meadow camp. "Not truly."

"What are you, then?" His voice sounded as queer as before.

"I don't know," she faltered.

They were silent after that. To say goodbye he only shook her hand and whispered very low: "God bless you." Then he strode away as if glad to be free of her. His wife . . . Almost she felt she was. Had he seen that? When she had stolen back to her buffalo robe she remembered he had never once mentioned Marie or his children to the Campbells. Marie hadn't come here . . . Delilah heard her father's uninterrupted snoring. Farther away, Simon stirred but didn't wake . . . What sort of wife wouldn't follow her husband as far as she could? Delilah tried, then, to pray for Charles's safety once more, but she soon gave it up. She could think of nothing but what Colonel Campbell had said, and how Charles had seemed so shocked and at a loss for the words which usually came so smoothly and easily to him. "This is your wife."

He thought, then, she wasn't proper to be here. *I don't care! I saw him and I talked to him alone. I had that.*

During the night she dreamed her old battlefield dream. She saw a figure running up a high hill in the sunlight; then a smoke cloud shrouded him and in its midst he clutched his chest and stumbled to the ground. But it wasn't her father at all this time. It was Charles, and he was flinging out his arms on red autumn leaves that grew redder as he lay motionless at last among them.

12

T HE HARVEST of 1780 was a better one than the last had been, for the wheat yield was seven bushels to the acre. Delilah went down with her grandmother to the mill, where they waited to load their gunnybags of ground corn and wheat and oats onto the broad backs of the horses. The mill had a strange atmosphere about it; for there wasn't a man in it but the blacks. Instead, women had gathered outside to rest briefly, leaning their shovels and hoes against its chinked walls, laying out their bullet molds to dry in the sun after having cleaned them in the millpond. Simon's mother was ganted and tired-looking. Her mouse-colored hair was tied back from her thin face in a tight knot; her gown was patched and muddy. She had been grubbing at thistles all morning, she sighed; she'd a sight rather tend posies than cabbages. Inside the millhouse where the noise throbbed from overhead Delilah expected to see a slave at the tollbox. Instead she saw Marie, scooping grain carefully into a wide sack a black man was holding open for her.

"You are surprised?" Marie raised her head. She was as pretty as ever, and her face had lost its pinched look. Her small body was slim once more, as it had been on her wedding day. "Maum Silvey tends my babies. Someone must see the mill is not cheated." The wheel thudded to a halt.

Charles had not asked her to do this, no, she explained as

she continued to scoop. But one disliked trusting the tithe to slaves; so one counted oneself, and one would present the tallies to Charles when he came back. Marie's mouth drew in this time as she spoke of Charles.

"You didn't come to Aspenvale." Delilah moved toward her.

"Aspenvale!" The bitterness of Marie's echo startled her. "No, I would not go after this mad Scotchman who takes my husband! He has a wife and two sons, has Charles. He has a duty to them. My father arranged matters at Vincennes. Charles could do it here. It is folly to think woodsmen can fight English troops when they are not surprised, when they attack. Charles left me and I do not forgive that. He understands it. Honor is to care for one's own, yes? Or perhaps *you* would not believe so." Angrily, Marie delved up another ladleful of buckwheat groats.

"*I* believe it," Gran answered dryly, coming forward herself. "I've always believed it." Then she smiled. "You taught yourself to use a tollbox, eh? You don't like looking after yourself but you can do it. I'm glad of that, Mrs. Bickley."

"You may call me Marie." A shower of grains fell into the bag. "Perhaps you would like to see my babies. They are John and William — after Charles's father and his uncle the baronet. They are very handsome. Willy is English because he never cries but only grows so red in the face. Johnny must be French; he cries much, but already he can smile." Marie laughed a brittle laugh.

"The raid — " Delilah began.

Marie's mouth shut tight. Then: "I cannot talk of it. Please. I had not known — "

Gently, Gran laid her hand on Marie's arm. "I understand. I bore my girl in a raid many years ago. Delilah's mother. It's the most humiliating thing can happen to a woman — to make her man tend her when he wants to fight, and she wants to fight by his side."

"That is where we differ, Madame. I never want to fight." Marie's red-brown curls tossed in a gesture of impatience. Then she went to the morocco ledger and noted the Winfields' toll for the day, her quill scratching purposefully in her small hand. From the carpenter's shed came the chink, chink! of an iron hammer on a wheelrim.

"Have you tried walink tea for your baby's crying?" Gran asked. "I know the simples of the mountains. Perhaps I could help you. Sang is overstrong, and whiteroot's useless." And while Gran went on offering friendly advice to Marie, Delilah began to smile mirthlessly. This was the greatest irony of all: for Gran to begin to nurse those children that should have been her own grandsons.

As September wore on, the hobblebushes fruited, and also the shrubs Gran called strawberry bushes but Simon Oscher's mother called "hearts a-bustin' with love," their crimson seeds dangling from long pink husks. Katydids scraped at night. Ninety days from first katydid to first hard frost, the black men murmured at the mill while Delilah waited for her father's wheat. Would this winter be like the last? Would the men return to see it? Where were they marching with William Campbell, who shouted and cursed and prayed and drank fiery corn liquor as he rode to battle with the cheers of his wife and his parson ringing in his ears? Sometimes, at day's end, Gran rode down the mountain to meet Delilah at the mill and they went to see Marie and the two babies who thrashed red-faced from the heat as they lay in the walnut cradle Charles had hewed out for them with

his own hands. He had once hewed out a fox cage too . . .
Delilah had to sit again in that cabin while Gran coaxed
herb teas down those little throats, while Marie spoke of
home-things like sweeping floors and baking cornbread and
curing venison and mending hose, and how in Alsace long
ago she had fattened geese by stuffing bread into their gul-
lets so they would grow big livers to make the *pâté*. Yes, she
would show Madame Mackinnon how to do that one day.
It was most delicious, *pâté* of goose liver. Marie spoke too of
the plantation, Bickley Mills. If only the stupid war would
end, and she and her Charles could build it. Charles had
told her the story of his family: how the first important Bickley had been a linendraper a century and a half before, how
he had grown rich and bought a manor in English Norfolk,
Attleborough Hall. True, years later the manor had been
lost. Charles had spoken of a small gold-framed latin motto
his father had inherited. It was said the draper's grandson,
Sir Francis Bickley, had written it for his wife Annie. "What
shame or limit should there be to love?" One had, however,
to be sensible. It was as easy to love sensibly, to choose
where one's love should rest. Charles's own grandfather, the
builder of Green Springs, had sensibly taken a rich wife in
Virginia — a Shelton of Rural Plains. He had known how
to rebuild the lost family fortune. And Marie would see to
it that she and Charles raised many strong sons out here, so
that the Bickleys could make this corner of the world their
own forever . . . While she talked, her slippered foot
rocked the cradle where her sons slept after Gran had fed
them her brewings.

Marie's was a beauty at once frail and hard. Delilah could
imagine her, at night, using it as a spur to Charles, drawing
him to herself and giving him his body's ease only to whis-

per unquiet urgings in his ears afterwards. She wondered if Charles would want his wife to be dreaming his own sort of dreams. It was hard to believe Marie could love his land as much as he did. Why didn't he ever tell *me* about his family in England, Delilah wondered resentfully . . . "What shame or limit should there be to love?" . . . She continued to shock corn on Sugar Hill and watch the calf nuzzle the brindle cow, and she finished her Sugar Fancy quilt and then laid it away without looking at the quilt underneath. Gran taught her how to load and shoot a rifle, how to snap the firepan and wad cartridges and draw a bead on her target. But the Indians, perhaps, were fighting in Tory regiments beside Colonel Ferguson's men down the mountains in Carolina — fighting against Colonel Campbell and Ben Winfield and Simon Oscher and Charles Bickley.

Surely Gran was dreaming of Ben Winfield while Delilah dreamed of Charles. "Lord," Gran prayed, "remember David in all his trouble . . ." But Delilah knew there wasn't any Lord to remember a thing. It depended how straight you shot and how good your enemy's eyes were.

It was Gran who spied the long line of men coming back to Cassel's Woods from the south. So many of them, praise God! Her old fingers were trembling as she bolted the cabin door, and in heedless eagerness she let the river wash over her moccasins and skirts as she rode through it. "He's there!" she shouted back triumphantly at Delilah. Moments later she was trying to gather her son-in-law's bulk into her thin arms, and he was smiling down at her. When Delilah had kissed him too he began blurting out his tale of King's Mountain, the hill in Carolina where four hundred and fifty Tories and only thirty Americans had been killed. The Almighty had triumphed once more. Ferguson had lost his white charger and his silver whistle, his silk sash and his papers — and his life. The men he called rebels had yelled at him and had stamped up that hill to victory, shooting yellow-and-scarlet-coated Royal Carolina traitors as they went. "I picked off one myself. Saw him fall." Campbell had charged with his claymore, and the Huguenot colonel from the Nolichucky River Settlements, Jack Sevier, who wore a plume in his hat, had charged beside him. 'Chucky Jack even swore when he'd finished with Ferguson he'd ride down to Chota and burn out Benge. After the battle every man had prayed on his knees in the field below the mountain: Simon, a fine soldier, and his father and Lawyer Dickenson too, and Joe Sawyer, and Henry Neece, and Jimmy Bush . . .

> "Come all you good people, I pray you draw near;
> A tragicall story you quickly shall hear
> Of rebels and Tories, who bred a great strife
> And chasèd old Ferguson out of his life."

In the mounting confusion of women crying with happiness in their men's arms, of squealing children and shouting fathers, someone was screaming out a marching song. It was then that Delilah saw Marie, whose face was as white as bleached flour. She was standing to one side: alone.

> "The drums they did beat, and the guns they did rattle.
> Our enemy stood us a very smart battle.
> Like lightning the flashes, like thunder the noise,
> Oh this was the charge of our bold mountain boys!"

Delilah shut her eyes. Make the man stop, she begged God unaware she begged. Where is he? Where's Charles? Why is Marie just standing there?

She opened her eyes as her lips formed his name. And she saw her father put a finger to his mouth, nodding in Marie's direction.

> *"Brave Colonel Williams, and twenty nine more*
> *Of all our fine heroes lay rolled in their gore;*
> *With sorrow their bodies we laid in the clay,*
> *In hope that to heaven their souls took their way . . ."*

The sudden roaring in Delilah's ears drowned out the raucous voice of the balladeer. The world blackened, except for the myriad of tiny silver stars dancing crazily in the void, merging and bobbing and tossing while her brain rang. And through it, she heard her father's words that she could not, at first, take in.

"He's alive. Barely. We got him on a litter. Dickenson's with him now, in the fort yard. We didn't want his wife to see so soon — "

"You dolt!" Gran drew back. "He must be gotten out of this. Delilah, bring Marie. A chest wound? Great glory, we'll put him on his pallet and keep him there." Delilah heard her own voice saying woodenly, "Come with me, Marie. It's Charles — but he's alive. Don't worry." She felt herself making her feet turn toward the fort, where she saw Dickenson and Simon and her father and Gran bent over a deerhide litter where a man's large body lay very still under a cover stiff with brown bloodstains.

It was Marie who screamed. She began screaming and never stopped until Delilah clapped a hand over her mouth.

Then Delilah knelt too. She wasn't shaking at all now. She could see clearly every line on Charles's face, his growth of beard on cheeks drained of color and seamed with pain. He'd fainted . . . Without thinking she drew down the cover; and she saw the swollen red flesh of his festering wound, the dried blood at its edges and the torn shirt with its powder burns. She smelled the violent odor of decay and disease and knew it for death. Her hand went quickly to his forehead. His suntanned skin was burning with fever. When he did open his eyes he stared blankly up at her, as if veils were covering them. Then she heard behind her a convulsive sound that froze her hand on the cover even as she turned. The sound was coming from his wife. And she was not sobbing. Instead, she was covering her mouth while her shoulders jerked uncontrollably. Shamelessly, in front of everyone, even Charles, she was trying to keep from retching, as if she had seen a thing so repellent to her she could not endure it. Her own husband was dying before her eyes and all she could feel for him was disgust.

"He'll *see* you!" Delilah hissed at her. "Stop it!"

He had seen, perhaps; for he had turned his head in his wife's direction and his glazed eyes stared up at her. But Marie, racked and heedless, paid no attention. Then, without even drawing near him or laying a hand on his head, she started stumbling toward the fort gate, her hair sagging at her neck, her hands still over her mouth. Charles's head did not move. His eyes only fixed themselves on the gate as she lurched through it and out of sight, and they stayed fixed on its emptiness afterwards. At last he closed them.

"Get him to his cabin," Gran rapped, the shock plain in her voice. But she straightened up and took charge. "Gently, Simon. Ben, hold up the other end. Delilah, you're to ride home and get me my bunches of sang and leopard's-bane — and the pokeroot and jimson too, anything you find. I want my mortar and pestle — "

"I think he's beyond us, Mrs. Mackinnon." Lawyer Dickenson shook his head sadly. "Poor devil."

"He's beyond nothing!" Delilah heard her grandmother bark. "Not even that idiot of a wife. Go, child, for the love of God. We've got work to do."

Delilah found her fingers moving with curious ease, her eyes seeing with curious clarity, as she helped her grandmother tie Charles's hands and feet to his bed with whangleather thongs. She was without any feeling at all. She only listened to be sure she was doing correctly what she was told to do. "The cloth," she heard. "Get it in his mouth, that's the way. Maum Silvey" — to the slave — "I'll want those pincers for the bullet. Then you'll hand me the poker; be sure it's as hot as you can get it. You'll hold him down too, Ben. Keep the flask ready, Delilah. If he comes round you'll put it to his lips, but be sure you get the cloth out first — "

Somewhere beyond the closed door a woman was sobbing: at last.

It was only surprise Delilah felt that a dying man could be so strong when she had to push him down as Gran probed for the bullet. With all her own strength she heaved her weight on his shoulders while her father held his legs fast. He was trying to cry out, but he couldn't. Ruthlessly, she pinned him to his shuck tick, and she tried to keep his head from jerking on the pillow.

"Missed the lung," Gran muttered. "Here in the tendon."

The poker sizzled in the flames that leapt up in the fireplace. Delilah turned away. When the sound of flesh burning came she threw her weight on him again; but after one great effort to rise he fell back. His teeth stopped their grinding, and she knew he had fainted once more. The smell of his rotten wound and its burning rose everywhere around her; but she breathed it in, the smoke and the smell alike, hardly aware. When the first cauterizing was over she began laying a soaked cloth across his forehead. His skin was as taut as parchment. Again the poker sizzled at his chest, again she threw her palms hard on his shoulders when his body started to arch upward. The poker couldn't be as hot as his flesh . . . His bearded cheeks seemed to be hollowing and sinking momentarily into death; but still he breathed, in choking rales that filled the room.

"A dressing, Ben. Quick."

Deftly, silently, Gran worked to bind his wound while old Silvey watched wide-eyed. Delilah's father moved back. There was no sound but the convulsed irregular breathing of the man in the bed. The distant sobbing had stopped. When Gran finished she covered him; she did not remove the thongs that kept him immobile. Then she too stood back.

"Go home, Ben."

"I'm staying here, Gran," Delilah whispered.

"Yes. Of course."

It was dark when Marie came into the room, her step soft on its puncheons. Her hair was tangled on her shoulders; but she had changed her dress. Her husband's breath had slowed and quieted. Woodenly, with a fearful glance at Gran from her blue-ringed eyes, she moved to the bed and stood over him. "He — sleeps?" It was a stupid question; even she looked as if she knew he must either sleep or be dead.

"He's unconscious." Gran's voice was clipped. "You can

help by keeping the children quiet. I'll watch him, Delilah too. Go. You can do nothing here."

"I know," Marie whispered. Then, as softly as she had come, she stole away, her eyes more immense and frightened than ever in her colorless face.

For two days he lay that way. Gran and Silvey and Delilah took turns keeping awake, changing bandages, sleeping on a makeshift tick in the corner. By day the pale November sun streamed in. By night a single taper flickered in the icy draft. Shadows of furniture danced on the rough walls: bedposts, chairs, tables. Delilah heaped two fresh quilts on him the second night. Sometimes Marie crept in to stare for a few minutes, as if apologizing for her intrusion. Mostly she stayed with her babies. It was Delilah who first knew his forehead had cooled. Gran was eating in the next room, and Silvey had gone to help Marie with the children. She bent over him to kiss him. He would not know. Then she heard herself whispering to him the words he would not hear. "I love you so. I'm here." She kept her hand on his, feeling its pulse begin to come stronger.

She was kneeling over him alone, her lips on his forehead, the morning he opened his eyes. She checked a gasp as she drew back. He was staring up at her. His lips tried to move. Then, ever so slightly, he smiled, and nodded his head on the pillow.

She untied his hands. Now he could understand he mustn't touch the bandage; he'd want his hands to be free. "You're going to be well," she told him softly, brushing back a limp strand of her hair. "You mustn't move, or loose your dressing. I'll give you broth tonight. I love you."

"Yes," he whispered, so faintly she could hardly hear him, "I know."

"Gran did it — saved you for me." She knelt beside him. "Your fever's down."

"Don't go," he whispered.

"I'll never go unless you send me." Again she kissed his forehead. He made no move to turn. Instead, his moist hands tightened a little in hers, and when she drew away he was smiling still. "They're strong yet — your hands." She knew she was smiling back. "I'm grown for you now. I love you."

His smile died. "I too," he answered her. When their eyes met, his were clear; and as they fixed on hers she knew he understood the sort of love she meant. The moment was theirs. He had forgotten his wife and family, he had forgotten his lands; he had perhaps forgotten even King's Mountain. Soon he would remember. But in this instant he belonged to her alone. And he was accepting at last the way in which she belonged to him.

13

THE MOMENT was not long. Rashly she had promised not to go; but she knew that, physically, she would have to go almost immediately. He knew it too when Gran bustled in. As he framed his first words of gratitude to Gran, his mouth slackened, and though he was trying to talk to her he kept his eyes on Delilah.

"If it weren't for — "

"Hush." Gran laid her hand on his. "I want you to listen to me. I only did what I know how to do. Your wife was upset when you went to fight. 'Twas only natural. She thought of your danger, and her babies. Can you hear me?" He didn't move. "You *must* hear me." Gran's voice grew urgent. "I don't know what happened to her in that raid when she bore 'em, but I do realize she can't stand such. That's what it is. You must realize too. You must forget what she did when you came back. We'll leave now, Delilah and I. We'll not talk of this again. I'll look in on you, never fear."

Delilah felt her eyes filling. What a traitor Gran was! She was actually trying to heal the breach between him and Marie! Even when she felt nothing but contempt herself for Marie, who had let a dying man see no love but only her selfish revulsion.

"I have to stay, Gran," Delilah tried to steady her voice. "The broth you made — "

"You have to go to your father. We must let Charles sleep. Marie can give him his first broth."

"Delilah — " She could hardly catch his call. But she bent down, ignoring Gran. "I — " he began; but a grimace of pain passed across his face, and he closed his eyes.

She said nothing to her grandmother as they rode to Sugar Hill, Gran clutching her bag of herbs tightly with clawlike fingers. Gran said nothing either. On the mountaintop, Delilah's father was splitting logs for firewood, his axe echoing in the grove. Briskly Gran told him that Bickley was tough, that he'd mend. Then she went into the cabin, motioning Delilah to follow her. The ring of the axe went on. She scraped flints at the hearth, put a taper to the tinder piled under a walnut log, and then sank wearily into a chair as the flames shot up in sputtering tongues.

"Sit by me, missy. I have something to say to you."

Delilah bit her lip; but she moved to the fire. Reynard scampered down from the loft, and she took him in her lap, pressing him to her while he yipped happily and bobbed his head. She shook back her hair. Then she looked down curiously at her gown; how worn and stained it was!

"I don't forget right and wrong. Don't you. All my life I've tried to live by my notions of 'em."

Delilah felt her mouth curl into a hard smile. "Are you afraid I'll burn, Gran?" Her voice rang out like iron. "Do you think God will send me to hell? I've been in hell on Sugar Hill."

"Delilah!" Gran's cry was low as she bent forward.

"He loves me now. He said it. That's all I care for."

"But" — Gran tried to rise from her chair; her thin arms

collapsed, and she fell back — "you're mad. You'll be punished."

"I knew he'd come back wounded. Gran, I'm in his life. He wants my love and I mean for him to have it. I've been punished already." She started when Reynard jumped from her lap. A stick fell from the grate onto the hearth, flamed up briefly and died. "I don't know what will happen. I can't think of the future. I don't care. And nothing you can say or do will change me."

"Your father will!"

"You'll tell him?" Delilah stiffened so that her shiver would not be seen. "Do it if you like — he'll curse you, and curse me and Charles. He's not like he used to be — I know that. But he won't leave here, and he can't watch me twenty-four hours a day. He'll just make us miserable with his rantings. And they'll only put my back up."

Unexpectedly Gran's mouth formed itself into a smile. For a long time she said nothing. Then she raised her chin. "You'd better be afraid of Charles, then, if not your father. Charles isn't like you. He has earthly gods in which he believes. He also has" — she held up her long fingers, their nails stained brown with tannin — "two children and a wife. Had you forgotten?"

No, Delilah thought dully in those first days back on Sugar Hill; I haven't forgotten . . . She longed to ride swiftly down to him again. But for a week Gran did not go near Cassel's Woods. "Visitors will tire him, Ben," she would say. "Delilah, mind you card all that wool today. Be sure you get the seeds out with the burrs. I'll not let you ride in the woods — or elsewhere. If Marie needs me she'll send. And she hasn't." A heavy mist closed down over the moun-

tain and the valley and never lifted, from morning until
night. It was not until the first afternoon of sun, when the
soggy ground had started to dry out and the trees glimmered
silvery bare, that Gran prepared to take down to Cassel's
Woods a piggen of arnica tincture she had brewed from her
leopard's-bane.

"I'll come too." Delilah smiled forcedly at Gran and at
her father.

"Very well." Gran compressed her lips. "We'll see him
together, then. You can go tomorrow, Ben."

At the cabin, its logs touched with powdery light filtering
through the shade of the cedars around it, Silvey opened the
door. When she muttered "Miss" was at the mill Gran made
a little sound of amazement. Silvey motioned with a stubby
hand to the open door of the room where Charles lay, and
Delilah followed her grandmother inside.

He had been shaved — or had shaved himself — and he
was half sitting against several pillows. His cheeks were
sunken below his eyes, which were heavily circled. The
blue color of his irises was so dull it was nearly gray: as gray
as his forelock. His neck was unnaturally long because the
cords of it were stiff and the fading skin slack in the pit of
his throat between them. His hands, thin and veined, were
folded on his quilt. When he smiled, it was not a happy
smile. It was wistful, tender, touched with wisdom and sadness. "I'm a good patient — only because I have to be, Mrs.
Mackinnon." His voice was calm, lifeless for him, very low
and gentle. He eased himself gingerly back. "I wish it were
spring. I'd like to look out the window, if I could sit up that
far." Delilah doubled her fists as Gran uncovered his
wound; she saw him sink his teeth into his lower lip. But
Gran approved of what she saw.

"Marie's done well."

He nodded. "The mill will be a change for her. She likes the work there."

How long Gran sat in her chair Delilah did not know. Gran talked endlessly of trifles: how few eggs the Dominecker hens were laying, why she needed a new flax swingle, how she meant to bring down the bull-tongue plow to the mill for straightening. Charles listened and nodded. But he was watching Delilah, who found the room beginning to blur before her. Yet she had to sit like a stick until finally Silvey shuffled in to ask Gran to come to look at baby John, who was sniffling. Gran shot a quick suspicious glance at Charles; but he too seemed surprised. Gran's eyes bored into Delilah before she left. I trust you, she seemed to be saying; think of him, not yourself.

When she had gone Delilah took her chair. Mutely, she clasped Charles's hand. He pressed hers. Then he began to talk. "What I did to you — I didn't know."

"Hush. Don't worry." She ran her fingers along a callus on his left palm, then up to the crook of his arm. "I'm happy now."

"But I've seen you sad. I made you sad on the mountain." His dark brows came together as he drew a long breath and fell silent. He sighed at last. "It was all I could do to send you back that night. I felt I'd nearly betrayed a child — that I was so starved and bitter I'd wronged a girl scarce out of her cradle who didn't know what she was doing. I hated myself. I couldn't bear the thought of harming you — I could stand even your crying, to save you worse. Your father'd sheltered me and I'd repaid him pretty badly." He gave a short laugh. "So I hurt you more. What a rum job I made of it."

"You're tired. You'll hurt yourself. Hush."

"Did *you* hate me that night?"

"My body did. Never my heart."

"At Vincennes — it was so cold, Delilah. I never told you, did I? I was so damn tired after slogging through that mud. I remembered you, kept seeing your face and the way your mouth always looks just about to smile."

"And then Marie came." Softly.

"Yes." He paused. "We were alone very much — hated the fort and got out every chance we could, we — " He broke off. A titmouse whistled in a cedar beyond the window. A branch cracked in the wind. "I'd like to be outside." He closed his eyes. "In my fields, wind or no."

"You will be."

He put his hand on hers once more. "Campbell scared me when he called you my wife. It seemed right. You were there for me and she wasn't. She wouldn't come. I'd asked her to but she wouldn't."

"I was brave at your wedding."

He gripped her hand so tightly that he hurt her. But she let him. The very life in his hand gave her joy.

"The raid — I wanted to help her. She couldn't understand I wanted it. But" — his voice dropped — "I made her sick when my time came." He raised his head. Delilah smoothed her hair. "There's no way for us. I'll have to see you sometimes, though."

Then you can't think of the future either; were you explaining all that to me or yourself? . . . She said quietly: "There's a place on the shore, on our side. It's a hollow where I go. There are some willows there, near a rock. When you're well you can come."

"And you'll want that?"

"Yes."

Silence.

"I'm a scarecrow. I saw myself this morning. She brought a mirror."

"I love you any way you are."

"You've turned beautiful. Did you know it? Your eyes have a way of shining like candles."

She could smile. "You're lying."

"You're strong. Give me some strength, Delilah."

"I'd give you my life."

"You gave it to me — for what it's worth."

The sound of the millwheel came down on a fresh gust of wind, and the mixed smell of pines, teaberries, and rotting logs.

"Bickley Mills," he murmured. "Listen to it." Then he fell asleep.

You've turned beautiful. She did know it for the lie it was; but it was a lie of his love, and even while she knew its sham the memory of it warmed her. What did he see? Her straight black hair, thicker and coarser than ever. Blue eyes Gran said were very large; heavy brows; smooth skin — but bruised hands nothing would ever heal. A tall body, wide-waisted and broad-shouldered. The word her father had once used for it was "Junoesque." She had hated the word then. I don't want to be Juno! she had longed to cry. I'm no goddess married to an old fool god who doesn't love me! I want to be tiny and frail, and sniff little tow handkerchiefs I make myself and have fainting spells and wear ruffles on my gowns and have a handspan waist and dance a reel where a score of handsome young men try to partner me and afterwards open doors for me because I'm so helpless . . . She could smile at that too now. She could laugh at a tale

Ann Neece had once told her. Ann had set her cap for Tim Fraley. Big, red-faced Ann had tried to flatter Tim. Watching him split rails, she'd squinched herself down, looked up at him, and sighed, "You're so powerful, Timothy." He'd grinned back politely, "You're right powerful yourself, Ann." Then he'd gone on heaving his axe into a walnut log and invited her by his gesture to join him until she'd simpered, "Oh, I couldn't!" Well, power was not always so bad a thing after all.

Delilah knew she must wait until Charles had gotten better before she disturbed him again. And so, to explain future trips to Cassel's Woods, she began going down to the mill when her father had hides to send. She waited for his grain barter without seeing Charles at all. Several times Marie was there. Courteously, Marie nodded to her from the high stool where she was perched and kept scratching at her ledger, the feather of her goosequill bobbing in quick rhythm in time with the gears. Once Simon was there too.

"You did remember *I* came back?" His smile was skewed as he pushed up his fur cap.

"Of course I did! It's just we've been so busy — "

"You aren't going to see him today?"

"Oh no." Casually. "He's mending, they say."

"Nasty gouge." He drew her into a corner where Marie could not hear them and a beam muffled the noise of the burrs. "Listen, Delilah. If you do see him maybe you ought to tell him a thing. *She's* going to cause a heap of trouble. She's not a bit proud of him, and she spreads all kinds of talk she doesn't care who wins the war if it only stops. Henry Neece thinks she's a Tory and so does Joe Sawyer. If it has raids or the like there could be a right smart of trouble. She's been bragging on Sir Will'am Bickley too, his title. If folks figure Tory connections, and what she says, they'll watch e'er thing he does trying to trap him someways, or — "

"But it isn't true!" Delilah broke in. "Simon, if they only knew. I could stop the talk in a minute if — " *If he'd let me. But I promised to keep silent* . . . She swallowed; then she stared at Simon. Could she trust him? In a moment, she decided she had to trust him, because if any trouble came she might be on Sugar Hill. "Would you swear to keep a secret?"

"For you? I suppose." He wiped his hands on his hips.

She whispered: "He's Patrick Henry's cousin, cousin to Madam Campbell too. Colonel Campbell himself trusts him. She told me, Madam Campbell did — at Aspenvale. Would you tell that if people got — restless? But only then?"

Simon whistled. For a minute he seemed unable to take it in. Then his eyes went to his feet, to his worn jackboots. She was startled, later, to hear him laugh deeply with a man's bitterness. "So he's loyal for a reason. Now we know how he gets land grants when Patrick Henry's in office."

"No!"

"How do *you* know?" Simon countered scornfully.

"You'll *not* tell. Not unless — "

He shrugged. "Not unless I thought you'd want me to. No." Outside, he quickly changed the subject. He was going to start his second cornfield this spring. Some one of these days — he gave her a sidelong glance — he was going to start his cabin too. He was still hunting wolves for pelt bounty, and he had enough money to buy a heap of tools — froes and adzes and scythes and a wheat cradle — if there was any way to get such from the Settlements. He was alive and kicking, was Simon.

"You ought to wed." She tried to chaff him. "You ought to take Ann Neece's mind from Timothy Fraley." Simon did need a house of his own. He had a pent look about him.

"Surely," he said levelly. "Ann Neece." Then his jaw came up. "But there's another I'll take when the time comes."

She didn't dare to think about that.

One day she rode down to the mill with a deerskin her father wanted her to trade for extra buckwheat. Marie was counting bags in the grain storage room: again. She had begun, Delilah noticed, to tie back her hair, but it fell soft and still shining into a knot at the base of her neck. Her skin was as white as ever. She had her Negroes, so even her hands were not red. The change in her was hard to pinpoint. It might be the squint between her eyes, or the tiny lines starting at the lower corners of her mouth, or the very slight rounding of her shoulders — from bending over ledgers? Oh, yes, Marie smiled stiffly, Charles improved every day. He had begun walking about the cabin. He played often with the little ones. We will agree not to remember anything, you and I, she was really telling Delilah. I am grateful; leave it at that. And yet, quite abruptly, she began to tease: "How is your tame fox, Delilah? Charles gave it to you, I hear." Lightly, she laughed, showing a set of white teeth as she threw back her head a little. "Is it not dangerous to be able to tame foxes? In Alsace we think only witches can do it. You are brave, to have such a familiar."

News came that 'Chucky Jack Sevier had at last gone to burn Benge's town as he had promised. He had led a whole battalion of mounted soldiers across the Tenase into Chota and they had razed the place, torture stake, wigwams, and all. Benge was furious. He had screamed that holy things had been defiled. Now he was swearing revenge, and Hargis with him. Maybe miller Bickley ought to think twice before he built the new sawmill over on Big Spring Branch, and the barn where he planned to store sang and pelts. It wasn't a healthy idea, sending tykes into the forest to get sang when Benge was madder than usual. Surely it wasn't, people murmured. A blessing General Russell was back at Cassel's Woods. He'd doubtless herd folks into the fort fast enough if need be, and command 'em to stop digging.

Charles must be well by now. I can't stand this waiting much longer.

Delilah didn't know why she went down to the hollow that first warm afternoon. She had had no message. The water of the Clinch was still far too cold for even a thought of wading. But she sat on a fallen willow log and watched Farmer George chew low-hanging brush at the shore where the cane had used to grow. She breathed in the smell of new-flowering serviceberries and she sighed, wanting to share all of it.

"I knew you'd be here."

She gave a cry as she turned to see Charles standing over her. She hadn't heard a thing. Then she covered her mouth. Oh, how pale he still looked, how dull his eyes were! But he was here, he had known and sensed and felt. He had!

"I'm still a clever woodsman. I saw you."

He had not touched her yet. But she could feel the very power of him drawing her. Slowly, in a giddy dream, she got up. Then she was in his arms, pressing herself to his chest. She heard him catch his breath — in pain? — but he gripped her closer with one arm while he raised the other and then began running his fingers down through her heavy hair. He put his mouth on hers, holding her so tight she could scarcely breathe.

Then she was crying. How stupid, always to cry! She was trembling, too. His hands went to her shoulders to steady her, and there was a question in his eyes.

" — so glad," she stammered foolishly, "wanted you — waited — "

"Ah." Softly. He drew her back to him again. "I'll let you cry about that." When she looked up, he was smiling. Incredibly, his face had gone red. "I've been waiting too. Watching every day, I've wanted to see you so long." Shakily, he laughed. "Why didn't you come here before? Didn't you believe I really meant to?"

It was strange afterwards to remember what they had talked about. Such silly things, each one touched and transformed simply by their closeness. The way he'd botched his books on his first day back at the mill. What Reynard had done last night: gotten up on his hind legs and stolen a corn-dodger from Gran's skillet. What a sorry nag Chick was. Delilah ought to have an Arab horse. He'd get her one some day. Why beavers built dams, and how they knew enough. How the Clinch River was named for Billy Clinch who'd fallen into it and drowned after a Long Hunt and too much Monongahela. What she'd have if she could have anything in the world: a great green brocaded ball gown. Yes, she would, right here on her mountain; she wouldn't have to wear it to any palace, she'd just like him to see her in it, and she'd sit happily in her cabin wearing it while she spun flax or the like . . . It was easy to forget the real world. A strange, deep peace came to her as she sat with him. Why, if this was all he wanted to give her, if he wouldn't take her in

his arms again, still it was enough. They were making a
world of their own and nobody else could come into it. She
could look at him all she liked, at the gray streaks in his hair
and his proud thin body and hard hands. She wasn't afraid
of hurting him. She could tease, and he wanted her to, and
he could tease back, and tell her irrelevant escapades he'd
been in as a boy — smearing blueberry conserves all over a
chambermaid's pinafore when it lay on the board ready for
the sadiron, tying his tutor's bedsheets together —

"What did he *say*, Charles!"

"Well, my brother helped with it, you know. Oh, he
roared a good bit and gave us piles of latin verses — poor old
boy, I must have shortened his life. The worst we ever did
was dumping a gallon of ginevre into Uncle William's fruit
punch when nobody was looking. Lord, Uncle said it was
quite the most delicious punch he'd ever served and
we watched him fairly stagger away from the bowl and the
parson was staggering with him — "

All the while the specks of sunlight in the river flashed
like jewels, and the bright sky shimmered over the edge of
Sandy Ridge. She heard the buzzing of warblers and the
quick jumps of squirrels. But when Charles started talking
again she forgot every sound for the sound of his voice:
warm, intimate, humorous. He was giving her his childhood
too. Then she danced with him in mirrored ballrooms, and
he bowed her into dining rooms where chandeliers flickered
over long tables laden with jellied meats. "Some day," he
told her, lost in the dream too, forgetting the bitterness of
losing Green Springs. She'd see it all. It was the world of
his family, the Connection, who planted their smooth
acres and also made pilgrimages to each other's houses and
the capital where they danced and watched players twice a
year . . .

"We had a little schoolroom," she told him. "It was on South England Street. It wasn't much, I reckon. I can remember my mother spinning, though, and Papa reading out loud to us from Homer every night — that was before he took to reading the scriptures so much. Sometimes you might have been right outside, and we didn't know. And when we came west you didn't talk to anybody."

"God, I wasn't fit to talk then." He was smiling again. The sun had started to sink before either of them knew it, its last rays making a thousand shapes of light all around them and then fading to an afterglow in which she became freshly aware of the tang of the serviceberries. New noises of the forest echoed in her ears: the trill of a thrush, a coon's wary footfall, soughing pines.

"Come back," she pleaded when he held her. Once more she smelled the mixture of tobacco and resin in his clothes. He kissed her eyes, her cheeks.

"Yes. I must, you know." Then he let her go.

Benge raided Cassel's Woods twice in quick succession. Once the very men in their fields had to throw down their hoes, Charles among them. He'd run to the fort from the field near his sawmill. He'd shot like the devil, but in the fort itself do you suppose he could shoot? No, Johnny had of course begun screaming at the fire arrows and Marie couldn't manage him or Willy either because she was hysterical, and when the blessed thunderstorm came Johnny perversely screamed more than ever; and somebody had to quiet him, didn't they, and tell him he was safe where he was, poor poppet? (They were only other people; not his wife and children. Not for Delilah Winfield, sitting with him in the hollow.) Thank God Benge seemed to have a fear about raiding Sugar Hill where he might be picked off

climbing the trace. But Charles had been crazy with worry
all the same, half his mind on stilling Johnny and the other
half on her . . . The second time Benge came Charles had
been in his house — couldn't get to the fort at all. He'd shot
through the loopholes and downed an Indian skulking under a crabtree in the yard. The door had bulged from the
pressure of red bodies outside it, and he'd shouted "Hold,
boys!" to nobody but cowering Silvey and Marie and the
children, scared worse by their mother's babbling than by
the Indians . . . Christ, he'd breathed easier when that
door had stopped bulging. But they'd gone on to a family in
Abb's Valley, Benge's men had; they'd broken into a cabin
and hacked everyone to death with tomahawks. Afterwards,
thieves had appeared from nowhere to loot it. Charles had
had to give some land for Cassel's Woods' own graves.
They'd had one funeral already, for a scalped man with a
limp. Russell read from the English Book of Common
Prayer; it was very stately. A fellow had a right to decent
obsequies.

And so she found that their private world could also be
the world of other people. But as she and he confided trouble and fear, the trouble and the fear changed. They were
eased because they were known together. She went to one
funeral herself. Her father and grandmother went with her.
She was afraid General Russell might begin barking at them
for not coming to the fort. But he wasn't its captain now, he
said somberly, he couldn't force them. Jimmy Bush didn't
seem to mind. Gravely, Russell bowed to the Winfields.
Then he prayed a dignified prayer over the shrouded body of
a child who had lingered in the woods and been massacreed
by a lone Cherokee.

Please, God, not a child digging sang. But Delilah never

asked Charles that. She kept her eyes away from him and his wife as much as she could.

It was just as Russell — his beard had gone quite gray — was intoning the last words that she heard hoofbeats. "Glory be to the Father, and to the Son . . ." Startled by the intrusive sound, she turned to see a lone rider in a uniform of blue and buff. Surely that was the Continental Army uniform Charles had described to her. Charles went to the man and took something from him. When Russell finished and the rider galloped on, Charles opened a paper. Then, savagely, he crumpled it and threw it down, looking back to the gaping bury-hole.

Afterwards, when he had left with his stiff-faced wife, Delilah picked up the paper. It was so muddied all she could read was the single word "Peace." Perhaps it had to do with the war in the east. Here, Henry Neece and Joe Sawyer were beginning to shovel clods of red earth over the tiny wooden coffin, and men and women were beginning to speak of the approaching year as another Year of Sorrows.

14

D ELILAH and Charles could not meet until the trees had leafed out in their hollow and they would be hidden. When April came they both rushed to the hollow so quickly that they laughed at each other, she in relief that he had come after all, he in amusement at his own relief. They were able to snatch a few hours together every week that followed in spite of plowing and planting. Sometimes they poured out in jumbled sentences everything that had happened to them in the intervals alone; sometimes they said very little. He kissed her a few times, but always he stopped, shaking his head. "No, my dear." For he had a wife. That was a cold fact which had to be faced. Dreams were not life itself. Whenever he left, Delilah would stand on the riverbank watching him ride Mercury across to Cassel's Woods. And often then, staring across to the distant peaks touched with a lavender light as transparent as rain, she would remember a little song her mother had used to sing at her weaving loom:

> *The water is wide; and I can't cross o'er;*
> *And neither have I wings to fly.*
> *O bring me a boat that will carry two —*
> *We'll row away, my love and I . . .*

At night, tossing on her pallet in the loft while whippoorwills cried in the forest, she tried not to think of Marie. But
always the knowledge of their being together while she lay
alone haunted her. Did they still come together as husband
and wife? Could they? He never said anything about his
secret life with Marie. He never told what he felt about her
as his wife, what she felt about him as her husband, how
she managed their house. Marie, and the credits and contra-
credits of his growing plantation, were hidden areas. In the
arithmetic of his business Delilah had no interest. She could
see the growth of Bickley Mills with her eyes, and seeing it
was what she cared for most: knowing he now owned Red
Oak Ridge, that slope behind Copper Ridge so heavy with
trees, knowing too he'd gotten all the shore along Big Spring
Branch, where a waterfall roared down over the rocks —
perfect site for his new mill, he explained. She didn't want
to know why certain families had gone on to Watauga or
into Kentuk or back to Lynch's Ferry. She didn't want to
know how he got so very much sang to trade to the Settlements; enough that she saw the great canvas bags hung on
his swaybacked packhorses while two of his blacks shoul-
dered new rifles and mounted their cobs and prepared
to guard the sang from robbers and Indians on the long journey east. But Marie! She now spent more than half of
each day at the mills, Charles said casually, now talked of
carding machines and watched each shilling and pistole and
réal and Spanish dollar and deerhide and grainbag and could
add column after column with lightning speed. Surely
Marie was turning into a clerk! Her face was sharper every
time Delilah saw it. What had been frail white-skinned prettiness was turning into grim-eyed pallor.

The worst times of all were when Delilah caught affection

in his tone when he said Marie's name. If only he would hate her utterly! Marie had tried to keep him from the battle he thought was his duty. She had all but repudiated him as he lay dying. Who was Marie to chain him, to keep him from the woman he truly loved? Why couldn't *she* be laid in a bury-hole at Cassel's Woods?

That's murder, Delilah realized, suddenly horrified; I must stop this. Loving him can't make me so bad as that!

The afternoon she found herself riding Farmer George along the muddy path to Big Spring Branch, Charles was away with a party of salt-makers on the Holston. Her heart always contracted at the danger of his going out in the raid-ing season to hack raw salt from the buffalo licks there, then to stand day and night over kettles while they boiled and hissed to the countryside for miles that his scalp could be had for the taking. There were men who had sacrificed their lives for salt. She had longed to cry at him: don't you give yours! Think of me. And if you have to go, give me a thing to remember — an hour, a minute . . . She had had to try hard not to say it. But he'd done enough. Didn't he under-stand? Why did he feel he must do more?

She rode on along the branch, hearing the muffled clop-clop of her gelding's hooves and the rustling of beech leaves that glistened after a morning shower. Then she heard the pounding of the falls and the roll of the new-made sawmill wheel. There were many rocks on the path, most of them embedded in the clay, their tops clean gray. One, she no-ticed suddenly, was not. It had been overturned. Leafmold showed where its underside had lain. It was a small thing; but she remembered her father's warnings, Charles's stories of his days as a Kentuk surveyor on Indian trails . . . She looked up; and in a tall beech she saw a foxgrape vine broken so recently its severed stem hung green at both joints.

She felt the sweat breaking on her forehead. She was alone. She had no rifle. Her hands went icy cold on the reins. Slowly, automatically, she turned back toward the fort. Then she saw the stocky figure of a bareheaded girl farther down the branch, basket and hoe in hand. It looked like — it was Ann Neece. She was digging sang.

"Ann!" Delilah screamed on impulse. "Come back with me!" She had no sooner cried out than she choked on her words; for a group of Indians sprang from the hill close beside her in a tangle of bodies, their breechclouts flapping, their arms raised. They screeched, they waved their tomahawks, and those with rifles began to shoot.

Without knowing what she did in her terror she dug her heels into the horse's belly. She couldn't look back, not now. "Ann!" she screamed again. Her horse began racing ahead of the Indians. Bullets started whistling by, and the whooping rose. "Ann! Run!"

Her horse began racing. Oh, she hadn't known he could race so fast! A bullet grazed her sleeve. She could hear the guttural cries coming faster, and the sound of firepins snapping harder, but never the Indians' feet. No, Indians ran softly . . . And so she rode on, her head bent against the summer wind that felt like January on her cheeks, her horse stumbling over rocks . . . Were the yells growing fainter now? Please God, they were! She hardly knew she had reached the fort until she heard the great stockade gate clattering shut behind her. Dazed, she pulled at Farmer George's reins. He was panting and snorting but she stopped him near the opposite row of cabins. For a while she sat astride, covering her eyes and listening to the rifles

and the cries. Then she was aware of Simon helping her
dismount. Shuddering and cold and damp, she let him hold
her and she was glad of him. She tried to breathe more
slowly and she couldn't. She blinked and saw men — Jimmy
Bush, Henry Neece — darting wildly in opposite directions,
the fringes on their shirts flying. Neece was already pulling
down piles of cartridges stacked on a wall shelf. Jimmy
Bush snatched a powder horn from a high nail, ripping its
thong. Frantically he wiped his rifle stock and barrel on his
leggings.

"It's Ann," she gasped at last. "She's still out there. I
couldn't wait — "

Simon gripped her tighter, but didn't answer.

"Get that musket, Oscher!"

He had to let her go. He seized a powder horn and began
dumping powder into his firepan. Rifles clacked out in a
fresh burst of fire; the rotten-egg smell of powder gathered
in the air. A half-naked Indian scaled the palisade and
Simon shot him. At a loophole Lawyer Dickenson was
shooting too, his wig pushed grotesquely back from his forehead. Two painted faces grinned from the blockhouse overhead. Delilah backed against the splintery wall of a cabin.
When she heard the frantic snorting of her horse she knew
she would have to take the reins. Henry Neece had pulled
one Indian down by his moccasined feet and was dragging
him toward a hominy block. She heard a skull cracking but
she did not know she heard it. She pushed her horse into the
first cabin door she found, slamming it after him.

The Indians were trying to set fire to the fort; she heard
flint scraping outside. But the ground was wet from the
shower and the logs were damp. They gave it up soon and
another appeared on top of the palisade, his roached stiff

black hair twisted, his breechclout flapping in the breeze. She heard his amazed cry as Simon shot him in the groin, and heard the thud of his body on the ground outside. A wail went up, then sank low in the Indians' throats. She tried to stop the chattering of her teeth and the shaking of her arms and hands.

The sun was low when silence came. At a loophole she saw the Indian's body outside; she saw too the rest of the band stumbling aimlessly into the woods beyond, two of them limping. They were going! But Ann, Ann . . .

"They're out o' cartridges, most likely." Jimmy Bush kicked at the body of the Indian Neece had killed near the hominy block. When Jimmy opened the fort gate Delilah moved to it just in time to see a figure staggering slowly from the forest. It was a woman. Her arms, her bared breasts, her ripped and twisted yellow madder gown, were covered with blood. Thin streams of blood were matting too what hair she had left. Her mouth hung open. She swayed, and still she walked ahead, heedless of the mud puddles that turned crimson as she passed over them.

Henry Neece gave a strange sound.

In Ann's hand still swung her sang basket, and she kept on walking toward her father: alive.

The rumors began slowly. It was hard to know at first who was starting them. Gran was the first of the Winfields to hear them whispered near the mill while she was waiting there to be paid for a batch of her son-in-law's beaverskins. When she repeated the whispers afterwards over supper on the mountain, passing her cabbage and stewed chicken all the while, her voice was calm enough but perplexed. Charles Bickley was in league with the Indians; Mrs. Bush had hissed it to her as a fact, but as a fact she'd heard from somebody else. That was why he had contrived to be away when he knew an attack was coming. By his treachery he had saved his mills. His wife's screaming and shutting herself up with her slaves all around her was only a clever trick. And when Gran had laughed outright at Mrs. Bush and demanded to know who had filled her with such nonsense, Mrs. Bush had only shaken her head. A few days later Delilah's father went down with a deer carcass and heard the same tale from Mrs. Sawyer, with the added feature that somebody else, some other spy, must be running Bickley's messages to British generals at the Northern Lakes. Winfield, too, had laughed. Who? he had asked Mrs. Sawyer. Nobody stayed away long enough to travel to the Lakes and back, did they? But she had then muttered to him that some might call militia duty what others didn't. It was not until he heard the story a week later from Mrs. Duncan, a woman whose child had been killed playing downriver, that he understood how it had started. For Mrs. Duncan had said: "A body can't blame Henry Neece for thinking such. I know how he feels. Don't try to tell me the war is over — that it's all independence and England has no say. They still send their redsticks, don't they?"

Ann still lived, lying in bandages on a cornshuck pallet. She had a mind, but no detailed memory of what had happened to her. Her father himself had pegged the crown of her head and then wrapped it in strips of tow. It would be at least a year before she healed. Everyone pitied her, and in Boone's Chapel she was prayed for every Sabbath. Why, her father shouted all the while to anybody who would listen, had Bickley told her to dig sang at Big Spring Branch? There was sang closer to the fort than that. Oh, Bickley had meant her to die! She had only wanted a few pence for a sunbonnet and now she'd never be without one. And Delilah Winfield had left her to be murdered, not caring.

Delilah didn't want to believe Henry Neece had said such things. But her heart sank as she knew it might be true; he would have reason to say them, to strike out blindly at whatever cause he could find. "I didn't know what I was doing," she faltered to her father. "I called her. If I hadn't, the Indians might have waited, I know it. But my horse bolted — "

He understood, he said kindly in his old voice. But he compressed his lips before he told her another thing Neece had said — this at last to his own face outside the mill. Neece had seen Delilah Winfield and Charles Bickley together by the river, alone, not once but twice. What they had been doing he would not say.

"It's a lie, isn't it, Delilah? Neece is mad?"

She kept her hands at her side. "Yes." Her father's breath came easier. But after a pause he told her the rest. There was more still. Henry Neece was also saying she was a witch; he was talking heathen superstition, because of Reynard. She had bewitched Bickley into becoming her lover. It would be best to draw flour crosses on the paths where she had ridden. Next she would be bringing the ghost hound, the specter that trotted beside a doomed man and then rose up in the air breathing fire. That was how everybody would know who was going to die next; they'd see the hound. Somebody had heard it already, baying out its fearful cry at midnight by the river. Delilah and Bickley: they were against all Christian folks on the Clinch . . . The skin at the corners of Winfield's eyes folded as he repeated the nightmare aloud in his cabin.

"He's not my lover." Delilah could hear Gran stirring her rose jam in the corner; she could feel Gran's eyes on her too.

"I suggest it's time for Delilah to wed," Gran said presently in a dry voice. "She'd be alone if we were murdered ourselves, Ben. She needs to be looked after. Simon's a good lad."

"That Cohee?" He turned.

"You could letter him — you've said as much. Delilah's twenty. It's over-old for maidhood. No man will fit every measure you've made out. Don't wait for a William Campbell."

"No," Delilah told them tightly. "I can't do it."

"Of course she can't!" her father flung at Gran. "I never liked Simon as her *husband*, Madam."

"Soon you might settle right quick for any husband," Gran answered tartly. "Remember it. Meanwhile you'd better go down to Neece yourself; with Delilah."

No, Delilah begged silently. Not to see Ann this way yet, and have to hear the only thing I have left dragged out where people can tear at it and worry it . . . But she knew she would have to go. The day her father took her he stopped first at the mill. Simon was there trading coonskins, and began repeating the slanders — and the truths — she already knew. He too would go to Neeces' with her. She tried to stop him, to hold him off; but her father shrugged and then muttered, "Very well. It might help." That was the final humiliation: to have Simon hear what she might not be able to deny convincingly enough, perhaps to have him too caught in her web of lying and half-truth and her fear for Charles.

The Neeces had hung blankets over their windows. The cabin was dim, shut off from the brightness of the afternoon.

Ann lay white-faced and heavy-lidded but conscious on her pallet. Delilah was surprised to see her so little changed, except for the wrappings on her head. The memory of Ann half naked and bleeding, groping her way toward the fort, rose before her and she shut it out. Now Ann was merely pale; she tried to smile, as if to say, I can't help what my father does. Soon enough, in the half-darkness of the adjoining room, Henry Neece's curses began coming venomously. Delilah stood beside her father and Simon and tried to tell him her horse had bolted and she had called, that Ann was her friend . . . She heard Simon and her father reminding Neece how she went to the chapel, how she prayed and sang hymns and knew her Shorter Catechism. All the while she looked into the sorrowing eyes of Ann's father, and the eyes looked back, as if to shout: I know! I may be mad, but I know!

It was then that she remembered what Marie had said about Reynard. She pulled at her skirts with hard fingers. "Was it Mrs. Bickley who told you I was a witch?"

"Hell's delight, she didn't have to!"

"Because I have a fox her husband gave me once? Because she and her husband quarreled when he went to King's Mountain where he nearly died for all of you — you'd forget that?" She choked back the sob starting in her throat.

"Kill your fox, then. Decent folks don't tame varmints. You listened to a Tory scheming and left my daughter to be skulped! You're well named: Delilah."

"The miller isn't a Tory, Henry," Simon put in quietly. Ann tossed on her pallet in the next room; they could hear her. "Even Ann doesn't believe that — any of it."

"How do *you* know so much?" Neece raised his red-rimmed eyes.

Quietly still, Simon told him what Delilah had confided to him. When he had finished, Neece blinked at him. "Campbell? I heard he's been killed back east."

"But Madam Campbell must live on at Aspenvale. She can swear to the miller."

Neece stared dumbly ahead. At last he said with a drawn mouth: "So we got to see the miller taking e'er thing we own and stand it, because Patrick Henry might be governor again. Is that it? It's worse than the other." Oh, everybody knew how Bickley had gotten his ten thousand acres. (So much! Delilah wondered. So much, now!) It hardly mattered, maybe, for what a man hated the miller. He, Neece, had let Ann go out to dig because she'd wanted to deck herself for that Fraley boy, and now she'd have to deck herself forever . . . And Delilah Winfield was a witch, a Jezebel, she had a lover and she'd left his daughter to be skulped . . .

"I have no lover." She heard herself saying it just above a whisper.

No? Could she deny she'd been on the riverbank with him? Could she? Henry Neece had been standing there to watch 'em both through those willows; he'd seen the Arab stallion Mercury, that rich man's horse, tied close by. He knew!

"Don't!" she begged senselessly, "don't!" She knew no denial would help her. If only Charles would come back!

When she left with her father and Simon they stopped briefly together by the millpond in the twilight. Nothing, she knew, had done herself any good. The shadow of the motionless wheel was soft-edged, barely perceptible across the grass between. Dark pools were already spreading in the hollows, but the distant line of Sandy Ridge was still gold at its rim as if touched by invisible flames. She could hear footsteps. Someone was on the way to feed his stock, going to his barn as if the routines of life had never been broken. The ridge faded slowly to gray . . . *Fire on the mountain, run gal run* . . . There were times you couldn't run.

"Thank you, Simon," she said at last. They were waiting for her to speak, she knew. "You did right. It was time to tell it."

"They haven't got the Tory thing against him now. They'll want another. They'll gossip — I mind that's worse." He turned to Winfield. "Sir, I'm asking your favor for Delilah. It's time for that too."

Winfield tensed. Delilah could see the muscles of his forearm tighten. Then he laughed, remembering. "Ask her, boy."

She could only shake her head.

"You see?" She felt her father's arm coming around her waist. "She's in no state to give you any answer."

"She's in no state to think of e'er thing she does, neither, seems like." She knew what Simon meant. She felt a great fondness welling in her for him, even as she shook her head again. She knew he understood now that she truly was meeting Charles, that Henry Neece had seen one thing clearly. Simon knew, and he could stand such a blow to his pride to save her. But she was committed. It was too late to be saved anything. All her life was flowing like the river toward an unknown end she could not understand but knew could not be changed.

It was a beautiful night on Sugar Hill. The trees towered high and stately, rustling their leaves. The smell of raspberry roses came strong in the tangles. How many times before she had stood here with her father as a child! But now she could wish her father weren't with her at all, that it was

Charles beside her instead and she was letting him gather her to him and nobody would see.

"You believed me, Papa?"

"Why, yes, my dear. I believed you." His manner was so easy, so reassuring, her last fear of him passed. When Reynard scurried out to meet her as he always did she actually smiled to see her father stoop to pet him. "You're tired, Delilah. I'll walk him tonight."

And so she went inside, thankful the ordeal was over, grateful to her father for his blind trust which would make her feel guilty on the morrow but which now she was glad to accept. She was asleep on her pallet by the time he came back to the cabin without her fox.

15

"H e ran away." That was Winfield's explanation. "I must have frightened him by some noise, or perhaps it was a noise in the woods. I'm sorry, my dear."

"He wouldn't do it! He'd come back!" she cried out.

"He's wild, Delilah. You can't keep a wild thing pent forever."

"No," Gran agreed, with her narrow look. "But it's a wonder how many try."

Day after day Delilah searched the woods for Reynard. There wasn't a sign of him. She called him. She put out scraps at night, but when they were gone in the morning she knew it was only some coon which had stolen them. She knew too that Charles was back when she saw Mercury tied to a tree across the river, so she waited. She was supposed to be gathering pokeroot for Gran while she looked for Reynard. Perhaps Charles would help her gather it later and she could return with a full basket. But he didn't come to her after all, and toward nightfall she began by herself to pick as much pokeroot as she could. Perhaps Gran wouldn't be too angry. Gran knew how she felt about Reynard's disappearance. Perhaps Gran even suspected what she suspected — that Winfield had taken him so far from the cabin he was lost.

He wouldn't do more, Delilah tried to tell herself; he wouldn't do anything like — like killing him; he wouldn't hurt Reynard just to punish me. Yet she went to the barn to look at her father's axe. It was clean, without a trace of fur or blood. He was very careful, she remembered then, about keeping his axe greased. What a horrid thought of her father, that he would kill Reynard whom she had loved so much. But all the same she wondered. He might have done it not to punish her but to save her from Neece's taunts of witchcraft . . . Oh, it was surely wrong to love an animal almost more than a person.

One afternoon Mrs. Neece came up the mountain to tell Delilah that Ann wanted to see her. "You got to excuse her pap." Mrs. Neece nervously wiped her hands on her berry-streaked skirt. "He was wild. Ann spoke to him some." Her eyes grew hard and meaningful. "For Ann's sake he wants to say he's sorry, to your face. He'll say he lied to hurt the miller."

"For Ann's sake?" Delilah felt the heat in her face and breast, but she stood erect.

"For Ann's sake," Mrs. Neece nodded. "She needs e'er friend she has these days."

How Ann must have begged, Delilah realized when Ann's mother had left stony-faced, how Ann must believe in her goodness — though she truly had none. Miserably she remembered all the times past she had ridiculed Ann in her heart for her awkwardness and her dowdy gowns. What did such things matter? Ann needed her, and now she needed Ann — and Ann's father.

"I trust you've learned your lesson, missy," was all Gran said.

The shame of hearing Neece's apology would be worse

than the shame of his accusations; but she would have to bear it. How bright a thing her love had started, but what dinginess it was making of all her life. When she rode Farmer George down to see Ann she stopped first at the mill; one of the blacks there told her the miller and his wife were inside reckoning salt bushels. They'd been doing that ever since he'd returned from the Holston. It was all she could do not to go in and confront him then and there, crying: "I'm alive too. And I'm waiting for you!"

The second time at Neeces' was as terrible as the first. Ann pressed Delilah's hand and asked her to forgive Neece while he stood sourly by, his face colored with a mixture of contempt and anxiety. "I been takin' it back," he grated. "All of it. It's what Ann wanted. You too, I reckon?" His mouth curled on the question.

"Yes, I — thank you," Delilah whispered, turning as her face began to sting.

"I hear your fox run away." He spat into the fire.

"Yes."

Later Ann's eyes, still strangely pretty in their brown clarity, filled with tears as she motioned Delilah to bend close. "Tim Fraley won't want me now. No man will. What can I do, Delilah? It worries Mam and Pap so. I can't go through my life lorn, I can't."

"You won't have to," Delilah said gently, knowing her lie. She could do nothing for Ann beyond pressing her hand and smiling down at her and promising to make her a fine muslin cap embroidered with ivy leaves. Some day when the war was over Ann could send to the Tidewater for a wig; but a cap would look fine, meanwhile, with the hair at her forehead curled. Gran had an old set of curling tongs. She'd bring them down later. She'd bring down, too, some of

Gran's elderflower water for Ann to smooth her hands. If the small, everyday things Gran called girls' needful fripperies sounded as ludicrous to Ann as they did to Delilah while she chattered, Ann didn't show it.

"You going to wed Simon?" Ann arched her brows. "He thinks a heap of you." Then: "I wish Tim'd thought of me that way. It would be a thing to remember now."

Afterwards Delilah wondered if men talked of their own fripperies when such things happened to them — new knives, maybe, or good liquor or fine saddles. The men had changed in this war. Henry Neece, once a great lumbering humorous farmer with a red face, fond of his cider and a fiddle, had turned into a fearful man who believed in witches. Simon did what killing he had to do and was proud he could do it so brave, but between times he was growing tender. He was independent in his ways but he could see, now, into her heart with a truth that frightened her. He wasn't any longer the rough Simon who had tried stealing a kiss on the trace. Now he would know exactly what she was feeling even if she didn't herself. Charles, people said, was growing more grasping, more greedy of land. But he had had to fight so much for it: he had the right. The women were changing too. Once, Delilah thought, her grandmother would have stopped her loving Charles any way she could. Now Gran was saddened by it, but didn't seem to know what to do. Delilah herself had changed. She had seen things she could never have guessed at the night she had felt sick to see a doe shot by the river downstream. She could see anything now and not flinch. She wasn't a believer any more. She wanted a married man. Oh, yes, things had happened in this war to change everybody! It was curious how people just went on talking about the little things: how Ann, who had been scalped and lived through it, could ask with perky interest what Delilah was going to do about a man courting her. If the war stopped tomorrow the men would doubtless go on talking of hunting while the women talked of receipts and infares and babies, and it would sound as if everybody had forgotten the time when any day you woke up might be the day you were killed in your own house. But the children might go on playing one of their games: the one where you filled a hollow reed with sand from the river shore and blew through it pretending it was a gun while you shouted "Dead, Injun, dead!"

Tomorrow: herself and Charles. She had such need of him, and yet he didn't come. *Let them talk! We love each other already! We've already wronged and cheated Marie but she deserves it, with her squeamishness and her book-keeper's soul. It was I helped him live, not Marie. I have first right to him.* Quite as reasonable was the other argument: *We haven't done a thing.*

The shoemake bushes turned scarlet and the chinquapin trees grew heavy with nuts. The river foamed faster over its rocks during the afternoons Delilah waited in the hollow. The pokeroot season passed; her father and Gran believed she was picking witch-hazel. She always managed to gather enough blooms to pass muster when she went back. At the dinner table she always answered coolly and politely when her father spoke to her. He too was cool and polite. They never talked of Reynard. I know I've lost my daughter, he seemed to be telling her; I understand. And Gran's eyes darted from one to the other, wondering, trying to figure.

Charles came at last on an afternoon turned misty, a day full of dripping leaves that stuck to each other in a feeble wind. His face looked healthy again but it was a remote and unreadable mask as he stood over her. "Not here," he said shortly. "We've been seen."

"Is that why you stayed away?" She led him up the trace into a thicket of beeches, catching at her skirts to keep them from tearing on briers.

"I heard everything. Oscher came to me directly I got back. This is dangerous for you." His voice was tight and angry, but she knew the anger wasn't for her.

"He's got no call to interfere. I had to tell him about Madam Campbell — to save you, I thought. I reckon I only made it worse."

He took her face in his hands, reading in her wide eyes all her love and all her unhappiness. His heart was beginning to beat in dull, sickening thuds. Could she really know how he wanted her, how she was a part of him and it was all he could manage now not to crush her to him right here and make all that love and eagerness and pain his forever, to set his seal on her and hers on him?

"Could you save either of us?" he managed. "I — Delilah, I decided we had to stop. For your sake. I'm afraid. I can tell you so, you see. If anything happened to you I couldn't live with myself."

"Stop?" She choked on the word. He dropped his hands and sank down to a smooth rock, pulling her beside him.

"No. I'm not strong enough either." Briefly he held her away, his fingers digging at her shoulders. When he let her go she picked up a stalk of goldenrod and began to twirl and strip it, her face averted.

"But you count salt bushels with your wife. You eat her food and play with your children. You share a heap of things with her. Maybe she thinks you still love her, maybe you give her a reason."

"My God, Delilah — " She saw his jaw come up.

"I have the right to say it." She kept her voice steady. "You're all I think about now. You're all my life."

As quickly as it had grown hostile his mouth gentled. "You're my life too." He began to dig at the leafmold at his feet with a beech stick, making the dirt fly out in clumps. "I made a marriage vow."

"You're not religious," she said scornfully. "No more than I am."

"I'm not much good at reeling off psalms, no." He jabbed at a stone. "I think, you know — I've made promises to you, to her."

"She's saying I'm a witch." Her face had begun to smart.

He nodded, hunching his shoulders. "Yes. She may understand what's happened. I'm never sure."

"You can't care for her!"

"Not as she is now. I cared once. She was warm then, and — and brave."

The wind murmured. In the distance a waterfall was running. "I'm so weary." Delilah leaned against his shoulder. "I wish there was nobody else in the world but us. I'm weary of trying to live with other people and thinking about them all the time." She could feel his hand on her hair, beginning to stroke it. "Papa must have killed Reynard. I don't believe he ran away."

She felt every muscle in his shoulders and back go hard. His hand left her head abruptly and he sat bolt upright. "When?"

"After the night at Neeces'." She moistened her lips. "He says he lost him walking in the woods."

Slowly, Charles whispered: "How *could* he?" And then they were together again. This time their embrace had a searching despair, an urgency born of time passing and time lost and the hostility they knew lay around them both. His mouth crushed hard on hers, and she ran her hands over his back as if she must learn its dimensions only from touch. He tried her name, his voice just at the edge of control until he stopped to kiss her once more. It was only when he let her go that she realized his hands were shaking. In an instant she saw them stiffen.

"I love you so much. I do know what I'm doing! I don't care what happens!"

"I do," he whispered; and she saw the defeat in his eyes.

"I've loved you a hundred times over in my dreams."

Stiffly he got up. "This is worse." His voice was suddenly dead, but very clear. She felt the wind sting as cold on the side of her face as if he had slapped her. He began to pace, his boots cracking irregularly over the twigs underfoot. "You can live in the moment but I can't, Delilah. Don't deceive yourself. I'm married. I wouldn't undo it if I could because I've got my boys. They'll turn out what I am, live up or down to — to that. Boys do. I've botched your life pretty thoroughly too, haven't I?" He gave her an ironic smile. "No courtship and poems, just hiding behind trees; and lies — many, I'm sure. Just possibly the tortures of hell — if not in this world, in your father's idea of the next. A very pretty girlhood. Christ, I wish I could tell you I never wanted to see you again."

"Then don't, if you're so ashamed!" She jumped to her feet. "You make it sound horrid!"

"Isn't it?" he asked quietly. His eyes turned distant again. "Can you tell me there aren't times you wish we'd never started?"

"Let me be, then!" she taunted. "You hate me — say it!"

In the same dead voice he answered: "You know better. Nothing ever happens to me but I want to tell you, touch you — If you can make me forget, go ahead. If you really do want to make me forget."

"Your precious honor — that means everything, doesn't it? That nice Tidewater word! It's not your thought of me at all. It's you, what *you* feel, what *you* don't want to do. D'you think it's your stupid honor makes me love you?"

He barely smiled as he answered levelly, "I hope not. I have very little of that left."

As the moments of silence passed, the heat began to leave her body. In its place flowed a coldness that froze her until she felt she could scarcely move. This wasn't happening. A part of her was involved in every word she had spoken, every gesture she had made. Another part watched herself acting out the drama as if detached from it. He was staring at her steadily now, his lips still curved in a faint cruel smile. Finally she faltered: "No shame or limit in love, Charles, I — "

"And the limits are there." It sounded softly in the heaviness of the air around them both. He showed no surprise at her knowledge of the words.

"Why?" She moved to him. "Not for me."

"The shame too. For me, always. I'm sorry."

"But I won't have you that way." Her voice began to rise again. "Loving me and not wanting to — *trying* not to!"

"Trying hard." How could his smile have turned so tender? Every one of his features stamped itself on her brain in that moment: his peppered hair, caught back into its club by the same faded ribbon; the crook in his nose; his wide mouth, quivering slightly; his high neck and prominent cheekbones; the stiffness in his right shoulder, under his buckskins, nearest the scar she had just been touching, running her fingers along the raised streak of it. He came to her quietly this time. "My darling," he pulled her against him with iron arms to stop her struggle, "don't fight me. Hush. I'll 'let you be' — at last. Yes. You've made it easier. Oh, Christ, I — " His voice shaking, he broke off. Finally he said: "Only stay here with me a little now. This once. I'm sorry. You'll forget — my love — " When he buried his mouth in her hair she could not move. When she heard the twigs cracking outside the thicket she could not turn. At the unmistakable sound of footsteps she still stood rooted to the ground with him.

"Adulteress!"

She recognized her father's voice full of hatred as he croaked out the word, but it was Charles who broke away to face him. Between two beech trunks stood Ben Winfield, his feet planted wide apart, his hand on his rifle, his shoulders high and defiant and the cleft of his chin deep in shadow.

"It isn't true, Ben." Her father's hand only clenched harder on the stock of his Deckhard. "We're saying good-bye." Charles walked slowly toward him. "Ask her why; she'll tell you."

"We're not!" But neither man heard her.

"Get out of here, Bickley. This is my land. You trespass. Great God, how you trespass!" He turned to Delilah. "You're worse than a witch. You have no decency. Look at you — caught!"

"You've done enough to her."

"Have I?" Her father laughed unevenly. "I wonder."

Charles had stopped not a foot from him. Delilah, trembling, could only hold to a sapling and keep watching. "Hurt Delilah more and I'll make you pay for it, Ben. I'll know.

The hardest thing I've ever done is to leave her to you."

In a deliberate movement Charles turned once more. Briefly his eyes met Delilah's. Then she watched him walk quietly out of the beech thicket, leaving her to her father. His cold appraisal made her shudder.

"Did he have you?" His voice was thick. "Did he?"

"No," she whispered finally, knowing in that instant how she hated her pride and Charles's. Soon she heard her father's questions and felt his arm tighten mercilessly on hers as he started to push her up toward the cabin. She heard Gran's cry when it came, heard her ladle drop to the puncheons and the cornmeal mush boil over in the caldron and sputter down to the floor. She heard the beginning of her father's new quarrel with Gran, the name of Simon and the cry of Adultery being shouted into a hundred corners. They were the corners where Reynard had used to sleep. His cage stood shining in one of them still. The fire crackled, and the smells of dittany tea and cooked-out mush hung all around.

" — mazed!" Gran's voice was gravelly. "Not God yourself, Ben! Can't dare to touch her or keep her a prisoner — try to help — said himself it was over for 'em — "

"Stop," Delilah said dully at last. "I can't stand any more." Slowly she got up to slice bread as she always did for dinner. But at the first stroke she cut her left forefinger. Stupidly she watched it bleed until she realized neither her father nor Gran saw or cared. They were still glaring at each other. She would have to tear off a piece of tow herself. She almost could have laughed at that.

She began a new quilt after a few weeks. Whenever she was free of stock-tending and furniture-rubbing she sat quietly at her frame, finding it easier there not to flinch under her father's sad steady gaze. Truly there was no need to flinch. He couldn't hurt her; not where I am, she thought, so far from his life . . . Gran's face was as sad. Delilah forgot she had ever dismissed Gran as unknowing. To manage to grow old was a wonder. The lines in Gran's face were deepening. Gran was nearing seventy. The liver spots were spreading over her neck. Gran might forgive her some day. She had heard her father's promise of silence to Gran and could be freshly grateful Gran had asked it.

About Simon, Delilah had nearly forgotten. The afternoon he rode up the mountain with Timothy Fraley she was surprised. The boys hobbled their horses at the cabin door, scraped their feet on the rock near the stoop, and inside threw themselves down on the settle at the hearth, rubbing red hands. Simon grinned at Fraley while he hemmed and hawed about the cold snap. "Ask her," he finally charged. "Straight out!"

She hadn't realized a boy like Tim Fraley could turn so red with shyness and embarrassment. But he did when he started trying to sort out his words. It was Ann. She had such grit. He'd never thought much of her when she'd giggled and prattled at him all the time. Right silly, she'd been. But now Ann was quiet, stately in her ways, not addling a man with her chatter. Ann only watched you, fingering her curls under that funny little white cap with the ivy leaves; she never took it off — of course. A body could nearly forget what — well, what had happened, what was underneath. There was something in Ann's eyes when she watched you; something gentle, like her hands when she touched the shoulders of little ones. Would Ann have him, did Delilah think? Would she believe he just felt sorry for her? You needed a woman who could stand life out here (there were few enough), who'd be good to your younguns and give you some peace. But how could you say that? Tim had his own cut-log cabin; buckeye, it was. He had three hundred acres ready for plowing against spring came.

That was the first time Delilah smiled because she really wanted to. She could forget herself and Charles and her father. She thought instead of Ann. Ann at least had lived for a purpose — for this straight clumsy farmer who had come to cherish the strength she had tried so hard to hide from him. "I'll tell her it isn't pity. But she'll know it, Tim, if you tell her what you've told me."

"I'm not a handy speaker," he mumbled.

Simon laced his fingers together at the knees of his leggings, coughing as if to remind Delilah of his presence. "Mostly it isn't speaking that counts. You'll come to the marrying with me, Delilah?"

She nodded slowly. "We'll have to think of a thing to bring her."

"Look here, what makes you two so sure — "

"Oh, Tim!" She couldn't help even teasing him. "Haven't you *ever* had to do with a girl?"

"There weren't always much time," he answered, grinning sheepishly.

Simon was smiling too. "We'll surely bring you a fine thing, Tim. Both of us." He ran his tongue over his lips, as if waiting for the effect of his last words. But Delilah passed them over.

A week later she went down to the blacksmith with Gran to have Chick and Farmer shod. Standing with Gran at the shanty to wait, she was surprised to see a small file of men, women and children shuffling slowly out of the forest close by, led by a black man with a rifle slung over his shoulder.

Their backs were bent; their eyes stayed on their feet. As they came closer she could see baskets slung over their arms and short hoes clutched in their fingers. A familiar but nameless sharpness came into the air. The hair of the women straggled over their thin faces as the men lumbered after them. The children stepped softly, as if the earth were so fragile a careless footfall might destroy it. Their little hands were clasped tight on their baskets as if the wind might sweep the baskets away. Haltingly they filed past the shanty on the trace toward the mill, the guard clumping ahead of them, never raising their eyes to Delilah or her grandmother either. As they climbed the rise near Mill Creek their bodies were silhouetted for a grotesque minute against a reddening sky, the tiny line of them like a line of ants. Delilah tried a deep breath, and knew the smell about her for sang. The sun vanished behind an immense thin cloud. The sky grew redder behind the small figures. When they disappeared over the crest the sky flamed; then the sun emerged low and yellow, and the sky around it faded. She heard the churning of the faroff millwheel.

"Maussa he sang-diggers." The blacksmith nodded briefly toward the ridge as he led out the horses. But she had known that before. Even as her life was going on, so was Charles's. So was the building of Bickley Mills.

III

"I lookèd all around me, and
found I was alone . . ."

—*Old Virginia Ballad*

16

I T W A S not long after Delilah and Charles had stopped meeting that she first heard herself called an old maid. Perhaps it had been at Timothy and Ann Fraley's infare eight years back; she couldn't remember now. Ann had three children by this spring of 1790, the last, a boy, just birthed. Ann had a good stout body again; and though at first her husband had had to stay with her during the raids because she was as terrified as Marie Bickley, she had learned once more to swallow her fear and take her place at the fort loopholes with her rifle beside the men . . . But perhaps somebody in the fort had first whispered "old maid" as Delilah passed. She had spent several stretches in Fort Bickley with her father and grandmother, the times Benge's Cherokees and the Ohio Valley Shawanese alike came down on the Clinch valley nearly every month with British rifles and freshly sharpened tomahawks. Vexing stretches they had been, rank with the stench of combined humanity, full of the quarrels and pettinesses of people without privacy. There was no such thing as solitude in a shut stockade. It was hard for Delilah to think any longer of definite years at all, for she remembered a particular summer only as the summer of Mrs. Bush's feud with Mrs. Neece over the use of a washboard, a particular fall as the fall of Freelove Duncan's tiff with Tivis English after a three-year courtship, Freelove swearing she'd never wed a man who drank himself senseless every night; she said she could smell it on his breath. Delilah could understand. Boredom in a crowd was the worst kind. She was grateful at least that Charles preferred to garrison his house and not live in the fort himself. She could not have faced him intimately with Marie.

She was never humiliated to hear the taunt of her spinsterhood. She could have ended it in a moment with Simon by one lie and a false promise. She had a mirror; Simon had bought one for her at the mill store Charles had built with new dollars from his sang and peltry trade. Since British lobsterbacks no longer overran eastern Virginia trade plunder from the Settlements was beginning to come in and would keep coming. The women of Bickley Mills (few still called it Cassel's Woods) were buying ribbons and combs and riding crops these days, ticking and brass pins and pewter trenchers. Not every season was spent in the fort. The first time Delilah looked in her mirror she was startled; why didn't her face show what had happened to her? She only saw the same wide eyes and unlined skin and full red mouth. If there had been any reason she would have tried making a wave in the front of her hair, just beside the peak on her forehead. Once Charles had called her beautiful. Her features were too big for that — her nose not small or delicate enough, her chin a shade too firm. Yet long ago she had known how a beautiful woman might feel pride; she had known what it was to be cherished.

Gran had at last stopped harping on Simon. She was even speaking of him half contemptuously sometimes. "Like a hound dog traipsing after his mistress. He'd go to Jericho and back for you, missy." But Simon wouldn't make a fool of himself. Delilah knew it because there had been the day soon after Ann's infare — Delilah had worked Ann a sampler and Simon had made a frame for it — when he had taken her into his cornfield near Copper Ridge and shown her the first foundations of his cabin. She remembered the great oak and cedar logs lying crossways near a clump of crab-trees. She could still, when she shut her eyes, see Simon pacing the cabin's unbuilt rooms, his yellow forelock bobbing while he gestured out his plan to her. He'd surely have a dogtrot, and glass in the windows, and a summer kitchen in back, and a well close to the house so that ne'er woman would have to drag heavy water buckets up the Ridge to the spring. In the front room he'd hang a sampler like the one Delilah had made Ann. "Order is Heaven's First Law," it would say, the same motto.

It's come. You have to tell him now. He's building it for you . . . She'd actually wanted to go to Ann's infare with him. There were many things she wanted to do with him — forget herself by dancing to Tivis English's fiddle in a long barn on nights when there weren't any Indians to raid, or ride along the riverbanks where the sycamores were dappled by sunlight. She hated being really alone as much as she hated being crowded in the fort.

Her face, that afternoon in the cornfield, must have shown a glimpse of the inner hurt she had suffered. For Simon, standing in front of his logs, frowned: "You afraid I'll snatch a kiss? When I get one from you again I won't be stealing it."

She had tried to laugh. "You think I'll beg for it?" But she saw his brown eyes darken quickly. She couldn't fool him by clumsy flirting.

"I think you'll give me what I want. Yes." He started toward her. Then he motioned her to a wide boulder and they sat down together on its cold, ridged surface. "You know I mean to wed you. It's time we spoke some of the miller."

She turned away. "You know about him."

"I know you had a fancy for 'im years ago. I know he married *her* — and then he came back from King's Mountain and you tended him. It was then he started to love you, wasn't it? So you sneaked off with him when you could, and how far you went I don't want to know. Then a thing happened; and you stopped. Was it his new babe?"

"No." Dully. Sebastian Hatler Bickley . . . but he'd been born afterwards.

"Neeces'?"

She only shook her head.

"I'd think you'd have more care of yourself than to take a woman's leavings. At first I thought I could take a man's leavings to save you. But I can't. Do you love him — still? I mean to see you in this cabin. But it's got to be over with the miller. I'll not bed you knowing you're dreaming of another all the while."

She felt herself flush. "Please — "

"I don't speak proper? Seems like I ought to speak of bedding when I speak of marriage with you. You're not unknowing yourself." How straight Simon sat! She had never noticed how wide his own shoulders had grown, how his lean boy's face had filled out into a man's and had become almost craggy-featured with its narrow nose and pointed jaw and the sun lines at the corners of his eyes. "He's right handsome, the miller. He talks in the Settlement tongue and his ways are grand. But I haven't been wasting my time. Lawyer Dickenson, he's taught me to write my name, read in the spelling book too, and cipher to the rule of three. Did you know it? I can tell your pap. I won't stick so much in his craw now, it may be."

"For me? You paid the lawyer to know — "

"For me too. A man around here's got to be thoughty to deal with Bickley or he'll lose every acre he's got in the tithe books. But tell me how it stands with you. Will you wed me now, or do I wait?"

Slowly, she turned to Simon. A pair of bluebirds were twittering overhead in an oak tree. Paradise weeds rustled in the wind, their thick red stalks bending stiffly and their blossoms bobbing loosely around the floppy leaves. "I couldn't wed you now, Simon." Her words were spaced, deliberate.

"Because you love him yet?"

She put her face in her hands. He rose to stand over her.

"Then I'll not take you into my house."

"Take another," she pleaded. "While you have time — before I make it worse for you. Oh, Simon — " A dry little sob of pity threatened her poise, and she broke off.

"I may do that some day," he said quietly. "Maybe I can, later. Maybe I can stop caring for you, though it seems now I'll never stop. But I'd tell you. Meanwhile you can think of me nights. I'll be down here planing tables for you, hammering your cooking crane, weaving your hammock and pegging your bed."

"You don't want to see me," she said listlessly.

"If you like me truly I do. But I'll not endure to be used — take you to dances where the miller goes, or such."

"I do like you!" She heard the pleading again in her voice as she started up. "Ever so much! It's just — "

She was amazed to see him smile. "Delilah, that's about the nicest way of telling a man to go to hell I e'er heard."

Simon hadn't lost his pride yet. She'd been too kind to tell him she couldn't bear to think of wedding him at all. She would let him keep his pride. So they had fallen into

the habit of seeing each other at cornhuskings and barn-rais-
ings and play-parties and chapel and in the fort. Bickley
Mills, doubtless, gossiped behind hands. But its people still
whispered "old maid" and Delilah was content to let it be so.
Sometimes, however, on long nights when the fire leapt in
the grate and she and Gran sat knitting before it together
while Ben Winfield bedded down his stock in the barn, she
wanted to ask Gran: what do I do with the part of me that's
wife, that's mother too? How can I kill that woman I once
wanted to be?

Her father had become very considerate in his manner toward her, treating her as a grownup at last when she no
longer cared, neither hoped for it nor feared it. Often he
talked to her of rye-planting and sheep-raising and the year's
wheat yield and his troubles with cutworms in the vegetable
patch. Once he asked her advice about feeding more milk to
the hens. He never mentioned either the disappearance of
Reynard or, true to his promise, the scene in the thicket.
When he talked of Charles at all it was merely in terms of
his trading.

He selected his scripture carefully, of course. She'd heard
so many times of the woman taken in adultery and brought
before Christ that she could repeat it in her sleep. But her
father seemed convinced of her actual innocence if not the
innocence of her heart. Perhaps he was ashamed. He prayed
often about his own sins. Sometimes Delilah could hear his
voice from her pallet in the loft as he prayed alone below:
"Suffer me not to set myself above Thee, who hast said
'Judge not' . . ." Every spring she sugared with him, facing
the wind and the darkness and the cold beside him. But —
was it because he really hated Charles? — he said it was
wrong to own human souls, to have blacks. There was no-

body to trade his sugar in the Settlements but Charles's blacks, and he had to pay a heavy transport price and a commission besides. There was nobody to tend any extra sap buckets either. Charles's old plans for a north and south bush, for hammering out extra hogsheads, had come to nothing. The Winfields had enough, if Benge left them alone. They had their land and their living, they kept a step ahead of the hungry times and occasionally they could barter for fripperies at the mill store: hair combs for Gran, a beaver hat for Winfield, new slippers for Delilah.

Sometimes, at the store, she would see Charles in a far doorway explaining to a slave how to count dollars in the new government money or how to measure yard goods. But she only nodded to him, and he to her, while she waited for her change. She had never seen him alone again. His face revealed nothing to her. He had stopped going to Boone's Chapel. Ann Fraley said he read English Church family prayers in his house each Sabbath.

There had been many changes at Bickley Mills. As Simon had predicted, Charles and Dickenson and General Russell had begun to fight for acreage. Each one had wanted Copper Ridge. Then General Russell had started being away very often; and Bickley Mills learned of his astonishing courting and then celebrated his marriage to Madam Campbell, a widow at Aspenvale. Russell had sold out to Charles and gone to operate new salt mines on the Holston and live at Aspenvale himself. Madam Russell, his wife was called now. His first wife, the frail woman who had always had the flush of fever on her and whose son Henry had been massacred with Jim Boone long ago, lay forgotten in the Bickley Mills cemetery. The second Madam Russell, people grinned, had taken to wearing a fur cap in winter, her voice boomed louder than ever, and Russell's was starting to boom too — in pure self-defense, more than likely. Since Charles had outbid Lawyer Dickenson in the purchase of the Russell lands Dickenson had removed himself to a tract east of the Ridge which he called Dickensonville and had started a new plantation there. Four years back, when Russell County had been created out of Washington County because the western settlements were filling up so fast in spite of the raids, Dickensonville had been made the county seat.

Charles, therefore, had all of Bickley Mills except for small farms like the Neeces' and Bushes' and Fraleys' and Sawyers' and Munseys' — and Winfields'. He needed those farms for the business of his mill; that, people grated resentfully, was why he let them stay. He had built a new house for himself and surrounded it with tiny boxwood bushes he had sent for to Lynchburg. It was a handsome house, Delilah thought, with its two large wings and half-enclosed dogtrot. Night and day his blacks guarded it from the threat of Benge's torches. They wouldn't have to, if 'Chucky Jack Sevier ever put down the Cherokees everywhere as he was always promising, and the United States government attended to the Indians in the Ohio Country as it kept promising too. Charles, Simon told Delilah when he came — watching her face so carefully she wanted to wince — was talking too now about weatherboarding and pillars. The brick for his chimneys had been made at Bickley Mills in a great firepit next to the sawmill. Day after day his workhorses had circled the pit with their stirring bar and his blacks had tended the fires and molds in the kiln. The old cabin belonged to the overlooker he had hired on a trading trip east. He was a county justice and captain of the militia; often he was away for weeks at a time.

It was Ann Fraley who talked most of all about Charles.
She would smile obliviously to Delilah ("only my pap's being beside himself that time") and finger the satin ribbons
on her cap, and go on how Charles often played on his lawn
with Johnny and Willy, his ten-year-old twins, wrestling
with them or catching their beanbags, and how he was teaching little Hatler to ride and had gotten him an English saddle and a pony, and how he had once laughed to Tim he
could do with a daughter or two. He was going to adopt a
raid orphan, Ann had heard, a girl. Always, during the
raids, he stayed with his children, trying to keep them from
hearing their mother.

"You'd think she'd get used to it," Ann sniffed. "I did."
Then she dropped her eyes. "When she looks at me, though,
I know why she's afraid." Brightening: "She's finicky in
her ways, isn't she? Tim wouldn't stand such. Looks
ganted, too. Hush, baby." Ann bent down to the cradle
beside her. "Benge will get you if you pester your mam.
She's got a visitor."

As Delilah rode home from Ann's at twilight she often
saw two little black boys shinnying up the pole of the Bick-
ely Mills plantation bell beside the gristmill to swing it back
and forth and call the field hands to their quarters. The oaks
would be sighing in the cemetery; the sentries at the fort
would be changing shifts; and one by one the candles would
begin going on in Charles's windows. Her own cabin seemed
empty when she reached it on such days, though Gran had
lit the lamps. Simon's cabin seemed empty too whenever
she went there — not often. He lived in it with two big
good-natured black and tan coon hounds, and the first time
he asked the Winfields to dinner there he teased Gran for
being pranked out in her best black gown. Afterwards De-

lilah's father began praising Simon again and decided to give him his copy of the *Farmer's Letters*, which few people bothered to read any more. Wryly, Gran told him not to waste his teaching. He needn't worry over Simon's learning. The time for that was past.

There were warmth and comfort in Simon's cabin: a fire and full grainbags and clean wooden dishes. It was all waiting, Simon told Delilah once more. It would be as safe as Sugar Hill. And she began to think at last: you can't keep faith forever with a ghost . . .

She was surprised to see Lawyer Dickenson riding up Sugar Hill one day when she was beating counterpanes in the yard. The lawyer brushed mud from his sleeves when he dismounted his cob. Inside, he sipped Gran's dittany tea for a while and ate her corncakes and made pleasant conversation about the warming weather. But at last he knitted his spiky eyebrows at Ben Winfield, cleared his throat, and announced: "I have unfortunate news for you. I warned you long ago about your title."

Winfield frowned impatiently. "Are we to go through that again? The Englishman named Smith who owns Sugar Hill? I told you I'd never give you a fee for legal tricks and I meant it. Surely Virginia's confiscated her land from England."

Dickenson answered quietly: "No. All titles stay as they were. I'm afraid Mr. Smith has done something which affects you. Letters came to the courthouse today — he's sold your mountain and Virginia's duly recorded the deed. Cornrights" — the lawyer laced his long fingers together across his rounding stomach — "unfortunately can't be read in Richmond any better than they could in Williamsburg."

17

FOR A LONG time they were silent: Dickenson, thumbs locked on his vest while he waited to see the full effect of his news; Gran, speechless half in shock and half, perhaps, in her very acceptance of a thing she had long feared; and Delilah, unable to realize yet what it might mean, this news of Richmond and England and a deed she had never really believed in.

"Who bought it?" her father asked carefully at last.

"A Frenchman." Dickenson leaned forward, straightening his wig. "Not for cash, mind. Smith traded it for a block of London real estate the Frenchman had. He's called Tubeuf — Baron Pierre François de Tubeuf. Lives in Paris. I inquired."

"Then he'll do nothing, will he?" He got up to tap out his pipe on the mantelpiece in a series of sharp blows that made Delilah wince. "It's all ridiculous, surely? For a minute I thought you were telling me the buyer was coming out here. The man's only a speculator, as Smith was."

"I said he's a baron." Dickenson leaned back. "The French rose against their nobles last summer — you heard it? They took a leaf from America's book. Their king reigns from his palace a prisoner. Courtiers can't be finding Paris very pleasant. They'd have reason to buy Virginia land."

"Impossible. A foreign aristocrat would never come to

this place. He'd have," Winfield finished with a tart laugh, "to be mad."

"You came yourself. A schoolmaster wasn't bred to the Clinch either. No," Dickenson recrossed his legs, "I think now the only thing for you to do is try to buy. I don't like this trade. It's dangerous, Smith's holding to his claim."

Slowly, Winfield sat down again. He seemed to want to steady himself as the lawyer's words sank in. It was not he who broke the silence but Gran.

"I've ten pounds saved." Her voice was empty. "All these years I've hoarded it in my trunk. It's our sugaring money — what was left after we got our axes and plows. Would he take that, do you think — the baron?" Then she smiled wistfully, as if she knew the answer. "Or do court tricks win every time?"

"You'll all have to borrow a very great deal of money, Madam." Dickenson coughed, and his cough had a dry finality in it that sent a fresh shiver through Delilah. "I can lend something, of course. You'll have to sound out everybody you know. Try for your four-hundred-acre cornright — a few hundred dollars might get that for you." Carefully, pedantically, he began explaining the fluctuating price of western land. He explained too how Virginia held land surrounding the mountain and how the baron himself held the mountain's ten thousand acres in addition to the cornright. Those ten thousand acres would demand an impossible sum whatever the current exchange rate of the dollar, whatever the value of the ground. Times had changed. No, the Winfields would have to scrape together everything they owned and then borrow more to pay merely for their clearing. If the baron did nothing else he might sell in his turn. Eventually the top of Sugar Hill would pass to somebody who intended using it to live on, unless the Winfields acted now.

"But — I could go to law. Surely I could go to law?"

"You haven't a leg to stand on. Once I told you a lawyer was needed here. Now you know why. Principles don't win a man his holdings in the end. He needs hard cash."

At supper nobody ate much. Tactfully, Dickenson had left, closing the door softly behind him. Delilah heard her father mention names vaguely, as if still dazed: General Russell on the Holston, who had led them out here; the Preston family upcountry near Brushy Mountain — they were reputed to be rich. Did she remember how Colonel William Preston had fought in Dunmore's War? Perhaps the Prestons would loan money to a veteran of it . . . And all the while Delilah knew whose name they were trying not to mention. Gran wasn't angry. Delilah had never seen her more gentle, just as if she had never warned any of this was coming. It was so long ago, the day Delilah had first gone to the lawyer's cabin with her father. Charles had been away fighting with Clark then.

It was Delilah who first spoke the name in all their minds. "Go to Charles." She swallowed after she had said it.

Winfield straightened in his chair at the head of the table. "No."

"Do you still think he was my lover, Papa?" She sighed, leaned back, and smiled sadly as she folded her napkin. There was no fear of her father in her tonight. This crisis had purged her of any fear which might have lingered. "I know we've kept from talking of what happened. But it's what's mattered most of all to us, isn't it? For eight years? I wanted him to be my lover. I have to tell you that. But he wouldn't be. Now he's our only chance."

"And you think he'd do it for *you?*" Winfield pushed back his chair, got up, and began to walk in the room, his steps echoing in its corners. Abruptly, he swung around. "By heaven, what do you take me for? Am I to go to him and say, 'Give me a fortune because you lusted for my daughter'? Am I?" He had started to shout. "Answer me!"

"What else can you do?" Her voice was quiet and tender. "There would be other words to use."

"No! I'll go west again before I crawl to Bickley! I turned him out."

"You're forgetting a thing, Ben." Gran's voice was as quiet as Delilah's had been. It seemed only to be whispering with all her seventy-four years, with the whisper of dry leaves in an autumn wind. "I'm too old" — her veined hands gestured around her — "to begin all this again."

Yet it was not Delilah's father who went to Charles Bickley. Instead, the next morning, she heard a knock at the door she knew could only be his: brief and muted, as if he were paying a casual call. How many years ago it was since he had paid calls here, and since he had lived in this house after the first raid! Bracing herself, she went to the door and let out the latchstring, stilling the trembling in her hands. When she saw him standing over her it was he who had to smile first. She couldn't help her little indrawn breath of shock. His head had gone as gray as her father's — she hadn't noticed that at the mill. Had she truly not seen him close in so long? There was a slight stoop in his shoulders. Yet he wasn't more than in his late thirties. What had happened to him? His features were still sharp-cut, his eyes bright, his mouth warmly humorous as he smiled. But in his shoulders there was a tiredness which came either from his work or his life, perhaps from both. This was the man she had loved. She had laid her head on those shoulders, drawing strength and solace from their firmness. Now he seemed a stranger as he faced her.

"Aren't you going to let me in?" His voice had changed too. It had always had a soft slur in it, but today it had a tiredness like that of his body. To think of him unhappy and weary of life sent a new stab of pain through her. *Couldn't one of us have found peace?*

Her father was as stunned at Charles's coming as she was. Gran had to begin saying the courteous commonplace things that might ease the tension nobody else could. Would he take tea? Did he fancy any cornbread or bacon? The ash chair was still too small for him . . . Those were the hands which had held Delilah Winfield and caressed her. She had dreamed of him in her loneliness and now she didn't know him when he had come to her. His eyes on her had turned wide and questioning as they searched her too. Perhaps he didn't recognize what she had become either. He leaned forward, his elbows on his knees, his hands clasped. He no longer wore a hunting shirt, but a broadcloth suit. Finally he spoke.

"This is damned awkward, Ben. Dickenson came to me last night. I've spent every minute since wondering what to say to you. Dickenson and I can manage to raise your money. We'll give you fair terms. I know what you must be thinking, but think this too — we don't want a stranger coming in. This is business, no more. I'd do the same for Tim Fraley or Jimmy Bush." The speech out, he cleared his throat, as if something he had dreaded was over.

Winfield's answer was rough. "Does your wife know you're here?"

Charles nodded. "Marie's very anxious for you to take the loan. Her life is bound up in my place as mine is." Slightly, he smiled again, and Delilah felt herself go cold. His smile seemed to be telling her that if an old happiness had turned sour he had managed to find a new one. "I've got three boys, and an orphan from the last Copper Creek raid. There's a baby on the way too. Marie and I fancy the idea of interest coming in through the years." In the silence which followed, Gran clinked spoons against plates as she washed them at the wooden sink, dipping them in the cedar bucket she had used when Charles had slept in this room.

Delilah's father laughed. "You're mad. Is my daughter part of the transaction?"

Charles sprang to his feet. "We won't drag her name into this. It's an insult to her and me, yourself too. Leave Delilah out." The ring in his voice sent a surge of pride through her even as she thought: I can't be left out. You know it as well as I do, Charles.

"I find it interesting" — slowly, her father began turning an egg-stained spoon on the table in a series of dull raps — "that your wife didn't come with you."

"She isn't well." Then Charles burst out: "Christ, you haven't changed at all, Ben! I'm here to talk price and the past is the past. Listen to me."

All Delilah's pride left her as quickly as it had come.

"It's never the past." Her father's voice was cold. "Look at my daughter. The old maid: they call her that. Once I found a flour cross a pack of children had drawn on our trace — maybe yours among 'em. I stamped it out before she saw. My daughter: the witch. If you didn't take her maidenhood you took her life. Once I looked high for Delilah, to a man like William Campbell. Now I look to Simon Oscher."

"Do you think I wanted that — what's happened?" Charles turned away, his voice tight. "Do you think I wanted what I had to bear either? But it's over. We can't change it."

What I had to bear . . . Oh, but this was private, this was between themselves. It didn't belong to anybody else. How could Charles and her father be dragging it out now and fighting over it before her very eyes? It was for thinking, not talking!

"Stop!" She hadn't meant to scream it, but she did. "You're acting as if I wasn't here and I am! Stop, both of you!" Then she covered her face with her hands and went to Gran, whose arms came around her as they had not done in years. She longed to hide her face in Gran's warm breast, herb-scented and sheltering, the way she had done as a child.

"Your diggers," Winfield charged relentlessly. "I know how you get your money. Don't think I don't. You've robbed men of everything they had to get your land. You rob children, bend their backs and dim their eyes. For what? Your kingdom? I'll have no part of it. I won't end *my* days grubbing in a forest!"

"You'd all be lost without my kingdom." Charles faced him steadily. "Some people are born to fail. I'm not. I only use the failures, use 'em honestly. It's how I've gotten what I have and I'm not ashamed. Without me they'd starve. Now I offer you my help to see you don't fail."

"I'd die before I'd take it!"

"And Delilah — what about her?"

"Stop!" she cried. "Please!" She tried to hold back her tears.

"Leave!" her father was shouting again. "I'll take my chance. I'll trust Providence, not a thief who turned his back on his wife. Get out!"

Dimly, in her misery, she heard the other angry shouts which followed. But what she knew she would never forget was the last thing Charles Bickley said in that room where he had had a pallet of his own for the winter of his early loss. He said it at the lintel, and though Delilah could not see his face she knew what fresh bitterness must be in it as the words came from him: "God help you if Benge ever kills me, Ben. You'll have to deal with my wife."

That alone told her what his life had been for eight years. Didn't it?

The Winfields took no loan from anybody. General Russell was very polite in his drawing room. He asked Delilah's father to sit on a soft upholstered chair from the Tidewater and listened gravely, and then explained as gravely that his saltworks took every penny he had. Afterwards Madam Russell had come into the room fresh from her garden, an empty seedbox in her hands. "Why, Mr. Winfield! We've a saying here, 'Never pay a lad ninepence to climb a tree and look into the middle of next week — 'tis money thrown away.' Your Frenchman's not come yet, has he?"

Perhaps nothing would happen after all (though Gran smiled a tiny smile and said it was generally the rich who advised a body not to worry over money). Perhaps Smith's title had been worthless; it hadn't been tested in a court, had it? Perhaps the Frenchman was too gullible to know it, or else he meant to swindle another Frenchman into buying it from him in turn. There could be so many things behind the sale. If they all shut their eyes to the trouble, Delilah decided, it might pass. But suddenly she began to wonder if there mightn't be a God after all, if He mightn't be punishing her for her scorn of Him. That would be fearful indeed. Perhaps, then, there was a thing she could do in her own turn to save the mountain: stop mooning, as Gran would put it, stop going over the past, start praying and repenting in earnest. All these years she had gone to Boone's Chapel acting a sham. She had taken her very Sealing Ordinances in hypocrisy. She had fed greedily on her memories of Charles. Well: now she had seen him again, and she had survived it. Perhaps it was time she thought of starting life afresh, of accepting life the way it had to be. The real Charles of today didn't even look quite like the man of yesterday she'd been conjuring up. If she turned her heart and mind ahead, not back, perhaps God would relent and give her Sugar Hill to keep. She remembered, too, couldn't help remembering, that Simon had a cabin just large enough to hold a homeless family . . . Oh, there had to be more in life than this worry eating at a body all the time! She must have the courage to do *something*. If she thought she could keep Sugar Hill the courage might even come for what she ought to do about Simon . . .

She was hardly surprised when the two preachers came to Bickley Mills. It seemed a sign.

They were curious-looking men, the preachers, in their black mud-stained cloaks and wide-brimmed hats which could not hide their sunburned faces. Mud streaked their saddlebags bulging with the books they took out to distribute, each one labeled in large gold letters HYMNS OF MR WESLEY. Was it possible, they asked, that no man of God but Parson Doak had ever dared to come here before? The

one who called himself Brother Asbury promised that if
Bickley Mills would feed and house a Methodist he would
send one to ride a circuit on the Clinch right away. It was
the English Church, sneering and scoffing at its own great
saints of God the Wesley brothers, that feared the dangers
of the overmountain lands. But he had broken off the shack-
les of that church. He was no Tory, and it took more
than heathens to frighten Methodists.

Asbury began then, on that sunny morning in the field beside the gristmill, to explain what he called the grievous
error of the Presbyterians. Salvation was not just for some
but for everybody. God would forgive anything if the sin-
ner repented. He had prepared a table where men might
come to feast on His love. He did not damn babies and send
some people straight to Hell without hearing them. "It's
heart-religion I preach!" he shouted, his voice beginning to
ring like a bell, louder and louder in Delilah's ears. "Christ
is in you all. Glory!" . . . A shudder ran through the crowd
when he had finished. A single voice throbbed out a subdued "Glory!" which died on the wind. He let his hearers
savor the silence before he began to line out a hymn from
his book:

> "Amazing grace! How sweet the sound
> That saves a wretch like me;
> For I was lost and now am found,
> Was blind but now I see."

But even while everybody sang, the old words leapt at Delilah to deny the hymn: Election. Justification. Predestina-
tion. Abomination. Adultery . . . Her father and grandmother were standing stock still on either side of her. Two

rows ahead, however, sang a woman whose red-brown hair gleamed in the sun as her body swayed back and forth, from side to side . . . Marie! Charles stood erect beside her, his hand on the shoulder of one of his boys, and Simon was near him, his voice loud and a little offkey . . . When the hymn ended people began milling around Asbury to count out pence in little clinking sounds. They questioned him in a rise and fall of voices, muttering of sanctification and repentance. Charles bent over Marie; then he made his way with authority, smiling and nodding as he swung his elbows. Marie stood apart, her pregnancy only half hidden by her cloak. Her face had lost some of its rigidity; frown lines were still creased between her eyes, but her eyes themselves were vague and she was smiling faintly. The children were clustered around her: black-haired Johnny and Willy, so like their father in their straightness, and redheaded Hatler who laughed and chattered so often at the mill half in French and half in English but who now stood obediently quiet, and the raid orphan, a blond girl in calico who hung shyly behind, her eyes fixed adoringly on Charles. Charles and Marie, together always . . . A family of one's own . . . With a jerk Delilah turned away.

As the preachers trudged up to Charles's house for the noon meal, she heard her father dryly asking Simon to Sugar Hill for their own dinner. Simon was full of Brother Asbury all the way up. Right enough, he'd gotten the miller to pledge a church. A lot of folks were saying they'd be glad to be shut of the Scotch God that only threatened them. Simon himself hadn't ever cared for Him much. The new One gave a body some reason to try to do his best. Didn't Mr. Winfield agree? Simon's eyes settled on Delilah while he waited for an answer.

"Ridiculous." Her father's clipped verdict came at last, but not nearly as violently as she had expected. At the hearth Gran set out her iron grate over the logs and began to fry a chicken in the spider, bending stiffly in her worn blue cambric gown, wincing from her rheumatism.

"Methodists converted General and Madam Russell too," Simon continued. "You heard it, sir? The General got on his knees in his own garden." The chicken sizzled at the stroke of Gran's fork. She turned to him, her knees creaking as she straightened: "I've seen many ways to the Lord myself, Simon. Mind you don't always judge a creed by its followers."

Delilah was setting out the trestle table, frowning in concentration over the number of serving spoons she would need. After a while she managed a laugh: "Maybe I ought to turn Methodist too. They seem to set less store by the past than the future."

"Heresy," her father snapped. "I forbid it for you."

Quickly Gran came to stand squarely in front of him. "Would it be her first heresy? Or are you blind to the others that have plagued this house?" Then, with a hard backward look, she returned to the spider where the chicken began sputtering furiously at every poke of her tines. "Liberty of conscience — have you forgotten why you came here, Ben?"

Winfield stared at her; then he bit his lips to hold back an answer. Simon's eyes were still on Delilah. "You're speaking truly? You'd take the new religion with me? I mean to take it, for a fact."

Carefully she put down a table fork and two spoons at her father's place, intent on their arrangement. That way she wouldn't see in her mind Charles and Marie and their children . . . No, you couldn't love anybody forever; not if

you decided not to. She'd faced Charles in this room and
now Simon was here and she was thinking of him, and how
could a body bore you by kindness and quietness? . . .
Slowly, she raised her head. How open Simon's eyes were,
how honest as always. A man to put dependence in . . .
"Of course I might take the new religion. More than
that, I — " she swallowed, "I mean to."

The silence in the room after she had spoken was punctuated only by the sound of Gran's cooking. "Do you know
what you're doing?" her father asked gravely at last. "To
cast all your life aside? All I taught you?"

"Yes. My life?" She stood rigid at his place. She heard
her next words sound in her brain even before she said them,
and she knew she would say them all the same. "I'm telling
Simon I'll marry him, Papa. His way. It's time."

18

THE ONLY person who showed much emotion at her announcement was Simon. Her father and Gran only stood silent, apparently waiting for her to say more. What more could she say? Defensively she moved closer to Simon, whose eyes were rounded, his mouth set in proud restraint.

He got out finally: "I've spoke to you before, Mr. Winfield. I reckon you might not be surprised."

"No." Dully. Even now it was cruel to see the resignation in the cast of her father's shoulders. Delilah knew she had hurt him. But she knew too she had hurt him worse before.

Gran forced her thin lips into a smile. "I think it's fine." Nervously she smoothed her apron. "We'll drink the last of the wine to it, then."

"You know I got my place. She'll have a good home, Ma'am. You've seen my place."

"Yes. It's very nice, Simon." It was Gran who toasted Delilah and Simon after the grace; and it was Gran too who explained to Simon the legal tangle over Sugar Hill. "You've a right to expect inheritance of it some day, lad. But you ought to know how matters stand with us. Mr. Winfield may yet be a schoolmaster instead of a farmer."

"We won't lose it now." Delilah refilled her wineglass.

During the meal she kept her eyes on Simon: on his stubby hands and his weathered face with its freckles, his long neck with its Adam's apple. But Simon *was* handsome in a way. He had the angularity of his Scotch-Irish mother's forebears and the fair coloring of his father's Palatine German ones. His mother cared for beautiful things like flowers, no matter how drab her work had turned her face and body. She wanted to be, in her own way, moved. His father was a hard powerful man who loved his wife and son. So emotions ran deep in the Oschers as they did in the Winfields, it might be.

Simon was still quiet when she and he walked together on the trace, his arm light on her shoulder. "I reckon you know what you've done. You said 'my way.' That means it's over — the miller."

She stopped. Do it now, she thought; kiss me; I'm ready; I know it's coming. "Yes."

But he didn't draw any closer. Instead he colored and laughed: "It goes queer. Now I've got you and I keep thinking of what's fit." He scuffed his boot in a hill of wet clay on the path. "I guess we ought to wed soon with summer coming on. They'll be things you want to do with the cabin. I got to make a house outside for the dogs, you won't want 'em underfoot."

"Oh, Simon!" She couldn't help laughing too. "That kiss you tried once — take it!"

His color deepened. He glanced back at the cabin to see if anybody might be watching. But he embraced her as gently as if she were fragile. There was nothing rough in his touch of her today. The feel of his lips on hers was not unpleasant. When he let her go he smiled self-consciously. She felt no desire for him to take her back but she was aware of warmth and affection in her heart if not her body. He did not repel her; no. It was all right. He merely did not quicken anything in her. But that, doubtless, would come. No woman, perhaps, could feel with a second man the exaltation of her love for the first. Such wildness came only once. A woman's task with the second was to watch ever for the ghost and put it down and accept what had come instead, taking gladly the gift of that for what it was.

"I better ask the miller when that circuit preacher's coming." Simon began swinging her hand in his as they walked on. "We can have Parson Doak, though, if need be. I'd like to wed you against midsummer comes."

"Do ask Charles," she said evenly, proud of herself. "You'll come back tomorrow?"

"At night, when I'm shut of the farm chores. E'er night you'll have me here." And he repeated: "It goes queer — getting you when I'd about given you up."

Her father made no further protest at her conversion — if, she thought dryly, a body could call it that — or her engagement. It was evident from an exchange of glances that he and Gran had talked it out. Gran herself repeated her congratulations formally when Delilah was alone with her for the first time. And then, with her narrow look, she asked: "You'll use the old marriage quilt?"

"I may as well." Again Delilah was proud of herself for her smile. "We ought to go down to look at the cabin once more, Gran. I can't remember what he has."

"Can't you?" Gran asked politely, her eyes narrower than ever.

So Delilah unfolded the quilt with the white dogwood stars and blue rings and golden wheat sheaves, and when she pressed a corner of it to her cheek she was sure that no one saw her do it. She hung out all her quilts in the yard to get the camphor smell out of them. She'd be using each one: Sugar Fancy, Willow Branch, and the last one she hadn't yet named, and the Star of Bethlehem Gran had made her when she'd been a child. She began to spend her days at the loom weaving tow for her sheets, and when Gran gave her rows of crocheted edging for her pillowcases she began stitching it onto them carefully and perfectly. Simon would like pretty house things. His mother hadn't many, Delilah suspected. When she went down to the Oschers' with her father and Gran she saw she was right. Their cabin was bare of everything but necessities: two tables, one bedstead, a pallet, three chairs, a few cookpots. Well, she'd give Simon the pleasure of her fancy embroidery and her quilting and weaving while she could, before the little ones came. Then, naturally, she would be bound up in the care of them. Beforehand she would make as fine a cabin for her family as she knew how, keep it swept and be sure its chinking and logs were sound everywhere so that she wouldn't have to keep brushing away flying ants. Gran never tolerated flying ants in the Sugar Hill cabin, though she spoke of slatternly women who did in theirs. In time these ants ate clear through a house and it fell like a pile of rotten sticks. Such was a disgrace to any housewife.

"Mind you keep your hearth swept," Gran advised. "I mind a bride who had mice nesting in her hearth, so busy she was thinking about other things." Gran smiled a secret smile. "I suppose I needn't worry with you." Her smile stiffened.

A welcome peace came to Delilah in these days of the spring while the crabtrees bloomed around her. She had repented of her sins and was giving Simon what he wanted. Now God would reward her. It surprised her that she still loved her father so much. She had thought she hated him when he had come upon her and Charles; but he had cried out his accusation in love of her after all, in fear for her. It saddened him that she was settling for Simon. She could see it.

"Papa — I'm sorry." While he sat hunched over the hearth and his face looked so worn in the long light of the flames, she took his callused hand and spoke the inadequate words, bending over his shoulder. He looked up at her, studying her.

"Are you?" he asked at last. He didn't smile; mostly now he smiled in battle, perhaps thinking it was the one thing he could do well. "I'm sorry too, my dear. We've seemed to be at cross purposes for years, haven't we? Now you deny even the faith I taught you. But never mind. Do you care at all for Oscher? I hope so." He leaned back in his tall chair and closed his eyes. How old he looked! He had had gray hair ever since Delilah could remember; Gran said he'd had it in his twenties. He was only in his fifties now. But his cheeks were sinking in — why hadn't she noticed that? His eyelids bulged on each side of a nose growing hawklike, and from the corners of his mouth hard bitter lines ran down to his jaw. "I killed Reynard," he said tonelessly. "For your sake. You must believe it if you can. I — I buried him. It wasn't easy. I've always tried to care for you."

She was hardly surprised, only relieved to know — at last. Still she pressed his hand, but if he felt it he gave no sign. She could hear the thump, thump! of Gran's loom from the room beyond, and the sputtering of the fire close by. "You cared for my mother too."

"Yes. She was my faith once. I paid for it." He didn't move. "It was wrong. I see that now. And you're formed as I was. I tried to fight that evil in you, tried to spare you. The flesh is a terrible burden. And yet" — his eyes opened, and they were bewildered as he looked up at her — "there must be something between a husband and a wife. You can — can endure the thought of Oscher, can you?" His voice had sunk so low she could barely hear him.

"Yes." She knelt beside him. "I can put dependence in him. And I didn't believe in anything at all before. Maybe," she lied to comfort him, "I'll come back to your faith. Meanwhile I need this one."

He patted her hand, sighing. "Your grandmother told me. I suppose I'd known."

"I'm praying again — that you'll keep Sugar Hill. I think — now — you can."

The Methodist preacher's name was Brother Whitaker and he was coming to live in Bickley Mills by mid-June. From there he would ride his circuit as far down as Fort Blackmore. His congregation would throw up a log house for him and the Bickley blacks would begin a second church. His first wedding would be that of Simon Oscher to Delilah Winfield. That would be fine, Mrs. Oscher smiled to Delilah. That would be a good start, surely. Was Delilah's grandmother preparing for the infare? Had she enough flour left for tarts and pasties? It would be a large infare because Simon had many friends: the Bush boys, the Sawyers, the Fraleys, Peter Munsey and Tivis English, the rest. Delilah mustn't remember the old gossip about herself, the whispers. Mrs. Bickley had been a mean one right enough, with her sly little hints of witch; but now she'd been

Saved, and they must forget what she'd done. She'd got religion sure enough. Mrs. Oscher didn't believe for a second that Delilah and the miller had ever taken a look at each other. Poor Henry Neece had never really got over what had happened to Ann. Ann had used to have fits; did Delilah know it? They'd stopped, though, since she married.

"You'll have things different from what I had," Mrs. Oscher went on dreamily while she mended her husband's buckskin leggings with a length of rawhide. Her fingers were pitted from the stabs of her needle. She had no thimbles or gloves. "You'll have a plot o' your own from the first. You never knowed what it was to be indentured and bound, neither. I'm glad for you, honey. Some day I'll show you how to stitch with this rawhide. I'll stay a day over, if it don't misput you. I guess you never worked deerskin for your gran."

At the mill Delilah stopped to buy a yard of blue ribbon at the store. She held it up before the slave boy behind the counter to examine it in the ray of light streaming from a high loophole. It was watered silk, right enough; well, she had a few pennies saved for pretty things. She had always wanted some for her bridal day.

"You must not pay us for it." The voice was Marie's. Quickly Delilah turned to see her coming into the room from the back. "We will give you another wedding present, but take this from us now — from me. My husband is much pleased with your news." She smiled. It was hard to say whether she meant her smile or whether it hid a malice so deep it could not be seen in her eyes either.

"Thank you." Delilah moved toward her; it was best to swallow her pride. "Are you well?" Marie's baby must be coming very soon; Marie always looked grotesque in pregnancy because she was so small. In her face the lineaments of her old prettiness remained, but a network of tiny lines covered her skin and while Delilah could not be sure she wondered if her lips and cheeks weren't faintly touched with the carmine powder she had once seen lying on the counter in a tiny packet.

"I am well." Marie's smile had always been fixed. "Walk with me."

Near the millpond they stopped in the same patch of snapweed where Delilah, at twelve, had begged Charles Bickley not to take her father to war.

"Do not think I am stupid." Marie straightened, brushing a speck of sawdust from the gray sleeve of her frock. "I know it is not easy for you to marry Oscher. But you do it even so. It will be easier if I tell you Charles does not care any more and scarce remembers. I've always known you wanted him. It was hard for him too once; not now. He loves *me*. That will help you."

"Marie, we'd best not — "

"You will please listen to what I tell you." Marie's voice hardened, the color of her lips and cheeks garish in the sun as she drew closer. "I have a weakness. I hate it as you do, as Charles did before he could understand. It was fear I had when I saw his wound, not disgust. You never bore children while savages cried and the shooting went on and all the time the pain was so great you could not help what you did. You never had the shame of such a thing — for your husband to see you so. I cannot stop what happens to me in my mind when I am afraid. My father was killed by savages. I cannot forget that either. For years you tried to take my husband by using my fear. But he is happy now. And" — her voice fell, as if all the energy of her outburst had left her

— "I find I do not hate you any longer, because he loves me."

A shower of white petals fell from a nearby crabtree. A mockbird trilled from the woods.

"You're right," Delilah said at last. "It helps to know." She held out her hand. It was steady. Firmly Marie took it. Then she turned back toward the mill, where Delilah could hear one of her children shouting for her to come: "Maman!" She thought it might be Johnny. He was old enough not to cry but only shout loud that way if he needed her. Soon she herself would have a boy of her own. Marie was right. She had made everything much easier. But Delilah wished she had seen the last of her all the same, and feared she hadn't. She would have liked to cast away her guilt, her pity, her resentment, forever.

They were full of the smell of the crabtrees, those nights Simon came up the mountain to court her. The atmosphere of May, heady and warm, began to envelop them both. At first they stayed in the cabin while she showed him her linens and her blue and cream-color towels, her cookpots and the infare gown she was making of bright blue cotton that Simon said matched her eyes. Gran wouldn't show her the wedding gown she was stitching every night by the betty-lamp after Delilah had gone up to the loft. Simon said he was sure it would be a fine one. But soon he and Delilah grew restless in the house. The world seemed at once permanent because there had been other years of May, and impermanent because this May so soon must pass. Deeper and deeper into the woods they walked together, heedless of any danger, he speaking of his plan of raising blooded cattle and horses some day, and of his hope to give her everything she could ever want. Her wants were modest, for a fact, untroubling and so doubly important to him.

One night as they walked a painter screamed close by. Instinctively Delilah thrust herself against him. She had always hated painters so! The warmth of the darkness turned cold. She clung hard. At first he held her as if to soothe her, but then his breath started to come faster. His arms tightened. Briefly he held her suspended as if every muscle in him had frozen. When he began to bear down on her, she stiffened as he had done. It had been so foolish, to throw herself at him from fear, to break the peace of the night. But she mustn't flinch. She was going to be his wife. She made herself relax, concentrating first on her mouth, then the tendons of her neck, then her upper arms and forearms and wrists, untying each part. What were the words he was trying to say? That he loved her? She knew it, but she listened. It was amazing, how little stiffness was left in her. She had banished it all by will, knot after knot. She let him speak of his love because she owed it to him. He had been the truest person in her life and she wanted to make him happy for that.

"Delilah, honey — " His hoarse voice came to her as from an infinite distance. Had he disarranged her hair? She put her hand to a curl and smoothed it surreptitiously. When he drew her down to the mossy ground, gently and carefully for all his tautness, she whispered: "Wait." For she wanted just to arrange her skirt so that it wouldn't wrinkle. The green gown she wore had ever been hard to press out, being mostly woolsey.

Abruptly he let her go. His breath seemed now to be all the sound there was left in the night, though dimly she heard the distant river. He was peering at her. Even without a moon she could see the shadow of him against the faint glow of the starlit sky.

"Simon?" she tried. "It was only my gown."

He sprang to his feet. "You could think of your *gown?* I thought you wanted — "

She reached up to him but he didn't help her get to her own feet. "Maybe it's best, now, not to — "

"You *lied!*" he charged her. "You've lied all along! Why don't you shout 'beast' at me the way you did once? Or have you got so far you can just stand me? Are you that brave, Delilah? It's a wonder! So brave you'll even wed me? Say it! It's true."

"Hush! It isn't!"

"You lied," he repeated, his voice steadying. "You think I don't see. I love you and I deserve better than your pretending." When she caught his sleeve he shook her away. "Don't. There's no need. What did you want of me, then, to take me?"

"Please understand! It's not my way to be — "

"Babies of your own?" he cut in savagely.

"I don't love him!" she cried out.

"Don't you? You surely don't hanker for me." Far in the distance the painter screamed again. Now the sound was hardly believable above the croaking of the frogs and the running of the river and Simon's breathing and her own. He turned, finally, and began walking away from her.

"Stop!" she begged. Again he shook her off.

"I don't want a brave woman." He swung around to face her again. "I don't want a dutiful one. That's the way of it with you and I won't have such. I'll go away. I'll sell out in Bickley Mills and I'll go anyplace where you'll be shut of me for good. Kentuk, it may be, Tenase, I don't know. I'll start as soon as ever I can."

"You're stupid! Because I tried to save a gown you — "

"Because you acted like you'd forgotten everything but

me and you hadn't. Because you lied." Through the darkness she saw the hatred burning in his eyes. She couldn't
help flinching.

"I wanted to forget him!" she pleaded when they had
come to the clearing's edge. "I did! I'd have been different
after, I know it."

"You wanted," his voice scratched at her. "But you
couldn't."

She couldn't believe he was leaving her, either. Yet she
saw him tramp carelessly across the field full of young
wheat stalks heedless of its rows and stakes. She saw him
disappear over the rise beyond the cabin, his steps dying
away on the trace. The wind came up full of her father's
orchard, and she breathed it in naturally before it brought
the memory of Simon's embrace in the woods when she had
smelled blossoms too . . .

Once more she was alone. How could that be, when she
had schooled herself to think of life with Simon, caring for
him well and tenderly to the end of his days? She was not
frightened. She was only sorry for him. Kentucky! Exile,
when she might later have loved him more. He would give
up everything he had simply to escape her. She had never
dreamed him capable of such quick hate, had never
dreamed what passion had underlaid the loyalty she had
found so comforting.

Overhead, the trees stirred. Above their jagged tops she
could see the constellations of the Chair and the Polestar
blinking softly down on Sugar Hill. Why, she wanted to
cry out suddenly, did everybody and everything she loved
have to come to trouble? Why did her loving twist people
and then lose them to her forever, so that she could give
them nothing at all?

IV

"The army were marched in a body, but I do not remember the year. I remember only the unusual number of successive hard frosts without any intervening bad weather."

—*Charles Bickley*

19

A̶FTER Simon Oscher had left Delilah nearly on the eve
of their wedding ("jilted," she knew people said behind her
back) the cabin he had built for her stood empty.

"It's bad luck, that house is." "Raised for a bride that
ne'er came to it. I'd not admire to live there." "It's a ghost
place, built for a thing that ne'er happened." Delilah could
hear in her mind the low voices of the women. "Why did
he go?" "You reckon Henry Neece was right that time —
you reckon she's truly a witch, and Simon learned such?"
Mrs. Oscher herself, bewilderment and pain in her eyes, had
first reported these sayings. Why had it happened, she
had asked? What *had* happened? Simon had only muttered
"It wouldn't be right between Delilah and me, Ma'am,"
and had left forever, his rifle Sairey in his hand and a stout
pack on his cob. Four years ago, now; it might have been
four lifetimes ago. Once a peddler passing through Bickley
Mills brought a note which Brother Whitaker, the circuit
preacher, had read to the Oschers. The note had been from
the Illinois Country; it had said Simon was well and strong,
and was building himself another house on a Clark grant
he'd bought from an old militiaman, and he believed this
house would be lastier than the first he'd made . . . You
took my son, Mrs. Oscher's eyes accused Delilah all the

while her voice dully and evenly reported the facts of Simon's distant living.

Briefly, Delilah smiled. "His cabin here is lasty too." And she added lamely: "We — we quarreled. Please don't ask me about it."

Doubtless Mrs. Oscher had repeated the tale of a quarrel. It explained her own loss, at least. Ann Fraley, full of questions she was too tactful to press, told Delilah Mrs. Oscher always loyally denied Delilah was a witch. So, for a wonder, did Marie Bickley deny the rumor she herself had begun. Once Ann had heard Marie at the gristmill when she had broken into a knot of gossiping women. She had told them to hush their talk. Miss Winfield was not happy, and it was not kind to dwell on her unhappiness, whatever had brought it about. She, Marie, had grown to have a pity for her. To be jilted was a hard thing . . . Delilah had blushed hotly as Ann repeated those words to her. She had wanted to cry back: But *he* loved me once! She knew she couldn't.

She did not stop going to the church. It was an increasing comfort to her, Simon's religion — hers, she could call it too now. It helped, to think somebody could forgive you even if you couldn't forgive yourself. Sometimes, in the periods of silent prayer when the chapel was hushed and lanky Brother Whitaker stood at the front with his balding head bowed, his rifle propped against the pulpit, she would see Simon's face before her as she had so often seen it: the steadfast eyes and serious straight mouth. I gave you my trust as long as I could, the vision's lips moved soundlessly; remember it. Try to remember that.

In those first years after his going she busied herself on Sugar Hill. She tried not to snap at her father and grandmother during the long winters they were cooped up together in the cabin. She tried to be efficient, not to forget bread loaves in the hearth when she was remembering what she ought not to be remembering. Every year Gran's rheumatism grew a little worse, so she had to take over more of the cooking, all of the gardening in the herb and vegetable patches, and any cleaning that required bending or reaching. This was not spoken about between herself and Gran; Gran hated admitting her weakness. As it was, Gran took to making sassafras brooms and spinning and weaving almost constantly. She would never give up her sitting jobs unless she had to — and of that time, Delilah did not want to think. Then Gran might need a doctor, and the nearest one would be two hundred miles away at Lynchburg. Gran's dark eyes still sparkled in her seamed face. She still chuckled when Delilah tried making jokes, and her voice was as steady as ever. No, Gran's increasing stiffness and the threat of losing Sugar Hill were two things always pushed out of the lives of Ben Winfield and Delilah and Gran herself as long as they could be.

Once, Delilah couldn't help asking: "You knew everything, Gran — Charles and me?"

Slowly, Gran raised her face from the reed basket she was plaiting. Her thin hands became still. She nodded. "But you ask me now? Is he still so much in your mind?"

Delilah bit her lip. "I think, that's all."

Slightly, Gran smiled. "I'm not a fool. I know why Simon left you. You were a good play-actress but not good enough. I respect him for it — so should you." She leaned back in her chair, closing her eyes, her lids spotted with tiny flecks of brown.

"You blame me." Delilah held her hands at her side, her

fingers tight on the wet cloth she was using to scrub the table.

Gran opened her eyes quickly. "For your wrong. Never for what you are." There was comfort in the paradoxical gentleness of her deep gaze, the intensity of pride and care in it. "Only for what you do."

With that, Delilah had to be content. But all the same she knew she had been hateful to Gran the day she had seen Charles and Marie coming back to Bickley Mills from Lynchburg, where they had been visiting his father. They had been riding splendid new Arab horses with Mercury behind them, and two packhorses and three wagons carrying house plunder they had gotten themselves back east. Their children had all rushed out to meet them: Johnny and Willy, Hatler, Lisbet the baby, and the orphan girl too. Black Silvey had been clucking at the children to keep them back, but even Lisbet had run on her stocky legs and cried out "Papa!" and Charles had lifted her up, laughing . . . That night on the mountain Delilah had nearly screamed at Gran when Gran had been sweeping crumbs: "You're so slow, let me do it! We'll never be finished at this rate."

"I'm sorry," Gran answered coldly, drawing herself up and laying aside her broom. "You're right, of course. I am slow."

And then the fresh tears, the useless apologies, and Gran holding her close and saying: "Hush, hush, I know . . ."

That had been near the end of their time together on Sugar Hill. For Baron de Tubeuf finally had come to the Clinch as Dickenson had predicted. The Winfields after all had to leave the cabin they had built and the land they had cleared to cross the river to Bickley Mills. Ben Winfield was shocked into reality at last. Dickenson could do nothing to help him. It had not been easy, moving into Simon's empty cabin and starting a school there. The school fees would pay the Oschers for it. These days when she saw Mrs. Oscher Delilah tried to keep her head up with what tattered pride she had left. But she knew the women were whispering more than ever, that even the children giggled sometimes when she left her classroom. Worst of all she knew Marie Bickley herself still pitied her. Once when she bought a packet of indigo from Marie at the store Marie said softly as she counted out Delilah's change: "It is too much — to lose your home too."

The Baron had not seemed real when Delilah was still on the mountain; he had seemed only the old threat, lived with and therefore capable of being dismissed. But his documents, his train of Frenchmen, his young son, his trunkful of gold and the snake-proof hip boots which were all he had for life on the Clinch: these had all become abruptly real when Delilah saw them for herself. Her father's dull stare, then his squared shoulders and his resolve to keep himself by doing what he had done long ago: these had been real too. Even now she could see the Baron's face as he had told of the mobs which had driven him from his Paris house with their torches. It was a stern face, white with powder, arrogant and delicately cut. His cheeks were high, his eyes narrow and appraising. He expected submission. His face even more than his deed to Sugar Hill had sealed the Winfields' defeat. For the Baron had a power Delilah had known in one other man, Charles. The cool voices of such men, the way they stood, the appropriate and even charming condolences they could bring out while they were taking something from you: these things were the essence of that power. In his banishment the Baron merely demanded new homage of new people. He took what he could get in a wilderness. Somehow he made men work for him and for his settlement planned to be a haven for his friends: Sainte-Marie-on-the-Clinch, he called it, "in honor of the Blessed Virgin who has saved my life." The Governor of Virginia had himself loaned him money for the scheme.

And somehow — because the Baron and his men had been watching — Delilah had ridden erect down the mountain the last time without so much as a sigh. All summer afterwards she spent trying to find places for everything in a house far too small to hold her father's and grandmother's and her own goods: books, cookware, clothing and piggens and egg cups and hair combs. She spent nights bending over the volumes her father had told her she would need to use when she helped him. The dry pages of *Newtonianism for Ladies* rattled as she turned them biting her lip, hating them, thinking of nights on the mountain now called Sainte Marie. She made herself a red calico gown and soon the children appeared calling her father "Schoolmaster" and herself "Mistress" and Gran "Ma'am." The gown dared those children to call her anything else to her face, at least. It became her banner.

But she loved the children from the first; even when, with unconscious cruelty, they told her how Baron de Tubeuf was commandeering Bickley and Dickenson slaves for more clearing and building the widest road and the biggest chimneys on the Clinch: how he paid his day workers in Spanish gold: how he'd paid the special militia the Governor had sent him against Benge in the same heavy gold pieces and then screamed at them in a foreign tongue when they had left him to garrison a fort downriver. She could forgive the children all their gossip, for she found to her surprise that it pleasured her to teach them as much as it had pleasured her to make quilts. It was the same: you watched a thing grow, and had a part in it, and put yourself into it at the same time it turned into something in its own self. She taught the girls all the more simple stitches she knew — the cross and feather and butterfly and backstitches — and watched them try their first clumsy towels and pothooks. To some of the boys she taught penmanship. Her father taught the slowest ones, half the time shouting at them and the other half clapping them on the back to praise their grubby attempts at letters. Her own scholars were the ones who could practice by themselves.

The Bickley boys held themselves somewhat apart. Hatler Bickley, who was ten, spent his time sullenly copying the latin verbs her father had given him. Often he stared out the window, running a stubby hand through his mop of red hair: wanting perhaps, like his father, to be in the fields. Willy scratched at ledger pages. Johnny, his twin, was clever for thirteen, and as the days passed he grew more talkative. He had an engaging smile that sent a pang through her, so like Charles's old one it was. He had heard nothing, then . . . Johnny wanted to learn everything he could about mathematics and machines. When he grew up he'd help his father build newer and bigger mills. He meant to learn surveying too. His father had bought tracts in Kentucky and Illinois because Willy and Hatler might want them when they grew up. At tax time his father grew very gruff, and you had to be careful what you said to him. Only Lisbet, the baby, could get round him then. Mamma never tried; but he always knew anyhow what Mamma wanted, and he gave it to her.

Stop it!

"How interesting, Johnny. Land in the west? No, I didn't know."

Among the girls, the orphan Charles had adopted also chattered heedlessly of what life was like at the Bickley house. She'd learned to bake her first cake a few days before. It had been a mite heavy, but "Papa" had said it was very tasty. Whenever he had time he read aloud to them all from books he'd brought back from Lynchburg from Grandfather's house. Once when she had had a nightmare he had stayed with her until dawn. He had heard her screaming, and he'd sat beside her in his old woolsey robe and tried to tell her that her dream didn't mean anything bad was going to happen. It only showed what had happened to her already. He had talked a long time, his voice very low, and kept his hand in hers as if he had nothing else in all the world to do. She'd promised him at last she wouldn't be afraid any more. That wasn't true, but she knew it pleasured him to hear it. Did Mistress Winfield ever have nightmares? "Papa" said they weren't things to be ashamed of. What mattered was what you did, he said, not the fancies you had that you couldn't help.

During the school hours Gran generally sat silent, close by the fire. Sometimes, when Delilah looked up from her book, she would see Gran's head nodding in its stiffly starched cap. It was a mercy that the "hard winter" had been so many years ago; for at seventy-seven, as Gran was now, she might not have endured it. Life on the wrong side of the river was settling slowly into its new tasks. In spite of his loss her father seemed happy enough, for he was doing what he had planned to do with his life before "the Trouble." Delilah helped him oil pinewood for bookshelves and could even smile with him about the cabin's lack of space, and when he teased her in turn about her red gown and then told her it became her she could flush with pleasure. "I suppose I always knew," he told her wryly once. "About the mountain, I mean. I don't keep things well, my dear." And the children continued to prattle breathlessly to Delilah about the Baron, sure of her consuming interest. They told her about his new grindstone, his axes and his latest messages to the governor, his trunkful of gold. He'd clink the little pieces for a body if he had time, and smile to think a body hadn't seen gold before . . . It was Tim Fraley who stopped by on a sharp winter night to tell her the Baron and his Frenchmen had all been bludgeoned to death by thieves. The Baron's young son had hidden in her father's old sheep pen and then escaped down the trace, and a maidservant had been drowned trying to swim the Clinch for help. Tim and Charles Bickley had found the dead men . . . Oh, it was a fearful thing, how far the talk of the gold must have spread . . . And as Delilah listened to Tim she thought to herself in all her shock: there's still a house on Sugar Hill but it's not the Baron's. There isn't any Sainte Marie. He couldn't keep it either . . . Later she realized she could scarcely remember the sound of the Baron's voice. Again he wasn't real. He wasn't real even when she saw the stone which Bickley slaves placed beside the tallest sugar tree in what had been her dooryard:

Here lie Pierre François de Tubeuf, César Lefebre, Eusèbe de la Planche, Simon Perchet . . .

"So?" Gran raised her brows. "But we still can't go home to the land of the French boy. That's real enough, is it not?"

20

Nobody called the mountain Sainte Marie after the murders. But Bickley Mills began to whisper that Sugar Hill was surely cursed. Hadn't the hornets been building their nests low in the bushes there? Hadn't there been too many fogs on the slopes? Oh, a heap of signs had been ready for the reading.

"You're well off the place, Delilah." Ann Fraley shuddered. "Think what might have happened to *you*." Lawyer Dickenson had posted a large reward for the murderers, but they hadn't been found yet. Even so, almost immediately Delilah's father began to talk of trying to buy back Sugar Hill on credit from the Baron's son, who was staying with Charles Bickley.

"I've my teaching fees now," Winfield said hopefully. "We could at least try for the four hundred acres we cleared."

"Wouldn't you teach any more if you got them back, Papa?"

"Afraid I'd take you from the children?" He smiled. "Yes, my dear, I'd teach. I doubt if I could stop again. But all the same I'd like to leave this cabin to go home at night. Sugar Hill is mine, and it was meant for you. It was to be yours," his mouth twisted, "and your children's."

But when Delilah rode into Dickensonville with him she learned Charles had already begun procedure for the legal adoption of the French boy and was trying to arrange with his trustees to buy the mountain. As Dickenson announced it matter-of-factly, she heard through her own astonishment her father's cry: "My God, he can't! He wouldn't dare."

"The boy has no one, Winfield." Dickenson leaned back in his chair. "He's but fourteen. The trustees are far away. It's best."

"It's a ruse!" Winfield rasped. "Homeless orphan, my foot! Don't you see it? Bickley's going to work round that boy and coddle him until he defrauds him. You can't sit there and say you'll let it happen!"

Dickenson smiled. "I thought you had small use for courtroom tricks."

"I've small use for thieves — Bickley's stealing from a child!"

"Even when the child swears he wants no part of the mountain where he saw his family killed?"

A year ago, even many years ago in the time of Charles's love for her, Delilah might have believed he truly was stealing the land. But she remembered now the picture the orphan girl in his house had given her: a man in a woolsey robe comforting a nightmare-ridden child in her room, sitting there with her to ease her of her fear. That man could not steal, could he? Delilah tightened her fingers in her lap. The near-certainty filled her even as Dickenson explained to her father that he could not interfere. She longed to cry out he needn't, that she believed; but she knew it would only roughen her father's heavy breathing and goad him into worse anger than he felt already. And in her ears, too, whispered nameless voices: the Cowans. Long ago they were the first to leave, in the early days of the war. Remember the sang-diggers in the hollow behind Red Oak Ridge; remem-

ber the line of them that day near the blacksmith's shanty.
Remember what Charles said, "I only use the failures, and
use 'em honestly." Remember how he's built Bickley
Mills . . . He wouldn't take Sugar Hill, answered her
heart. Not unless . . . unless he might want to sell it back.

For she wanted Sugar Hill herself. The Winfields had
shaped it into order long before the Baron had built his road
and chimneys. She knew too it would take her father years
to pay for the mountain and that Charles could buy it in an
hour. Was he going to begin sugaring next winter in the
very bush where he had taught her how to boil sap? Or
might he, one day, consent to sell the mountain to Ben Winfield? She hardly dared to hope it, but began to believe it
might be true. She had to find out. Charles had talked of
debts when her father had sheltered him, when Gran had
nursed him. Maybe he meant to pay those debts.

Johnny Bickley was delighted the following afternoon
when she said she would go home with him. He'd be proud
to have his teacher for tea. Toward the west as she walked
up the path from the schoolhouse the soft winter light
touched the peaks of Sandy Ridge. When Johnny left her in
the parlor to find his father she sat gingerly back in a high
wing chair. The house was soundless. As the minutes
passed she began to stare around the room. How it had
changed since she had seen Charles's older parlor! Her eyes
caught gleams of silver everywhere: candelabra, sconces,
bowls. There was a streak of gold on a table: the edging on
a thin china plate. Surfaces were polished to a sheen.
Trained slaves must have hewed out these tables and chairs
of pine and cherry at the mills. The owner of this room cared
for his possessions. She realized then that her feet were resting on a real rug, not a braided or hooked makeshift but a
Turkey carpet such as she had not seen since Williams-

burg. At the windows, long gold hangings stirred in the draft: moreen. The walls had been painted white, the chinking plastered over so that they were smooth and unflawed. The floor at the edges of the rug was burnished with polish. The bright and improbable vision was before her. How could there be forests beyond, with thieves and savages to roam them? But there were. And even so, Charles Bickley dared to fling his challenge. And perhaps he would need all the land he could get to make it good . . .

When he came in, alone, he smiled a quizzical smile at her, but she couldn't imagine any contact with him closer than the handshake he gave her. Even when he did that she shivered a little from the strangeness of it. When she looked up at him she saw that his mouth was softer than it had used to be, its seam less marked. Perhaps that was because he was so obviously puzzled. At once she felt silly. What could she really do here? He wouldn't care for what her father wanted. He'd offered a loan only when he himself hadn't had a chance at Sugar Hill.

"I take it you did want to see me without Johnny?"

"I've come to ask you a thing." She cleared her throat.

"It sounds serious." He sat down opposite her. "I remember when you came to do that before." Think of the mill, and your first times here, he was warning her. Not afterwards. "Johnny? The school?"

She tightened her hands in her lap, staring at the figured red of her gown as she shook her head. "My father's saying things about your buying the mountain."

"Ah. So that's it. He would, of course. And you've come to plead for him."

"Yes." She could not look at him. "Some day, when he has more money, I thought — "

"Go on, Delilah." He had leaned forward.

"You're not robbing the French boy. I know that." She almost whispered it. Oh, she was mad to have come, and she was saying all the wrong things! But she had to finish what she had begun, so she swallowed: "You'll be fair. But some day, if you could be fair to my father too, if you could let him buy Sugar Hill from you because he wants it so much, I — "

Slowly, emphasizing each word, he answered her: "I'll never sell it to him, Delilah."

She raised her head. He was making a temple of his fingers as he leaned back. Dumbly, she stared at him while the light fell across the dark broadcloth of his breeches. His legs were hard and muscular. The white stock at his neck was neatly starched. It accentuated the tan of his face and throat. He looked impressive, remote, immovable.

"I'll never sell it to your father," he repeated deliberately. "He had better know it."

She could not speak.

And then, inexplicably, almost tenderly, he smiled again. "You trust me about the French boy. Can I ask you to trust me to be fair to your father too? But in my own way?"

"It's Sugar Hill he longs for," she stammered miserably at last. "You know he does. There is no other way."

"He couldn't pay for it, my dear. Ever." Then his voice turned rough. "Please go." He rose abruptly, wondering even as he stared at her sad, drawn face that she did not know what he himself was feeling . . . She could not, of course: Delilah in her unlikely red gown, Delilah of the haunting eyes and breathless questions and waiting mouth that was red too now, though it waited no more . . . He said: "It's no use. I have to tell you I can't — "

But just as he started to tell her what more he couldn't do Delilah heard Marie's light step. When Marie came into the room she stopped in surprise. For a moment she stood irresolute; then she smiled the smile of a hostess and turned to her husband. A frown line came between her eyes. "The overlooker was here just now. The diggers are packing the sang with whiteroot again and one of the gears is jammed at the gristmill."

"Delilah's just leaving." Charles's voice was as smooth as it had been grating a minute before. "She came to inquire after young Tubeuf."

"Charles! I — "

" — offered to help us with his care, and I've told her you give him enough of your own time, my dear, he'll soon be ready to go down to the school."

"How kind of her." The line between Marie's eyes deepened. "Will you go to the mill or shall I? I think it will be the same gear that failed last week. The men are stupid about a simple shaft pin."

Charles gave his wife his old grin, boyish and wide, as if he had not been lying at all. "Try. Maybe you'll put some starch into 'em where I can't."

Firmly, Marie nodded, the curls bobbing at the neck of her gray gown. Those youthful curls were an incongruous frame for her shrewd preoccupied face. Charles had lied to spare her, no doubt. How he must hate me! Delilah thought. And he must hate Papa too — enough to be glad he can refuse him . . . . She felt a fresh tinge of revulsion toward Marie, for surely it was she who had caused such hatred. Charles had never been vengeful. Yet Marie had been kind once or twice, it was odd . . . Delilah would have to walk with her as far as the cabin, for it was on the way to the mill.

"I'll remember your coming," Charles said as he helped

Marie and then Delilah with their cloaks. "Thank you." But Delilah didn't answer him.

Outside, the ground was dry and frozen hard. It had been a strange winter without snow, she murmured to ease the tension she felt.

"Yes, one sees the tracks of the horses from days before but not one's own. We have commenced hauling corn." Marie's mind was evidently miles away.

"Marie, I wanted to know — " Delilah broke off.

"Of course," Marie said evenly. "The boy. But I speak his language, you understand."

It was an afternoon of perfect stillness. The very flutter of dry leaves was startling when it came, and the whistle of a titmouse and its far-off answer were startling too. In the crisp cold the sounds were magnified what seemed like a thousand times. Once a jay screeched. Delilah drew her cloak more closely around her, trying to think of something else to say. They were walking silently, two women who possessed an uneasy understanding of one another that was masked as surface friendliness. The titmouse whistled again, and again was answered. It was just as she and Marie neared the cabin that she saw the shadow of a man at its side. The outline of the roached head on the sunlit ground betrayed it as the shadow of an Indian. It did not move.

Even as she stopped still to put a hand gone rigid on Marie's arm, even as she concentrated on not screaming but only waiting, she could not believe what she saw. This was winter! Indians never came in winter! But the Indian was there. Inside the cabin were her father and Gran. Their guns would not be handy. The Indian was waiting to strike them, and she could not prevent it. The world began to swim before her eyes. She was aware of Marie frowning at her, puzzled, and knew the moment Marie guessed the trouble they themselves were both lost. If she and Marie stole away they at least might have a chance . . .

She swallowed. "I — I thought I saw something." Stupid! What she saw was Ann Fraley, lurching toward the fort gate long ago . . . Her throat went dry. Again she let her eyes look at the shadow. It had not moved. Why was it standing as still as herself for so long? In a moment it would surely go inside, would kill her father and Gran in a few swift strokes and they would scarcely know what was happening until the tomahawk fell. Then the mills would burn as they had burned before, what had happened then would happen again . . . She could try to fool Marie and hide with her. Or she could let her scream and then try dragging her to the fort and ringing the bell and warning everybody. But how many Indians were unseen, close by?

The whistle of the titmouse sounded again, and she knew this time it was no bird. The jay's screech answered from the shadow. A raid, nobody armed or in the fort . . . She and Marie might be shot where they stood the minute Marie cried out, but that would make a noise . . . Drawing a deep breath, Delilah told her: "There's an Indian by my cabin, Marie. Look."

Marie did scream; her hand flew to her cloak pin; but her screams soon died in her throat. Her eyes went wide and vacant, her face pasty-white. The sound was just enough for the shadow to spring into view.

"Run!" Delilah shouted at her then. "To the fort — the bell — run!"

But Marie didn't move until Delilah clutched her arm and began pulling her. Soon both women were running swiftly, stumbling over the rough ground toward the hill where the stockades of Fort Bickley stood empty. The Indian was in close pursuit; Delilah could hear his leggings flapping as he ran. She tried to scream herself but she couldn't find breath to do it. Her feet carried her still faster over the tufts and stones of the ground, and though she was digging her fingers into Marie's arm she knew Marie was running as swiftly, all her own terror in the lightness of her feet. As shots began to ring out Delilah could hear bullets whistling over both their heads. Faster! she wanted to urge. As she had taken the Indian from her father's door she believed beyond a doubt she would reach the fort. She had to! Nothing else was possible! She stumbled on, the pain beginning to throb down her side, and Marie stumbled with her. Over there was the Fraley cabin, its logs bulking silent in the winter light. No one was stirring from it. Where were the Sawyers, the Munseys, the Bush family, the Duncans? On and on Delilah ran, the bullets whizzing past as she pulled up her skirt higher from her ankles and heard it rip. Then she heard whoops and saw Indians swarming down from a thicket of oaks. Only when she saw they had closed around her did she understand she could not possibly get through. Still her legs believed in safety; they were running as crazily as Marie's were. It was not until the first Indian had actually seized her shoulder and was grinning down at her that her body as well as her mind realized she had no chance. The chase was over. She gave a low cry and Marie began moaning, falling to her knees. A second Indian pulled up Marie by the arm, and she struggled uselessly to break herself free before she slumped in his grasp.

From the loopholes of a single cabin, a volley of answering shots clacked out at last. It's too late! Delilah's panic told her while the Indian hardened his grip and began dragging her toward the woods. A chorus of whoops rose once more. The landscape was full of Indians now, their rifles banging as they ran forward. She did not know how long afterward it was that the fort bell began to clang over and over, its soundings rending the air above the cries and the shots. She only knew she and Marie were being carried off to be scalped and nobody was noticing. There was nothing either of them could do. When she heard fresh screams not hers and not Marie's she thought they might be the screams of children but she could not be sure. Above her grinned the painted face of her captor. In the distance she saw a tangle of figures running wildly up the hill where she had been running seconds before. The hand on her arm tightened harder. Already they had come to the first thicket beyond the fields. The Indians, four of them, were taking them into the forest. *I'm going to die. It can't be true but it is.* The bell clanged more faintly. The distant cries receded, and the shots and whoops. Closer she heard the strange voice in her ears: "You squaw. You come." The words were guttural but firm, the savage's breath warm and fishy.

A rifle jabbed the small of her back when the savage let her arm go. Marie was walking beside her, staggering as she herself must be staggering. Visions began to torment her: Gran and her father lying in pools of blood, Charles lying beside them and Johnny too . . . The faraway echoes were the echoes of battle but she scarcely heard them as she tripped and fell and was wrenched up. She could not yet fix on the pain in her body as her own. The procession wound deeper into the woods over a way she had never taken. Real titmice started whistling and real jays screeched; cedars began to sigh . . . Sometimes the Indians laughed. She could not see them, for they walked behind her. Often they grunted as if with satisfaction. On and on they all plodded, Delilah and the Indians and Marie too, who could not yet find voice for her terror but only breath to walk ahead of the gun that jabbed her as another one jabbed Delilah. Twilight fell in a glade so far from the mills and the fort it was unknown to Delilah. The ground seemed to grow harder as the pain stabbed her feet and surged up her legs, recognized in its force but still a thing apart. Over an eastern cliff rose a scarlet moon, and she heard then the wolves in the forest ahead start to howl.

21

"WE'RE STILL alive." Her words echoed in the night as if somebody else had said them. Snoring Indians held fast the ends of the thongs that pinioned her and Marie to separate lashorn trees. The Indians had drunk from the flasks they carried. They had squatted around their blazing campfire while they roasted the squirrels they had shot. Drunkenly at last they had tumbled to the ground, but they had not been too drunk to forget to tie the thongs tight to her own broad wrists and Marie's thin ones. "We're still alive, Marie. Think of that."

Marie did not answer. Perhaps her fear had turned her too mad for speech. *Am I mad too?* When the laughter welled from her own throat she knew it only as one more sound of the lunacy from which there was no escape: *Hurry, Charles. You too, Papa. Climb out of your graves and save us.*

The sound of Marie's struggling in her thongs was slight. It was just enough to wake her Indian guard, who staggered up, belched, and slapped her face several times hard across the cheeks with the back of his hand. When the sun rose Delilah could see Marie's chin down on her shoulder, her burnished hair loose and disordered on her collar. She had fainted. The Indians had to poke her with their rifles to make her begin marching again.

Delilah wondered if the knives at the Indians' belts were scalping knives. The blades were long and thin, catching glints of light. The sun was on the left; they were going south, then. The Indians must be Cherokees. Desperately she tried to collect her thoughts into a pattern which made sense. There must be a thing she could do. If she and Marie had been spared so far, there might be a way they could free themselves. Delilah's pain was not dissociated from her any more. She believed it at last, as she could start to believe everything. She wished she could think ahead one step more, instead of thinking only of the present and the savages beside her. But it was useless. All her mind was lost in a red void of panic.

All that day they passed along a narrow trail through dense forest where laurel covered the ground in monstrous tangles on either side. The earth steepened and plunged. There were no open places. The blood on her feet dried brown in the wind as fast as it oozed from the cuts and scratches on them. She thought once of leaving pieces of her red gown on twigs, so that she might be followed. She had heard a tale of a woman doing that in Kentucky. But she knew she dared not try. The savages were watching her too closely.

It was strange about Marie. The vacancy had left her eyes, and she was starting to march obediently, almost willingly. Perhaps she wasn't mad after all. Delilah's feet continued to blister in her moccasins. Leafless briers scratched her chafed calves and forearms. Late in the afternoon her left sleeve ripped off in a brier patch. When the Indians built their fire the second night one of them shoved her a hunk of what she recognized as pemmican. Her father had carried pemmican to Dunmore's War.

Marie ate the pemmican too. Her flimsy gown, spattered with blood from her cut arms, was in shreds at her swollen ankles. She stared dully ahead; but hers was certainly the face of a woman who knew in reason what had befallen her. Perhaps she had passed beyond fear altogether into despair.

"I'm thirsty," Delilah said finally to her guard, wondering if he would understand her. She opened her mouth and pointed down her throat. He mimicked her gesture, then brought her a gourd he filled from a stream running over nearby rocks. She cupped the gourd in her hands and leaned back against the tree, finishing the drink in a gulp. Remembering then, she pointed to Marie. Again the Indian mimicked her; but he brought the gourd to Marie too, who drank it silently.

Delilah chewed her pemmican. A half-formed plan began to nag at the back of her mind. The savages had let her and Marie stop in thickets when necessary in the afternoon. Perhaps if they both pretended a need now while they were yet untied . . . But she did not know how much cunning was left in Marie. One thing became clear above all the rest: she could not escape alone. Marie must remain with her to the end. No reason presented itself to her for it; it was simply a fact, to be accepted in all her thinking, in whatever haze her plans took shape. Like, dislike, love and hate had no meaning here.

She heard her voice to the guard come evenly once more. "We want to go over there." She pointed to a laurel slick, and with a slight motion of her hand tried to make Marie understand too. She must have done so, for Marie nodded and with a grimace of pain got to her feet. There was fresh laughter from the Indians. One whose face, arms and chest were tattooed in dizzy red swirls pointed to the stream. He made a lewd gesture of squatting down. Marie swayed as she stood alone, not seeing. But Delilah knew Marie had started to follow her when she heard her irregular steps over the brush and she whispered back to her: "Come!" The painted Indian must have quickly understood she meant to run away. He began pulling her back by her unbound hair. "You stay." Another Indian jumped up to push Marie to the stream and dump her into it. The men slapped their thighs as Marie's arms flailed until the tattooed Indian dragged her back onto the bank, sodden and shaking in her tatters. "She wash," he turned a grim look on Delilah. "She not run." That night the guards put them both on the ground on their backs. Across their chests they laid long, straight branches to which they tied their arms. Then they staked their ankles and knotted bare grapevines around their necks, twisting the vines together and fastening them to a tree. The ground was cold and wet. Delilah's teeth began chattering.

I must be cleverer. The resolve drifted through her mind as if someone else was fashioning it, but she was too exhausted to think more and she fell asleep in her pinions even as she strained not to. Marie had not said a word since the Indians had thrown her into the water.

On the third day Delilah fell. Her gown was already in ribbons from the brambles. The foul-smelling savages were wearing stiff buckskins, but she and Marie were unprotected in their rags and were bleeding and raw. The pain now rose and fell in great waves and she knew what every surge of it would be like before it came. She wanted to stay on the ground where she had fallen. They would kill her and it would be over: the march, the choking at night from the bonds, the smells, the pain, and the cold. But she knew they weren't going to kill her yet when her guard dragged her up and jabbed her on, kicking her throbbing ankles while she stumbled. When Marie fell she too was dragged up. At twilight the Indians shot a bear. They patted their stomachs and smacked their lips as they ate its flesh and entrails by their campfire. Delilah forced down a chunk of raw meat, at once wanting to keep her strength and also to die to be out of her torment. The wind was chafing mercilessly at her exposed skin. Afterwards her guard handed her a yellow strip of bear fat and made motions of rubbing his body with it. She realized he was telling her to grease herself where her gown had torn. She began to coat her arms and legs and face, her will if not her mind pushing her hands and fingers. Soon she saw Marie greasing herself the same way.

Staked to the ground, while the smells of the bear meat and fat and blood hung over the camp from the carcass by the fire, she heard Marie whispering to her after the Indians slept: "Always I knew." She tried to raise herself on her elbows, but she could not. "It is no use, Delilah. They had to kill me some day."

When they came to the river, a few brown oak leaves were drifting down in a thin mist of rain while others clung limp to the branches above. The wind moaned across the water's gray ripples. Delilah would have shivered at the sight had she been conscious of anything but the agony of her gashes and, unbelievably, her sunburn. She turned from the water to stare at Marie, who had been shoved beside her. She knew she must look as Marie looked; she shut her eyes. But she could still see Marie, the last shreds of her underclothes and gown wrapped around her greased arms and legs to protect them, her ragged petticoat bunched as a breechclout, her hair matted with mud and leafmold and twigs and dried blood. Marie's face was swollen and distorted; she too had crossed the wide meadow and climbed the mountain to its unsheltered bald. Days ago — but there were no days any more, there were only light and dark — they had both had to begin stripping themselves to make their rags into these coverings. Delilah had stripped her own body first and then she had helped Marie because she had seemed too weak to do it herself. Delilah had split the cloth with her teeth and tried to bind Marie's feet with the rags; she had bound her own when her moccasins had worn through. The cloth had torn too, however, and had fallen away on the unceasing struggle over the trace. By now many of the blisters and sores on Delilah's feet had hardened to calluses; she saw Marie's feet hardening too. How long they had been gone she did not know. Sometimes the Indians smiled at them furtively and she wondered what they were thinking. She heard the cunning that had become so much a part of her voice as she said: "Bring grease" or, ingratiatingly, "You feed us now." It would have been a wonder, this insinuating craft she possessed; but there was no wonder left, only the dull hope of escape that was hardly a hope at all, and the unspoken prayer that when death came it would be swift. Now she did not want to die at all. Even in this hour she did not want to give up the aching body that was hers. She had stood this much and she wanted to go on. But she knew how senseless she was being. It would be better to accept again the idea of dying as Marie still did, to know the threat of the long Indian war had come true for herself at last too. She ought to be praying aloud for speed and mercy in her death as Marie was praying; but she could not do it.

"Don't be afraid," she had tried to comfort Marie one night.

Slightly, Marie had laughed. "There is no reason. It has already happened to me."

Wind shuffled through the dripping oak leaves at the river. Showers fell even as the rain stopped, and the droplets stabbed like needlepoints on Delilah's arms. She blinked. Vague forms sharpened before her at the bank: old ramparts overgrown with winter-killed weeds and bare saplings, heaps of rubble, remnants of a wall which followed a narrow ridge to a bluff that plunged to the water below. Greening cannon lodged in disused bastions.

She tried to straighten herself and her bones fought her effort. "What place is this?"

Her guard didn't answer. Only when he had half pushed and half hurled her and Marie down a slope beyond the ruins to the edge of the water did he order: "Swim." The water was ice. At first Delilah could not move her arms and legs. She began to sink down through the swirls of it, her body without purpose or strength. The ice closed over her head. But her sudden struggle for breath surprised her, and her limbs relaxed as she felt herself being pulled to the top by her hair. She thought it must be the guard who pulled her, but she was not sure. The roots of her hair ached. Behind, she could hear Marie's shortening breath. She knew her arms had begun to splash rhythmically when a white shower of ice fell against her cheeks. She was swimming across the river despite its cold and her weakness. On the shore she fumbled to pull up her sagging breechclout. Her guard pursed his lips at her. When she coughed the ice fell from her mouth to her bare throat. Marie was swaying; again she had to bend to help her fix her rags.

They had come to a village. Rows of long, narrow log houses stood beneath the rocking trees, small mud huts scattered between them. Delilah and Marie were prodded past a great chinked house in the center, then past a clearing with stakes at either end and a pole in the middle. Delilah saw and smelled and heard the milling Indians beginning to press around. Tiny silver bells jangled on the shirts of the men. White feathers waved in their black roaches, and some wore cloaks of scarlet feathers which ruffled in new gusts. They swirled around her as the water had swirled only they were worse, blue- and vermilion-painted, jangling, stinking of urine and beargrease. Topknotted women stood in buckskin shifts, their streams of bright ribbons waving in the wind. The crowd moved back when two old men in short cloaks of dirty white feathers walked toward Delilah and Marie to look them up and down.

"What place is this?" She heard her question again. This time the answer came shortly: "Chota."

Chota . . . the Tenase River . . . 'Chucky Jack Sevier burning Chota, Benge's town . . . "Torture stake, wigwams and all; Benge swears he'll have revenge". . . She did not know what happened then, for her exhaustion became a tyrant to which she had to yield above all else. When she woke she thought she must have wakened from what had been a nightmare, for she was warm. When she stared up to mud walls she knew the warmth came from a fire that glowed red-gold in the center of the hut where she lay beside Marie. Half naked as she was, Marie turned to her with open eyes. The distant, reedy notes of a flute hung in the air.

"They will do it now."

Delilah felt her fists clenching. "They can't. Not after they've brought us this far." As she inched her way closer to the fire she could feel the thongs on her wrists cutting at her flesh.

Marie said softly, almost tenderly: "You are such a fool."

Delilah shut her eyes, repeating: "I'm alive."

At night a white man brought them venison, pemmican, and a gourd of thick soup in which dead hornets floated back and forth. Delilah managed to raise herself on her elbows: "Who are you?"

"Trader," he mumbled, shoving a chunk of meat into her mouth. "Got you hornet soup. Good."

"British?" Her eyes went up and down his length trying to focus on the details of his seamed brown face, sandy hair, and gnarled hands.

"Your service, Ma'am." As he squatted, he gave a mocking bow from his waist. "I've seen too many of your kind in my time. Had to go beyond the treaty line, didn't you? Paying now for stealing Cherokee land. This here's Chota, as they told you. Their 'old beloved town.'"

"I'm Delilah Winfield from Bickley Mills. You must help me get word —" But she fell back, her mouth full of pemmican, her last piece of venison slipping from her fingers. Childish tears sprang to her eyes at her renewed hunger and her sense of futility. Marie had turned away; she did not even care. Marie would never help her. She would have to plan everything alone. It was not fair.

The trader narrowed his eyes, and squatted closer, hams on his moccasin heels. "No word to be got, Delilah Winfield."

"But this is Mrs. Bickley herself —"

"If they black your faces, you'd best run and get shot instead. Black faces mean burning. I can't help you. They'll never rape you — don't fear it. Warriors take vows. Best thing, both stay here and take men from amongst 'em if you aren't burned or skulped. White Deer — this is her hut —

she come from the Clinch Settlements ten-eleven year back. From Poor Valley, she told. She stayed."

"No!" Delilah choked.

"I'm right sorry. Baynton, Wharton Comp'ny ain't in business to save lives, but I'll try to speak some for you."

"You're American! Oh, if you're decent you'll send word to Bickley Mills!" A quick surge of rage shot through her and she was glad of its vigor.

"Send word by Benge, maybe?" Derisively, the trader guffawed. Then he left, stopping at the hut's low door, looking back only briefly before his broad figure disappeared into the dark.

In the morning a wrinkled old man prodded Delilah and Marie out of the hut. He handed them a pair of buckskin shifts, unbound their thongs, and pointed to a woodpile close by. "Carry." His teeth were yellow and stained in his copper face as he smiled amiably. "Chop. Benge come soon. See you work." The feathers of his cloak ruffled in the wind.

Benge was still on the Clinch then, burning, murdering, looting . . . Delilah's eyes went to Marie. Overnight she seemed to have turned ancient, her face gaunt and lined and empty of paint, her green eyes birdlike, her throat hollow and her shoulders round. A sudden rage at Marie filled Delilah and sent that surge of strength through her limbs and trunk once more. How could Marie dare to be so sure of dying? Of course there was hope! Even this wizzened old Cherokee was trying to give them a little hope, to tell them Benge might spare them if he saw them working. Why settle for death when there was a single chance?

In a mixture of defiance and gratitude Delilah told the old man they would try to work. "Bring us skins too. We're cold." When he left, nodding, she knew he would do as she had dared to order him. Marie still stood dejectedly in her rags, but Delilah pushed her closer toward the woodpile. "Start!" she hissed. Taking for herself an axe which lay before her on the ground, she commanded Marie: "Trust me." Marie stared at her and did not move; but when Delilah threatened to prod her again she nodded and took up a second axe, her arm as slow as if the axe had weighed a hundred pounds.

When the darkness had closed down and they had tumbled onto their pallets in the hut Delilah could hear a fire crackling in the clearing beyond. A crowd of Indians had assembled at the stakes by the faggots she and Marie had made ready. As they had come in together after hours of chopping the wood and dragging it to a pile beside the stakes they had seen a blond girl with a blackened face being led toward the center pole by two men in scarlet cloaks. The girl had been trying to cover her nakedness. *I won't think about it. Dear God, I can't.* As if through a wall Delilah heard the start of the beating from her hut, the girl's screams, the clatter of rifles, the roaring of the crowd. She knew Marie heard too but she willed not to think of what was happening and hoped Marie could will the same. When she turned to her she saw Marie had sunk beyond all of it into the refuge of sleep. She too let herself sink, caring and not caring, down and down into a hot black silence beneath the smell of burning flesh beginning to hover everywhere. A soul might be lost forever in such blackness and heat: her soul, her body too, Marie's . . . When sunlight streamed through the door of the hut Marie's bloodshot eyes begged her for help, for a fresh command. Did Marie remember the night or know a white woman had been burned alive

outside her door? She did not seem to. *There was a path
through that forest. I must get a knife to kill us both in case
we can't find it when we get away. Marie might scream
when she mustn't* . . . Marie truly was stupid, yes. She
depended on another woman cleverer than herself. It was
scarcely possible to believe they had ever shared any life
but this one at Chota: hacking at logs and dragging them to
the clearing, gulping what food a trader brought them, rubbing more beargrease on pitted arms and legs and faces.
Cleverness with numbers was useless here. Cleverness with
living was what counted.

It was surely Benge who stopped by the woodpile one
afternoon to watch them, his trophies. From the corner of
her eye Delilah could see hair as red as Marie's; she could
see a tall, bronzed figure in fringed skins, the scarlet spot of
a feather clashing with the color of his hair. His voice was
low as he murmured to the old man who had first set them
at their task and who now stood sentry beside them. She
did not dare to stop to study even Benge or try to read his
face. She continued to chop at the stubborn hickory log at
her feet, hoping Marie would continue chopping too. At
last, with a shrug, Benge moved on.

That night she found herself sitting with Marie on a cornshuck pallet in another mud hut and she narrowed her eyes
to study the woman who sat in front of them. The old man
had led them to this place. Flames were casting long rays of
light over the bright yellow of the strange woman's buckskin
gown. Silver ornaments on her breast gleamed. When she
moved her hands a deerhide bag tied to her left wrist swung
tauntingly. Her black hair was tightly drawn back from a
round face with slitted eyes.

"Benge is here." Her voice was low and her English clear

and even meticulous. "He has spoken in the council that you must die. I am sorry."

"No," Delilah charged wearily. Marie's lips moved too, but she was shutting her eyes. "We've worked, he can't." In the firelight Marie's snarled hair was more grotesque than ever.

"It is not my wish," the woman answered. "You come from Benge's land. The gods, whose prophetess I am, were silent. I could not change Benge's heart tonight."

"Are you going to scalp us?" Marie's eyes opened and her voice quavered. Then she cried out: "I cannot stand to wait more, I tell you! For the love of God, do it! Here!"

"Hush." The order was so quick, so contemptuous, that it silenced her and she fell back on her pallet only to sob with her fist in her mouth.

"Who are you?" Delilah asked the woman, whose eyes were beadily calculating. "Why did you want us?"

"My whiteman name is Nancy Ward, but it is not polite for you to ask. I am the Little Carpenter's niece. He was a very great chief. The English King received him over the water as our ambassador. I am the Ghigau, the Beloved Woman of Chota. It may be the gods will speak through me yet." In a corner of the hut, on a perch, a raven fluttered its feathers. Nancy Ward smiled, fingering the silver brooch at her neck, glancing at the raven, then running her hand down the yellow buskin on her right leg. "There has been much killing." She dropped her eyes. "I have warned your people many times. Always I tell them to leave before we make war. The gods commanded me to do this. I was your prisoner once. You did not kill me because of my warnings. All must heed the gods, your people and mine — the Yun-wíya that you call Cherokees. We are the True People."

"Spare us." Delilah brushed back a strand of her long hair from her face. "We spared you."

"Do not look for mercy, whitewoman." Nancy Ward's voice grew colder. "You have broken every treaty you ever made with us and warred against your own king. We welcome your traders even so and they rob us. We asked only to live by ourselves and the King promised us this, but you stole our hunting grounds. Benge was tricked out of his by the gift of a butcher knife."

Marie's face was still in her hands. She was sobbing more softly. Her hair hung down on her shift. Delilah looked away, trying to ignore her even as Nancy Ward was ignoring her. Nancy Ward fingered her brooch again. The flames burned higher, making a monster of her shadow on the wall. "I wish to know a thing," she said at last. "You can make whiteman butter and cheese?" Her eyes fixed themselves on Delilah's.

Delilah stifled an impulse to laugh insanely. Then she answered steadily: "Yes."

"You would teach us if the gods spoke, if you were spared." It was not a question.

Delilah nodded. Marie uncovered her face to peer at her. "I've been a teacher a long time," Delilah said, the hope mounting in her voice. "I could show your people how to make butter and cheese and this woman could help me."

"You would wash your white blood away in the river and bear us children to take the place of those Jack Sevier has killed?"

Delilah checked every instinct she had to answer: "Yes." Time was all she needed. If she could remember that and bargain for it, surely there would be a way to flee Chota yet. She would bend all her will toward the chance. She tightened her fingers and repeated: "Yes. You are hungry here, then?"

"We have stolen cattle but they must serve us better." The firelight brightened Nancy Ward's dark eyes. As the smoke around her thickened, the rest of her face blurred and her voice came lower. "I shall listen for the word of the gods. If they speak I shall speak in the council myself. Go."

At their own fire Delilah tried to whisper to Marie what they would do. Of course she didn't mean to stay in Chota with any Indian! But she and Marie had left no trail in the forest. Charles and her father — if they had survived — could not hope to trace them to Benge's village. Instead they must make their way back to the Clinch alone. The Cherokees must first be made to trust them, to relax their watching. That would take weeks, months. Churning butter and stirring cheese would at least be a rest from the woodpile. Somehow the savages could be put off. If not . . .

"Never!" Marie's eyes were wide again, absurdly vulnerable in her old woman's face. "You would not!"

"Sh! You'd rather be burned? Don't you realize the gods of Nancy Ward do what she wants? We'll live if we mind her." Delilah crept to the fire as the wind howled in the trees outside. She must get a knife very soon against the possibility of failure. Never would she trust Marie to be steady enough to succeed at running away alone afterwards. For her own clumsy try on the trace she had nothing now but regret. No, Marie was a millstone round her neck and must be reckoned with. Marie was staring into the fire, seeing what disordered visions she did not know. It was Marie who had so much to go back to, to live for . . . "Think of Charles, Marie. Your children."

"They are dead." Marie folded her hands and went on staring, her face more emaciated than ever in the flames. Delilah saw the light flickering over her hair. Was it mud, a trick of the fire, or had Marie's hair started to come in white at the roots?

Afterwards, from the great log house in the center of the town, the murmur of echoing voices floated through the clearing under the oaks: a man's voice, subdued and angry, and a woman's, clear and inexorable. Once a raven cawed.

22

INSTINCTIVELY Delilah did her new work in the weeks that followed, stirring at the new voices, warming to new friends like the old man who had set her to chopping wood, and chilling to new enemies like her guard on the trace, who often scowled as he passed her in the village. She was in Chota and she was learning its rhythms until they were as much a part of her as those of Sugar Hill and Bickley Mills had been. She knew too that she was becoming a habitual sight. So was Marie. There were even times Delilah saw Marie's shoulders straighten at her task of churning, perhaps in a pride that she had at last put fear behind her. The rains of early spring pelted Chota and the winds blew cold and warm again through Delilah's buckskin dress. She tied back her hair with a length of rawhide and bathed her face in cupped hands whenever she went to the river to gather water. She could feel her scars. She was glad she could not see them in the muddy water. It was enough to see Marie's.

She wondered at first if she would see Benge again. She knew now that Benge and Nancy Ward were rivals in Chota. Both wanted power in the village. Benge wanted to lead the Cherokees to war and kill every white man on Cherokee land. Nancy Ward believed this was impossible and sought to bring her people the ways of the enemy so the Cherokees

would not starve without their hunting grounds. Nancy
Ward had not saved her and Marie from any mercy. They
were merely tools. Nancy Ward wanted to learn dairying.
Whether she was capable of pity Delilah did not know.
Who could ever tell, with savages? Even when they laughed
she couldn't always be sure they saw anything funny. Actually Benge stayed in Chota for only a day or two at a time.
He was otherwise raiding, she supposed. But she couldn't
help breathing a sigh of relief at his absence, refusing to
think further of what it meant. She would have shown
Benge her fear at close quarters and he would have used it
somehow to hurt her more. In the distance Benge was
straight and stolid, very tall and hard-muscled, his red hair a
strange crown. He wore jangling silver bracelets and from
his belt hung long streamers of dried hair, one of them red
too . . . Sometimes, as Delilah pushed her churn up and
down at the door of her hut, she would see Benge grinning
at some dark child's antics by the water buckets. Traders,
too, came and went in the village. She wondered once if
any of the white men who appeared so briefly might be Hargis, the renegade. Several of the men had ruddy faces and
the receding black hair Hargis was supposed to have; but
she did not ask, and nobody volunteered to tell her people's
names. Doublehead, Hargis, Hanging Maw, Bloody Fellow
. . . these were names in her mind. If she heard their Cherokee equivalents or saw their actual faces she did not know
it. The Cherokees grunted their English only to her, not
among themselves except for the traders' company names:
Panton Leslie, Baynton Wharton. Once a trader brought a
horseload of rifles and the Indian men gathered around him
eagerly. She believed they were British rifles until she heard
the murmur "Wharton." That was the American Company
again — in Philadelphia, the capital, her father had once

mentioned. Impossible! But with a sickening pang she realized it had not ever been the British generals arming the savages against the Clinch. American merchants were arming them too — and for money, not caring, which was worse.

She had thought long ago Benge was a leader all Cherokees must follow without question, like sheep who knew no other course. Now she had learned he was but one of many chiefs, with his own comings and goings, his own plans and doings. He had an equal in Nancy Ward, the Ghigau, the Beloved Woman or prophetess, and was not even the only war chief. But still Delilah would be afraid of Benge until she died; she was glad she had not had to face him alone. In a contest of hatred she reckoned she would surely have been the loser.

Bickley Mills grew more and more distant to her mind. Sometimes it seemed as if Chota were her only life, the making of butter and cheese before a knot of stinking savage women her only occupation, the guiding of their greasy hands her only task. Evenings she tended black-haired babies with dark faces and wide eyes and — for a wonder — smiles like white babies' smiles. She would sing to them in their winter huts because she knew it pleasured the squaws; and when they were pleasured, she soon found, they forgot to watch her so closely.

> "As I was going down Shinbone Alley,
> Hoozen John, a-hooza;
> As I was going down Shinbone Alley
> Long time ago . . ."

Gradually the Indians stopped watching every move she made with Marie. It became possible for them to go by themselves to the river for water, for instance. The first time

they tried they had come back to find the old man in the
feathered cloak berating the toothless squaw set to watch
them. But soon, at twilight, the squaw began grinding corn
at her pestle all the same, watching merely from the corner
of her eye. At last she gave up even this pretense.

Delilah knew she had a name, Unigatíya. It meant Tall
Woman, the squaw mumbled when she asked. Marie did
not seem to have a name at all, but perhaps she had one and
Delilah merely could not figure it. Her own she had guessed
from the pointing, the pursed-out lips. She knew she and
Marie must make their break when a particular Indian
started to stand by more often to watch their churning. He
was a short, fat man with a purple scar running from his left
ear to the corner of his mouth. He had a habit of wiping
his hands on his thighs. Delilah heard her Cherokee name
in his mouth and felt a wave of revulsion, then indignation.
If this was the man Nancy Ward thought to give her she
would learn differently! But of course Delilah couldn't yield
to any savage at all. That had been a desperate piece of
bravery contemplated when she had wanted only to live a
day more, an hour more, a minute more, when she had been
dickering for any time she could get.

One night the fat Indian came to the door of her hut with
a long strip of venison. Smiling fatuously, he held it out to
her. She knew it was a gift and she sensed what it meant.
If she took it, she promised herself to him . . . Quickly
she turned to Marie who was stirring cheese in a caldron
over the fire. Marie did not see . . . What was there to
do but take it? So she forced herself to smile back, wondering if the fat man saw her lips quivering, and she held out
her hands. He walked away then but she knew he would
come back.

"Tonight," she whispered to Marie as she passed the fire. "When we get water." Startled, Marie stared up at her, but she moved on to her pestle.

At twilight, when the first thrushes were ending their songs in the greening trees of the village, they took their water buckets together and tried to walk as aimlessly as possible down the path to the shore. Slowly they sauntered along the mud street. Delilah was glad she had the venison under her shift, and a knife. Once a trader had lent the knife to her when she had been skinning raccoon meat for a squaw. She had never returned it. Perhaps the trader had thought she would use it to kill herself: it did not matter . . . She did not speak a word to Marie; she only swung her empty birch bucket as carelessly as she could, walking on. By the shore Marie began to talk but Delilah hushed her. It would not do to be seen talking now. She began instead to take a long time washing her face, then to dangle her feet in the water as if cleaning them. Marie followed her example. A last thrush sang out. The stars began to flicker. She breathed easier when nobody came to fetch her. She and Marie had been forgotten as usual. The fat man was going to creep later into their hut in hopes of finding Delilah waiting on her pallet. Only then would Chota learn the truth, its men start bawling quarrels with their wives, its children whimper . . .

A canoe was tied a few feet down the bank to a willow bough. Marie could not be trusted to swim the river, perhaps; it was better to be safe. When the darkness had deepened she whispered only "Come, Marie" and she put down her bucket. Then, softly so that no twigs would crack underfoot, she crept along the bank to the canoe and untied it. The water plopped at its bow but she could not help that.

"Get in." She prayed Marie would make no noise. If they were caught it would mean burning in case she couldn't manage to use the knife; it would mean crying the same cries that had come from the naked girl in the clearing . . . It would have been better to stay until the nights were warmer, but there was no help for the shivering which came half from cold and half from fear, or for the noisy teeth that already sounded in Delilah's ears as if they must rouse the whole village. The only fresh sound as she climbed into the canoe with Marie was the water, a splash that might have been a beaver. When she took the paddle in her hands the canoe had already started gliding across the river, and she cursed the moon beginning to rise in the east. Silently she pushed the paddle down through the water, thankful for its silvery calm. At the opposite shore below the ramparts of the abandoned fort she stepped out without a word, Marie after her. She laid the paddle in the dugout before she let it go, its shape sidling slowly off with scarcely an eddy. Briefly she turned to look back at Chota. Already it slept: she hoped.

The moon rose higher to hang like a lemon over the pitted earth beyond the village. Delilah tried not to stumble, not to make a sound. Marie was lighter; fortunately she understood the need of silence too. Delilah would look after her to the end. She would pay her own debt to Marie with Marie's life . . . When the moon set and daylight came she made a shelter among some laurel boughs and a half-fainting Marie tumbled into it. They won't see us here, Delilah thought; later there will be the cane to hide in. Before she too fell into the cradling hollow of her tiredness and her tension she dreamed of Marie's husband as he had used to be. Almost she could hear his low voice in her ears, telling her to have courage and to go on. Almost she could feel his caresses, this time healing her bruised arms and legs and breasts . . . She tried then to pray; but she didn't want God as she wanted the lover of long-ago to banish all her pain. Marie was doubtless dreaming of Charles too: as he was now, if he lived. Delilah did not begrudge her that. Such was her right.

But what a burden she was! On the second night when she moaned she still wanted to die because she was so tired, Delilah longed to strike her face. It would be so easy to leave her in this forest! But she belonged to Charles. *I mustn't think. Oh, God, yes; I have to keep thinking as long as I can. Where are we?* Doubtless search parties were already on every side of them. A series of cautions stamped themselves on Delilah's brain: step softly in the dark. Go slowly. Cover footfalls. Stay from the trace when you can. Watch for campfires. Listen. Sleep by day under the boughs. Watch everything. Wake at sunset . . . At sunset first of all there were the little fires to see, the rows of animal eyes in the night, frightened eyes she thought must be like her own. Tiny feet scurried everywhere. Once a painter howled down from a distant mountaintop and she put her hand on Marie's arm to reassure her, forgetting her own shrinking.

"Hungry," Marie whispered.

Delilah's own stomach was contracted, begging and racked. But she gave Marie a slice of the fat man's venison and not until Marie had swallowed it in a gulp did she realize she must snatch back the rest of the meat. It had not been clever to take so little. But how could she have foreseen Marie's greed, her failure to know it was more necessary for her, Delilah, to eat because she must lead?

"Please, Delilah!"

"No," she snapped.

The wind was cold when the trace started to leave the laurel slicks and needle-strewn stands of evergreen to mount to a windy height where stunted bushes pushed up from boulders at the edge of a grassy bald. Had they passed this way before? Delilah, her hand on her forehead, could not remember. The climbing, the wind, became eternal. There was a great storm when forks of lightning severed the black sky and the thunder crashed down to split the forest below. All the earth turned to a screeching, keening, rocking, swishing nightmare in her ears, by turns lurid and void in her eyes. There was no shelter on that bald high above the tiny world. It was a doll-like world when morning lit its river threads and yellow-green puffs of trees. She and Marie clung sodden to each other at the bald's edge all day. They raised their faces and opened their mouths to drink when the sunlit trees shed glassy droplets. They started to crawl toward the sun again until Delilah remembered they couldn't dare.

The wind was always colder on the heights, she learned.

It was wiser to travel by dark with no clothing to leave telltale shreds on twigs. They had their buckskin gowns for the light, for sleep. And their bodies had weathered much already. Whenever she felt the heavy coating of grease and grime on her arms it reassured her. Carry the buckskins, yes. Soon perhaps she would not be able to reason out any necessities. *Cane shoots when you find them, sassafras shoots. Eat. If a black bough is warm draw back, for it's a snake and it must slither away. Stay alive.*

The screech of an owl rent the darkness. They stopped in their tracks. An owl answered. So close! Indians already so close! Then they stumbled on because there was nothing else to do. The laurel branches everywhere turned to tentacles to be silently slipped aside, each noisy break a disaster. The vines too were a maze, but the moon moved from east to west. *Remember, north and east. The way back. Bickley Mills.*

The owls called again but their calls receded. When they vanished the sky ahead was reddening. Delilah beckoned Marie toward a canebrake. When Marie did not move she pulled her there. She squatted with her to eat. "No venison. Cane."

"I — cannot."

"They'll catch you. You'll burn."

Later Marie murmured: "Do you — pray?"

He maketh me to lie down in green pastures . . . Old words danced on nameless yellow pages before Delilah's eyes, but they were without sense. She shook her head. "North" and "east" were the only words that mattered. One day she and Marie heard a shout and whoops. They were both sleeping, side by side at the edge of a stagnant pool. Delilah had fallen into a half-dream of the way it glided rankly through the sheltering thicket, the foulness of its green scum and the skunk cabbage around it hanging in the still air, the green thin branches overhead so sinister and yet so welcoming . . . The shouts rose higher. There were sudden hooves to pound and shake the earth under her body.

"It's white men. Horses!"

Delilah slapped the palm of her hand against Marie's mouth to stop her cry and hoped the noise of it had been drowned by the horses. Crawling to the edge of the thicket she peered through a maze of honeysuckle to see a brace of savages in breechclouts furiously driving a gang of saddled horses. Stolen . . . The hoofbeats retreated into the distance behind. The Beloved Town lay behind, and the Beloved Woman, and the stakes and the naked girl who had burned, and Benge if he were not following. *They didn't see us. Not this time.* Or was Benge playing cat and mouse: laughing?

Keep thinking. It's your only chance.

A second voice soothed the first beguilingly: *You're tired. Rest. It's easier.*

When the venison ran out she taught Marie to break young grapevines noiselessly and eat the leaves. Always now they were hungry and thirsty. Gnawing stomach, parched lips and tongue, were constant torments. They slept less and they dreamed of food and water. Delilah had visions of heaped trestle tables with Gran at the head of them, passing shimmering jellies and bubbling stews and mugs full of persimmon beer. Eat! cried the voices. Drink! But she did not know how to find a spring where she was, and when she and Marie came haphazardly on branches or creeks they gorged themselves at first until they understood their retching came from the cold water. Then they drank slowly, cautiously. One night they heard a sound of tearing and grunting. Delilah crept ahead. In a tiny glade a giant black bear was eating a deer carcass in the light of the half-moon.

"We'll get some," she whispered.

Together the women watched the furry bear lumbering through his feast, pawing and ripping. When they could watch no more it was Marie who crawled forward. The bear growled. Shaking, she crawled back again. "He won't let us," her voice broke pettishly as the tears streaked in tight drops over the grease on her face. So they groped on, hungry until they found a brier bush with dried hips still clinging to its thorny canes.

Days later they came to a large shelving rock which jutted into a blackberry thicket. Under it Delilah spread a bed of dry leaves. Through the briers Marie hurled herself into the leaves. Then she turned. "I — must stay," she whispered. "I cannot go on. Leave me."

Doggedly Delilah shook her head as she forced her arms up into her buckskin. Silly not to wear it always; surely they had left a trail anyhow. Cold; keep it on. Hungry. Thirsty. Hours had passed when Marie's voice came once more, this time with the sound of reason in it; and with reason too Delilah could understand. "I hold you back. We will die together?"

Delilah turned on her bed of leaves and nodded. "If we have to." Impulsively she reached for Marie's hand. It was moist and cold. They lay still, hands touching, only their breath sounding in the hollow. When Marie spoke again her voice was fainter, but it was clear. "Delilah — "

"Yes?"

"I am — weak, now. But truly I am not afraid. Thank you." She was sinking into sleep. As her eyes closed her breath slowed until it only rose and fell like the wind in the new leaves overhead. When her grasp loosened Delilah buried her face in the leaves on the ground. Later, when her bones ached so much and so fiercely she could lie still no more, Marie got up too. Marie passed her hand across her forehead and again she smiled that smile of ridiculous tenderness in her disfigured face, its gashes cutting across it in a web of scabbed lines. "Let us go on."

At the head of a steep gully where a waterfall poured over craggy cliffs Delilah crawled to a boulder to rest. Great veils of water sparkled in the dawn. Above the roar of the waterfall new words, lost words, started to ramble through her darkening mind: *Were I sold on Indian soil, Over the hills and far away* . . . Soon they became the only words she heard at all, because neither she nor Marie were talking any more. Yet there had to be other words too, she knew as she braced herself to continue: Light no fire. Drink slowly. Reach into the brook under the rocks, trap the little fish with your grapevine net as they spill from the beaver dam . . . With cunning pleasure Delilah could smile down at the net she contrived. She would scale the fish with her knife, and give Marie more because she herself was so very strong . . . Stumble ahead toward the dawn. Over the hills and far away, *o*-ver the *hills* and *far* a-*way* . . . I am Delilah and I am alive. Delilah. Remember. Alive.

A gap yawned below them. Delilah clung to tiny partridgeberry bushes as she gripped her way down. She heard her buckskins tearing but there was no time to pick off the shreds. Halfway down the cliff she had to reach out one hand to Marie, who was clinging to a root. The root broke and when Marie grasped her for support they both began to hurtle downward, over the rocks and rotting boughs, and finally there was the hard blow of earth and no breath and dancing stars and the battle for breath once more, and they lay together. In the darkness she tried to pray again: light, oh, light my brain! A gap in the mountains: near! Think! Try!

They crawled to a stream and they drank. When they found they could stand again they went on. The sun rose and set four times before they left the cliffs and the stream below.

Sometimes now, trusting ears and what was left of brain, they climbed by day. The afternoon sun was stretching through a stand of beeches when they heard hooves. Delilah jerked her head. When she saw the tiny hole in a wall of mossy rock she dragged herself into it. For a while they could crouch together in the cave. There was light, but there was still the sound of the hooves, hollow and close. As they crept farther a wall of rock hung down and they fell to their stomachs and began to crawl over wet pebbles into the darkness where no Indian might find them. They crawled until they slid down a solid wall of rock. The wall and the ceiling vanished and Delilah stood, sensing space, sensing void. In the darkness she cast out her arms. One of them hit a sharp point hanging from an unknown height. With Marie she slumped to the floor.

Soon the darkness began to lift: a little, a very little. She heard dripping and in the low, faintly yellow light she saw the grotesque shapes of a wilderness of points, a very forest. Somewhere there were voices, soft and sibilant, and there were echoes too, and the steady hollow dripping. The glow burned feeble. The only things she could not see were Marie and herself. When she raised her hand before her eyes she could not make out its shape. The voices drew closer. She could not catch their words, but they were not Cherokee words. Help was coming, somebody knew . . . Blind in the light, she stared at the forest and still could not find her hand.

When she woke nobody had come after all. The glow still hung over her and still she saw the wilderness of fantastic rock shapes but not Marie or her own hand. This was not the way, then. No food here: get out: somehow . . . She touched Marie, whose breath was escaping her in soft quavering sounds, the hollow echoes bouncing back from unknown limits. Delilah helped her toward the tunnel and they crawled and crept once more, they grasped and climbed and crawled again, their stomachs bleeding from the points of the stones and the scrape of walls, their buckskin rags sodden with water and stiff with mud. Still the glow hung down. Delilah knew it now for madness, as the voices had been madness.

At the door of the cave the light pierced hot into her eyes. For a while she staggered and Marie with her until she could make out the shapes of the world: trees and branches and earth. Together she and Marie gathered more sassafras and cane. Once they came on a patch of wild chokecherry blossoms and they gorged until they vomited and everything in their bodies turned to water. The sun waxed and waned several times in a green mist of griping sickness. There was no shame: only the cramping pain, the doubling, the crazy whorls of light taunting closed eyes.

Painters screamed louder in the descending night that finally gathered the pain to itself and freed them. Under a hanging boulder whose moss Delilah had probed for snakes with her halting fingers she and Marie lay sleepless, forcing out their rattled breath. When the dawn came she turned to see tiny gray tufts of fur scattered among twigs red with crumbled clay. She jammed the tufts into her dry mouth for the skin still clinging to them, she drove herself to sit and lean back against the boulder. She was all instinct now, no mind; all hunger, all thirst, all driven to reach the goal she hardly knew but which had once pulled her and so she must push to it with her broken body and her broken brain. The next night they stayed too because Marie's feet were bleeding. In the morning Delilah could make out fresh tracks so close she might have touched in her sleep whatever had made them. Desperately she scratched in the earth for traces of food the animal might have left behind. She clawed at part of a rabbit's head, and threw the ears and nose to Marie, saving the neck for herself.

Rain again: it drove down through the sugar trees and the

beeches, it roared through the hemlocks, it swept the steep world clean. Delilah and Marie climbed and slipped and fell and clutched at sleek grapevines and grubbed in strange leaves and roots because there was no cane. They sprawled at creek beds to drink because the rain was not enough to stop their choking thirst. When the sun rolled out it stiffened their buckskins to boards, and still they struggled on. At twilight Delilah raised her eyes at a long, hollow cry. Atop a ledge of rock a brown elk raised huge horns, spreading them with poised head into a silver and violet sky. Then he turned and bounded into the laurel. Unseen turkeys began to gobble mockingly at the cracking of branches he made.

Afternoons became hotter. Beneath her buckskins Delilah felt trickles of sweat wetting dried scabs. At night the sweat turned to ice like the ice of the Tenase which had not been ice. A bed of ivy drew her down into its shiny reddish tangles and she did not sleep but fainted. Yet she could get to her feet when the rim of the sun climbed over the mountain range ahead. A new torment began: her arms and legs and face and feet and neck turned to swollen pulsing blotches of red. The itching drove her to flailing; the more she scratched the more she throbbed. Her body swelled on until the swellings burst to spread acid trickles that burned under the rakings of her curved fingernails.

Marie was crying again, raking too. She threw her festering body into a creek bed before Delilah could stop her. But the creek was shallow, and when Delilah herself crawled onto the stones the water flowed over her like a soothing balm. Only later did she realize it had washed away half the grease which had covered her. When she closed her eyes she heard the nasal droning of Brother Whitaker. Why did he preach of lepers? Ah, she was a leper, Marie was a leper too, that was it, burning, rotting . . . There was one small stand of cane near the creek and when Delilah fumbled with a stalk and found her hands were too sore and too weak to break it she sucked. She watched Marie suck too, cheeks hollow, breath coarse, eyes glittering beneath a rat's nest of pied hair.

On a hot morning when mist smoked up from the valley floor and water droplets plopped from flat-leaved sycamores and a ghost sighed somewhere they came to a wider trace. The sun; always the sun, search for that! But the mist hung down in billowy folds and there was no sun. Delilah turned her eyes upward; they stung and watered and she clawed at her lids in desperation. Where had the sun gone? Should she go left? She turned. She knew Marie was following her when she heard her dragging footfalls. "Uh-coo, coo, coo!" cried the mourning doves. But it was not a dove that began to flutter at Delilah's side. She stopped, confused at the tameness of the tiny brown sparrow. She could see its very eyes, ferocious and dark. Then she started on, Marie after her. Again the bird fluttered at her knees. Flies buzzed at her blisters. She brushed the bird away. It fluttered still, beating its wings upward as it swooped, whirring away, whirring back.

She did not know why she turned once more. She kept her eyes on the bird until it flew high and disappeared. Then she kept her eyes on her red feet that were pointing ahead the new way. Quietly she plodded on. She heard Marie plodding too, but with ever more irregular steps. Her stomach begged and twisted, and she gripped her belly, and when that did not stop the pain she jabbed her fist at it to drive it away.

When they came to the great river, flowing silently between tall sycamore banks in the sunset, she knew they could not go on longer. She had become a mass of all her pain, gelatinous, without shape or form, expanding and contracting and gnawing. She was blind, she was deaf to the world even while her ears rang with giddy music. She staggered; she reached out to grasp Marie, but when she did it Marie fell too and Delilah heard her head knocking hard and hollow like her own against the boulder. Automatically she reached out again. Her hand fell on warm flesh, it knew the throbbing of a heart still beating, and she tried to raise her head. She could not. It fell too on the flesh, over the beating heart, and she remembered the sound so dimly, from a past she could not remember at all . . . Oh, the world was wide and vast, and the river flowed on, and the trees sighed . . . But soon the world began to shrink. It gathered itself around her in the sighing and the beating and the flowing, and then it was smaller, smaller, softer, until it was a dark shell and she lay within, curled and silent, waiting for her last breath in the darkness and the quiet. Just as the sides of the shell were about to press her forever within them, all feeling, all knowledge, stopped.

It was over at last.

23

THE CLINCH valley never called 1794 by a name such as other war years had had: The Year of the Bloody Sevens, the Year of Sorrows. For Delilah it would always be, simply, the year of the great wonder that she lived. It was weeks before she could understand what had happened to her. At first, when she woke in her own bed, she hardly knew it was her grandmother who supported her back and was spooning broth to her lips. Her body would have felt as flimsy as air except for its pain. She did not know her father. Gradually she sensed the sound of footsteps in the room, and knew her throat was swallowing from time to time. She became aware of people coming and going and understood touch, sound, taste, and smell. As her strength began to return she obeyed blindly the impulses to cry out in agony until she heard the low voice that said, "I'm with you," and recognized it for her father's at last. Long before her mind began to stir her body began to heal. Later she would learn of the poison ivy blisters, her near-starvation, how she and Marie had been found by a passing trapper as they lay dying only thirty miles down the Clinch River just below Fort Blackmore . . . It was harder, she would understand then, for her reason to begin working than for her body to begin responding to its needs.

Consciousness began for her in scattered memories: a bird fluttering at her side, her turning, the hand of a woman clasping her own, a stag poised on a cliff . . . More slowly came knowledge: that she had been saved by a miracle from going into Kentucky, that the woman with her was Marie, that her father and grandmother were alive and beside her now, that she had come home after all. She began to be able to smile in her grateful disbelief, to move her fingers on the counterpane and watch them curve, to turn herself without pain. She and Marie had done it after all. They had pitted themselves against the savages and the wilderness and won. All her life now there would be that closeness with Marie. Her first whispered words were for her, and her grandmother laid a cool hand on her forehead and answered "Yes, very brave," and she could nod. She had saved two lives, her own and Marie's. Or had God done it? In time she would be strong enough to tell her father about the bird. She would never tell much more: how she had had to sink to the level of a grubbing animal, how (as she could remember) she had eaten fur and tried to share a bear's kill. Marie would know these things. It was enough. The bond of their survival would be between them always, and nothing else they had felt before it mattered.

As the weeks passed Delilah lay in her bed and felt the soft summer wind on her face. When she ran her hand over her face she wondered at the healing of its scars, even the one near her temple where her head had hit the boulder at the shore of the Clinch. Her bones began to feel less jagged at her neck. Some day her body might yet be round and hard and not a skeleton . . . But that was not important. The sweetness of life came to her in things like the scent of sheepmint and raspberry roses, in the gentle touch of the wind on her closed eyelids, in the knowledge that her family was with her, in the very sound of her breath.

Was she strong enough to understand more, Gran asked

one day? When she nodded Gran told her what had happened at Bickley Mills: how the people had driven off the Indians in the raid, how her cries and Marie's had warned them in time. Everywhere the men had searched for their bodies, and when they had not found them Charles had organized an expedition into the woods. He alone believed his wife and Delilah might yet be alive, captives of the savages. But his party had lost the trail after the first charred campsite. Later there had been nothing to follow, no sign.

"I couldn't manage —" Delilah began, but Gran motioned her to be quiet. Her father was there too now, smiling down as he talked . . . He, Charles, Gran, everybody had believed her and Marie to be dead after the trail had been lost. They had both become heroines who had perished to save their neighbors, as Brother Whitaker had said in his memorial sermon. Her father and Charles had vowed they would never rest until they found the graves, and many times they had ridden into the forest alone together, searching, wondering, forgetting everything but their common loss. When the trapper and his friends had carried Delilah and Marie home Gran had fallen to her knees . . . That had been in May, in the time of the crabtrees. It was July now, Gran said, and Mrs. Oscher's marigolds were blooming in her dooryard down the road.

July! Broth; milk; then beef and greens and sang tea . . . yes, it was possible for so many weeks to have passed. As Delilah realized it she knew too there was more to be told, for her grandmother's head was cocked, as if she were waiting to go on.

"Benge's dead, Delilah."

"But I saw him, Gran! I —" She tried to sit up.

Her father cautioned her to lie back. In turn he told her

of the expedition the men of the Clinch and Holston valleys had organized in the spring to find the man who had murdered their families and burned them out for twenty years. Her own disappearance and Marie's had been the last straw. Instead of each man trying to get Benge for himself, they had planned out the search in unity this time. Charles had been one of the grim-eyed leaders. They had studied Benge's habits, learned the trails he used when he came from his village. They had tested each other's marksmanship beforehand, calculating. Near the Cumberland Gap at Prince's Flats settlement they had surrounded him in a pass on a morning bright with sun. Her father wished he had been there; he would have left her sickbed for that hour . . . Benge had fallen at the first shot.

"Who —"

She was surprised to see her father grin broadly and suddenly. "A circuit rider," he said. "One of your Methodists, God bless 'em."

Benge dead, peace on the Clinch at last, the government seeking a treaty with the Ohio tribes, the committees of vigilance her father called posses to watch for thieves, news of the Baron's murderers having been traced to the Illinois Country by Lawyer Dickenson's handbills . . . It was so much to take in. As Delilah grew stronger, able first to sit and then, leaning on her father's arm, to stand, she found it incredible that there was nothing more to fear. She wondered if she had lost fear in the wilderness or here. Marie had said something about losing it, but she could not remember what. She wanted to see Marie, to go to her. It was her father who told her she could not.

"Why?" She clutched her pallet as she sat at the edge of her bed. "She's not — mad, is she?"

He laid his rough hand on hers and shook his head. "No. She's dead."

For a time Delilah sat very still, her breath slow. When she could ask how it had happened, knowing she had saved Marie for no purpose, her father's voice was as full of compassion as she felt. Marie had regained consciousness sooner than Delilah had. "Too soon, perhaps. I've seen Bickley — she told him about your time at Chota, how you tended her and made her go on. She told him she loved you."

Marie, too, had tried hard to live. But the hardiness of her body hadn't matched that of her mind. In her own bed, in her own room, she had grown weaker and weaker from the effects of her ordeal until one night she had pressed her hands to her chest, given a little moan, and died. "Her heart stopped beating. He was with her — the children too."

"Then she did it for nothing," Delilah murmured bitterly, her mind on the woman with whom she had shared those months. "It was worse for her than me — and for nothing." Faintly, she laughed as she lifted her eyes to her father's. "Can you think the sparrow came just for me?"

"I think there are things no man can explain." When she saw the mixture of humility and love in his eyes she could wonder at that too, and she pressed his hand again. Later he added: "Bickley's pretty broken up by it. He asked for you when I saw him, but it's easy to see his mind's not on anybody else."

When she asked for her mirror her father and Gran wouldn't let her have it. It was too soon, Gran said. The scratches on her face were still too red; they would frighten her. But they would fade. She'd better know her hair was streaked gray at her temples. Yet she would look her thirty-two years in time. She must be patient. She would put on flesh and her eyes would brighten. Meanwhile she mustn't worry. She understood then how ugly she must have turned — so ugly it would take courage she didn't yet have merely to see herself. How odd that her looks were becoming important to her again. Her father and Gran had masked their shock well. As Gran, needed and skilled in nursing, seemed to have grown younger and more limber, she herself had turned old. Then she shrugged. She had her life. Never again would she utter the childish pout, "I wish I were dead." Marie had nothing but a grave in the Bickley Mills Cemetery.

Many people began coming to see Delilah: Brother Whitaker, who prayed with her; Granny Sawyer, who hobbled over with a raspberry pie and wheezed affectionately; Ann Fraley, whose eyes were full of sympathy and who said little but only took her hand, as if welcoming her into a sisterhood; Mrs. Oscher, who embraced her tearfully. "Let me send to Simon, honey — "

"No. I couldn't think of such. Please."

"I reckon not yet, you've had that bad a time. I ought to have knowed."

In the manner of everybody but Ann there came a strangeness. She began to see strangeness even in her father and grandmother. It was awe, almost fear. She knew she talked far less these days. But whenever she did speak everybody else fell silent as if to catch every word. All naturalness seemed to forsake the people around her. She was being treated as a person apart, as if she had come back from the grave, a person other people could not understand but only study. Even Ann had a little of this when she murmured her own time had not been as long or hard. Delilah thought: I remind them of what they've been through and they'd rather forget. But I'm lonesome . . . She might as well shout "twenty years of war!" at them, for the way they shrank. Marie had hated facing Ann Fraley because Ann had reminded her of what could happen. Now Marie was gone, her early beauty and her later disfigurement both memories. Delilah felt that she herself had turned into what Bickley Mills would ever after regard as a statue, unapproachable and remote, moving among them like a monument to tragedy. The children would think it too when she began to teach again, as she meant to do. In the wilderness she had prayed for strength; now she was too strong to live in a world where there were everyday weaknesses and the tedium of common things. Her strength, she reckoned, had removed her a step from the human race.

But you're not really strong, her mind taunted all the while. Why fool yourself? You know you want him to come to you and he hasn't, nor any of his family. That house has been as silent as your own.

She longed to cry out: I don't want to wonder. I'm tired!

Yet on a hot afternoon the first week in August when her father had gone down to the sawmill, Gran coughed at the door of her room. Delilah had been dozing, and she still felt as sleepy as the buzzing of the jarflies sounded in faraway trees.

"Charles is here now," Gran said simply. "You had better comb your hair."

Frantically then — and she had not been frantic in so long — she ran the comb through it. It was still thick and difficult. She twisted it into a low knot at the nape of her neck and fumbled for a pin. She wiped her face and brushed her old black gown and tried to sash it more tightly so that it wouldn't fall in such limp and ill-fitting folds from her waist. It had been stupid not to know he would come eventually. Their lives, hers and Charles's, were so tangled together his coming was inevitable whatever he would say, whatever he felt.

What *would* he say? "Thank you," perhaps. Gratitude, grief, guilt, lost love and pity: there were so many things that might be in his heart, a thousand conflicting emotions he was no more ready to name than she was. He would be managing the business of day-to-day living as she was doing; that, God knew, was enough . . . He'd seen death and dealt it out, he'd been wounded, but he'd never fought it like a wildcat as she had. Gran had fought it for him. Perhaps he would be like the others: silent, watching, nervous of her because of what she meant. They might have everything to say to each other or nothing. Wildcats had no fine manners, no ambitions. They had only claws. Biting her lip, she went to the door. A moment later he was walking slowly toward her from the front of the cabin into the room. If he was horrified at what he saw, he did not show it. His weathered face was very grave and gentle. He did not say anything, but only laid his hands on her shoulders, holding her away from him as if he could not believe she stood before him. One of his hands jerked; he steadied it. After a long time of silence he drew back, and when she sat at the edge of her bed he sat opposite her. Her breath began to feel hot on her parted lips. If only he would say something, because she couldn't! She stretched taut the muscles of her neck and jaw and fumbled with one of her hairpins.

"Were you waiting?" he asked at last, and she was surprised at the huskiness of his voice. Irrelevantly, while he groped for more words, she thought his kneecaps looked larger than ever in the chair he had taken. He needed big furniture as much as she did . . . Where was Gran?

He fingered his cravat, then the ribbon at his club. "Were you?"

"I — I reckon so." She could hardly hear herself.

He laced his fingers together, elbows on his knees. "She said you had no thought but for her." His voice could have been about to break but Delilah wasn't sure, so quickly did he steady it. "That's helped."

"I'm sorry." She let out a long breath. It whispered back at her from the corners of the small room. In a ray of sun from the open window, dust motes were streaming. A cluster of gnats was buzzing at the sill. "I did try."

"It must have been — unspeakable for her."

"Don't. I can't tell you."

His eyes were searching hers. They were baffled now, uncertain. "No. It's not a time to tell much, is it?"

She turned away, brushing a mosquito from her sleeve. "I want to forget."

"I've wanted to forget things too. Some I couldn't. When you came to me about the mountain you were wearing a red dress. I remember what you said, the way your eyes looked. That day pretty well undid me, you know — even while you were there."

"It was the day I — "

"Look at me, Delilah. I love you. I think she guessed that at the end — that I could never forget you. If there's a hell I've been in it: thinking what it must have meant to her. Just before she died she said 'Marry her.' That's what I've been living with." He got up and came to stand over her, his fingers resting on her shoulders. "I think now we ought to be honest. We don't have to pretend any longer. Her dying means we can have each other."

Staring up at him, she whispered: "No. Oh, no. Not now — "

His fingers sank deeper into the hollows above her collarbone. "I dare to think you love me too — still. If we tried to be hypocrites it wouldn't help her."

In spite of her inner knowledge that this had to happen, she was shocked. Where was his honor — as he would call it? Was his love a lie of his pity? He had surely loved Marie. She, Delilah, had seen them together . . . "You loved her, not me," she told him tightly.

"I spend weeks thinking you're dead and I try to find you, I can't stop seeing how they must have killed you — I remember everything we ever did and said and try to think of her instead and can't — then when you're here I have to know it and not see you alive — how much do you think I can stand?" His voice did break, but he went on: "Help me, for God's sake. I love you more than anything in the world."

"Look at me," she laughed deep in her throat.

His hand went to her hair. "You've never believed you're beautiful to me. You'll have to live with your jealousy. Try."

She shook her head, got up, and walked to the window. A pair of swallows were swooping near the barn Simon Oscher had built. The long grass of the yard, dotted with blue specks of chicory, was bending in the hot wind. Children were shouting; a hand saw whined away beyond. She heard him follow her, yet when he turned her and took her wrist she said again: "Don't."

He would not let her go. He drew her to him hard, and when she struggled briefly from his hands and his mouth he only held her tighter. His lips closed on hers. In her shock and all her temper she had to yield. Even when she struggled once more at the deepening of his kiss he held her

fast. When she began to feel the old weakness, the old wanting and surrendering which had once been all her life, she
despised herself for it. Today he was seeking her in a way
he had not long ago and it made her more defenseless than
ever, though she did not know exactly what the difference
in him was. She knew only his breath, his warmth, his near-
ness to her. Slowly she began to give herself to him until she
found herself learning the shape of his shoulders and back
again, the sound of his heart, the roughness of his face.
When he stared down at her she could not look away. "You
said once you trusted me. Don't you still?"

"I can't think." She buried her face in his coat, smelling
its tobacco smell.

"You love me too. Don't deny it." He rocked her in his
arms. "We've tried to keep faith with the others — it's time
to keep faith with ourselves."

When she didn't answer, he kissed her temples, her brows.
As he did it she felt as if nothing had changed. She could
not tell herself she had not known years of misery, for she
had. Yet now she wanted him as he wanted her: less with
passion in this moment than as a part of herself regained, an
extension of herself long lost and this day drawn back into
the very center of her being. She hadn't been able to give
herself to Simon because she had not had all of herself to
give . . .

"Simon!" she whispered. "If you only knew — "

Quickly he held her back from him, his mouth and eyes
grim. "You were pretending that for me. Tell me! Weren't
you?"

"No! I wanted — " But her breath turned to a sobbing
sound and she could not continue. I wanted children too! I
wanted something! His fingers were digging into her shoul-

ders, and she could only shake her head. Then she burst out: "Twelve years! Where were you?"

"Did you love him?" he demanded. "Did you?"

"You're hurting me! We're not the same. Twelve years!" And she couldn't have them back. What could wipe out the gray of his hair and the scars on her face and her trial of Simon and his of Marie, or his children? They couldn't make believe life had never happened to them both in twelve years. "Let me go." She hardened her voice. Again she turned to the dappled leaves and windblown grass outside. It was too late: too late for them to think and breathe together, as they had done once. Too late for a singlehearted love, the only kind possible.

"I'm sorry," he said dully at last. "I promised myself I wouldn't do this. My God, Delilah, haven't you put me through enough?"

"We've lost too much."

"Don't mock our decency. I need you. I couldn't wait more."

Something truly was different in him. As she looked up at him again, she realized what it was. He had lost his mastery, his sureness. He was talking of need and help. His kiss today had asked more than it had given — that was it. He was stripping himself even of pride for her, showing her his weaknesses and asking her to accept them. Gran had said long ago there was no room for people in his heart, but she had been wrong. He had sought them from the start. Of course Charles Bickley was afraid of loneliness. He had said it, and in an instant Delilah was more deeply sure of it than ever. He had been afraid of loneliness from the time he had come west. He wanted the world to accept him for his power. He wanted, also, a home that could never be taken away from him as Green Springs had been. Herself, Marie, the children — his own and the ones he had so eagerly adopted — he had surrounded himself with people. He had known loneliness once and so hated it he refused to bear it again. Now he wanted her, Delilah Winfield, so much he was ready to defy the world's opinion and marry her out of hand when he was supposed to be mourning. As she kept staring into his begging eyes she remembered how he had come alone to the Clinch, had begun to build alone, had always had to fight a battle of honor against need. If he hadn't been a Tory in early years he could have had friends. If he hadn't been too careful of her youth he might have had herself. If, later, he hadn't kept his marriage vows he might have had her once more. How much his decency had cost him! Why, that too was why she loved him! Of course she did. He was not perfect; he seized land and drove sang-diggers and rode roughshod over the feelings of helpless men, "failures." But she wasn't perfect either. Perhaps the twelve years could be forgotten after all in his very longing to take and hers to give. That itself was a singlehearted thing. If Simon had loved her, he had still not been willing to take her on any terms but his own. But Charles was willing, he wanted and needed her however she might come to him, however bitter his jealousy might be. His love for her was larger even than his pride. And he loved not what he wanted her to be, but what she was.

So she could smile at him, even feel shy of his vulnerability that he had let her see and admitted in words. That was his own gift: to cast off his armor for her. "I — I mind we're being silly." His eyes widened as she said it in her shyness, but his mouth stayed grave. When she came into his arms of her own will he did not speak, but pressed her to him so tightly he hurt her ribs. Once more they began to find each other, driven, as if to obliterate all the past in a single time of striving. Yet she knew it was the beginning of a lifetime of striving, because his heart was as restless as her own. They would both have their jealousies, their doubts: but later. Not now. When she felt giddy with weakness and had to sit down he quickly knelt beside her, his hands on her wrists.

"I'm all right," she laughed jerkily. "Just shaky still."

"But how could I quarrel with you?" He took her back to him, this time very gently, holding her as if he feared she might break. She heard him starting to whisper the words of his love, and in her dream she smiled. She formed her own words of love, knowing they had never been far from her heart. She listened while he told her his children knew he had come here; that too would be a thing to face later. She would be ready. Now it was enough to hear him saying he wanted her forever. He was still holding her when Gran came to the door, and he did not let her go even then.

"When," Gran asked laconically, "is the wedding?"

She was smiling broadly at him all the same.

Epilogue

This Indenture made the first day of October in the Year of our Lord One Thousand Seven Hundred and Ninety four between Charles and Delilah Bickley of the county of Russell and State of Virginia of the one part and Benjamin Winfield, of the same place of the other part, Witnesseth: that Whereas Charles and Delilah Bickley for themselves, their executors, administrators and assigns for and in Consideration of the Sum of One Dollar ($1.00) in silver to them in hand paid by the said Benjamin Winfield: the Receipt whereof the said Charles and Delilah Bickley do hereby acknowledge: do freely, fully and absolutely give grant Bargain and sell unto the said Benjamin a tract of land commonly known as SUGAR HILL: Ten thousand four hundred acres on the west side of Clinch River beginning at the dogwood sapling by the first round boulder, thence ninety degrees west two hundred and forty poles, one chain, ten links to the sugar tree next the Springs, thence sixty degrees South two hundred and thirty poles, two chains, eighty links to the Cave at the turning of the Frenchman's Trace, thence one hundred and ten degrees south-east three hundred poles, five chains, one Link to the beech clump at the point athwart Bickley's Ford on the said Clinch River . . . To have and to hold the aforesaid tract of land all and singularly the *houses and barns stables Orchards Ways Watercourses, Rights, Liberties, Privileges and Hereditaments whatsoever . . . This indenture to be and remain in full force and virtue Any Thing to the contrary Notwithstanding. In Witness whereof the said Charles and Delilah Bickley hereunto set their Hands and Seals. The Day and Year above written.*

Charles Bickley
Delilah Bickley

Signed sealed and delivered in the presences of:
Henry Dickenson
Benjamin Winfield

It was surely the strangest of the law's tricks that a single piece of paper and a few words about saplings and poles and boulders could presume to measure out so vast a thing as Charles's gift to her father of Sugar Hill.

The Bickley Connection

Francis Bickley, Bart.,
of Attleborough Hall,
Norfolk, England
b. 1644

Other children   Joseph Bickley —m. Sarah Shelton
of Virginia
1685–1750

William Bickley,   John Bickley   MARGARET, widow
Bart. b. 1705   b. 1713   of Angus Mackinnon
(title outlawed by   ("Gran") b. 1716
U.S. Constitution
1788)   BEN
           WINFIELD   m. Peggy Mackinnon
           b. 1732   1740–1768

Other children

MARIE, daughter —m CHARLES —m DELILAH
of SEBASTIAN   (1)   BICKLEY   (2)   WINFIELD
HATLER   b. 1753   b. 1762
b. 1753

JOHN   WILLIAM   SESASTIAN   ELIZABETH
BICKLEY   BICKLEY   HATLER BICKLEY   BICKLEY
    —twins—   ("Hatler")   ("Lisbet")